Resounding Praise for
New York Times **Bestseller**

PHILLIP MARGOLIN

"Phillip Margolin knows how to
pack in the thrills."
Tess Gerritsen

"A splendid writer."
Seattle Times

"Margolin keeps reeling out the surprises."
Orlando Sentinel

"He is a master of plot and pacing—and one
of those rare authors who can create
a genuinely surprising ending."
Lisa Scottoline

"Margolin knows about the types of people who
kill and about those whose lives have
been destroyed by crime. . . . [He] never has
stinted on making his books seem real."
Statesman Journal (OR)

"Margolin knows his way around
a police precinct and a courtroom."
Columbus Dispatch

"Margolin will have you turning pages furiously."
Otto Penzler

By Phillip Margolin

LOST LAKE
SLEEPING BEAUTY
THE ASSOCIATE
THE UNDERTAKER'S WIDOW
THE BURNING MAN
AFTER DARK
GONE, BUT NOT FORGOTTEN
THE LAST INNOCENT MAN
HEARTSTONE
EXECUTIVE PRIVILEGE
SUPREME JUSTICE
CAPITOL MURDER

Amanda Jaffe Novels

WILD JUSTICE
TIES THAT BIND
PROOF POSITIVE
FUGITIVE

PHILLIP MARGOLIN

HEARTSTONE

HARPER

An Imprint of HarperCollins*Publishers*

This is a work of fiction. Names, characters, places, and incidents are products of the author's imagination or are used fictitiously and are not to be construed as real. Any resemblance to actual events, locales, organizations, or persons, living or dead, is entirely coincidental.

HARPER

An Imprint of HarperCollins*Publishers*
10 East 53rd Street
New York, New York 10022-5299

Copyright © 1978 by Phillip Margolin
ISBN 978-0-06-198388-7

First Harper premium printing: December 2010
First HarperTorch paperback printing: February 2005

Visit Harper paperbacks on the World Wide Web at
www.harpercollins.com

10   9   8   7   6   5   4   3   2

For Doreen, Amy and Daniel,
beside whom even the publication of
a first novel seems unimportant.

With special thanks to Martin Bauer, Jed Mattes, Ned Leavitt, and all the people who helped me with the research and editing for this book. And with additional, and no less special, thanks to Jean Naggar and everyone at her agency and to Irwyn Applebaum, Elisa Petrini, and all the terrific people at Bantam Books, who have been so kind to me and my novels.

HEARTSTONE

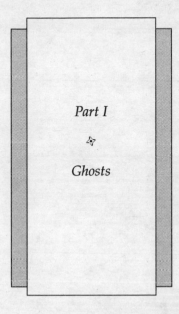

Part I

Ghosts

Prologue

It was two days before Christmas and Louis Weaver's only friend was dying in a dollar-a-night room at the Hotel Cordova. Louis stepped into a doorway to rest. It was hard to breathe the icy air and the whirling snow had made him half blind. He wiped his nose and took a drink of cheap whiskey from the flask that he had jammed into his raincoat pocket before leaving the hotel.

Willie told Louis that he was going to die when they were in Salt Lake City. He made Louis promise that he would take him home to Portsmouth. There was something Willie had to do in Portsmouth so that his immortal soul would be saved. They had stolen aboard a freight train and Louis had spent the hours on a hay pallet in the corner of a boxcar watching his friend decline.

Willie had been talking about heaven and hell a lot lately and Louis could tell that there was something terrible on his mind. Louis could not help but think that Willie's tribulation was all the fault of the preacher in Fort Worth who had given Willie religion, because he never used to be so troubled. Louis wished he could help his friend, but Willie only talked about the thing that was bothering him when he was real drunk or delirious and then it would come out in mumbles and groans and Louis could never get the drift. All he knew was that it had something to do with a girl and had happened long ago.

Louis sighed and returned the bottle to his pocket. He was so tired and cold, but he was almost there. The courthouse was only two blocks away. It would be warm there. Louis wished he was back at the hotel. He had spent his last few bucks on their room, but he sure wasn't getting any use out of it.

A blast of cold wind whipped a sheet of snow across Louis's face and he was immediately sorry for having thought about the room and being gypped out of his money. Soon Willie would be cold like this for eternity and Willie was his only friend.

The radio alarm switched on and Albert Caproni tried to deny its existence with his whole being. Logic demanded that he stay under the nice warm covers, nestled next to his nice warm wife.

"Honey," a voice purred. He felt soft lips kissing his ear lobe. He half wished that they would go away.

"Honey, you have to get up now," the voice said.

"Go away," he mumbled, burrowing deeper under the covers.

"You have to get up," the voice repeated in its sexiest tone and he felt a warm hand snaking through the fly of his flannel pajama bottoms and soft fingers curling around his penis.

"Please, Mary," he begged. "I want to sleep."

Even though he had not opened his eyes, had not seen the snow or felt the wind, he knew that it was going to be a miserable day. One much better spent in a cozy bed.

He felt Mary move her large, curvy body so that her entire weight rested on him. Then he heard her running her dampened tongue across her lips to make them as wet as possible. Finally, he felt her lips as they covered his face with damp, slobbery kisses. Enough was enough. He conceded defeat and opened his eyes.

"I hate you," he groaned, shifting so that he could hold his wife.

"I love you," she said. She moved her weight off him and they cuddled together. He kissed her gently and began to stroke her backside and leg.

"None of that," she said. "And you are going to be late if you don't get dressed right now."

"Not even a fast one?" Albert asked playfully. He felt sexy, the way he always did when he held Mary close. After all these years of marriage, she still aroused him.

"No."

"I knew I shouldn't have married a frigid girl."

"Tough," Mary said, giving him a peck on the cheek and rolling out of bed. "You knew what you were getting when you married me. Now scoot or you'll be late and Commissioner Hadley won't give you the salary for those extra attorneys you want."

"Hadley. Shit. To think I'm giving up this warm bed and the best piece of tail this side of the Rockies for that old fart. Next time I run for office you make sure that the public knows about the sacrifices I make."

"They know already."

"Listen, make it two eggs this morning. I'll need the extra energy."

"What about your diet?" she asked as she left the room.

"For one day I can skip my diet."

Caproni stretched and walked sleepy-eyed to the window. The snowstorm outside obliterated any trace of the beautiful landscape that he usually saw upon rising. He yawned and scratched. Despite the ugliness of the day, he was happy. In fact, he could not remember a day in the past few years when he had not been basically happy. True, there had been minor disappointments, but he had a wife he was crazy about, two beautiful kids and, at thirty-five, he was the youngest person ever elected to the office of Portsmouth district attorney, a job he loved almost as much as he loved Mary.

Al was a career district attorney in an office that was traditionally staffed by bright new law school graduates who stayed the two years it took to gain trial experience and make contacts and then moved on to practice corporate law.

Al had enlisted in the army after college. After the army he had entered night law school and had worked days as a Portsmouth policeman. His last year in law school he had been assigned to work as an investigator with the district attorney's office. His contact with the criminal side of legal practice quickly dispelled any thoughts he might have had of practicing corporate law. And if he had ever pictured himself as a criminal defense attorney, one year with the D.A. had changed that.

Shortly before graduation Al had asked Herb Holman, then the district attorney, for a job. The deputy district attorneys he had worked with had given him glowing reports. Albert Caproni was sworn in as a deputy district attorney on the same day that he received a letter from the State Supreme Court informing him that he had passed the bar examination.

That was many years ago. In between there had been a rapid rise through the office, which had resulted in his appointment as Chief Criminal Deputy when Harvey Babcock, one of Al's closest friends, was elected D.A. It had been a time for celebration. Then, as soon as the excitement of a new administration had begun, it had ended. A car driven by a drunk driver had hurtled the lane divider on the Interstate and had killed Harvey Babcock.

Albert Caproni had been the unanimous choice to fill the vacant post. In November of this year Albert C. Caproni had run against State Representative Sylvia Marshall and had won election by a landslide.

Albert glanced at the clock as he took off his pajamas. It was a little after 5:30. Al always worked long hours. Even as a kid he had held down a part-time job after school to help out the family. He did not mind the hours. He had been working like this so long that it had become routine. When he was a trial attorney, it was those extra hours of added preparation that had made up for his lack of brilliance. He always took extra satisfaction in whipping one of the boys from the prestige firms or law schools on an obscure point of law that he had dug up after hours of diligent research.

Albert dropped his pajamas on the bed and started for the bathroom. He stopped in front of the mirror and looked at his body. He was neither pleased nor displeased by what he saw. True, his short body was not as compact as it had been when he first joined the office and his hair was thinning out. On the other hand, he was still hard underneath the extra fat.

"Let's just say that I am keeping my perimeters in check," he thought.

Still, he regretted getting out of shape. When he was younger, he always seemed to have energy for handball or basketball. He'd even done a little boxing in the service. It was harder now. He did pushups and situps when he had the time. And there was an occasional game of golf. Oh, well. He had made his choice. He knew the demands of the job and he accepted them willingly. He would die someday, anyway. Getting into heaven was not going to depend on the size of his waistline.

"Give me an extra slice of bacon, will you, hon," he yelled before turning on the shower.

Fanny Maser had been the receptionist at the Portsmouth district attorney's office since 1958. She had come in with the Republicans, stayed through the Democrats and remained at her post when the office became nonpartisan in 1970.

Fanny's husband had been a policeman for sixteen years when he was killed trying to stop a service station holdup. The two months it had taken to pull her world back together had been the only lengthy period that she had ever taken away from her job.

Fanny was the ideal receptionist. She looked, even in her younger days, like everybody's idea of what a mother should look like. She was a small, gray-haired woman with a perpetual smile. Her voice was soft and soothing and she had an ability to put people at ease. This trait was essential in an office whose customers were irate citizens, tired, off-duty policemen who were waiting for court after spending a night shift in a high-crime area, nervous witnesses and, occasionally, rapists, robbers and murderers.

The criminal element was one of the most exciting facets of Fanny's job. She would often tell her bridge group about the "headliners" she had greeted. There had been the slow morning she had spent passing the time with Carl Billingsgate, the hammer killer, while he waited to be interviewed by the Chief Criminal Deputy. Carl had confessed that very morning.

And what about Marie Louise Renoud? What a nice lady she had appeared to be. Who would have guessed that she and her lesbian lover had shot her husband and left him for dead on Switchback Mountain, only to have him crawl back, as Fanny would tell it, from the "Portals of Hell" to testify at Marie Louise's trial. Marie and Fanny had had the nicest chat.

With all the exciting things she had seen, and all of the interesting people she had met, it was no wonder that Louis Weaver made no particular impression on Fanny Maser when he pushed through the glass doors that opened into the reception area.

It was ten-thirty and the reception area was empty. An hour earlier it had been filled with young district

attorneys and their witnesses, but court had started
and they had all left. Louis spent the first few seconds
sopping up the warmth from the courthouse heating
system. He stood in the doorway shivering and casting nervous glances at his new surroundings. He was
a mouse of a man. His worn raincoat, tattered suit
coat and stained white shirt were all that he had between him and the sharp, winter wind. His baggy
pants were tied to his waist by a knotted rope and
they appeared to float around hips too narrow to
hold them up.

Fanny knew that greeting Louis Weaver would be
distasteful. She disapproved of drink and Mr. Weaver
was obviously intoxicated. He also smelled. Nonetheless, she smiled and inquired, in her most pleasant
tone,

"May I help you?"

Louis took off the cheap gray fedora he had been
wearing. His fingers worried the frayed hatbrim as
he shuffled unsteadily toward the bar that separated
Fanny from the three rows of permanently installed
plastic chairs that filled the reception room.

"Is this the district attorney's office?" Louis managed. Fanny could see that the poor man was upset
and frightened and her initial dislike was replaced by
a feeling of concern.

"Yes, it is."

"I got to see the D.A."

"There are fifty district attorneys in our office. Is
there someone in particular that you would like to
talk to?"

"Ain't . . . isn't Mr. Caproni the D.A.? Willie said
to say Mr. Caproni."

"Mr. Caproni is the elected district attorney for Portsmouth County, but he doesn't handle cases himself. Perhaps I can direct you to someone if you will tell me what your problem is."

Louis ran the back of his hand across his grayish stubble. This was getting more complicated than he had expected. Bureaucracies, even those populated by Fanny Masers, frightened him. He wished that he could take a drink, but that was out of the question.

"It's my friend Willie. He's dying, so I promised him I'd do him this favor. He said to see Mr. Caproni and no one else. He said it was important and that Mr. Caproni would want to see him."

There was something about Louis Weaver: the tone of his voice and his obvious desire to be somewhere else. Fanny made a decision.

"I can't guarantee that Mr. Caproni will see you. He is a busy man. But, if you will tell me the subject matter of your visit, I will see if he has time to talk with you."

Louis's mouth was dry and his heart was pumping. Willie had said only Mr. Caproni, but, if he didn't tell now, she would make him go.

"I'm to say Willie Heartstone is dying and he wants to tell who killed Elaine Murray."

Despite the awful weather, the day was turning out beautifully. He had concluded his meeting with Hadley in a half hour and had extracted a promise that the Commissioner would actively push for two more staff attorneys. This was a necessity. There had been a large jump in recent years in the number of criminal cases that were going to trial. The deputies he had now were overworked. In District Court, where misdemeanors, like drunk driving and shoplifting, were tried, his deputies were going into court with almost no preparation. True, these cases were often simple and required little more than asking the only witness what happened, but Caproni did not want a criminal beating a case because a deputy did not have time to prepare.

After his meeting with Hadley, he had returned to his office for a conference with a young man that he had recently transferred to Circuit Court, where the more serious crimes, like murder and armed robbery, were tried. The deputy had been assigned his first major case. After months of work, Portsmouth police and Federal narcotics agents had finally caught one of the state's biggest heroin dealers before he could get rid of a large shipment of heroin. Now it looked as if the entire case might be lost because of what the defendant was claiming to be an illegal search. He and the young man had spent a half hour trying to figure out a way to salvage the case.

Caproni liked the young man. He reminded Caproni of himself at that age. Both came from similar backgrounds and Caproni appreciated the grit of a boy from a poor family who had worked his way up the hard way. The case was a tough one, but the kid had sunk his teeth into the only positive approach and it looked as if he had dragged forth the germ of an idea. Caproni could see how badly the kid wanted this bastard and he approved of the effort he was putting out to get him.

Having cleared his desk of the morning mail, Albert now turned toward a stack of recent Supreme Court cases he had been meaning to read. He leaned back in his chair, a comfortable, oversized, leather-upholstered lounger, which was one of the few luxuries he had permitted himself.

"Mr. Caproni?"

Albert smiled at Mrs. Maser. She was one of the few people who outranked him in seniority. He still felt funny when she called him Mr. Caproni instead of Albert. The change had taken place when he was appointed district attorney. It was one of the negative aspects of growing up and assuming a position of authority. It caused subtle changes in your relationships with the people around you.

"What can I do for you, Fanny?"

"I hate to disturb you, but this could be important."

Albert noticed that Mrs. Maser was tense. Now that was unusual.

"There is a man at the front desk. He has been drinking and he looks like a derelict, but . . . well, he said he had a message for you. I don't think he is a crank. He looks sincere."

"What was the message?"

"He said that he had been sent to tell you that Willie Heartstone was dying and that Mr. Heartstone wants to tell you who killed Elaine Murray."

The room shifted and Caproni felt faint. One minute there had been solid ground beneath him and then it was gone and he was floating, light as air.

"Mr. Caproni, are you all right?"

William Heartstone. He fought for control. A deep breath. The dizziness passed, leaving him disoriented and unsure of himself.

"Get Pat Kelly. I want that man back here. Tell Pat no rough stuff, but don't let him leave. And bring me a tape recorder. A portable."

His voice was quivering. Quite unlike him. It seemed to come from far away. From the past. He could hear it echoing in the solitude of a dingy hotel room on the one and only day that he had ever seen William Heartstone.

Caproni filled a glass with cold water from the tap in his private bathroom and wished it was Scotch. He straightened his tie, tucked in his shirt and put on his jacket. The Murray-Walters case. After all these years.

The morning paper was resting on the corner of his desk. There was a picture of Philip Heider standing arm in arm with the President. There was talk that he was being considered for Attorney General. What effect would the reappearance of William Heartstone have on his career? None, probably, Caproni mused bitterly. Heider was one of those indestructible people who gain strength from the things that corrupt and sicken most people. His tracks were too well covered anyway. Thanks to him and Shindler there was no evidence. Only shadows and whispers.

Heider had never been the person responsible for what had happened in the Murray-Walters case anyway. From the beginning it had been Roy Shindler. In the years that had followed the dramatic ending of the trial of Bobby Coolidge, Caproni had tried to find out if there was any truth to the ugly rumors that he had heard about Shindler's part in the case. He had always come up against a wall of silence.

Shindler was too well respected in the department to be crucified for one lapse of faith.

Maybe Caproni, with his influence, could have discovered the truth if he had really tried, but his reflection in the mirror stared out accusingly, reminding him that he, as much as anyone else, was responsible for what had happened. There was a point in time when he could have made a decision that would have made a difference, but he had lacked the courage. Maybe he had never really wanted to find out the truth. All the guilt and uncertainty that he had stored in the attic of his mind pressed once more against his shoulders. The weight made him tired and he slumped in his chair.

Pat Kelly, Caproni's chief investigator, entered the office. The thin, frightened man beside him was obviously down on his luck. He looked like a child next to Kelly. Caproni decided that Weaver did not appear to be too steady on his feet and he signaled him into a chair as soon as the introductions had been made.

"Mr. Weaver, I understand that you are a friend of William Heartstone?"

"You mean Willie? Yes, sir. We go way back. I met him at the V.A. after he lost his leg."

"He lost a leg? I didn't know that."

"He was in an awful accident. It done somethin' to him up here," Weaver said, pointing to his head. "But he ain't mean and he never hurt no one, honest."

"Why did you feel you had to tell me that he wouldn't hurt anyone, Mr. Weaver?"

Louis bowed his head and stared into his lap.

"It's about why I come. Willie got religion in Fort

Worth and ever since he's been talkin' about his soul and the bad thing he done. Only I ain't never seen him act like he says he did.

"Then he got sick and he wouldn't talk about anything else except coming back to Portsmouth and seeing you."

"Where is Willie now?"

"He's at the Cordova on Tenth Street."

Caproni knew the Hotel Cordova from his police days. It had changed management a dozen times since then, but it had not changed. It was still one of the many dollar-a-night flophouses in the lower Water Street district that catered to alcoholics, drifters and pensioners.

"How sick is Willie?"

Louis's fingers kneaded the brim of his hat, twisting and curving it. Caproni's question made him think of Willie, alone on the hotel bed. Poor Willie, coughing and sweating and moaning in his own personal hell.

"I think he's going to die."

"Has he seen a doctor?"

Louis shook his head.

"We didn't have the money. I spent my last dollars on the room. And when I talked about the V.A. or the County Hospital he would get all excited. The only thing he talks about is seeing you and making his peace."

Caproni gave his secretary instructions to have a doctor sent to the Cordova. Then he, Kelly and Weaver took the elevator to the lobby. Kelly ran into the cold to get the car and Weaver and Caproni stood in the lobby.

"Willie's not in any trouble, is he, Mr. Caproni? We've been good friends for a while now and I know he done some small things. I mean we both pinched some wine now and then. But I ain't never seen him do something real bad."

Caproni stuffed his hands into his overcoat pockets and stared out at the snow-covered trees in the park across the street. The park took up the whole block across from the courthouse. It was small and, during the summer, it was overcrowded and dirty. The winter had emptied and purified it, transforming its tired and beggarly trees and grass into royalty by draping them with cloaks of smooth white snow. It was nice to think about nature's ability to change the sordid and unclean into something regal, but Caproni knew that the dirt still existed beneath the snow.

The Murray Walters case was like that. The years had smoothed over the questions and the doubts, but Caproni knew about the dirt. He had never forgotten what Shindler and Heider had done and he had never forgiven himself for his lack of courage when he had been faced with a choice between his own career and another man's life.

"Willie's not in any trouble, is he?" Louis repeated. Pat Kelly drove the car in front of the entrance.

"I don't know, Mr. Weaver," Albert Caproni said as they moved into the storm.

Part II

Death

1

Elaine Murray was so excited that her hand shook and she smeared her lipstick. She rubbed her lips together to even the Tahitian Passion. She saw the spot the smear had made on the skin beneath her lower lip and used a tissue to wipe it away. She said, "Oh, damn," when the spot resisted. Then she giggled. She liked to swear in the privacy of her room or when she was with close friends, but using swear words always caused a nervous giggle, because she knew her folks would never approve. They were both very square.

Her hair looked fine. It was natural auburn brown. Sometimes, when the sun was just right, Richie said it looked like it was on fire. She patted the edges with approval.

Elaine stood up and walked over to a full-length mirror that hung on her closet door. She struck a pose and smiled. Her body was trim and athletic. Her stomach was very flat from exercise and her hips were wide and curvy. When she looked at her breasts, she frowned a little. They were beautifully shaped, but small. She knew that men liked large breasts and she hoped that Richie would not be disappointed. She had thought about wearing falsies, but rejected the idea. She was sure that tonight would be the night and she did not want to be a phony. She wanted Richie to know exactly what he was going to get. Besides, Richie was a gentleman and he would never tell that she was smaller than she usually appeared. That would be their secret. One of the things that they would share—maybe forever.

Forever! Elaine closed her eyes and lay back on the bed. She tried to imagine Richie and her married. Of course, that wouldn't happen for some time. After all, they weren't even going steady . . . yet. But after tonight . . .

Elaine didn't want to think about it. Maybe she was guessing wrong and he would not ask her. After all, they had only been dating seriously for a month. A month. It seemed like forever. She could not remember when she had been so happy. Richie Walters. It seemed like a dream come true.

Elaine had had a crush on Richie Walters since her sophomore year, but he had not even noticed her until this summer when they had both worked at the Empire Department Store. At first he had just talked with her at breaks or when he passed through her department. Her father, Dr. Harold Murray, knew the Empire's store manager and he had gotten her the job for the summer. Richie had gotten his job the same way. They had joked about being rich and having pull. Elaine was sure, though, that Richie could have gotten any job he wanted on his own. He was so handsome. She loved his curly blond hair and blue eyes. His nose was so perfect. And he was so smart, so deep. Richie knew all about things. He had worked on President Kennedy's campaign this fall and had actually met the President when he had campaigned in Portsmouth. She knew Richie had applied to a lot of colleges and was so smart that he could probably go where he wanted, but she hoped that he would choose State, where she was hoping to go. It would be hard to go steady and be separated. She knew that she would remain faithful, but . . . There she went again. He hasn't even asked you, dope, she thought. Then, again, she was sure, positive, he would. Wendy Blair was going with Frank Coppella and Frank played football with Richie and was his best friend and he had told Wendy that Richie had been thinking about it and Richie had been acting funny this week.

Elaine pulled herself up and sat down again in front of her dressing table. She applied eyeliner and mascara and turned her head back and forth. She thought that she was pretty. Not beautiful like Alice Fay, the queen of last year's prom, but pretty. And there were plenty of boys who thought so, too. She was a cheerleader and had been a princess in Alice's court, so she was no wallflower.

Elaine slipped on a pair of white panties and hooked up her bra. Then she put on tan toreador slacks and a white blouse. She pulled a red and black ski sweater over the blouse. It had been a funny winter, she mused. Here it was, just after Thanksgiving, and it was not all that cold. That was fine with Elaine. She never did like the cold weather.

Elaine doublechecked her blouse and noticed that one of the buttons was undone. As she rebuttoned it she felt a thrill of excitement. She closed her eyes and tried to imagine Richie's strong fingers unbuttoning the blouse, one button at a time. Very slowly and deliberately. Her mouth was suddenly dry and her stomach tight. Her nipples were growing taut beneath her bra and the friction between them and the cloth was not unpleasant.

Richie was a gentleman in every way, but he had the urges that all men had. Elaine had talked to her mother about sex and men. Her mother had told her to hold on to her virginity, because she would lose a man's respect if she was too free. She had followed her mother's advice even though it had been hard at times. Like when she was in Richie's arms and he was caressing her breasts through her blouse. When he did that she just wanted to let him do it like he asked. But she was glad she had not given in yet. A woman's body was a gift for the man she married. Her present to him. It would be so much better if they were married. And what her mother had said about respect was true. Look at the way the boys talked about Eleanor Strom behind her back and everyone knew how far you could get with her. But, tonight, she had made up her mind. Tonight, if he asked her to go steady, she would let him touch her breasts. It would only be fair and she would want him to have a reason to stay with her.

She looked at the clock. Holy cow, it was after eight and he would be here any minute. She slipped on a pair of tennis sneakers and looked at herself once more. Downstairs the doorbell was ringing.

* * *

Bobby Coolidge was standing in front of the mirror in the men's room of Bob's Hamburger Heaven, admiring himself. With great precision he raised the black plastic comb and drew it through his thick, greasy jet black hair. First, he swept the hair on the sides straight back. The hair on both sides of his head resembled wings and there was a little "tail" where the hair on each side joined behind his head. Bobby surveyed his work. A perfect duck's ass if he had to say so himself. He twirled the curl that he had placed in the center of his forehead one more time. Presley never did it better, he thought.

"Lend me the comb when you're through, grease-ball," his brother Billy said as he zipped the fly on his tight-fitting jeans.

"Just one second, man," Bobby said. There had been a hair out of place on the left side of his head. He stepped back from the mirror and ran the comb through again. When he was satisfied, he rinsed off the comb and handed it to Billy.

Billy stepped in front of the mirror and Bobby leaned against the bathroom wall, taking a cigarette out of the pack he kept in one of the zippered pockets of his black leather jacket.

"What do you want to do?" he asked.

"I don't know. What do you want to do?"

"What I don't want to do is stick around this joint anymore tonight. That pussy Delores is giving me a pain."

"The waitress with the pimples?"

Bobby nodded and Billy saw him in the mirror.

"The word's out on her, Bobby. Harry Capri says she toots on the root."

"Well, I got more class than Harry Capri. Do you ever see the pigs he goes out with?"

"Listen, Capri says she gives a hum job to the tune of Yankee Doodle and makes you come on the last note."

"You're full of shit."

Billy shrugged.

"Would I lie to my own brother?"

"If she's so hot, how come you ain't made a play for her?"

"Too ugly. I save the ugly ones for you."

Bobby laughed. He was lucky to have a brother who was also a good friend. The Coolidge brothers stuck together. They fought together. They screwed together. He smiled, took a drag on his cigarette and tried to picture Delores giving him a blow job. Nah, he couldn't do it. Shit, he'd never be that horny.

Billy straightened up and handed Bobby his comb.

"You still didn't answer me."

"About what?"

"What to do."

"I don't know." He shrugged. "We could crash Alice Fay's party."

"She having a party?" Bobby asked with interest.

"That's what Rog says. We can ask him when we get back to the table."

Billy pushed open the bathroom door and they wound their way through the usual tables of squares and teeny-boppers to their table in the far corner of the restaurant. Roger Hessey and Esther Freemont were eating their hamburgers and Esther, as usual, was finishing an extra shake. Bobby absentmindedly scratched his crotch when he looked at Esther. She had big tits, and Bobby liked big tits, and she wasn't bad looking, either. All the same, she fucked anything that walked and Bobby's personal opinion was that a good-looking guy like Hessey could do a lot better for himself. Also, she was a pain. She had a crush on Bobby and was always making cow eyes at him and giving him the big come-on. Bobby knew he could fuck her if he wanted, but he knew a broad as dumb as Esther wouldn't keep his interest long and he couldn't hack the big scene he knew would happen when he told her to get lost. He was also a little nervous, because he knew that Esther had stabbed a guy at Stuyvesant High who had tried something funny when she wasn't in the mood and he didn't want any of that scene. Nah, all in all, it was best to leave Esther alone. Now Alice Fay or Elaine Murray—there was class. Too bad they were such stuck-up bitches. He'd sure like to pop one of them.

"Rog, didn't you tell me that Alice Fay was having a party tonight?" Billy asked.

"Yeah. Why?"

"I don't know. I thought maybe Bobby and me would go."

"You ain't invited," Roger said.

"I know that, asshole. That has nothing to do with whether we go or not."

Roger shook his head.

"That's just gonna mean trouble."

Bobby grinned.

"You ain't afraid of a little trouble, are you?"

"Shit no," Roger said uneasily. "I just ain't in the mood for it tonight."

"Who says there has to be trouble?" Billy asked.

"All I was thinkin' of doing was going to a party. I ain't gonna start any trouble."

"One of those jocks will."

"Jocks are basically candyasses, right, Bob?"

Bobby nodded in agreement.

"Well count me out," Roger said.

"Oh, Rog, can't we go? I never saw Alice Fay's house," Esther said.

"What do you want to see her house for. It's just another spoiled rich kid's house."

"I know, but I'd like to. Couldn't we, please?"

"I told you, I ain't going to no fucking party where I ain't been invited. Alice Fay has got her nose stuck up her ass anyway."

"I know something I'd like to stick up her ass," Billy said.

"You watch your mouth," Esther said angrily. Billy just grinned.

"Look," Billy said, "I'm crashing. Who's gonna come with me?"

"Count me in," Bobby said.

"I'm just going home," Roger said.

"Can I come with you guys?" Esther pleaded.

Bobby looked at Billy. It would be a real pain to have to take Esther along, but, if they said yes, Roger would probably come so as not to lose face.

"Sure, Esther, come on."

Roger looked at his plate.

"Ah, if you're going, I'm coming."

"Good. I knew you weren't chicken."

"Who's chicken?" Roger bristled.

Bobby and Billy laughed.

"No one is chicken, man. We were just riding you."

"Yeah, Rog. Everyone knows you're a good man in a fight."

"Almost as good as this," Billy said and Bobby heard the familiar click as the long steel of Billy's switchblade snapped out under the table. "The Old Equalizer," Billy liked to call it and it had sure come in handy in the past. Bobby smiled as he remembered the time they had gone to the movies and the two niggers had sat down behind them and made all that noise. Bobby hated niggers. Bobby and Billy were Cobras and from time to time the Cobras would ride over to the nigger section of town and beat the shit out of one or two. But that time at the movies there had just been the two of them and these two noisy jigaboos and Billy had asked them real polite to shut up, but they started with this wiseass jive and just kept making more noise and talking cool about white boys and one nigger leaned down next to Billy's ear and whispered real low about how he was going to wait till the show was over and follow Billy outside and stomp him good. Bobby had started to turn, but he had felt Billy's hand on his knee and had heard the sound of the blade being withdrawn from Billy's pocket. The nigger's lips were practically touching Billy's ear and his nose was leaning down over Billy's left shoulder. The nigger never saw the knife in the dark until it was too late. Billy brought it up real slow with his right hand and pressed the button. The tip of the blade had shot out just right, poking the tiniest hole in the tip of the nigger's nose. The nigger had screamed in pain. Blood was pouring out of his nostril and Billy was up on his seat screaming. Those coons sure had run fast. Billy always ended the story by saying that it was the only time he ever saw a nigger turn white.

Esther was finishing her shake and Billy and Roger went over to the cashier and paid the bill. Bobby knew where Alice lived and Roger did not, so they decided that Roger and Esther would follow Bobby and Billy. Bobby felt good. He knew that something would happen tonight. He had that tingly feeling in his stomach that he would get when he was nervous, but cool. Like before a rumble or before he would start to put the make on some chick. The clock in the hamburger joint read eight fifty-five.

Richie Walters parked his '55 Mercury next to the curb in front of Elaine Murray's house. Before he got out, he checked his face in the rear view mirror. He had taken care of a pimple on the left side of his chin with Clearasil and he wanted to make sure that he had done a good job. The pimple was almost invisible under the flesh-colored cover-up. Richie smiled. He looked good. He had made a special effort to look good, because tonight was going to be a special night.

It was chilly out and Richie tucked his hands into the pockets of his letter jacket as he headed for the house. He felt funny: half elated, half depressed. He had never asked a girl to go steady before and the idea frightened him a little. For all his good looks and popularity, he was awkward with girls. He always felt that he was saying or doing the wrong thing when he was with them. Then he had started dating Elaine and everything had changed. He felt at ease with her. She thought his jokes were funny and his views incisive. And she responded to him sexually—to a point. That was the only problem they had. When he was kissing her or holding her, he lost control. Elaine would let him go so far and then stop. He knew she trusted him, because she let him go as far as she did, but he always left her with a mixture of fulfillment and frustration.

Going steady was a big step to take. He had thought about it for some time before deciding to ask Elaine. The biggest problem would arise next September. Richie was crazy about Elaine, but he knew that she was not as smart as he was. She had applied to State and a few other local colleges, whereas he had applied to mostly Ivy League and other eastern schools. State was his last choice and he did not really want to go there.

Richie did not think that he would have much trouble getting into a top school. He had excellent grades and he had letters in three sports, plus an honorable mention All-State as a halfback his junior year. Coach thought he would make first team this year and a few schools had already offered him athletic scholarships.

Richie had turned the athletic scholarships down. He wanted to play sports in college, but he was more interested in his education. He had listened hard to what John Kennedy had said during his campaign for the Presidency. Kennedy had talked a lot about public service and the disadvantaged. Richie felt that he had had all the breaks and he had decided that he wanted to help those who had not. He was not sure if he wanted to be a doctor or go into law or perhaps science. He was certain, though, that he wanted to work with, and help, people.

Richie rang the doorbell. He took a look at his high school ring. It would not be on his finger after tonight. That was, if Elaine accepted. For a second he felt a surge of fear. What if she rejected him? No, she wouldn't. He was sure that she felt for him the same way that he felt for her.

Richie heard footsteps approaching from inside. He took a quick look at the sky. It was a beautiful clear night. There had been some rain earlier in the day, but the sky was unclouded and star-sprinkled now. He had certainly picked a romantic evening to ask Elaine to be his girl. He had planned how he would do it. First he would take her to the movies. Alice Fay had invited them to a party, but he felt that the movies would be more intimate.

After the movies, they would cruise downtown. Richie's car was out of character for a boy who was basically introverted; but he loved it. He had customized it himself and it was the talk of the school. No one could touch it in a drag race.

Afterward, they would have something to eat. Or maybe they wouldn't. Then he would drive her to Lookout Park and ask her to go steady.

The door opened and Mrs. Murray invited him in. He liked Mrs. Murray. She was always very cheerful. He told her how nice she looked and she thanked him and called upstairs for Elaine.

Myron Krauss was in town to sell hardware, but the market was lousy, he told everyone at the bar who would listen. Myron was forty-eight, fat and balding. He lived in Minneapolis with his wife and three children. After twenty-five years of marriage he found them all boring.

Myron was pretty boring himself. Maybe that was why no one was listening to him. After a while Myron even bored himself, so he decided to try another bar. He stumbled when he pushed himself off the red leather bar stool. He had to grab for support. "I'm a bit high," he thought. He knew he wasn't drunk, though. Myron was proud of the fact that he could hold his liquor.

When Myron lurched out into the cold night air, two young men in black leather jackets and tight blue jeans followed him. Both men had their hair combed back at the sides and forward in the center, until it curled in the middle of their foreheads, like Elvis Presley's. The hair had been heavily greased and what little light there was in the bar reflected off it.

The wind gusted as the two men exited the bar. They pulled on leather gloves and followed after Myron at a fast pace. There was an alley a little bit ahead of the drunken salesman. The two men timed their actions perfectly. They reached Myron just as he reached the alley.

Ralph Pasante slammed both hands against Myron's shoulder and Myron stumbled into the alley. Myron was too drunk to realize what was happening. His face registered puzzlement instead of fear. Willie Heartstone knew that his prey would react just this way from past experience. He hit the little man in his solar plexus. Myron grunted. He could not breathe. He thought he might die from lack of air and he opened his mouth wide and wheezed. Willie thought Myron looked like a fish. He let him wiggle around for a second before driving his knuckles into Myron's nose as hard as he could. Willie felt bone crack and crumble and he saw blood gush out. That felt good. Ralph kicked Myron in the groin. Myron fell to his knees and his head bounced off the alley floor when it hit. Ralph stomped him once for fun. Then they went through the unconscious man's pockets. When they had his wallet, watch, rings and small change, they ran out of the far end of the alley. Their car was four blocks away.

After they had driven a few blocks, they pulled over on a side street and Willie counted the money.

"How much?"

"A hundred and sixty bucks and change," Willie said in a matter-of-fact tone. The muggings did not excite him like they used to, unless the victim put up a fight. Then he enjoyed it. He liked beating someone with spirit. It made him feel masterful. This punk tonight was a zero. Willie knew that he would not fight when he saw him flashing his roll at the bar.

"What do you want to do now?" Ralph asked.

Willie ran his tongue across his lips. The two beers he had had in the bar had made him loose and easy. While sitting and waiting for the fat man to leave, he had daydreamed about a woman: his dream woman. The one who came to him at night when he was alone. She was blond and long-legged and she always cowered on the floor before him. Sometimes he would beat her. Sometimes he would please her.

"I don't know," Willie answered casually. "We

could cruise downtown. It's almost ten-thirty. The movies'll be letting out."

Ralph smiled. He knew what Willie was thinking. Friday night movies meant unattached high school snatch. Willie headed for downtown Portsmouth.

Bobby Coolidge stopped the car in the yard of Alice Fay's house. Alice lived in a modern, three-story stone house which was located on several acres of Portsmouth's wealthiest suburb. Her folks were in Hawaii on vacation, so Alice had the house to herself. Bobby and Billy checked their hair in the car mirror. Bobby could hear the sound of a rock band vibrating the night air and he could see the silhouettes of people talking and dancing inside the house. He told Billy to hurry up and Billy zipped up his jacket.

Roger's car pulled up behind them and they walked up to the porch. Bobby knew that the four of them would not be welcome, but he didn't give a shit. Most of the people at the party would be candy-asses. Jocks, brains. In general, squares. He knew the squares felt uneasy in his presence. He enjoyed that.

Bobby pounded on the front door and a boy in a white shirt and chinos opened it. When the boy saw who had knocked, he looked nervous. The boy was Arnie Klaus, a jock. Arnie looked strong, but, like most jocks, he was chicken when it came to a fight. A year ago, when Arnie was a freshman, Billy had made him cough up a quarter for protection. Billy had outgrown that phase, but Arnie still avoided both Coolidges.

"Hi, Arnie," Billy said politely. "Good party?"

"Yeah, Bob," Arnie answered, a little too enthusiastically.

The four of them drifted into a corner of the room. They had noticed the buzz that had accompanied their entrance. It gave Bobby and Billy satisfaction.

The living room was big. Alice's family had plenty of dough. Everyone looked freshly scrubbed and fashionably casual. Bobby hated them. He tried not to brood on it, but he felt that it was so unfair that these snotnose punks should have it all, while he and Billy had to work so hard for everything they had ever gotten. It had been like that ever since their father had died. Both of them holding down jobs after school. Living poor. Watching their mother drink herself away.

Billy scanned the room. He stopped when he saw Alice Fay and Tommy Cooper standing near the punch bowl. Alice was going steady with Tommy. Tommy had his arm around her shoulder as if he owned her. Billy felt a mixture of anger and despair. It was not right that he should have no chance with a girl like Alice. She was tall and slender with large breasts. Her eyes sparkled and her teeth were perfect. She was perfection. At night, Billy fantasized about her. But it was just a dream and he knew that it could never come true. Alice and her friends were rich. They would graduate high school and go on to college. Bobby and Billy were nothings in their eyes. Their futures were obscure and gray.

Tommy Cooper told a joke and Alice laughed. Billy hated Cooper. He was a jock and a brain. He was tall. His black hair was cropped in a crew cut and his skin seemed tanned even in winter. He wore his letter sweater proudly over a plaid shirt and tan chinos. He looked relaxed and at ease in white socks and loafers.

Bobby noticed the way his brother was looking at Alice. Billy had never told him, but he knew about Billy's crush on her.

"That Alice is all right," Bobby said.

"She's okay."

"I'd sure like to get me some of that, hey, Rog?" Roger leered.

"Cut that out," Esther said. "We shouldn't even be here, so don't cause any trouble."

Arnie had walked over to Tommy and Alice while they had been talking. Arnie said something and motioned in their direction. Cooper turned toward them and scowled.

"I don't like that prick," Billy said.

"Me neither," said Bobby.

"You want to have some fun?"

"Hey, I told you I didn't want no trouble," Roger said uneasily. "Besides, we're outnumbered."

"I didn't say anything about trouble, Roger," Billy said, grinning. "I said 'fun.'"

"Billy, I know you. Look, Esther, I don't feel right being here. I'm going home."

Esther looked at Roger and at Billy and Bobby. Roger was her boyfriend, but he was acting like a coward.

"Let's stay, Roger. Please."

"I told you no. Now come on."

"You never want to have fun. I want to stay."

"Well I don't."

Roger started for the door. Esther went after him. They were talking in angry undertones as they went out the door. Five minutes later Esther came back in. She was crying. "Oh, shit," Bobby thought. Now they were stuck with Esther for the evening. Roger and Esther were always having fights. They usually ended with Roger slapping her around and Esther crying.

"That bastard left me," Esther whimpered.

"Don't worry. We'll get you home," Bobby said. He was watching Cooper carefully. Cooper had gone over to a couple of the bigger boys in the room and they were talking in the corner.

"I think I'll get some punch," Billy said.

Bobby followed his brother over to the refreshment table. His brother filled a glass of punch and munched some potato chips. The people at the table ignored them. There were a few comments made in guarded tones.

Bobby noticed Cooper approaching. He was having second thoughts about what they were doing. He had been in a fighting mood all day, but now that it looked like they were going to get into it, he didn't like the odds.

"Hi, Alice," Billy said.

"Hello, Billy," Alice answered stiffly.

"Nice party."

Alice forced a smile and walked off. Tommy Cooper talked to her in low tones. There were four guys behind him. Bobby knew two of them from school. He did not know the other two. They looked tough.

Alice looked upset. Bobby heard her say something about "no trouble" and he saw Tommy and the others push past her and head in their direction.

"Alice said she didn't invite you, Coolidge."

Billy was refilling his punch glass and he purposely kept his back to Cooper.

"I guess she didn't. We just heard that there was a party and decided to drop by."

"Well, why don't you just drop out."

Billy turned. He was smiling. Bobby had seen that smile before and he moved his body sideways so as to make himself tough to hit.

"Why don't you just fuck off?"

Cooper looked uncertain of his next move. The noise in the room had stopped.

"Now look here . . ." Cooper started to say. One of the two boys that Bobby did not know had moved beside Tommy. He was Billy and Bobby's size, about six two, and he looked lean and muscular. His hair was crew cut and he resembled Cooper. The other stranger was taller than the Coolidges, but he was fat and looked out of shape.

"Let's cut the talk," the boy who looked like Tommy said. "I've heard enough from this little fart. Now you two get out or I'll kick your ass out."

"You better listen, Billy. This is my brother. He's on leave from the service."

Billy's boot caught Tommy's brother in the groin. As he folded, Bobby hit him in the temple with a right. The boys standing with Tommy were too shocked to move. Billy had counted on this and he smashed the punch glass into Tommy Cooper's face and hit him in the stomach.

The fat boy was the first to react. He was deceptively fast and he put his bulk behind a right that exploded against Billy's head, knocking him backward across the refreshment table. Bobby hit the fat man, but the punch had no effect and two other boys had him down before he could move. They were not hitting him. They were just holding him.

"He's got a knife," someone screamed. Bobby could not see much from the floor. The fat boy moved into his line of vision and he heard his brother yell,

"Come on, motherfucker, and I'll cut you wide open."

"Stop this," Alice Fay was yelling.

"Let my brother go and we'll leave this shithole."

"Let him up," Alice said, and the two boys that were holding Bobby rolled off.

Billy was standing with his back to the table with the knife in his hand. The fat boy had a broken Coke bottle.

"Let's get out of here," Bobby said. The crowd moved away from the door and they edged out. Esther was already on the porch. She looked terrified.

People were filing onto the porch as they moved toward their car. Esther climbed in back and Billy drove off. Billy's face was tight. Bobby could see a pulse throbbing in Billy's temple.

"The bastards," Billy said in a taut, clipped voice. "Just once I want to be treated like a human being by those cocksucking sons of bitches."

"You were looking for it . . ." Esther started.

Billy jammed on the brakes and whirled in his seat. He held a rigid finger in front of Esther's startled eyes.

"Just shut your mouth or I'll ram a fist down it. You'd love to be one of those goody goodies, wouldn't you? Well, they're nothing but a bunch of leeches, living off of daddy's money. Not one of them is worth the shit off of my asshole. And someday . . ."

His voice trailed off into the darkness. The illuminated hands of the dashboard clock read ten twenty-five.

Elaine Murray checked her hair and lipstick one final time and left the ladies' room of the Paramount Theater. She had been grateful for the excuse to leave Richie for a few moments. She needed the time to catch her breath. She felt as if she was floating and giddy.

Elaine could hardly remember the movie. All she could remember was Richie's strong arms around her and the passion of his kisses. They had gone to the last row of the balcony and the movie had barely started when she felt him slide his arm behind her shoulders.

The movie was *Midnight Lace* with Doris Day and Rex Harrison. It was a thriller and it took place in London. It got tense and she moved as close to Richie as she could. Then he had been kissing her and she had kissed back, letting him slip his hand inside her sweater.

Their tongues had touched and she could feel his fingers caressing her nipples through her bra. She had lost control.

It was near the end of the movie when he had whispered that he loved her. She had almost cried. Then

the lights had come on. She told him that she wanted
to freshen up. Inside the ladies' room, she sat in a stall
until she was relaxed enough to go out again.

Richie was waiting in the lobby. He felt happy and
unsure of what to say now that he had said what was
in his heart. Elaine took his hand and they walked
out of the theater. The sidewalks were crowded with
Friday-night strollers and the streets were jammed
with souped-up cars that raced their engines and
honked at each other. Downtown Portsmouth was
the place to be seen on Friday and Saturday nights.

Richie and Elaine walked slowly despite the chill
in the air. A group of boys were standing beside
Richie's car. Elaine recognized Matt Shaw and Rudy
Pegovich. They said hello and talked for a bit. Elaine
wished they would leave. Soon Richie said so long
and opened her door. She felt proud to sit in Richie's
car. It was the talk of the school. She didn't know
much about cars, but she knew that the engine was
powerful and that other cars could not beat it. He had
dragged with her in the car several times and she had
always been thrilled by the car's speed and Richie's
daring.

As the car pulled into traffic, she snuggled up
against him.

"Do you want something to eat?" he asked.

"I'm not hungry," she replied dreamily.

Richie was stimulated by the softness of her voice.
He reached his right hand around her shoulder and
drove with his left. He kissed her when they stopped
for the light.

"Do you want to drive up to Lookout Park?" he
asked, knowing what her answer would be.

She did not say anything. Instead, she snuggled closer. Richie turned off the main downtown drag and headed for Monroe Boulevard. Monroe led out of the city to a large wooded area in the hills that was called Lookout Park by the City Park Commission and Lovers' Lane by everyone else. The park was large and sprawling, with several secluded areas that were used for picnics in the daytime and making out at night.

"It's so beautiful tonight, Richie," she said.

He wanted to tell her that he thought she was beautiful, but he could not. As intimate as they had been, he still felt tongue-tied. He had had so little experience with girls and he was afraid of saying the wrong thing or saying the right thing in a way that would sound phony. Gasping out "I love you" in the theater had taken an effort equal to anything he had ever put out on the football field. When she had accepted his profession of love without rebuke, he had felt like shouting through the theater.

He tightened his arm around her for a second and she melted against him, giving him a peck on the cheek. He shifted slightly and felt the contraceptive pushing against his buttocks from its position in his wallet. He had purchased a package of Trojans from a smirking pharmacist at a shopping center near his house. He had never done that before and it had been a nerve-wracking experience.

When he thought about the contraceptives, he wondered why he even bothered. Elaine was too nice a girl to go all the way. But what if she did. He wanted to do it with her so much that his body ached each time they made out. So far she had kept him off with affectionate but firm nos. But that was before they were going steady. Would that change now?

Richie was half afraid of what he would do if it did. He had only been with one other girl. There was a party after they had won the Division Championship last year. One of the girls had gotten drunk and he and three other boys had had sex with her. He had not done so well, coming almost as soon as he touched her. It had not been what he had expected. He was sure that sex would be different with someone he loved.

Monroe Boulevard was deserted this time of night. Richie and Elaine did not notice the car that pulled alongside at the traffic light until it raced its engine. There were two men in the front seat and a girl in the back. Elaine could not see their faces clearly. When the light changed, the car squealed its tires and raced ahead. Richie smiled at Elaine. He was grateful for the distraction. The car had stopped at the next light even though it was green. Richie pulled alongside and the light turned red.

Elaine squeezed the muscle of Richie's right arm and then moved over to give him room. She adored him when he was like this. He sat straight-backed, leaning slightly forward from the waist. His right hand gripped the shift lightly. His face was a picture of intense concentration.

The light changed. Both cars seemed to leap forward. Tires squealed. They floated side by side. Neither appeared to be moving. Then the Mercury pulled ever so slightly ahead.

The stretch of Monroe Boulevard ahead of them

was flat and had no traffic lights for several blocks. The other car lost more ground and then sped up, pulling even. Richie pushed the accelerator toward the floor. They were gaining. And then the other car was veering into them. There was a grinding of metal and the Mercury lurched sideways.

Elaine screamed and Richie fought for control.

"The bastards," Richie swore when they had evened out.

"What happened?"

"That son of a bitch rammed us. I'll show him who he's playing with."

The other car had gained considerable ground, but it seemed to have slowed, as if daring Richie to catch it. Elaine had never seen Richie so grim.

"Don't chase them, Richie. Let them go. Please."

"No one does that to me, Elaine."

The Mercury was pulling even again and as it drew alongside, the other car swerved into their lane. Richie reacted in time, pulling to the side, then cutting back into the other lane. Elaine screamed and there was the sound of metal grinding again. This time the other car went into a skid. It hit a wet patch of pavement and spun sideways. The driver fought for control and the car fishtailed toward the sidewalk. Elaine watched open-mouthed through the rear window as the car bounced off a telephone pole and then screeched to a stop, facing the way it had come. Richie gave the Mercury more gas to widen the distance between the two cars. Elaine could see a figure in tight jeans and a black leather jacket getting shakily out of the car.

Richie started to laugh and she laughed too. It was a release of tension and it sounded hysterical for a moment.

"Did you see that guy fishtail?" Richie asked.

She kissed him for an answer. Her heart swelled with pride at being Richie's girl.

They rode through the hills until they found a place to park. There was a dirt side road off one of the paved roads that twisted through the park. The dirt road ended in a meadow surrounded by evergreens. Richie pulled the car to the far end of the field. He switched off the lights, but left the heater on. With the headlights off, the only illumination was the pale glow of starlight.

Elaine had taken her coat off when the car had heated up and she had put it on the back seat. Richie looked at her and she did not trust herself to speak. Her heart was thumping and Richie looked as nervous as she felt.

"Elaine, I asked you out for a special reason, tonight," he said, the way he had practiced it. They were facing each other and he had placed his hand over hers. The sound of his own voice sounded strange and the words he was saying sounded terribly stilted.

"Elaine, do you . . . do you want to go steady?"

There! He had said it. Elaine thought that her heart would burst. She could not speak. Instead, she threw her arms around him and began to cry. He kissed her and she opened her mouth. Their tongues met.

When they parted, Richie slipped the ring off and gave it to her. She held it and turned it in her hand. He stroked her cheek with his hand and drew her to him. This time his kisses were gentle. She felt herself sliding down on the front seat and she could feel his hand move under her sweater and cup her breast. She arched her back and stroked his neck and ear.

He was unbuttoning her blouse and she did not resist as she always had before. Richie was breathing hard. He managed the buttons without fumbling. She was completely relaxed, accepting him.

He had the blouse undone now and he was caressing her nipple through the bra. His hand worked around her back and she moved slightly to assist him. He was elated and she was afraid and calm at the same time. No man had ever touched her naked breast before. She was terrified of the effect that his strong hands might have on her, yet she longed for him to cup and stroke her. To love her.

He was murmuring his love for her. Kissing her earlobes with the tip of his tongue. Her hand wandered down his leg, terrified of what she knew she would find there. He moved his weight and she touched it suddenly through his pants. It was large and hard. Her fingers pressed it gingerly, drawing back like startled fawns.

The bra was unhooked and she was aware of his fingers exploring the hard tip of her nipple. She was flooded by strange emotions. His penis was so hard and big. If she let him put it inside her, would she feel rending pain? She did not care. She wanted him inside her. She wanted to be driven insane by him, like the women in the books. She felt him loosening her pants.

"No," she said instinctively, pressing her hand on his.

"I love you," he said and she felt his fingers entwine with hers. His lips were kissing the hand that had tried to restrain him. His hand was on her stomach and below. Questing. Caressing her vagina through her panties. She was moaning now. Wanting it. Willing to do anything for him.

"What was that?"

He was sitting bolt upright, staring through the rear window. Her eyes snapped open, startled.

"There's someone out there," he whispered.

She was frightened. From her position on the car seat she could only see the car roof. She heard Richie opening the car door and felt a blast of cold air.

"Richie, don't leave me," she whispered.

"I'll be right back."

The door closed quietly. Her clothes were in disarray. There were tires crunching dirt and gravel nearby. She could hear it now. There was another car door opening and footsteps coming toward the car.

She fumbled with her pants. Richie was outside the car. The interior light was on, because the door had not shut completely. She was in a panic. She could not have anyone see her like this. She struggled with her bra, still lying down so that she would not be seen.

There were voices shouting angrily. One of them was Richie's. Her bra was fastened and she tried to button her blouse. A button popped and she cursed. Someone was grunting. No. More than one person. She struggled with the buttons. They would not fit. She wanted to see, but she could not sit up looking like this. Anyone would know what . . . The car shook with the impact and she could see Richie's back blocking the rear side window. Then it was gone, lunging into the darkness. She sat up. The interior light made it difficult to see into the dark. She reached for the door to close it and Richie screamed. She froze and Richie screamed again. There was the sound of men grunting from exertion and someone swearing. She slammed the door tight. Richie was kneeling and there were two men in black leather jackets standing over him. One man kept raising and lowering his arm and Richie kept screaming.

She had to get out. She had to get away. She looked for the keys, but they were not in the ignition. Someone was yelling in the dark. Someone was rushing toward the car. She turned to her left and screamed. There was a face pressing against the window. Fists pounding on the door. The glass on the other side shattered and she whirled around. An arm clothed in black leather was groping like some obscene spider for the door handle. She curled in a fetal position against the driver's door. She gripped the steering wheel and stared wide-eyed.

"Please. No, please," she whimpered.

The passenger door swung open.

2

It was 9:30, Saturday, November 26, 1960, and Portsmouth police officer Marvin Sokol was almost halfway through his shift. Marvin was in a funny mood. He was feeling good because he had just won five bucks from his partner, Tom McCarthy, who had had the temerity to bet against Navy.

Sokol was an old Navy man. He had been in for four years during the Second World War. He always bet on Navy and this afternoon his boys had walloped Army 17–12 behind the running of Joe Bellino, who Sokol thought would make a great pro, although McCarthy thought that he was too small. Anyway, with Navy winning, Sokol's mood was partly good.

On the other hand, he had read some sad news in the paper that morning and it was making him feel melancholy. He had forgotten about it while he and McCarthy were watching the game. But now, during the monotony of patrol, he had started to brood about it again.

Sokol was fifty years old. In great shape, but fifty nonetheless. Usually this did not bother him, but in this morning's paper he read that "Amos and Andy" was going off the air for good after thirty-two years on radio. Sokol had grown up on the radio. He had a TV like everybody else, but he still listened to radio and his favorite program was "Amos and Andy." He almost never missed it. When he heard it was cancelled, he thought about death.

When you are young, fifty seems ancient, but when you are fifty, fifty doesn't seem that old. You don't think about death being right around the corner. Unless they cancel a show you have listened to for thirty-two years and you realize that everything ends sometime.

Sokol looked over at McCarthy. A youngster. Twenty-two. Or was it twenty-three? He could never remember. "Amos and Andy" would not have meant a thing to him.

McCarthy was driving. Sokol did not care if he drove or not and McCarthy liked to drive, so McCarthy usually did. Sokol liked the Lookout Park section of his patrol. The park was peaceful and beautiful. There was hardly ever any trouble.

McCarthy swung the patrol car onto one of the unpaved dirt side roads that branched off the main paved road. There was a meadow up ahead. They could park for a bit and have a smoke. The car bounced a little and the jiggling motion of the headlights created an illusion that the trees were dancing.

The dirt road ended and McCarthy pulled the car to the side on the grass.

"Is that a car?" Sokol asked.

McCarthy had not noticed anything and he asked what Sokol meant.

"When you swung around, I thought I saw a car at the far end of the meadow."

McCarthy swung the car back in the direction in which Sokol had pointed. There was a '55 Mercury parked near the trees at the far corner of the wide meadow. It looked customized to McCarthy. Red body with red and yellow flames along the side. They drove across the field.

"Probably some kids making out," Sokol said half wistfully.

McCarthy laughed.

"You want to give them the full treatment?"

Sokol thought about "Amos and Andy" and said "No."

When they were almost to the car, they could see that there was no one sitting up in the front or rear seats. Sokol hoped that they were not going to find anyone making love.

McCarthy stopped the car at the rear of the driver's side. He walked toward the driver's door. Sokol skirted the rear and noticed that the window on the passenger's side had been smashed in.

McCarthy raised his flashlight so that he could see the inside of the car. The beam illuminated the front seat and Officer Marvin Sokol forgot all about his personal problems.

The coroner's assistants were trying to remove the body from the front seat of the car and place it on a rubber sheet. They were having trouble maneuvering the head and torso around the steering column, because rigor mortis had set in. One of the men twisted the arm around the steering wheel and Shindler flinched and turned away. When he lit his cigarette, his hand was shaking.

Shindler had been a policeman for six years and a homicide detective for three of those. He was supposed to be conditioned to scenes of violence, but this was something else.

Harvey Marcus, Shindler's partner, was standing over the rubber sheet, looking down at the blood-splattered still life. Shindler wondered how he kept his poise. When Shindler had viewed the body in the car, he had bitten his lip to gain control. The face had been pulp. The body had been a mass of blood-covered wounds.

"You know, I saw him play on Thanksgiving Day. I go back to the High School every year," Marcus said.

"Was he any good?" Shindler asked for no reason at all. Marcus shrugged.

"He was okay. He would have made a college team."

Shindler put out his cigarette. He was going to drop it when he remembered and stuffed it in his raincoat pocket. Clues. He smiled grimly.

"I think there was more than one, Roy," Marcus said.

"What?"

"I said, I think that he was killed by more than one person."

"He would have to have been. Jesus, Harvey, did you see his face?"

Marcus did not answer that question. There had been no face in the conventional sense. A young boy like that, Shindler thought. Someone would pay.

"I figure one stabbed him, or kept him at bay, then the other one hit him from behind. Probably with the same thing they used to cave in the car window."

"A tire iron?"

"It could have been."

They walked around the rear of the car. All around them policemen scurried with cameras and tape measures. Plastic bags and note pads.

"The ground about twenty feet from here shows scuff marks and there is some blood on a rock that wasn't washed away by the rain last night."

Shindler thought about what it would be like to carry the body, still warm, twenty feet to the car and then to stuff it into the front seat. He shuddered involuntarily. He could never have done it.

"Why do you think they moved him?"

"Concealment. Give them more time before it was discovered."

A young patrolman holding a plastic bag was casting nervous glances at the corpse. The bag was resting on the hood of the Mercury.

"That been dusted?" Marcus asked sharply.

The policeman looked up, startled, snapping his eyes away from the corpse.

"Yes, sir."

"What's in the bag?"

"Some of the objects we found in the car."

Marcus opened the top of the bag and peered into it. His eyes stopped on the purse.

"Where did you find that?"

"It was on the floor under the front seat. We found a woman's coat in the back seat."

Marcus started to say something when he was interrupted by a uniformed officer.

"We have a woman who may have seen something. We're keeping her over by the cars. Her name is Thelma Pullen and she lives on the border of the park near the Monroe Boulevard entrance."

Marcus and Shindler followed the officer toward a group of police cars that huddled together on the edge of the meadow. A young officer was writing intently in a notebook when they approached. He was talking to a bony, middle-aged woman whose eyes darted nervously toward the ambulance and the body every few seconds.

"I'm Harvey Marcus and this is Roy Shindler, ma'am. I understand you have some information for us."

"Yes . . . I mean I don't know if it's anything. I just heard about the . . . the murder on the radio this morning and I thought it might be of importance."

She stopped and looked back and forth between Marcus and Shindler, waiting for some word of approval. Marcus gave it to her.

"We appreciate your help. Now what did you see or hear?"

"Well, I live near the entrance to the park. My backyard runs right into the woods at the edge of the park. We used to get a lot of prowlers. Kids mostly.

"John—that's my husband—he's a salesman and he's away a lot. He was worried that someone might break in while he was away. We've been burglarized twice already. So he bought two German Shepherd guard dogs.

"Last night, I was sleeping, when the dogs woke me. They were out in the yard. I let them roam out there and they have a large doghouse. They're on a leash, but it's pretty long.

"Anyway, I got up and looked outside and I saw a girl running away. It was dark, and she was almost off of the property when I looked, but I'm certain it was a girl and she seemed to be coming out of the woods. At least, she was running from the woods."

"About what time was this, Mrs. Pullen?" Shindler asked.

"I thought about that and I really don't know. I didn't look at a clock, but I did go to bed at midnight, so it must have been after that."

"Well, thank you, Mrs. Pullen. This officer will take a detailed statement from you and we will be back in touch later. I appreciate your taking the time to come up here. If we had more good citizens like you, our job would be a lot easier."

The woman blushed and shrugged.

"I just thought it might be important."

She turned toward the ambulance again.

"The radio said he was . . . was stabbed?"

"Yes, ma'am."

She shuddered.

"The park used to be a nice place to live. In the last few years, it's gotten so bad we're thinking of moving."

She shook her head and Shindler and Marcus walked away. Marcus spotted a short, slender man in civilian clothes standing halfway across the meadow. He called out to him. The man looked up and waved and Marcus signaled for him to meet them by Walter's car.

"Giannini," Marcus asked when they reached the vehicle, "did you go through the car?"

"First thing," Giannini answered.

"Did you find anything that suggests that there was a girl with the boy?"

"I'm afraid so." Giannini glanced at the plastic bag that still sat on the hood. "You've seen the purse? There was a woman's coat in the back seat and I found a button that looks like it came from a woman's blouse on the front seat. Mort found a piece of broken fingernail with nail polish on it on the floor of the car below the steering wheel."

Marcus sent Giannini back to the field.

"A girl, too," Shindler said.

"It makes sense. A good-looking kid like that out here in Lover's Lane on a Friday night. There would have to be a girl."

"Then where is she?"

Shindler turned to the young officer who was watching the property bag.

"Has that purse been checked for I.D. yet?"

"Yes, sir. The purse belongs to an Elaine Murray."

Shindler mulled this over for a moment. Then he ducked his head inside the car and fiddled with the catch on the glove compartment. The metal door flopped down. There were some road maps, a triple A book and a package of Trojans. He remembered that the kid had one in his wallet.

"You don't think it's possible that the girl killed him, do you?" Shindler asked.

"It's possible, but she would have needed help."

"And, if she wasn't involved . . ."

"Then, my young friend," Marcus said, "we have something more than murder."

Harvey Marcus had been on the force for eighteen years. When Shindler had transferred to Homicide, Marcus had taken him under his wing. He had been fascinated by the shy and awkward young detective who seemed so lost inside his large, ungainly body. Marcus and Shindler had been partners for three years now and Shindler was still a mystery to Marcus. Marcus had noticed his partner's emotional response to the boy's body. He was surprised by it, but this was not out of character for Shindler, whose moods shifted unpredictably and who could be intensely emotional one minute and icily intellectual the next.

Shindler was a solitary man. He was a bachelor. A twenty-four-hour cop. He could be charming when his job required it, but Marcus had never seen him with his guard down in a social situation. Once, Ruth, Marcus's wife, had tried to fix him up with one of her fellow teachers. Marcus had warned her, but she had insisted. The evening had been a disaster. Roy had squirmed through dinner, saying almost nothing. He would not speak to Marcus for two days.

"This is it," Marcus said.

The Walters' house was a two-story, white suburban ranch constructed of brick. A beautifully manicured lawn sprinkled with a few large shade trees framed it. Shindler parked the car and they followed a slate walk to the front door.

A young-looking woman in her early forties opened the door. Shindler felt his stomach tighten and his throat go dry. After all the times he had done it, he had still not found an easy way to tell the survivors about their dead.

"Mrs. Walters?"

"Yes," she answered through the screen door.

He held out his badge.

"I'm Detective Shindler and this is Detective Marcus. We're with the Portsmouth Police."

In the space of a second, the woman's face showed fear, hope and puzzlement. She stepped back and ushered them in.

"Is this about Richie? Have you found him?"

"Yes, it is. Is your husband home?"

"Of course. I'll call him."

She walked a few steps down a hallway carpeted in powder blue and called her husband. Shindler looked into the stylishly furnished living room. Everything was done in soft yellows and blues. There was a comfortable-looking sofa.

"Can we sit down?" he asked. She would need to when he told her why they had come. There was a bar in one corner. That was good.

"Mrs. Walters, where did your son go last night?"

Before she could answer, a tall, thin man with a balding head and a warm, self-confident look entered from the hallway. He was a man who was used to being in charge. Even so, Shindler thought, that look of self-confidence would have to have been put on this morning. He had to be nervous about his son's disappearance.

The detectives stood up.

"Dear, this is Detective Shindler and Detective Marcus. They're here about Richie."

There was an anxious note in her speech. Mr. Walters shook hands. He had a firm grip. Businessman or lawyer, Shindler mused. He looked like he would be capable of handling his wife's and his sorrow.

"I certainly appreciate this quick service," he said.

"Pardon?" Marcus asked.

"We only called in about Richie an hour ago," Mr. Walters explained.

"I see. When did you last see your son, Mr. Walters?"

"Friday night. He had a date and he left the house about eight o'clock."

Mr. Walters paused. For the first time, a flicker of doubt intruded on his self-confidence.

"Is there something wrong? Is he hurt?"

They never imagine the worst. They never ask you if he is dead. They just prod a little, not really wanting to know.

"Who was your son out with?"

"His girlfriend, Elaine Murray. They were going to a movie. He often comes in late and we don't hear him. I thought he might be sleeping late. He always closes the door to his room when he is sleeping, so I didn't know if he was in or out. Then I checked his bed and it hadn't been slept in."

Mrs. Walters stopped talking. Somewhere during the speech her hand had entwined with her husband's and they had moved closer together.

"Why did you call the police? It's less than a day since he went out."

Mr. Walters looked relieved.

"I told Carla we should have waited," he said. Carla Walters turned toward her husband. She was beginning to think that he had been right. That she had overreacted.

"I . . . Maybe I was foolish. But I called the Murrays and Elaine hadn't come home either."

"I see," Shindler said. Now came the hard part. The part that he had been putting off. He tried to think of a diplomatic way of phrasing it. There was none.

"I'm afraid that I have some very bad news for you."

He could picture what they were going through. It was the same vertigo that he had felt years ago when he sat with his family in their living room and a balding detective with tired eyes told them that Abe was dead. He had felt himself spinning then as the Walters must be spinning now.

Shindler laid the autopsy report on Marcus's desk and pulled up a chair. The Homicide Bureau of the Portsmouth Police Department was no different than any of the other detective divisions. It was a large, antiseptic room filled with old wooden desks at which sat poorly dressed men of varying shapes, ages and sizes. The only thing that they had in common was their cynicism.

"It's all in there. I had a chat with Beauchamp and he said he thinks that there must have been at least two people with two different weapons."

Shindler picked up the report. The autopsy had been performed by Dr. Francis R. Beauchamp, the

County Medical Examiner. He had found multiple stab wounds to the body, a skull fracture and other abrasions involving portions of the body, all of which indicated that some type of severe altercation had occurred. There was blood on the body and stab and puncture wounds and there were abrasions and bruises around the scrotum. The head injury was a depressed skull fracture made from behind by some type of blunt instrument. The stab wounds were generally about one-half inch in length and about a quarter or an eighth inch in width. Some of them were three to three-and-one-half-inches deep, penetrating to the diaphragm. A total of twenty puncture wounds were found. Death was due to internal bleeding into the left chest cavity as one of the puncture wounds had passed through the lung.

"Beauchamp thinks that the wounds that did the damage were made by a sharp-bladed instrument. He thinks Walters was standing upright and that the killer approached from the front and left side to have made the death wound."

"What about the damage to the head?"

"After. It was inflicted when he was down."

"You mean they beat him like that after he was dead?"

Marcus nodded.

"What kind of animals are we dealing with, Harvey?"

"The worst kind, Roy. You see that sentence about the depressed fracture. Beauchamp explained that to me. There are two types of fracture, a linear fracture, in which the skull is simply split or cracked, and a depressed fracture in which the skull is physically driven into the brain, just like splitting a melon. Those boys did a lot of extra work on Walters and none of it was necessary. They must have known that he was dead, but they struck him on the head in several places. There was a prominent injury above the left ear where the wound gaped so wide that you could see the brain through the wound and another where the skull was so badly smashed that his brain actually spilled through the wound."

Marcus was speaking in low, clipped tones. Shindler was thinking of the boy's head, the way he had seen it in the car. All that done after he was dead. Then lifting him and putting him in the car.

"Have they found the girl yet?" he asked quietly.

Marcus shook his head.

"That park is nine square miles and it's all timber and brush. There are hundreds of ravines and culverts in there that are overgrown with vegetation. If she's dead and they've hidden her in the park, we might never find her."

The phone rang. Shindler answered it. He was grateful for the distraction. It was the secretary at the front desk.

"There's a Mr. Shultz calling with information about the Walters murder. Should I put him through?"

There had been the usual number of nut calls that the police get on any publicized homicide, but Shindler was not passing over any possible leads.

"Put him through, Margie."

There was a click and a man said "Hello."

"Mr. Shultz? I'm Detective Roy Shindler. I understand you have some information on the murder of Richie Walters?"

"I'm not certain it will help, but my wife told me to call. We went to dinner Friday night at a restaurant just off of Monroe Boulevard. We finished very late. About eleven thirty we were walking to our car, which we had parked on Monroe, when we saw two cars racing each other. I noticed one, because it was very fancy. I think they said customed or customized. The other one, I'm not sure about. I really didn't pay much attention to it.

"This morning I read in the papers about that murder in the park. The car I saw sounds like the one they described in the paper. If I could see it, I could tell for sure."

"We can send an officer out to drive you downtown, if that's all right."

"Sure. But I'm not finished. There was something else. The red car—the one I remember—it made the other car crash."

"It made it crash?"

"Yes. I don't know what happened, because we looked away and they were several blocks away when we heard it. But we heard a crash and the other car—the dark one—was spun around in our direction. I guess the car wasn't damaged too bad, because it drove away in a little bit."

"Well, thank you, Mr. Shultz. That is important information. I'll send an officer out to see you and to take a statement. Thanks, again."

    Giannini had called them down to the lab fifteen minutes after Mr. Shultz's call. They had found something at the scene and he wanted them to see it.

"First, the small stuff. We found no prints in or on the car. The car had been wiped pretty thoroughly. We found a man's sock under the car when we moved it and another man's sock near the area where the dirt road enters the meadow. There were some fibers that we have matched with the socks that were found under the windshield wipers. It's my guess that the killer used the socks like gloves and wiped the prints off of the car."

"Is there any way of tracing a person through the socks?"

"Oh, we know where the socks came from. Walters was barefoot. I already had someone check with the family. They're his socks."

Giannini glanced down at a sheet of paper he was holding.

"Next, it looks like the motive wasn't robbery. There was thirty dollars in his wallet and twenty in the purse. There was also an expensive camera in the back seat."

"You said that you had something important for us," Shindler prodded.

"Right."

Giannini walked over to a filing cabinet and rummaged in one of the steel drawers.

"One of my men came across this stuff in some bushes near the base of the hill that leads down from the meadow to the paved road."

Shindler had a rough picture of the place. The dirt road wound upward from the paved road for a while, then straightened out into the meadow. If you did not use the dirt road, a straight line would take you down an embankment that had several steep

sections. The embankment was covered with under-
brush.

Giannini pulled three items out of a manila envelope and set them on a table. There was a cigarette
lighter, a blue rat-tail comb and a pair of feminine
glasses. The glasses were constructed out of plastic
and metal. The temples were made of yellow gold
wire. The frames were reddish plastic on top and
yellow gold on the bottom. The top piece curled up
at the ends and was harlequin-shaped with rhine-
stone trim at the tips.

"Dr. Webber?" Marcus inquired.

"Yes."

"I'm Detective Marcus. I called you from my office an hour ago."

The optometrist had been unlocking his door
when Marcus approached him in the hallway of his
office building.

"I apologize for asking you to work on your day
off, but this is very important."

"Of course. Come in. I wasn't doing anything
anyway and this makes for an exciting break in my
routine."

The doctor turned on the lights and led Marcus
through a small waiting room into a large office
lined with medical books. The doctor sat behind a
paper-covered desk and motioned Marcus into an
easy chair.

"Greg Heller told me that you helped him out in a
burglary case a few years ago."

"Oh, that." The doctor smiled. "Yes. He needed

to trace a person through a pair of glasses and I showed him how to do it."

"I have the same problem that Greg had, but our situation is more urgent. Have you read the morning papers? The story about the boy who was murdered in Lookout Park?"

"The Walters boy. Terrible. His family belongs to my church. I don't know them well, but the boy was thought of very highly."

That was the general picture so far, Marcus thought. Nobody with a bad word about Richie Walters.

"What I am going to tell you is just between us. We are going to let the story break soon enough, because we don't think that we can keep it quiet for too long, but I want your word that you won't leak what I tell you."

"Certainly."

"There was a girl with Walters and she's missing. We are searching the woods and we didn't want thrill seekers out messing up the investigation. We also wanted to give the people who have her, if she is still alive, a chance to make contact, if this is a kidnapping.

"So far, we have only one clue to the identity of the people involved: a pair of woman's glasses. I was hoping that you could tell me how to find the owner."

"Did Greg tell you what was involved the last time?"

"No. He just said that you knew how to do it."

"I know, but it's not easy and it's not fast. Did you bring the glasses?"

Marcus fished an envelope out of his overcoat pocket. He handed the glasses to the doctor.

"Prescriptions are a lot like fingerprints," Dr. Webber said as he rotated the glasses in his hands. "It is highly unlikely that you would find two people with identical prescriptions and identical frames.

"We have four numbers to work with for comparison. When someone comes to me for glasses, I determine what his prescription should be. I don't grind the lenses myself, so I send written instructions to the people who construct the lenses. When they receive my instructions, they take an unfinished lens. One that has not been worked on. The curvature of the surface of that lens is called the basic curve.

"I instruct the workmen to alter the entire curvature of the lens surface to form a new curve. This new curve is called the sphere.

"Next, I instruct the workmen to alter the curve of the sphere at the point where the pupil is centered. The area of the lens that the wearer looks out of. This means that the lens will have two different adjustments on its surface: the sphere, which covers the whole lens, and the new curve, ground on the sphere, where the line of vision is. The smaller curve is called the cylinder.

"Finally, I will instruct the workmen to grind the cylinder at a particular angle. It could be 45 degrees, 30 degrees, etc. This angle is called the axis.

"The four numbers for comparison, then, are the basic curve, the sphere, the cylinder curve and the axis. I have a machine in my examining room that looks like a microscope. It's called a Lensometer and I can put these glasses under it and find the prescription for you."

"And no two people will have the same prescription?"

"They shouldn't. Of course, you also have the frames. This is made by American Optical. The name is stamped on the inside of the temple. It's a Gay Mount. That is the style. The size of this frame is 46–20 and that varies from person to person also. So you have another figure for comparison."

"That's just great. I'd appreciate it if you could get that prescription for me."

Dr. Webber left for five minutes. When he returned, he handed Marcus a sheet of paper with a series of numbers on it.

"This has the information you need. It will make sense to any optometrist. You will have to circulate this and get them to check their files. That is going to take some time, I'm afraid. I wish there was some quicker way."

"So do I, Doctor, but, right now, we have no choice."

3

Three days after Richie Walters died, winter began with a vengeance. Temperatures dropped near zero. People started staying indoors and snow and wind made the price of firewood soar. And through it all the searchers went out daily hunting for Elaine Murray.

The fact of Miss Murray's disappearance and the police search was revealed in the Monday morning papers. The Marine, Navy and Coast Guard Reserve volunteered 125 men and the Boy Scouts rounded up forty more. During the first few days of the search the weather was still mild and the area around the meadow was cluttered with thrill seekers.

The story dominated the headlines in the Portsmouth *Herald* and several of the eastern papers picked up on the "Lover's Lane" murder and the hunt for the missing girl. The investigation turned up no new clues and the only real lead, the glasses, was kept from the public.

On December 28, 1960, the search for Elaine Murray was officially called off. Then 1960 became 1961. A new President of the United States was sworn in and more current events took hold of the public imagination and the Murray-Walters case drifted farther back in the pages of the *Herald* until it disappeared.

Roy Shindler's six foot five inch body slumped in his favorite armchair. A book lay face-down in his lap and he stared hypnotically at the cold, sleeting rain that beat against the living room window of his small, one-bedroom apartment. The apartment was tidy, yet cluttered. Shindler tried to maintain order, but often failed through lack of interest.

The detective was a resident of the city. He had been born there and he had been raised in its poorer parts. His father had been a shoemaker at a time when nobody seemed able to afford repairs. His mother worked as a sales clerk in a department store. She was always tired. His father was always silent. His childhood, the life of his family, had been a canvas of grays, except for one spot of shining white. Abe.

Abe had been a shooting star, always on the ascendancy. A person to be looked up to. He transcended their drab apartment, the monotony of life behind a sales counter or in the backroom of a shoe repair shop where people never came. On Saturdays, the family could watch from the stands at the high school as Abe floated downfield, avoiding outstretched arms, to stand in the end zone, ball held high above his head as the crowd screamed its adulation. In heated gymnasiums in the midst of winter, the family would join the crowd, Roy's father more strident than any other, as it cheered on Abe, who could score a basket with the grace of a ballet dancer. He was the best in sports and a top scholar. But most of all he had been a warm, caring human being. After Abe died, everyone talked about him the way they were eulogizing Richie Walters now.

Roy had always done well in school and, for all his lack of grace, he had been good at sports, but his father never noticed. He saw only Abe. Had Abe been someone other than the person he was Roy might have hated and resented him. But Abe was Abe and Roy worshipped his older brother.

In the first year of college, on scholarship at an eastern university that would groom him for the medical profession, he had excelled. He had come home for intersession, at great personal expense to Roy's father, to tell in person the tales that they had read in the sports section of the *Herald*. He had died in the snow returning home from an evening with his old high school friends. The detective who told them was sorry. He had been a fan, but then who hadn't been. The detective said that the motive was robbery. The person who murdered Abe was never caught.

When Abe died, the family died. Roy tried night school. He wanted an education, and his grades were good at first, but he wore down. He had to work all day because his father could no longer manage. He had to do the cooking and the housework. The oppressive atmosphere of the small apartment drained his resources. He found himself sleeping in class, unable to complete his assignments. He was too tired to study in the late evening, the only time he could call his own, when his father and mother were asleep and he could finally be alone in the solitude of his room.

He was never quite certain why he had turned to police work. At first, when he was new to the tensions and danger of the job, he thought about his choice a lot. Perhaps, subconsciously, he felt that he would someday find the person who had murdered his brother. Perhaps he had joined because the job was night work and presented a justification for sleeping away the daytime when his parents roamed the apartment like lost souls, sitting silently for hours at a time, rising slowly and without reason to wander to another chair by another dust-coated window.

His father had died during his second year on the force and his mother had passed away two months later. It had been a relief to Roy. He had moved out of their apartment into another apartment just as small and just as barren.

Before they died, Roy had imagined that their passing would somehow liberate him, but it had only left a void. The patterns of a quarter of a century are difficult to change. He had re-registered at the night branch of the state university. There even had been a girl. She had been quiet and bookish. Their dates had been a series of long pauses punctuated by discussions intentionally abstract and intellectual, as if both were afraid to communicate anything resembling a true feeling. They had lived together for a short time, but the barriers had never fallen and they had parted friends for whom a closer relationship had not worked out.

Roy's fellow officers found him strange. Intensely emotional about abstract ideas, yet cold as ice in life-and-death situations. It was as if Abe's death had killed all personal joy for him, leaving only the hard shell of his intellectualism to shield him from life's realities. The Walters boy reminded him of Abe in so many ways that the investigation operated like a scalpel that was peeling through the layers of his own personal wounds and baring the grief that he had believed to be long buried.

An hour ago, Shindler had tried to read, but his mind wandered and he had given up the attempt. It was the case. Several times he had even dreamed about it. He could not stop thinking about what had happened to that boy.

"You can't let a case get to you, Roy," Harvey had said. "If you become personally involved, you don't do your job."

"Intellectually, I know you're right, but I can't help it. It's the things I'm learning about him. I've talked to dozens of people and not one has had a bad word to say. It's not just because he's dead, either. You can tell.

"And you know what hurts most?" he said. "I was at the house again, yesterday. His mother was beginning to handle it. Mr. Walters said she was back on her feet. They even went out to dinner. Then they got yesterday's mail. He was accepted at Harvard. Harvard. Jesus. That kid could have been a doctor, a scientist. Anything."

The phone rang and Roy sighed and walked into the kitchen.

"Roy?"

It was Harvey Marcus.

"Yeah. What's up?"

"I just got a call from a Dr. Norman Trembler, an optometrist in Glendale. He read the bulletin on the glasses and he thinks he's found the person with the prescription."

"Did you get the name and address?" Shindler asked. He could feel Marcus's excitement. There was a certain electricity generated whenever good, solid police work paid off.

"I've got it. We went over everything on the phone. He sold a pair of glasses just like the ones we found to an Esther Freemont, 2219 North 82nd Street."

The Freemont house had seen better days. The small front lawn was overgrown with weeds and no one seemed to care about cutting the grass that was left. The wood had a gray, weatherbeaten appearance. It had not been painted in some time.

Marcus and Shindler stepped over some broken toys and walked up the creaking front stairs to the porch. There were soiled curtains on the front window and over the small glass window in the upper half of the front door. A tricycle lay on its side on the porch. Marcus could hear a TV blaring inside. A baby was crying and someone was yelling. There was no doorbell so Marcus knocked loudly on the door frame.

There was someone shuffling toward the door. The curtain over the front door glass raised and a bloated face peered out. Marcus flashed his badge and the door opened warily.

The woman standing in the doorway was well

over two hundred pounds. The weight was collected in rolls of fat over large thighs and sagging breasts. She wore a soiled gray dress that covered her like a tent. An apron hung over the dress. Her eyes were bloodshot and held no sign of cheer. Marcus suspected that she had been drinking. A cigarette dangled from the corner of her mouth and medium-length graying hair straggled across her forehead.

The inside of the house was a reflection of the personality of the owner, Marcus decided. A heavy, unpleasant smell hung in the air. The rooms were dark and untidy. How could humans live this way? He was always asking questions like that and never finding the answers.

"Mrs. Freemont?"

"I was. It's Taylor now."

"Are you Esther Freemont's mother?"

"What's she done now?" she said with bored disgust. Without waiting for an answer, she turned her head and yelled angrily into the interior of the house.

"Esther, you get out here."

A voice answered unintelligibly over the roar of applause on a TV game show.

"Turn that goddamn thing down and get out here," Mrs. Taylor yelled.

The sound level did not diminish, but a young girl came around the corner of the living room. When she saw the two men in suits, she stopped, then continued toward them at a slower pace.

Shindler watched her walk across the room, the way a hunter watches his prey. Esther was tall for a girl. Shindler judged her to be about sixteen years old. She was wearing blue jeans and a white tee shirt that covered large, swaying breasts. Shindler realized that she was braless and the excitement generated by the police investigation blended subconsciously with an undercurrent of sexual desire.

Esther's skin was smooth and dark. Her long, dark hair was as dirty and unkempt as her mother's. Involuntarily, Shindler began to think of her in sexual terms.

"These men want to see you. They're police. What have you done now?"

Esther's large brown eyes moved from her mother to the detectives without answering. She appeared to be nervous, but no more than any other person confronted by the law.

"We have no reason to believe that your daughter has done anything wrong, Mrs. Taylor. This is just part of an investigation we're conducting. We just want to ask your daughter a few questions."

"Oh," Mrs. Taylor said. Marcus thought she sounded disappointed.

"Is there someplace we could talk?" Shindler asked.

Mrs. Taylor looked around the cluttered living room. The couch was covered with unwashed laundry and the nearest chair was occupied by a cat. Mrs. Taylor headed toward the back of the house. They followed her into the kitchen. A portable TV was resting on the sink. A baby in a high chair stopped screaming when they entered.

Chairs were arranged on each side of a yellow formica-topped table. Marcus and Shindler motioned

Esther into one and took two of the others. Mrs. Taylor hovered over her daughter.

"Could we?" Shindler asked, motioning toward the TV . . . Mrs. Taylor looked confused for a moment, then leaned over and turned the sound off. The picture remained on.

"Esther, this is Detective Marcus and I am Detective Shindler. We are investigating the murder of Richie Walters and the disappearance of Elaine Murray, who were students at Stuyvesant."

Marcus was watching her. There was no trace of fear. If anything, she seemed relieved when they said that the investigation was not about her.

"Is . . . is she dead?"

"Pardon?"

"Elaine. You said disappeared. Is she dead?"

"We don't know, Esther. We have men out searching, but we still haven't found her."

"Gee, that's sad. I knew Richie from school. I didn't know him real well. He was in different classes. But . . . you know, being from the same school and all, it's like he was a friend. I cried when I read about it in the papers."

"Do you know Elaine Murray?"

"Well, not to talk to, but I knew her. She was . . . is real pretty. I hope she's okay."

"We do too, Esther. Can you remember where you were on the Friday night that Richie was killed?"

Esther looked nervously at her mother, then back to the detectives.

"Why do you want to know where I was?"

"This is just routine, Esther. We have to check up on everyone," Marcus said.

"You don't think she had anything to do with that killing?" Mrs. Taylor asked incredulously.

"You ain't going to take me to detention?"

Esther was panicky. She started to stand. Marcus laughed. It was a made-up laugh that Shindler had heard before. Esther looked confused.

"No one is going to detention and no one thinks you killed anybody. Now just relax and tell me where you were so I can fill out my report. Okay?"

To Shindler, Esther looked like a trapped animal. Her eyes shifted from face to face and her hands were slowly washing one another.

"You tell them where you were," Mrs. Taylor said, suddenly angry. "I just remembered where she was."

Esther hung her head and bit her lip.

"She was drunk, that's where she was. She come home late and puked all over the bathroom."

No one can look more dejected than an embarrassed adolescent girl, Shindler thought. Esther looked as if she wanted to crawl inside herself.

"How did you get drunk?" Marcus asked.

"You promise I won't go to juvenile detention?"

Marcus smiled his best fatherly interrogation smile.

"Don't worry about detention, Esther. We are only interested in Richie Walters's murder. Look, I used to drink more than a wee bit myself when I was your age. So, why don't you tell us what happened."

"Well, to tell the truth," Esther said sheepishly, "I can't remember it all. I was pretty drunk and it's kind of hazy."

"Tell us what you can remember."

"Roger, he's my boyfriend, and me and Bobby and

Billy Coolidge went to Hamburger Heaven. Then, we went to a party. It was after the party that we got drunk." She stopped and looked pleadingly at Marcus. "Do I have to tell? I don't want to get anyone in trouble."

"Answer their questions," Mrs. Taylor barked. "I told you I didn't want you hanging around with that Hessey. He's no good, like the rest of those hoodlums."

"How did you get drunk, Esther? Don't worry about getting anyone in trouble. We won't tell anyone what happened," Marcus said.

"It was Billy. He swiped some wine while the grocer wasn't looking at one of these all-night places. He took a few bottles. We drank it in the car. That's where it gets fuzzy. I guess I don't drink so well and I must have had too much, because I really don't remember after the wine. Except I remember we drank it in the car and I think we went cruising downtown after that."

Shindler reached in his pocket.

"Do you wear glasses?"

Esther did not answer for a moment. She ran her tongue across her lips.

"Talk up. Yeah, she has glasses to read," Mrs. Taylor said.

"Do you have your glasses, Esther?"

Esther did not say anything. She stared at the table.

"Esther, where are those glasses?" Mrs. Taylor asked menacingly. "Goddamn it, if you lost those glasses again, you ain't getting new ones."

"I'm sorry, Ma," Esther blurted out. "They were

stolen. It was three months ago. I was afraid to tell you."

"Who stole them?" Mrs. Taylor demanded.

"I don't know. I swear. I was afraid you would get mad, so I didn't tell and I thought maybe they would turn up."

"What was the exact day your glasses were stolen, Esther?" Shindler interrupted.

"It wasn't just the glasses. It was some other stuff from my purse. And I can't remember the exact day. I just know it was in early November."

"Are these your glasses?" Shindler asked, placing an envelope on the table. Esther picked up the envelope and took out the glasses.

"They look like them, but I can't tell until I put them on."

"Go ahead."

Esther fit them on her nose. She picked up a *True Confession* from the sink and scanned a page.

"These are mine. Can I have them back?"

"I'm afraid not right now. They're evidence."

"Evidence for what?" Mrs. Taylor asked.

"Did you also lose a lighter and a comb, Esther?"

"Yes," she answered hesitantly.

"Where did you find those?" Mrs. Taylor asked.

"The comb, the lighter and the glasses were found near the scene of the Walters murder. It is possible that the person who stole your daughter's glasses was involved in the murder."

"So she can't get them back?"

"Not for a while."

"Well, that's fine. And how am I supposed to get her new ones?"

"I'm afraid I can't help you there."

"Damn it, Esther, this is your fault. You're always losing things. Well, this time you don't get new glasses till you pay for them."

They left the house with Esther in tears. Shindler watched her intently: slumped in her chair, head buried in her slim brown arms, shoulders raked with sobs. He felt an icy contempt for her and something else he would not allow himself to name.

"She knows something," Shindler said.

"That girl?" Marcus asked incredulously. "She doesn't know a thing."

"I can feel it, Harvey."

"You want to feel it. Christ, Roy, she was more worried about being taken to juvenile detention for being under age and drinking than she was about being involved in a murder investigation."

"I don't buy the coincidence. Her stolen glasses just happen to turn up at the scene."

"Now wait a minute. The glasses were found near, not at, the scene, down the hill and quite some way from where the car was located."

"Right where someone who was running from the scene in a panic might drop it."

Marcus shook his head.

"I'm afraid I'm not with you on this one, Roy. If you want to follow up on Esther Freemont, you do it on your own."

The radio crackled and Shindler lifted the mike and gave their call letters. The radio dispatcher told them that they had found Elaine Murray.

They had been looking in the wrong places. The girl had never been in Portsmouth. There was an offshoot of the main highway that led to the coast. It was not heavily traveled, especially this time of year. Walter Haas and his wife, Susan, had been headed for their folks' house in Sandy Cove when their car got a flat. Walter had pulled onto a shoulder and had gone out into a torrential downpour to change the tire. The ground was muddy and slippery and he had lost his balance, sending the jack handle over the embankment. He could see the body when he looked over the side. It looked to Shindler as if it had been tossed over the edge of the grassy downslope from the road like a sack of wheat.

The rain was making it difficult for everyone. There was no possibility of finding any tracks. The roadway would leave none and the shoulder was a miniature swamp.

Shindler half slid, half scrambled down the embankment. A small group of officers were beating the tall grass for evidence. Marcus had gone over to a large man dressed in a rain slicker and wide-brimmed hat. Shindler looked down at the body. Someone had had the decency to cover it with a blanket. He raised the corner and looked.

He almost retched. The head was almost denuded of tissue and the scalp had practically rotted away. He moved his eyes away from the face. She was wearing tan toreador slacks, but the zipper was undone, as if someone had put them on her. Her only other piece of clothing was a white blouse. It was unbuttoned and the left side had flapped over, revealing her left breast.

Shindler was churning inside. He could feel the adrenaline conquering the initial effects of the nausea. Then he saw her feet and he started to shake. He did not know why the fact that she was barefoot should affect him so. What could it matter? She was dead. But then the whole thing was illogical. How could two young people such as these be struck down at the beginning of their lives.

Shindler covered Elaine Murray and walked up the hill with the rain stinging him. He stood by his car and breathed deeply until he was in control. Then he joined Marcus.

"Roy, this is Larry Tenneck, Meridian County Sheriff's Office."

They shook hands.

"It's a pity, ain't it?" Tenneck said. "A young girl like that."

"Any idea how long she's been down there?"

"Not a one. This stretch of road isn't heavily traveled in the winter. I don't think she was killed here. Course with the rain and all you couldn't really tell, but I figure she was just left here, because whoever killed her figured she wouldn't be found for a while."

"You're probably right," Marcus agreed. "The autopsy should tell us a few things."

"Speaking of autopsies, can we move her now? I told the boys to leave her till you got here, but I think it would be better to have her taken out of the rain."

"Of course. You took pictures?"

Tenneck nodded and signaled to two men who were smoking in the front seat of an ambulance that was parked alongside the road. One man nodded and flicked a cigarette out of the ambulance window. Tenneck shook his head.

"I wish they wouldn't do that. We have enough trouble as it is with littering. You boys'll want to see the clothes, I guess."

"Clothes?" Shindler asked.

"Oh, yeah. We found the rest of her clothes. Deputy found them over in that grass about a hundred yards from the body. I guess they dumped her, then threw the rest of her stuff over the side."

Tenneck reached into the back seat of his car and pulled out a plastic sack. Harvey opened the rear door and sat inside. Shindler sat next to him and Tenneck leaned in through the window, oblivious to the rain. There was a red and black ski sweater, a torn brassiere and a pair of panties in the bag. The panties were torn in several places and Roy realized that they had actually been torn in two at one point near the right hip.

"We better have Beauchamp check for signs of rape," Marcus said in a low, hard voice.

"That's the first thing I thought of when I seen them," Tenneck said. For the first time since they had talked with him, Shindler noticed that he had lost his country calm.

"You do me a favor, will ya. You get these boys and get them good."

Dr. Francis R. Beauchamp, like Roy Shindler, was a man of odd proportions. There, however, the similarities ceased. Where Shindler was tall and thin, with a small head and bulbous nose and overlong arms connected to oversize hands, Beauchamp was short and squat and possessed of a large melon-sized head that overbalanced his entire body, giving the impression that a quick, downward nod would pitch him forward. His tiny hands were heavily veined and his imperfect eyesight was aided by tortoiseshell glasses that perched on a thin, delicately shaped nose.

Shindler and Marcus were seated in the waiting room of the Heavenly Rest Funeral Parlor in Perryville, Meridian County's county seat. Shindler had smoked all the cigarettes in his pack and was debating with himself the pros and cons of braving the elements in search of pie and coffee when the door opened and Beauchamp flopped onto a couch upholstered in a peach-colored material upon which fluttered flocks of smiling cherubim.

"Strangulation," he said. He looked tired. They had called him from the Sheriff's office and made him drive out in the night. "Probably done with the cord that was found stuffed into the waistband of her slacks."

"How long has she been dead?"

Beauchamp pursed his lips.

"I'll say four to six weeks."

"The body didn't look that bad, except for the head," Marcus said.

"It's the weather. Gets cold out here. Cold retards the deterioration. Say, can I get a cup of coffee and some food? I'm really beat."

He looked tired, Shindler thought. We're all tired.

"On me. Grab your coat and I'll stake you at the first hamburger joint we find."

"Last of the big spenders. You bastards owe me more than hamburger for this job."

"Was there anything else?" Shindler asked. They all knew what he meant.

"Yes. Poor thing."

Beauchamp sighed and removed his glasses. He closed his eyes and rubbed the eyelids with his thumb and the knuckle of his index finger.

"There were hemorrhages on the front and back surfaces of the uterus. In my opinion they could have been caused by a blow to the lower abdomen or by vigorous intercourse. If it was intercourse, she would have had to have been unusually active.

"I also found morphologically identifiable sperm in the vagina."

"What is that? Morphologically identifiable."

"It means that I could tell it was sperm. It was dead, but it was there."

"And what does all that mean?" Shindler wanted to know.

"It means that I think that more than one man had her shortly before she died and it means that I think they had her over and over again. Then they killed her. That's an unscientific opinion, so don't hold me to it. But, then, I'm not feeling too scientific tonight. Dr. Harold Murray is a good friend of mine and I have been thinking of how lucky I am that I don't have to be the one who tells him what happened to his daughter."

4

It was April and Shindler was the only detective still working on the Murray-Walters case. The problem was that there was nothing to work on. The general consensus was that the couple had been murdered by persons unknown, for reasons unknown, which would remain unknown. Shindler did not buy that. He would not. He thought about the thirty dollars in Richie's wallet and the expensive camera on the back seat. Anybody cool enough to put Richie's body in the car would have been cool enough to take the money and the camera, if the motive had been robbery. There had to have been some other motive and if there was a motive it was created by something that happened prior to the killings.

So Shindler was searching for motive and finding none. He had compiled a list of everyone who knew the couple and from each interviewee he was learning that no one could possibly have wanted Elaine Murray or Richie Walters dead.

* * *

Alice Fay was one of the prettiest girls on the list and Shindler was grateful for some stimulation after the dull morning he had spent. It was Easter recess, so she was home from school. Her father was working and her mother was shopping. She would not open the door until Shindler displayed his badge. When he told her that he was investigating the deaths of her two schoolmates, she said, "Oh" softly and let him in.

He chatted about the weather and school vacation as he followed her down the hall into the kitchen. She had been seated at the kitchen table reading *Seventeen*. The magazine was turned to an article on fall campus fashions. She motioned Shindler into a chair.

"You're going to college next fall?" he asked.

"The University of Wisconsin."

"What do you want to study?"

Alice smiled and shrugged.

"I really don't know. I might go into nursing, but right now I'll just take liberal arts and then decide after I have some time to think."

"That's a good way to do it. You have plenty of time to be serious when you get old like me."

Alice laughed.

"You aren't that old."

"I get older every day."

He smiled at her and she asked him if she could get him some coffee.

"Do you think you will catch the people who murdered Richie and Elaine?" she asked as she turned on the light under the coffee pot.

"I don't know. We haven't made much progress.

That's why I am talking to everyone who knew them. Anything that you can think of that might be of help would be appreciated."

Alice sat down again. She appeared to be smart as well as good looking, Shindler thought. She would be a good catch for some lucky man.

"I would help if I could, but I honestly can't think of a thing to tell you. I knew them both real well and they were both so nice. Richie was so gentle. He really cared about people. He won all these honors in sports and he was involved in school politics, but it never went to his head.

"Elaine was like Richie. I remember in our junior year we both ran for prom queen. I know Elaine wanted very much to win, but I was named queen. She was so happy for me, even though she was disappointed for herself."

The coffee was ready and she went to the sink and poured Shindler a cup.

"Do you know a girl named Esther Freemont?" Shindler asked. Alice looked surprised.

"Yes, I do. Is Esther . . . ? She isn't involved, is she?"

"No. I just wanted to know if you knew her."

"Well, I know her in the sense that we go to the same school, but she isn't a friend," Alice said with a hint of distaste.

"What's Esther like?"

"I . . . I really don't know. She isn't too bright. She hangs around with a wild crowd."

"The Cobras?" Shindler interrupted. Alice nodded.

"She . . . I hear that she's, uh, free. If you know what I mean," Alice said blushing. "But I really don't know her that well," she added hastily.

Shindler changed the subject and they discussed Richie and Elaine some more. The time passed quickly and Shindler realized that it was getting late. He made a mental note to leave the interviewing of pretty girls to detectives with more self-control.

"Thank you for taking the time to talk to me, Miss Fay," Shindler said, rising. "If you think of anything that you think might help, give me a call."

He handed her his card and she placed it by the kitchen phone.

"You know, that's funny," she said as she turned. "I just remembered that Esther Freemont was at the party I threw the evening that Richie and Elaine were killed."

Shindler stopped.

"I thought you said that she wasn't a close friend."

"She's not. She crashed. She and the Coolidge brothers and someone else. I remember because of the fight."

"What fight?"

"It was pretty frightening. Tommy, my boyfriend, got mad because they had crashed. He tried to throw Billy Coolidge out and there was a fight. Billy had a knife. We were lucky that no one was hurt seriously."

"What kind of knife?"

"It was a switchblade, I think. One of Tommy's brother's friends hit him and he pulled it out. We stopped it after that."

"You mentioned a brother."

"Bobby Coolidge. He was fighting too."

"Why do you think they came to the party if they weren't invited?"

"I don't know. To cause trouble probably. Billy

always has a chip on his shoulder. His brother isn't as bad, but I really don't like either of them."

"Do you remember when they left the party?"

"Not really. I know it was dark and . . . No, wait. I do too know. Tommy got knocked down and he smashed his watch and broke it. I remember we all talked about it, because it was a new watch and he had gotten it as a birthday present. He was very angry. Anyway, the watch stopped at ten-twenty."

Shindler thought that over. There had been a police report of an interview with some boys who had seen Elaine and Richie when they left the show. The movies had let out at about eleven-fifteen. If Esther and her friends had driven downtown after stealing the wine, they would be in the downtown area near eleven-thirty. It was possible.

"Thank you for the help, Miss Fay. Would you do me a favor and write down what you just told me and mail it to my office?"

"Certainly. Do you think it's important?"

"I don't know, but it could be."

George DeBlasio had been a juvenile counselor for fifteen years. He first met Roy Shindler when Shindler was a patrolman. He had seen Shindler often during his first few years on the force and less often after he had become a detective, but the two got together for coffee whenever Shindler was in the neighborhood of the juvenile center, which housed juvenile detention, the juvenile court and the counselors' offices.

DeBlasio was in his early fifties. His hair was snow white and thinning and he had a narrow, angular face. His office was one of several identical cubicles that lined a long hallway set aside for the counselors. He sat on one side of a government-issue metal desk and Shindler sat on the other. The door was locked and DeBlasio addressed Shindler in conspiratorial undertones as he slid two folders across the desk to him.

"You know, I shouldn't be doing this. These files are supposed to be sealed."

"I appreciate it, George, and I wouldn't have asked if it wasn't important."

George grunted and leaned back as Shindler read through the files.

"You know, I was their counselor for a while."

"The Coolidges?" Shindler asked, looking up.

"For a year before they turned eighteen. Billy was a rough customer. I took an active dislike to him."

"Why was that?"

"There was just something about him. The other one, Bobby, was more human. I guess that was it. Billy was a cold fish. No moral setup. He operated on pleasure-pain principles. If it hurt him, it was bad. If it felt good, it was good.

"I think the first time I worked with him was when he was brought in for a rampage at school. He beat up three kids in the course of one morning. Really brutal stuff. He had been drinking and the judge just gave him a talking to and let him go, because no one was seriously hurt, but that was no thanks to Billy.

"Anyway, I was assigned as counselor, but I couldn't reach him. He showed no remorse. The only emotional reaction was his anger at the boys for telling on him."

"What about the other boy, Bobby?"

"He's a little different. I think he would turn out okay if he had half a chance. Of course, he doesn't. Father died when they were young. Mother's an alcoholic. Bobby is bright. So is Billy, for that matter. But they don't apply themselves in school."

"What was Bobby's problem?"

"Also fighting. He beat up a banker's son at school. The kid had it coming, but the father made a stink. The banker's kid had made some remark about Bobby's clothes. He told me that his mother had been drunk and he had washed them himself. He admitted, in an indirect way, that he was jealous of the other boy's clothes."

"You mean he disliked the other boy for being rich?"

"That was Billy's favorite theme. He's in a juvenile gang, you know. It's called the Cobras. I would get him talking about the gang and you couldn't stop him. He felt that the gang membership gave him status. He told me that he had earned his membership and that made him better than the kids at school who were rich only because of their parents. They both resent their parents. They feel that the father somehow betrayed them by dying and leaving them to fend for themselves."

"Have Billy or Bobby ever gotten into trouble for using a knife?"

George thought for a moment.

"Not that I can recall."

"George, do you mind if I keep these files for a day? I want to study them and I don't have the time now."

"I shouldn't, but go ahead. Just don't get caught. I'd be in real trouble if anyone found out."

"Don't worry, I'll have them back to you by to-morrow."

"This is important, huh?"

"Very. I'd tell you about it if I could, but I want to be sure before I accuse anyone."

"See you tomorrow."

"Tomorrow."

"I'll admit it's a possibility," Harvey said.

"Then you agree that I should bring them in for questioning?"

Marcus thumbed through the stack of papers that Shindler had put on his desk forty-five minutes ago. They contained police reports, notes from juvenile records and a psychiatric profile that had been done on William Ray Coolidge. The stack of papers painted a picture of two alienated, low-income juveniles who harbored a deep resentment against a society with which they could not cope. Shindler thought that he saw a pattern.

"They crash the party to see how the other half lives. They are jealous of these kids. One of the boys I talked to said he thought that Billy might even have a crush on Alice Fay, the girl who threw the party.

"Then, they're beaten up and humiliated by the very people they despise. They get drunk. Later, they run into Walters and Murray. They know them from school. They see two perfect representatives of the very social class they hate."

"Nice theory. But you have nothing to connect the Coolidges with the killings."

"Esther Freemont's glasses."

Marcus shook his head.

"Not enough. According to her, she didn't even have them on the evening of the crime."

"She's lying. I know it."

"But you have to prove it. Only don't go off half-cocked to the D.A. until you can."

"What about questioning the Coolidges?"

Marcus looked down at the reports again.

"All right, let's bring them in."

Shindler had developed a mental image of Billy Coolidge and he was surprised at how accurate it was. The thing that surprised him most was the physical reaction the boy produced in him. There was something there that repelled him. The boy was good looking in an almost effeminate way. His lips were too thick and they curled naturally into a sneer. The hair was thick with grease. Whenever he saw one of these punks with their slicked-back hair and black leather jackets, he felt a slow hate. They stood for too many things that he did not.

"Have a seat, Billy," Shindler said, motioning to a wooden chair on the other side of a wooden table. Shindler was seated in a comfortable chair on the far side of the small, bare interrogation room.

Billy took a cautious look around. There was nothing to rest his eyes on except Shindler, so he stopped there. His brother had been taken to a room on another floor by a policeman as big as the one who was standing behind him. There did not seem to be much he could do, so he looked at Shindler.

"What is this all about?" he asked.

"I'd like to have a talk with you," Shindler replied.

"Well, I don't want to talk to you. So let me go, or let me call a lawyer."

"You don't need a lawyer, son. All I want you to do is answer a few questions."

"About what?"

"Sit down, first," Shindler said in a voice still calm.

"I don't want to sit down and I'm not answering any questions. Now, let me out."

The defiant tone. The scared, defiant look. Like Nazis. Shindler hated them. He nodded and the big policeman twisted the boy's arm behind him and sat him down.

"Listen to me, asshole," he whispered, "when Detective Shindler asks you to do something, you do it. Do you understand?"

Billy groaned and writhed in the big man's grasp. He gasped out an "okay" and grunted with relief when he was released. He rubbed his shoulder and cast a frightened look behind him. He was scared now. That was good.

"Would you like a cigarette?" Shindler offered. Billy shook his head and Shindler lit one for himself.

"You were born in Portsmouth, weren't you?"

"You know that shit from my records, so why ask?"

The policeman took a step forward and Billy swiveled his head to watch him. Shindler raised his hand.

"All right. Yeah. I was born in Portsmouth. So what?"

"You and your brother have been pretty much on your own since your father died, haven't you?"

"I guess," Billy replied grudgingly.

"Are you working now?"

"You know I'm working at McNary Esso."

He was sulking. He had turned away from Shindler so that his profile was to him and his eyes were on the floor.

"Do you like working at McNary's?"

"What are you? Some kind of social worker? I want out of here and I'm not answering any more questions."

"Not even about what you were doing on the evening of Friday, November twenty-fifth?"

Uncertainty. Coolidge cocked his head and looked at Shindler.

"What's that?"

"Last November twenty-fifth. The Friday after Thanksgiving."

"How the fuck should I know what I was doing then. That's six months ago."

"Maybe I can help you. You had a little fight at Alice Fay's house. Do you remember that?"

"I don't remember nothing."

"Now you're being stupid, Billy. We have a dozen eyewitnesses who will swear under oath that you had a fight with Tommy Cooper, his brother and some other boys that night."

"Did that son of a bitch Cooper swear out a complaint on me?"

"No one has sworn out a complaint. We just want to know what happened that night."

"It was Cooper's fault. They tried to throw us out. I was just defending myself."

"With a knife?"

That stopped him, Shindler thought. He doesn't know what we know.

"Okay, so I had a knife. That fat bastard that hit me had a broken bottle, so I pulled my knife."

"Do you have the knife now?"

"The knife? No, I lost the knife."

"That's too bad. Where did you lose it?"

"I don't know. I just lost it."

"When?"

"I told you, I don't know."

"What did you do after you left Alice Fay's house?"

"I don't know. Cruised around, I guess."

"Who was with you?"

"You know who was with me. You got a dozen eyewitnesses."

"I want to hear it from you."

He clammed up again, half turning from Shindler and refocusing on the floor.

"How soon after you left Alice's house did you cop the wine?"

"Who said I took some wine?"

"We had a long talk with Esther Freemont."

"Then you know everything, so why waste my time?"

"I like your company."

Coolidge laughed suddenly.

"You must think I'm really stupid. You expect

me to come in here and just admit I stole something. Why don't you just give me the key to the jail so I can lock myself up, too?"

"We don't care about the wine, Billy. We care about what happened later."

"Later?"

"After you and Bobby and Esther drank the wine."

"Nothing happened later. What are you talking about?"

"You just tell me what you did after you drank the wine and you can go home."

Coolidge eyed Shindler suspiciously. When he answered, he answered in a slow, even tone. The anger and outrage had disappeared from his voice.

"Why don't you tell me what you think I did after we supposedly drank this wine."

"That's not the way we work things around here, Billy. Now I asked you a question and I want an answer."

Coolidge was staring at Shindler. His eyes were on Shindler's eyes. Shindler knew that this was high chess. Coolidge was straining to read his mind. Trying to figure out the move that would end the game for him, knowing that the wrong move would be fatal.

Then, Coolidge smiled and relaxed.

"Sure. Why not. You promise none of us will get in any trouble over . . . Well, let's say there was some wine. No one would get in trouble over that, would he?"

"No one will get in any trouble over the wine," Shindler said.

"Okay. Say, I'm sorry I gave you such a hard time.

It's just that I've been rousted by the cops before and I don't like it.

"About afterwards. We just sat on a side street and drank the wine. There was a couple of bottles, 'cause we had some in the car already. Then Esther got blotto and we took her home. That's all."

"Where was this side street?"

"I don't remember. It was a couple of blocks from the grocery store where I took the wine. That's over by Lake and Grant."

"So you drank some wine and Esther got drunk and you took her straight home."

"Not straight home. I think we cruised a little downtown. But Esther was feeling pretty bad, so we didn't stay downtown long."

"I don't suppose you remember the hour you were downtown?"

"Sorry, I can't help you there."

"We know it didn't happen that way, Billy."

"What do you mean? I just told you what happened."

"I'm afraid you left something out. Think hard."

Coolidge looked at Shindler. A little of the cool was fading, but the veneer was still there.

"I didn't leave anything out. We drank the wine, cruised downtown and took Esther home."

"You left out the park."

"What park?"

"Lookout Park."

"What are you talking about? We didn't go to Lookout Park."

He was nervous now. There was strain in his voice. Shindler could sense it.

"You can stop pretending, Billy. We found Esther Freemont's glasses at the park. We know you were there that night."

Shindler stared at Coolidge. The boy's eyes were bright with fear and Shindler sensed something alien and hideous in their depth.

"I wasn't in the park that night," Coolidge insisted. Coolidge's breathing had become more rapid and the boy was constantly shifting in his seat.

"You were there, Billy. Telling us about it will make it easier on you."

"Easier for what? I didn't do anything and I wasn't in the park."

"Did you know Richie Walters and Elaine Murray, Billy?"

Coolidge's mouth hung open and he stared wide-eyed at the detective.

"Is that what this is all about? You think . . . I want out of here. Now."

His voice had risen to a scream.

"You ain't gonna make me guilty of that. Let me out."

"I'll let you out, you little scumbag, when you tell me the truth," Shindler said in a voice tight with hate. "When you tell me how you stabbed that poor boy and gang-fucked that girl."

Shindler was standing. His body quivered and he moved slowly toward Coolidge. The boy turned to the policeman with a silent plea for help. His hands were thrust forward, palms out, as if to ward off some invisible blow.

The sight of the boy before him filled Shindler

with rage. He could see the girl, naked, pleading in terror for her life. He wanted to smash, to hit. The boy was yelling something. The policeman was looking at Shindler with alarm. Shindler realized where he was. His hand was shaking uncontrollably. He opened the door and left the room.

There was a men's room in the hallway. He plunged into it. He leaned against the wall. His body shook. His breathing was shallow. The face in the wall mirror frightened him. It was not his face. It was possessed of emotions as alien to him as the acts of the boy. It was the face of the primeval hunter. The killer in man.

He splashed himself with cold water. He sat on a folding chair. Slowly, he gained control. Harvey was on the second floor. He got up and walked downstairs.

Marcus came out at his knock. He looked at Shindler uncertainly.

"What happened?"

Shindler shook his head.

"I lost my temper. It's okay now. Are you getting anywhere?"

"Lost your temper? What do you mean?" Marcus asked, concerned. He did not like Shindler's intense interest in the case. He considered it unhealthy and unprofessional.

"It was nothing. How are you doing?"

"I don't think the kid is involved, Roy."

"Not involved?"

"He's been polite and cooperative. He answers all the questions. And he tells the same story as the Freemont girl."

"You're wrong, Harvey. You have to be. You didn't see that little punk. They invented a cover story, that's all."

"Or they are telling the truth."

"No, damn it. It's them. I know it."

"Roy, these feelings are all subjective. You don't have a single piece of evidence tying these boys to the killings. If you want to know, I think you are getting personally involved in this case and it is affecting your judgment. I'm going to release Bobby Coolidge and I think you should do the same with his brother."

That evening Shindler ate a TV dinner and drank a bottle of beer. Then he took off his shoes and tie and stretched out, still dressed, on his bed. He placed his hands behind his head and stared at the ceiling. He noticed a tiny crack in the ceiling plaster and traced it with his eye. A car hummed by outside. He closed his eyes and listened to his breathing.

Sometimes he felt that he was leaving his sanity behind. Moving so slowly into the world of the mad that he would not notice until it was too late. It was not healthy to encounter violent death so frequently. When death became part of each day, it started to lose its meaning. The next step was for life to lose its value.

Recently he had investigated the murder of a grocer who had been brutally beaten by two men. The face had been obliterated. The grocer had been a good family man with two beautiful children. Shindler had calmly directed the investigation at the scene. He had posed the body for pictures with bored detachment. He had conducted the interviews in a bored monotone. The death had meant nothing to him. When he realized this, hours later, it had shaken him.

The Murray-Walters case was a spiritual lifeline. He was grateful for a death that had awakened something human in him. Something that Harvey suggested was making it impossible for him to continue with the investigation.

He felt lost. Was that the choice? Did feeling lead to failure? Did success have to be purchased with a loss of human qualities? Were his emotions blinding him to the truth?

Harvey had talked to him for a long time after they had let the Coolidges go. He had tried to convince him that he should forget them. That the truth lay elsewhere. Shindler did not buy that. Somewhere there was a key. He had never been this sure about a case. Those glasses. The personalities. The knife. The fight on the same evening. There were too many coincidences.

Shindler looked at his watch. He had been lying in the dark for an hour. Esther Freemont. He could see her large brown eyes. Doe's eyes. Soft eyes. An animal at bay. She was not made of the same stuff as the Coolidges. She was soft. She would bend to his will. He could break her if she was lying. He closed his eyes and thought about it. He would see her in the morning.

Shindler had the plan worked out by the time he arrived at Esther's house. The day was sunny and warm. There were no clouds in the sky. He told

Esther's mother that he wanted to ask her some more questions about the glasses and that he would bring her home shortly.

Esther went with him reluctantly. She never relaxed. Her eyes moved constantly. Her hands would not keep still. Shindler approved. He wanted her nervous and without reserves, so that there would be nothing there but truth when the moment came.

Shindler engaged Esther in small talk so that she would not notice that they were not headed toward the station house. He headed up Monroe Boulevard and he noticed her looking out the window uncertainly.

"This isn't the way downtown."

"I wanted to show you where we found the glasses."

"Are we going to the park?"

Shindler nodded.

"To where Richie . . . ?"

"To where we found the glasses."

"I don't want to go there," she said suddenly. Shindler noticed that she was gripping the seat hard enough to make her knuckles turn white.

"There's nothing to be afraid of."

"I really don't want to go up there. Please, Mr. Shindler. It scares me."

"It shouldn't frighten you, Esther. The place doesn't look the same anymore. I'll take you to the meadow where we found Richie. You'll see. You would never know that someone died there."

She did not say anything more and Shindler continued until he reached the spot where the glasses had been found.

"Does this look familiar, Esther?"

She looked out of the car window. Shindler got

out and walked over to the exact spot. Esther did not follow.

"Come on. Take a look."

"I told you before, I wasn't here. I don't know why you brought me here."

"Just to see the place, Esther. I thought that you might be curious to see where we found your glasses."

She turned away and bit her lip. Shindler got back in the car and headed up the road to the meadow.

"I'm going to make one more stop. Then we'll go down to the station."

"Don't take me there. Please," she begged in a voice tinged with panic.

"I want to check something, Esther. You can wait in the car."

He parked the car at the end of the dirt road and looked around. The meadow had not changed. It had been peaceful even on the day of the murder. The violence had been added and subtracted. Shindler got out of the car and walked to the spot where the car had been. There was no trace of it. He waited a while for Esther to see whatever phantoms remained. Then he got back in his car. Esther was quiet on the trip to the station.

Shindler parked in the police garage. The garage was in the basement of the police station. They took the elevator up to the third floor and he brought her to the same room where he had questioned Billy Coolidge. This morning, before he picked her up, he had put the photograph in the small drawer in the wooden desk.

The matron tried to get Esther to relax. She only made Esther more nervous with her attentions.

Shindler could smell the fear in Esther. He had owned a pet rabbit when he was a boy. The rabbit had never adjusted to the cage. It would run round and round, darting into the mesh, trying to claw through. Esther's eyes reminded him of the rabbit's. They never looked at him. They darted everywhere, searching for an exit.

"You didn't tell me the whole truth the last time we talked, Esther."

"What do you mean?" she asked cautiously. She did not trust this soft-spoken thin man. There was too much of the deceiver below his surface.

"You didn't tell me about what happened at Alice Fay's house."

"I didn't do anything," she answered quickly.

"No. But Billy and Bobby did. Tell me what they did."

Esther stared away from Shindler at the floor.

"They fought," she said in a low voice.

"I didn't hear you," Shindler said.

"They fought," she said louder. "I told them to leave, honest. I didn't want them fighting. I just wanted to see the house."

"You didn't tell me how they fought."

Esther looked confused.

"What did Billy use, Esther?"

Esther's eyes widened.

"What did Billy use?" Shindler repeated.

"A . . . a knife," she said so quietly that her voice was like the tick of a clock in another room.

"That's right. And you held that back, didn't you?"

"No. Honest. I just . . . I didn't know it would be important."

"Not important, Esther? Did you know that Richie Walters was stabbed twenty times. Twenty different times. And you didn't think it was important that Billy Coolidge had a knife?"

"Well, we didn't go up there."

"Up where?"

"To the park."

"How do you know? You say you can't remember what you did."

"I just know."

"You just know," Shindler mimicked. Esther bit her lip.

"My mamma knows," she said suddenly, and with relief, as if she had grasped a lifeline.

"Wrong, Esther. All your mother can say is that you came home late and drunk. Richie was killed between twelve and two."

Esther looked down again. Shindler let her sit in silence for a moment. His eyes drifted toward the desk drawer. He could see the photograph through the wood and manila. It burned there, burning him with its fire. Any pity he might have had for Esther Freemont turned to ash. The picture dried him out and made him like cold stone.

"Tell me about the park, Esther."

"I wasn't in the park."

"How do you know if you can't remember?"

"That's what I mean. I can't remember. Please, can't I go home?"

"Richie and Elaine can't go home, Esther. You know that, don't you?"

"Don't talk like that, please, Mr. Shindler. It scares me."

"You don't like to think about Richie and Elaine, do you?"

She shook her head.

"Billy hated them, didn't he?"

"I don't know," she said.

"You aren't telling me the truth, Esther. Billy hates rich people. He envies them. I know. I've talked to enough people to know what goes on in Billy Coolidge's head. Now answer me. Billy hated rich people, didn't he?"

"Yes."

"Good," Shindler said, leaning back. "Now we are getting somewhere. Who did Billy hate, Esther?"

She wished he would stop saying her name. He made it sound dirty. Like it was scum in a gutter pool. She could feel tears coming.

"Who?" Shindler asked in a voice that cut to her nerve.

"Please, I don't know. Just the rich kids. He didn't like Tommy Cooper. I don't know. He didn't talk to me that much."

"You were with him that night."

"No. I was with Roger . . . Hessey. My boyfriend. But we had a fight at the party and he left me. That's why I was with Billy."

"And you can't remember the park?"

"I can't. The last thing I remember is hazy. It's downtown. I think we were cruising."

"Esther, I'm going to let you go, but I want to show you something first. Then I'll take you home."

She did not know how to take it. Whether to believe him. Going home. Out of this room. She relaxed like a balloon when the air is let out, deflating, shoulders sagging.

Shindler opened the desk drawer and drew out the manila envelope. He pulled the large color photograph out of the envelope facedown, so Esther could not see. Esther leaned forward out of curiosity. When her eyes were focused on the back of the print, he turned the picture faceup and leaned back. He could see the scene registering. Esther made a choking sound. Then she began to scream. He had not expected that. In retrospect, he realized that he should have.

She was standing and still screaming. Her hands before her face, half-curled, forming tiny claws. He watched her with detached interest. A lab specimen.

She could not look away from the picture and she could not stop screaming. The matron gave him a peculiar look when she helped Esther out of the room. People were looking down the corridor.

Shindler was suddenly aware that he had caused the screams. It began to dawn on him that his actions had been responsible for the girl's hysterics. His composure began to crumble. People were looking in at him. Still he did not move. He tried to think about the situation in terms of logic. He had done nothing wrong. This girl and those two boys were responsible. They had butchered two beautiful children. If Esther had to suffer so that the truth could be revealed, it was sad but necessary.

Someone asked if he was okay. He did not acknowledge him. There was a pitcher and water glass on the desk. He took a slow drink of water and contemplated the picture. He felt the same anger he had felt when he saw the boy for the first time.

The picture was of the body full length on the rubber sheet just before it had been taken from the scene. The angle showed the full facial damage. It had been cruel to show it to Esther, but Shindler was willing to do anything to find the people who had killed Richie Walters.

"I am taking you off this case, Roy. That is my decision," Captain Webster said. Shindler sat rigid, his mouth clamped shut and his eyes staring directly into the captain's. He did not trust himself to speak.

"I don't know what got into you with that girl. You're lucky if she doesn't bring a suit against you."

"Captain, I . . . I am certain that Esther Freemont is the key to the Murray-Walters murders."

"I know what you think. I had a long talk with Harvey Marcus before I called you in here. Now, damn it, Roy, I think you are one of the best detectives I have. But this is not the Gestapo. I can't have you torturing people to break cases. In no time we would be as bad as the people we are trying to catch.

"Besides, I think that you are way off on this one. Harvey thinks that this obsession that you have about the Coolidge brothers is preventing you from investigating this case effectively. He also thinks that your preoccupation with the case is affecting your other work. So I am taking you off of it."

"Because I showed her the picture?"

"Haven't you heard what I have been saying? The picture would have been enough. She's a sixteen-year-old girl, Roy. But that isn't why you are °off. I have reviewed the file and I have talked with several other people in Homicide. I do not think that it is in the best interest of the department to have you continue on this case."

Shindler took a deep breath.

"Who is getting the case?"

"I'm giving the file to Doug Cutler, but I am telling him to put it on inactive status."

"Inactive . . . ? Captain, that's like closing the case."

"I told you that I had reviewed the file. I don't think that a continuing investigation is going to solve this case."

Roy Shindler went home to bed. He did not sleep. He lit a cigarette and smoked in bed. He was so tired. He was so sick. The sickness was inside of him.

After a few hours, Roy sat up and called Mr. Walters at his office. He used to go to the Walters' home when something happened to tell them firsthand, but he had stopped because of Mrs. Walters. She always seemed to pull into herself when he came.

Mr. Walters was different. He had hardened since November. He kept in close contact with Roy, anxious to learn every detail of the investigation. Mr. Walters was in and said he would be glad to see Roy. Roy dressed and drove downtown.

"I wanted to tell you in person. They put the case on inactive status."

"You mean they closed the file?" Norman Walters asked incredulously.

"It amounts to the same thing. The file is still open, but no one is actively working on it."

"But you told me that you were on to something. That you thought that you knew who . . . who killed Richie."

"I think I do, but the department disagrees. I have been taken off of the case."

Mr. Walters stared at Shindler.

"They took you off the case. Who did that? I'm not without influence, Roy. Give me the names and I'll have you back on it by tomorrow."

Roy shook his head.

"That's not the way to do it. Even if you could get me reassigned, there would be so much resentment that I wouldn't be able to do my job."

"But I could get the Commissioner to order you back on it."

"I'm not so sure you could. And I know what kind of bad feelings would result."

"Then it's all over," Walters said dejectedly. "My boy is dead and no one will ever pay for it."

"No, it's not all over, Mr. Walters. It will never be over as far as I am concerned. I'll let this die down for a while. I still have access to the file and I can keep track of the investigation. What I do in my spare time is my own business. No, it's not over, Mr. Walters."

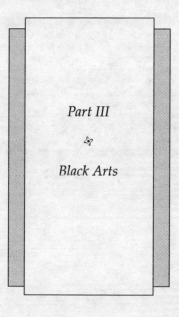

Part III

Black Arts

1

On the day after Thanksgiving, 1965, Norman Walters did what he had done on every day after Thanksgiving since November, 1961. After breakfast, he went into his study and wrote a check to the classified advertisement section of the Portsmouth *Herald*. Then he enclosed the check and a sheet of his business stationery in an envelope. Typed on the sheet was an advertisement that would run for a month. It read:

> $10,000 reward for any information leading to the arrest and conviction of the person or persons responsible for the murders, on November 25, 1960, of Richie Allen Walters and Elaine Melissa Murray. Please contact: Norman Walters, Suite 409, Seacreast Building, Portsmouth. Phone: 237-1329.

A floorboard creaked in the bedroom above. Norman glanced nervously toward the study door and sealed the envelope. Carla would be down in a moment and he did not want her to see the letter. She

had taken Richie's death very badly and there had
been a slow recovery. Even now he would come upon
her weeping quietly in a corner of the house, saying
nothing when asked for the cause. For the most part
she was his wife again, but he was careful to keep any
reference to their dead son from her.

The sun was shining when he left the house. It had
snowed the day before and the morning coat crackled
underfoot. Thinking of Richie made him think of
Roy Shindler. For a while after Richie's death he had
seen the detective often. At first Norman believed
that they shared a common grief, but he soon discovered that it was hate that brought them together. As
the passage of time dulled the sharpness of Norman's
desire for revenge, a rift had developed between himself and the detective. He was sure that no matter
how hard he worked to disguise it, the detective could
sense his growing aversion to the reminders of the
loss he had suffered. At times, he caught himself wondering whether his son's death meant more to Shindler
than to himself. Self-deprecating thoughts which
were, of course, not true. But they sowed the seeds of
guilt.

The posting of the advertisement each year had
become a ritual he engaged in to expiate his imagined sins. He felt compelled to do it so that he could
look upon Shindler's sad and accusing countenance.
In his heart, he prayed that there would be no new
clues. What great truth would be served if the killer
was discovered after all these years? It could only
lead to the baring of old wounds and new sorrow for
himself and his wife. There had been times during
the past week when he had considered not sending in

the ad. Then he would conjure an image of Shindler and his courage would leave him.

The lid of the mailbox snapped back, sending the sound of metal ringing through the still cold air. Norman's shoulders straightened as if a great weight had been removed.

The baby was crying again. It was harder to get up every time. Sometimes she thought about staying in bed until the cries became whimpers and finally stopped. Then she would feel guilt. It was an unnatural thing to want your baby to die. She loved her baby. It was just that she was so tired.

If John was here, she thought. But John had left Esther Pegalosi all alone. John had left because of the baby. No, it wasn't the baby. The others had left her and there had been no baby. She was to blame. She was the one.

The baby howled. Esther opened her eyes and looked at the clock. It was four in the morning. Still dark outside. She felt empty. What was she? A machine that ran on food. Get up, feed, go to the bathroom, sleep. No purpose. Less than a machine. At least a machine had a purpose. It capped bottles or pressed shapes out of steel.

Esther pushed herself to her feet. She could see herself in the mirror. She had lost most of the weight from her pregnancy and she was getting her figure back. She took off her nightgown and stood naked. Her legs were long and her hips wide. Her stomach was regaining its muscle tone. And then there were her breasts. John had loved her breasts. So had the others. He would kiss them and bite them. They were large and firm, nicely shaped even after the pregnancy. She had a good body. A beautiful body. They had all said so. But somehow it had never been enough.

How long had she known John? A year and a half? Two seemed more like it. She had been working as a waitress at Foley's Truck Stop near the Interstate. She was pretty, so all the customers used to joke with her and she got her share of propositions, many of which she accepted. But John had been different. He was quieter, more serious. He wasn't lewd like most of them. No pats on the rear or behind-the-back comments that were supposed to be overheard.

They had gone to the movies a few times and he had been a real gentleman. He had even brought her flowers once. The dating was sporadic, because he was on the road so much, but she started looking forward to seeing him. She didn't feel about him the way that the women in the confession magazines and romance novels felt, but she felt comfortable with him. He was gentle and treated her with respect and she appreciated that in him. She wanted to be in love, like in the books, but she settled for having someone nearby who, she thought, cared.

The baby's fists were tight and his color bright red. His mouth was so wide. Screaming. He was always screaming. Why couldn't he be a quiet baby? He never rested. He never let her rest. She picked him up and rocked him. Her motions were automatic. There was no love in them, only desperation.

Very little had changed for Esther before she married John. After high school, she had moved out and gotten an apartment and a job. There had been plenty of men, but they hadn't stayed long. They would say that they loved her and, with each new promise of happiness, she would give herself. But the affairs never lasted long.

Then John asked her to marry him. The proposal frightened her. She had prayed so hard for happiness and now that it was really there it terrified her. That night, she cried herself to sleep. He was a good man, she told herself. Then why does he want me? None of the others saw anything in me worth wanting.

She was sick with worry and did not go to work the next day. She was afraid that he would take the proposal back, as if it was a door-to-door sales offer. She could not have stood that. For once things were working out. This might be her only chance. Maybe she would be happy after all.

A judge at the county courthouse married them. They pooled their salaries and rented a small apartment. Then John lost his job. He tried real hard at first, but the job market was tight. After a while, he just gave up. He would sit in front of the TV all day. He started to drink more than usual and the frequency of their sex decreased. He had always been an ardent lover. It thrilled her when he told her how good she was, when he caressed her and kissed her. But after he lost his job he was always tired and on the occasions when they did have sex it was always fast, with little or no foreplay.

The baby sucked greedily at the bottle. Esther's head lolled to one side and she tried to stay awake. After he finished, she would change him. Then, hopefully, he would sleep for a few hours. He looked so peaceful sucking. It was an illusion. She hated him. She felt guilt as soon as she thought it. No, she did not hate her baby. She loved her baby. It was herself she hated. She blamed the baby for losing John, but he was just a baby. Only John would not have left her if she had not become pregnant.

When she told him that she had missed her period and thought she was pregnant, he had said nothing. It hurt her. She hoped that he would be happy. This would be their baby. Something they could have and love together. But the news had not made him happy. He became taciturn, sullen. There were constant arguments over finances.

She began to hate the baby even before it was born. She could see how it was breaking them apart. Wedging its tiny body between her and the only happiness she had ever known. She sensed that he would leave her. He never said anything about going, but the idea filled every room of their apartment. Then one day he was gone.

The baby's mouth sagged and fell off the nipple. He relaxed and his eyes closed. She would not change him, she decided. She could not risk waking him and starting the crying again. She placed him in the crib and left. Maybe he would sleep for a long time.

Esther crawled back under the covers and closed her eyes. The hardest thing she had ever done was to return to this apartment with the baby. The walls were her prison and the baby was her keeper. It was a life sentence. Sometimes she thought that she would be better off dead. If she had died in childbirth . . . She imagined the doctors in white. They would look solemn. The bouncing dot on the life monitoring machine would stretch slowly into a straight line. They would have told John that she and the baby were dead. He would have cried and there would have been roses at the funeral and a minister to say nice things about her.

But she wasn't dead. And, sometimes, she hoped. She tried not to, but when she was weak or tired, like now, she could not help herself. She wasn't much. She could see that. But there were other people like her who were somebody. All she really wanted was . . . was to be somebody. She started to cry.

Cindy Shaeffer heard her husband's troubled breathing and knew that he was awake. Outside it was still dark and she lay without moving, wondering what she should do. It was like this almost every night. She felt so helpless.

He was stirring. She knew he would be exhausted. He sighed and it sounded like a moan. She turned toward him and saw that he was staring at the ceiling, his forehead beaded with sweat. She put an arm across his chest and hugged him. Mark felt her embrace, but it did not comfort him.

"Do you feel okay? Do you want me to fix some hot chocolate? That will help you sleep."

Mark shook his head slowly. He felt scared and empty inside.

"I'm all right. I'll just go downstairs and read for a while. There's no need for you to lose sleep too."

"Mark, don't worry. Everything will work out. It just takes time."

Mark got out of bed and took his bathrobe off the

hook behind the bedroom door. He picked up his book from the dresser and started out of the room.

"Mark," Cindy pleaded. He looked so dejected.

"I'll be okay," he said, half-heartedly. "Don't worry."

She heard the door close and she lay back on the bed, fighting back tears. She felt so helpless. Everything was falling apart.

In the living room, Mark turned on the light and opened his book, but he could not concentrate. Eight months ago he had been on top of the world. He had always wanted to be a lawyer and that was the day he had received his notice that he had passed the bar. He was ready to start his career. The problem was that there were no jobs.

During the six months that followed, his self-confidence had been completely eroded. At first he had not thought much about it. That was when he was still expecting the lawyers who said that they would get in touch with him to get in touch. That was when he really believed that he would get a job. After a few months of broken promises and insincere handshakes, he stopped believing.

Cindy had been no help, because she did not understand. They had married young and she had taken a job as a secretary to help put him through law school. Like Mark, she expected to find gold on the day he graduated. Instead, there had only been frustration. She was from a poor family and very insecure about money. The longer he went without a job, the more pressure she began to feel and the more pressure she had begun to exert on Mark. She could not understand why he was unemployed. She began to blame him for not trying. There had been nasty scenes with Mark yelling and feeling guilty afterwards when she cried.

Then, shortly after the new year, tired of trying and failing, Mark had decided to go into business on his own. He had talked with a few sole practitioners and they had assured him that he could do it. It was a frightening thing to do. He was inexperienced and completely without connections. Still, the more he thought about the idea, the more it had excited him.

Unfortunately, it had not excited Cindy. She wanted to quit work. She wanted a baby. If Mark went into his own practice instead of working for one of the big firms that paid big salaries, it would mean more debts and it would mean that she would have to work some more—maybe several years more. There had been more scenes, but he had prevailed and two months ago he had rented a small office in the National Bank Building, an old, eight-story office building located three blocks from the courthouse in downtown Portsmouth. He enjoyed what he was doing, but business was slow in coming and he had begun to wonder if he would make it on his own.

He had not been sleeping well lately, because he was worrying. He needed his rest, but as soon as he lay down to sleep, he would start thinking of his expenses or whether one of his clients would try to stiff him. Then he could not sleep.

The fights with Cindy did not help either. They were going to bed mad more often, something they had rarely done in the first six years of their marriage. They usually made up in the morning, but the nagging and bickering were starting to get to him. He even caught himself wondering if they shouldn't separate for a while, but had rejected the idea. Still, he had no way of knowing how the relationship, which he had thought so secure, would hold up, if his business did not prosper.

Mark leaned his head against the back of his armchair and closed his eyes. In a few more hours he would have to go to work. If he could not sleep, at least he would try to rest.

"Slow down, will ya, Coolidge? This ain't a goddamn race."

The truck jarred and hopped as it hit a pothole and the Scotch in Mosby's bottle splashed over the rim, wetting his lap.

"Fuckin' A, Coolidge. This booze cost me plenty. I'll have your ass if you make me spill any more."

"Better you than the Viet Cong. You're cuter than the gooks anyway."

"Those little farts ain't gonna get your ass with me here to protect you."

"They may get both our asses if we aren't back at the camp by sundown."

Mosby leaned back and took another swig from the bottle. God, he could drink. They had both been doing their share since they hit Saigon last night. Bobby Coolidge could feel the effects of his share and he concentrated extra hard on the twists and turns of the narrow jungle road. The lush green foliage was packed tight along either side. The upper branches of trees stretched across the space between to cut off the scattered rays of light still left from the setting sun. The way was shadows.

He decided that he had been a fool to let Mosby talk him into waiting while he banged the bar girl he had picked up shortly before they were to return to camp. He knew how long it would take to return with the supplies and he knew the dangers of being in the jungle after dark.

The road curved suddenly and Bobby jerked the wheel sharply, just managing to keep the truck upright. Mosby cursed again. He shouldn't be driving after drinking so much. Shit! He had to drive. Mosby would wreck them in two seconds.

The hum of the motor and the monotony of the trip lulled Mosby to sleep. The almost empty bottle tottered over on a curve, spilling the brown liquid onto the floor of the cab. Coolidge glanced at Mosby's face. Mosby groaned and smiled in the midst of some obscene dream. It had been a long time since Coolidge had dreamed sweet dreams.

The old fears had resurfaced faintly in boot camp. A glimmer, a warning perhaps, but nothing he could put his finger on. He was still excited by it all then. Only weeks out of high school and primed on John Wayne. Then Vietnam did not work out the way he thought it would and he began wondering what he was doing there. The people he was killing did not look like the enemy was supposed to. There were too many women and children and old men. Sometimes he was not sure that they were enemies at all.

He became confused. One day he stopped firing his rifle in combat, although he told no one of this. What would Mosby say if he knew what was going on inside his head? Or the others? There were some who might understand or sympathize, but it was safer to keep his thoughts to himself. Only there was a price to be paid in the form of dreams that crept in when he was sleeping, bringing flashes and bodies and fire. Blood was everywhere.

The dreams began to control his life. They made him a lineman. He had to repair the damage to telephone lines in an area heavily infiltrated by Viet Cong. He would shimmy up the telephone poles in the dark. Then they would turn on a spotlight and he would have two minutes to work, praying the snipers would not find the range, each second stretching into eternity. It made him sick. He did not sleep during the day thinking about the nights and he did not sleep at night because of the dreams.

If it had not been for the liquor, he would not have made it. The bottle brought dreamless sleep and peace. It made the war softer and easier to survive. He began to see the war as part of some other life led by some other person. There were two Bobby Coolidges. One drinking and drifting and biding his time and the one that that one watched: the one who went through the motions of being a soldier. In no time at all, and without formal training, he was becoming a man of conscience. He was rejecting the violence of his youth. Questioning. There was no glory in it anymore. He had learned that on telephone poles in the dark and in side streets of Vietnamese villages from the faces of dying children.

The road was the same everywhere. The headlights hypnotized him and his eyelids grew heavy.

He must have dozed for a minute, because he could not remember seeing the old man dart into the road. He was just there, frozen in the headlight beams, a frightened deer, paralyzed and staring with eyes that begged for life.

Maybe Bobby could have given it to him if he had been sober, but he was too slow and the truck was over him before he could apply the brakes. There was a thud and the truck was tearing slowly through resistance for a moment. All Bobby could do was lay his head on the steering wheel of the truck that now sat sideways across the road.

The sudden stop had thrown Mosby against the dashboard. He saw his friend moaning and he saw the position of the truck. It took him a few seconds to take it in.

"What happened?"

"I think I hit a man."

"What?" Mosby asked, still confused by sleep.

"With the truck. I think I hit an old man. I swear I didn't see him. He was just there. I don't know how it happened."

Mosby stared into the darkness.

"I don't see anyone."

"He's probably behind us or under the truck."

"Oh, shit."

They sat in the cab for a moment.

"We gotta see if he's dead. He might just be hurt."

Bobby was afraid, but he followed Mosby, lowering himself out of the cab onto the hard-packed dirt. Mosby took a look around. It was pitch black where the headlights did not shine. He leaned into the cab and fished a flashlight out of the glove compartment. He flicked on the beam and they walked cautiously to the rear of the truck. At first they could not see the body, because it had been knocked into a thicket by the roadside. The beam caught a leg bent at the knee. The face was frozen in a state of disbelief. There were no outward signs of death except for a trickle of blood at the side of the mouth. The old man did not move when Mosby prodded him with his foot.

"Is he dead?" Coolidge asked over Mosby's shoulder.

"I think so. He ain't movin'."

"What are we going to do?"

"I don't know. Let me think for a minute."

Mosby shone the light in all directions. The area was deserted.

"Look, this was an accident, right?"

Bobby shook his head. He was still shaky and he felt loose inside, like he might come apart at any moment.

"This guy was old anyway and he's a gook. If we pull him into the bushes, he won't be found for days. And if he is found, who's gonna care? There's no way they can connect us with this thing if we don't tell anyone about it."

"I don't know. I killed him, Carl."

"Listen, Bobby. You got to start thinkin' straight. This ain't some white man. This is another gook. You don't know. He coulda been a V.C. Now, if we don't say nothin', there ain't gonna be no fuss."

Bobby had to sit down. He slid down the side of the truck and took out a cigarette with a shaking hand. Mosby reconnoitered the area looking for the best spot to dump the body. When he returned to the truck, Bobby was calmer.

"You're right. I'm okay now."

He stood up and approached the body with caution. Bobby licked his dry lips and bent down. His hands jumped a bit as he touched the still warm legs. Mosby had the corpse under the armpits and Bobby averted his eyes as they lifted and dragged the old man farther into the bushes. There was no blood on the truck and they sat in the darkened cab breathing heavily from the exertion. When they had recovered, Mosby drove the truck toward camp. It was finished. Nothing had happened. They agreed on that.

A few nights later, Bobby woke up screaming. He had been wandering through a village. The dead were everywhere. Their bodies were naked and their stomachs had been ripped open so that the intestines hung outside, looped in insane coils, tangling his heels as he walked among them. In the light of napalm flashes he saw the faces of the dead staring at him with the eyes of the old man.

"We're not gonna find 'em, tonight," Officer Stout said.

"You don't think so?" Shindler asked rhetorically.

"They're whores. They'll travel to L.A. or Frisco. They're like birds—they migrate. Be back next summer," Stout said, laughing at his own joke.

Shindler was in no mood to joke. He had been riding the streets all night with Stout, who knew the district, looking for two hookers who were witnesses in a murder case. Now it looked as if he might not find them. He was tired and depressed.

The police radio crackled, but Shindler paid no attention until Stout swung the patrol car in a U-turn with a squeal of tires.

"What's up?" Shindler asked, starting out of his reverie.

"Attempted suicide a few blocks from here," Stout said, the humor gone from his speech.

Stout pulled the car into the curb in front of a four-story apartment building. A woman in a bathrobe and curlers was standing in the lobby.

"She's in room 4B. It's locked. You better hurry."

But Stout and Shindler were already bounding up the steps. Shindler was puffing when they hit the fourth-floor landing, but Stout, young and in good shape, didn't show any signs of fatigue as he raced down the hall to 4B. Stout paused in front of the wooden door for a second, then swung his foot into it near the lock. The wood splintered and Shindler saw the end of a piece of chain whip through the air.

The girl was lying nude on the bed. An empty bottle of pills lay on the nightstand. Stout shouted that she was still breathing and Shindler dialed the phone in the front room that served as kitchen and living room. By the time that Shindler finished calling for the ambulance, Stout had her up and was trying to walk her.

"She left her baby at my door."

Shindler turned around. The woman who had met them was standing in the apartment doorway, staring past him at Stout and the naked girl.

"Pardon?" Shindler said.

The woman talked without taking her eyes off the tableau in the bedroom.

"I heard the baby crying. It was six o'clock and it sounded louder than usual. He was in his stroller in front of my door. She dressed him and strapped him in and left him. When I read the note, I called the police."

"You did the right thing," Shindler reassured her. He heard footsteps pounding up the stairs and walked into the bedroom to assist Stout. Two men in white carrying a stretcher rushed into the apartment. The tiny front room was getting crowded. Shindler watched the girl's face for signs of life. She was a pretty girl. Sensual was a better word. Pretty was for Miss America. This girl had a darker beauty.

The men with the stretcher were asking him questions. Something about the girl disturbed him. He felt that he knew her.

"What's her name?" Shindler asked the woman in the curlers.

"Esther Pegalosi," the lady replied as the men with the stretcher began to assist Stout.

Shindler looked at the face again. Esther! But not Pegalosi.

"I want to ride with her to the hospital," Shindler said.

One of the attendants nodded. They were working fast and Stout, relieved of the burden, was sitting on the bed, wiping the sweat from his forehead.

"I'm going with the ambulance," Shindler shouted as he followed the stretcher through the door. Stout looked up in surprise. He was about to say something, but Shindler was gone. He shrugged and took out his notebook. The lady with the curlers looked down the corridor after the stretcher bearers and the detective.

2

"She left the baby in front of the neighbor's door," Stout said.

"No kidding?" said the middle-aged nurse who had heard the story before in a dozen different forms and was only trying to make conversation.

"She's lucky she isn't dead," the policeman said.

The nurse agreed, even though she did not really care. Dr. Tucker was coming down the hall. The policeman was going on. Something about a note the girl had left before taking all those pills. She smiled at Dr. Tucker when he passed by.

Dr. Tucker nodded at the nurse. He was at the tail end of a hard day. One last patient and then home.

"The neighbor says the husband left her when she got pregnant. Then she was depressed after the baby came. They thought she'd gotten over it this summer."

"Maybe it was the change of seasons. I read someplace . . ."

Dr. Tucker missed the nurse's theory. I'll have to ask her someday, he thought. Change of seasons. As good as any theory about why humans try to destroy themselves. What was this one anyway? Caucasian, female, 22. He shook his head. What could be so bad that young? Well, it didn't matter now. She would be all right. Maybe they shouldn't try so hard to save some of them. It was their choice. Maybe this one would have been better off.

The door opened and Dr. Tucker looked over his shoulder. A tall, sad-looking man in a heavy overcoat had entered the room.

"Can I help you?" Dr. Tucker said, annoyed at the intrusion.

"I'm Detective Shindler, Portsmouth Police. I wanted to know how she is."

Dr. Tucker was about to reply when the girl moaned and opened her eyes. They were still glassy and she was having trouble holding her eyelids open. Shindler moved closer so that he could see her.

"How are you feeling?" the doctor asked in a voice he hoped sounded cheerful.

She was trying to work her lips. Dampening them with her tongue. It took effort to talk and she closed her eyes for a moment to gain strength. When she finally spoke, it came out slurred and barely audible and it sounded like "Is dead?" but Shindler couldn't be sure.

The doctor leaned forward and tried, "Your baby is fine," but she just stared at him with a confused look. Then she began to weep.

"He had no face," she cried. Her tears streamed onto her pillow. Shindler felt a cold finger touch the base of his spine. Dr. Tucker was exhausted, but he summoned his reserves and tried to comfort her.

"They wouldn't let him go. They just hit him."

"No one struck your son, Mrs. Pegalosi. Your baby is fine. He is perfectly okay."

She was confused again. She stopped crying and shook her head from side to side.

"No baby. Dead. They hit . . . didn't he? Died. Oh, God."

She was off again. Dr. Tucker sighed. Shindler moved to the edge of the bed.

"Esther, was it Richie?" he whispered.

The doctor swung around. He had forgotten about the detective.

"You'll have to leave."

"Was it Richie?"

"Hey," Tucker said sharply, "you're out."

"So much blood," Esther sobbed.

"Doctor, I . . ." Shindler began.

"I said out. This girl is in serious condition."

Shindler looked down at the girl. Her head lolled to one side and she was asleep. The doctor pushed him through the door.

"I don't know what you think you're doing here, but . . ."

"I'm sorry," Shindler interrupted.

"You should know better than to carry on like that."

"Doctor, I said I was sorry and I meant it. Now, I have to talk to you. That girl may have important information concerning a homicide. Could we talk for a few minutes?"

Mark Shaeffer opened the door to misdemeanor arraignment court and found a seat in the back of a crowded courtroom presided over by a young judge who was in the process of reading an elderly black man his rights.

"Do you understand that you have a right to have a lawyer appointed if you cannot afford to hire one, Mr. Dykes?"

"What I need a lawyer fo' if I didn't do nothin'? I been tellin' you, I'm innocent."

"Mr. Dykes, this isn't a trial court. The only purpose in having you in court today is to tell you what you are accused of, to ask you if you have a lawyer and to find out if you want to plead guilty or not guilty. You are charged with assault and that is a serious crime. You should have a lawyer to represent you in court."

"But see, that's what I been tellin' you. I ain't done no assault. It was my bottle of wine and when I wouldn't give that no good skunk some he grabbed me. So I natchally hit him. But it was my wine."

"Mr. Dykes, I don't want to hear the facts of your case now. I am going to appoint a lawyer to represent you."

The judge turned to a policeman who was standing in front of a door that led out of the courtroom and into the courthouse jail.

"Officer Waites, is this man in custody?"

"Yes, sir."

Mr. Dykes was standing in front of one of two tables that were set before the raised bench where the judge sat. A young man sat behind the second table, which was covered with files. The judge turned to him.

"Mr. Caproni, what is the position of the District

Attorney's office on letting this man out of jail on his promise to return?"

Caproni searched his files and pulled one out.

"Your honor, the recog. officer interviewed Mr. Dykes last night and he recommended that he not be released on his own recognizance, because he could not provide him with a residence address."

"Mr. Dykes, where are you living?"

"Now I'm at the Mission, but I wants to get to the DuMont Hotel. Only I ain't got the money now."

"Your Honor, in light of the seriousness of the charge and Mr. Dykes's transient status I would request that Mr. Dykes not be granted recog. According to the police report, William Thomas, the victim, required twelve stitches."

The judge's brow furrowed and he thought for a moment. Then he sighed.

"I suppose you are right, Mr. Caproni. Mr. Dykes, I will appoint a lawyer for you and continue your case until tomorrow morning."

"You mean I got to stay in jail?"

"I'm afraid so."

"But I ain't done nothin' and that skunk Willie Thomas knows it."

"We will take this up with your lawyer in the morning.

"Bailiff?"

An elderly man sitting at a table to the judge's right called a new case as Mr. Dykes was escorted back to jail.

"State versus Rasmussen."

Mark stood up and approached the table where Mr. Dykes had stood. The door to the jail opened and a grubby-looking man in his middle twenties, dressed in a tee shirt and jeans, was being led out. He had a stubble of light blond hair and he gave off the unwashed, urine smell that all new arrestees who have spent the night in the drunk tank exude.

"Your Honor, I am Mark Shaeffer. I was just appointed to represent Mr. Rasmussen this morning. I wonder if I could talk to him for a few minutes before entering a plea."

"Certainly. There is an interview room in the jail. We'll call another case while you talk."

"State versus Marsha LaDue," the bailiff said. The jailer led Rasmussen back to jail and Mark followed. A well-dressed young woman and an equally well-dressed older man with a briefcase were approaching the table.

The jailer put them in a small room with a table and two bridge chairs and locked the metal door behind him. Mark opened his attaché case and took out the case file.

"Mr. Rasmussen, my name is Mark Shaeffer and I have been appointed to represent you."

Rasmussen's hand was damp when they shook. He grinned sheepishly and ran his hand through his hair.

"I guess they got me good. I thought for sure that I could make it home. That damn cop got me a block from my house."

"Before you discuss the facts of the case with me, I should tell you the legal definition of "Driving Under the Influence of Intoxicating Liquor." You may think that you have violated the law, but . . ."

"Think? Hell," he laughed, "I was shitfaced. Look, I appreciate your help. I really do. But I did it and I just want to get this over with and get home to my wife. She doesn't even know where I am."

"All right," Mark said reluctantly, "but why don't you tell me a little about yourself. Drunk driving is a serious charge. Maybe I can work a deal with the D.A. and get you a light sentence or a plea to a reduced charge. Now how old are you?"

"I'm twenty-four."

"Any kids?"

"One. A boy. Four."

"Employed?"

"I'm going to college. This is my second semester. I got out of the army about six months ago."

Court was in recess and Albert Caproni was talking to Judge Mercante's secretary, a sexy blond who was laughing at something the young D.A. had just said. Mark waited until Caproni had finished. Then he cleared his throat.

"Excuse me. I'm Mark Shaeffer. I wonder if I could talk to you about the Rasmussen case?"

"Sure. I'm Al Caproni. What's the charge?" He asked as he rifled through his files.

"He has a drunk driving charge. I was curious about what kind of deal we could work out if, uh, well, if he pleads now."

Caproni found the file and took out the police report and a printout of Rasmussen's criminal record.

"His rap sheet shows that he's clean except for a speeding ticket a few years ago. Let's see. The report says that he failed to signal when he made a right turn. Officer followed. Weaving. Pulled him over."

Caproni skipped around, mumbling now and then.

"He was polite. No accident. Listen, he sounds okay. What does he do?"

"He's a college student. Just out of the army."

"Tell ya what. I'll let him plead to "Reckless Driving." Mercante will be easy on him and he'll probably just get a fine."

"Your Honor, I have talked with Mr. Caproni. He has agreed to substitute a charge of "Reckless Driving" for the drunk driving charge against Mr. Rasmussen. I have talked with my client and he has agreed to plead to the reduced charge."

"Is that your wish, Mr. Rasmussen?"

"Yes, sir."

"Is that agreeable to the District Attorney's Office, Mr. Caproni?"

"Yes, Your Honor."

"Mr. Rasmussen, are you aware that I could sentence you to six months in jail or fine you $500 or both if you plead guilty to this charge?"

"My lawyer explained that."

"And you still wish to enter a plea of guilty?"

"Yes, sir."

"Very well. Your plea will be accepted. Mr. Caproni, what are the facts of this case?"

Caproni handed the judge the police report. When he had finished reading it, he asked Mark if there was anything he wished to say on behalf of his client.

"Yes, Your Honor. Mr. Rasmussen is a college student. He just got out of the army and is married and has a child. This is his first scrape with the law except for a speeding ticket in 1962. I think probation would be appropriate here. If the court is considering a fine, I hope you will take into account the fact that I am court-appointed and Mr. Rasmussen and his family are living off what his wife makes as a secretary."

"Thank you, counsel. Do you have anything to suggest with regard to sentencing, Mr. Caproni?"

"Your Honor, I agree with Mr. Shaeffer. Probation sounds appropriate in this case."

"Thank you. You know, Mr. Rasmussen, you are going to get off easy this time, because your record is excellent. Your insurance would have gone sky high and you would have lost your license for a month if you had been convicted of "Driving Under the Influence." Your lawyer did an excellent job getting this charge reduced. Next time you may not be lucky enough to have Mr. Shaeffer representing you.

"Even more important. Next time you might kill somebody. Think about that the next time you have too much to drink and decide to drive.

"I am going to sentence you to thirty days in jail and give you credit for time served. I am going to suspend the imposition of that sentence and put you on probation for one year. If you are arrested for drunk driving again, you will have to serve your time. Do you understand?"

"Yes, sir."

"There will be no fine."

Shaeffer thanked the judge and walked Rasmussen back to jail.

"I want to thank you," Rasmussen said.

"I'm glad I could help."

"I mean it. I would have just pleaded to the other charge and lost my license. I didn't realize that I could get a reduced charge."

Mark smiled.

"That's why they appoint a lawyer for you."

"Say, do you have a business card? If I ever get in trouble again, you're the guy I'll call."

Mark laughed and gave him several of his cards. They talked for a few minutes and Mark returned to his office.

Eddie Toller stood outside his office door and looked over the early customers who were starting to fill up the dark red interior of the Satin Slipper Lounge. Eddie was thirty-nine years old and five feet nine-and-a-half-inches tall. He was skinny and, at one hundred and forty pounds, he was considerably under what he had once read was the proper weight for someone his size. Eddie stayed thin by not eating. He just did not have an appetite and, besides, he had an allergy to dairy products.

The early crowd was mostly businessmen stopping for a quick one before heading home to the suburbs. The people who came later in the evening were a different type. More working people and singles. Eddie smiled. He had a nice smile that went well with his features, which were often described as "kindly." The first time Joyce saw his sad eyes and the droopy salt and pepper mustache that he had cultivated in prison she thought immediately of Shep, a terrier that had lived its life with her family. In his later years, the dog lost his spark and loafed around the house all day, relaxed and content. Eddie looked like someone who had passed by youth and its illusions. He was tired and not inclined to race.

Eddie wandered over to the bar and said hello to the bartender, Sammy White. Sammy was an ex-boxer who had worked for Carl for years. He was friendly and he had given Eddie a few worthwhile tips when Eddie started as assistant manager a few weeks before.

Eddie looked at his watch and glanced toward the door. Joyce should be arriving any minute. He couldn't wait to see her. During the last few years he had been in and out of jail a lot. Never anything real serious. Mostly burglaries and one auto theft. Anyhow, he had spent a lot of time in the joint and the one thing he never got used to was that there weren't any women.

Eddie was a guy who needed women. Wait, that was not right. Eddie was no ladies man or womanizer. What Eddie needed was one woman. Someone to take care of him and tell him what to do. Not that he admitted this to himself, but it was a fact, borne out by thirty-nine years of history, that Eddie could not take care of himself.

When Eddie was young, his mother had looked after him so much that he never learned how to do it himself. Then the army had looked after him. It was after the army that Eddie started trying to think for himself. That, by coincidence, was when he started getting in trouble.

Joyce walked in and Eddie waved at her. Eddie met Joyce his second day as assistant manager. She was a cocktail waitress in the bar. She wasn't exactly a beauty, but she wasn't a dog either. Eddie liked her figure right off. He didn't go for those busty girls that were always throwing their tits around. He liked them skinny, but with long legs. That was Joyce. He didn't mind that she was taller than he was. He liked looking up at her blue eyes and touching her long blond hair.

Eddie was sure that he was falling in love with Joyce. He had never had anyone who cared about him the way Joyce did. Oh, he'd had girlfriends, but they were temporary things. With Joyce he found himself thinking about something permanent. And why not? He wasn't getting any younger and things were starting to go right for him, for once. Here he was only a month and a half out of the joint and he had a steady job. His first since he could not remember when. And a girl, too.

"You're late," Eddie kidded, looking at his watch.

"Whatta ya gonna do, Eddie, fire me?" Joyce asked.

"I just might," he said and kissed her on the cheek.

"You ain't got the heart, you big lunk. I got your number."

He looked at her real serious and said, "You do and you know it."

She blushed and he did too. Then she looked troubled and unsure.

"What's the matter?" he asked.

"Eddie, let's go to the office and talk."

"Sure," he said, uncertain, because of her sudden change of mood. They walked over to the office. The main office belonged to Carl, who owned the Satin Slipper and managed it. Eddie had a small office down the hall. It was the first office he had ever had, except for a desk he had had in the army when he was a supply sergeant. The office was not much. An old wooden desk, a filing cabinet and some hard wooden chairs. But he was proud of it.

"Eddie, I've been thinking a lot about us."

Oh, Jesus, was his first thought, she wants to stop seeing me.

"I like you a lot, Eddie. And I know you like me. Don't you?"

"Well . . . Yes. I . . . I like you."

He stuttered and looked down at the desk. She touched his cheek.

"Eddie, I want you to quit working for Carl."

Eddie looked up, shocked.

"Quit? Are you nuts?"

"Eddie, I'm worried. Carl is taking advantage of you and you are going to get in a lot of trouble."

"Carl! Taking advantage! Honey, Carl gave me this job. I owe him. What other guy is gonna take a chance on a guy with my record. Besides, I ain't done anything I could get in trouble for."

"You know that's not true. There's a lot of dirty money that comes through this bar. There's numbers and don't think I don't know about the drugs."

Eddie sat up at the mention of drugs.

"Honest, Joyce, I ain't foolin' around with drugs. I'm through with that stuff."

"I didn't say you were using drugs, Eddie," Joyce said, laying her hand gently on his forearm. "I'm close enough to you to know that."

She said the last in a low voice and they both felt suddenly shy and very close.

"It's just that there is selling going on here all the

time and someday Carl is going to get busted and they'll take you along with him, because you got a record."

Eddie knew that he was in love with her then. He held her hand hard.

"Look, Joyce, you have to have faith in me. I just know I'm gonna stay clean this time. I've been feelin' it ever since I got paroled. I can handle anything that comes up here and now that I met you—well, that's the biggest reason why I ain't goin' back to the joint."

Joyce could not think of anything to say. They just looked at each other. Then they were holding each other and kissing. Eddie realized that Joyce was crying.

"Hey," he said, wiping away the tears.

Joyce sniffed and blew her nose. She looked at her watch.

"I gotta change. My shift starts in ten minutes."

"That's okay. Take an extra five."

"I can't, Eddie. Carl will get mad and I'll get in trouble."

Eddie laughed and puffed out his chest.

"You take that five. Carl is out of town for a few days and I'm the boss."

The waiting room at the State Penitentiary was tiled in green and lined with cheap, leather-covered couches that were made in the prison as part of its rehabilitation program. Bobby did not know it, but he was sitting on the handiwork of a timid book-keeper who had solved his marital problems by roasting his wife and her lover alive.

Two guards stood behind a circular counter in the center of the room, answering inquiries. Bobby glanced at the clock on the far wall. The visiting hour would start in two minutes. He wriggled nervously in his seat and looked at an attractive Negro woman who was talking quietly to a small boy, explaining that he would have to stay with grandma while she saw daddy, because little boys were not allowed inside the prison.

One of the guards left the counter and moved to the side of a doorway that led down a ramp to the prison area. A line formed and the guard searched purses and made everyone empty their pockets.

There was a gate with bars at the end of the ramp. The guard signaled to another guard who sat at a desk in a celllike room and the gate rolled aside with a metallic groan. The visitors walked down another hallway and were shown into a large visiting room. There were more prison-made sofas and several chairs. They were set up facing each other across wooden coffee tables. Automatic soft drink, coffee and candy vending machines stood watch from a corner of the room. The color scheme was the same antiseptic green that was used where cream was not throughout the prison.

Bobby found a pair of chairs in a corner and watched the doorway nervously. A prisoner stood at the entrance and looked around. It took Bobby a few seconds before he realized that the prisoner was his brother. He had put on weight and he seemed thicker, especially in the face. He wondered how he looked to his brother.

Billy spotted him and waved. When he strode

across the visiting room, it was with a swagger. His handshake was firm and he showed no embarrassment at the prison clothes he was wearing.

"You're still as ugly as ever," he said, a grin spreading across his still handsome features.

"I should be. I look like you," Bobby said, but the levity in his answer was forced and Billy sensed it.

"Momma didn't tell you, huh?"

"She wasn't much of a correspondent."

"Well, it wasn't her fault. I told her not to. I figured you'd have enough to worry about in Nam and I didn't want you worrying about something you couldn't do anything about."

"What, uh, what happened? I mean, I only got hazy details from Mom."

Billy shrugged his shoulders.

"Things just didn't work out. I had a job that paid peanuts and no prospects. Johnny Laturno said, 'Let's hit a liquor store' and I went along. The clerk was an old guy. We didn't think he'd give us any trouble, but he decided to play hero and I hurt him pretty bad."

"What did you do?" Bobby asked. The question was almost rhetorical. He had been with Billy during enough rumbles to know what had happened.

"I stabbed him." He shrugged. "It was his fault. I told him to be cool and nothing would happen. He just didn't look like much so we forgot about him for a minute. Next thing, he tries to hit Johnny with a bottle. What else could I do?"

"Yeah, well . . ."

"Look, I don't want you worrying about me. It ain't so bad here. I'll be out in a few years. And I got enough friends in here so I'm not messed with. But look. Tell me about you. Mom said something about college. What's that all about?"

"I'm starting next week. It's something I thought about toward the end of my hitch. I never really gave school a chance and I want to better myself. I don't want to pump gas my whole life. When I was in the army, I started thinking about things. Not anything in particular. Just a lot of things. I realized that there was so much I didn't know, so I decided to give college a try."

Billy slapped Bobby on the back and grinned again.

"I'm proud of you. Really. You always had the brains in the family. I know you'll do great. Hey, maybe you'll be a lawyer and you can get me outta this dump."

They laughed and Bobby could feel himself relaxing. It was the same old Billy after all.

"What are you gonna study?"

"I don't know. I'll just take general studies until I figure it out."

"I hear business is good. That's where the money is."

"Yeah, well I'll see."

They sat back again and Bobby tried to think of something to say. Billy looked around. The other people in the room were huddled together, talking in low tones. Trying to preserve their rationed moments of intimacy.

"Say, do you want a Coke or something?" Billy asked. "I can get it from the machines."

"No thanks. I ate before I drove down."

"Yeah. Uh, well, how was the ride?"

"Okay. Boring. It's just the Interstate."

They looked at each other again. There did not seem to be anything left to talk about.

"How was the army?"

"Not good. I'm glad it's over."

"You see much action?"

"A little. I really don't like to talk about it. Do you ever hear from any of the guys?" Bobby asked to change the subject.

"A few visited me when I first was sent down, but I haven't seen any of them in a while. Most of the guys wandered off after high school."

Bobby glanced at his watch and Billy saw him.

"Say, if I'm keeping you, let me know."

"No, it isn't that," Bobby said guiltily. "I have to be back, that's all. I promised to help Mom around the house and I wanted to buy some stuff for my apartment."

"You're not staying at the house?"

"After the army, I wanted some privacy."

Billy smiled and motioned around with his hand.

"I can understand that."

Bobby stood up.

"Look, I'll be down to see you again next week. I'll bring Mom."

Billy stood up too. They shook hands.

"That'd be great. So . . . Take it easy. And let me know how you do in school, huh?"

"Sure. I'll let you know. Take care."

The hour was up, anyway, but he felt guilty when he left. Scared, too. It was a cliché, but it could have been him. He knew it. So did Billy, and Bobby wondered if his brother resented his freedom and his new life.

The walk from the visitor's area to the parking lot was tree-lined. The autumn winds were working changes on the yellow-brown leaves. It was beautiful enough to depress Bobby.

"Esther, I brought someone to talk to you."

Esther looked over Dr. Tucker's shoulder at the tall man who was standing by the door to her hospital room. Something about him frightened her. Why should she be afraid of him? She was too tired to think about it, so she lowered her head on the pillow.

"Esther, do you remember me?" the tall man asked.

She must have shut her eyes, because the tall man was towering over her bed instead of standing by the door. She could not remember him moving.

"She is still a bit sedated," Dr. Tucker said. His voice was a faint echo.

"My name is Roy Shindler. I talked to you a few years ago when I was investigating the deaths of Richie Walters and Elaine Murray. Do you remember that?"

She was remembering now. Very slowly. He was older and his hair had thinned, but it was that detective. The one who . . . And suddenly she was afraid.

"I remember you," she said in a small voice.

Dr. Tucker saw the fear on his patient's face and looked quizzically at Shindler. Shindler ignored him.

"There isn't any reason to worry, Esther. I know that I upset you the last time we talked, but it was unintentional. I really mean that."

"What do you want?" Esther asked warily. She was holding tight to the sheet that was drawn up around her neck, and memories, mirrored in her wide eyes, were pressing her deep into the bed, like an animal seeking protection in the shelter of its cave.

There it was again, thought Shindler. He did not think of her as human. He remembered his impressions of her on the two prior occasions they had met. It was always the feeling of the hunter when he traps his quarry. To him, she would always be an animal.

"When Dr. Tucker saw you yesterday, you had a little talk with him. Do you remember what you talked about?"

She looked at Dr. Tucker, then back to Shindler. She seemed confused.

"I don't remember talking to Dr. Tucker yesterday."

Shindler looked at Dr. Tucker.

"It's possible," Dr. Tucker said. "She's had a very traumatic experience. The effects of the medication may have contributed."

"Esther, yesterday, you told Dr. Tucker you saw someone hit someone until they killed him. Do you remember that?"

She opened her mouth and her eyes widened again.

"I saw . . . Oh, no. I never . . ."

"You did say that, Esther. I was there."

She looked pleadingly at Dr. Tucker.

"Please. I couldn't have said that. I never saw anyone killed. I told you that. You know I didn't have anything to do with Richie's death."

"No one says you did, Esther. But, if you did see this terrible thing happen, it might have frightened you so much that you don't remember."

"No. I never saw it. Please, Dr. Tucker."

She was crying and pleading. Dr. Tucker hurried to her bedside.

"I'm afraid you'll have to leave now. She's too upset. Wait for me in the hall, please."

Shindler closed the door behind him and took a cigarette out of his pocket. The door opened and he turned around.

"Sorry I had to push you out, but she was starting to become hysterical."

Shindler brushed the comment aside with his free hand.

"It was my fault. I should have realized that she was getting upset."

They started walking down the corridor toward the doctor's office.

"This business about not remembering. Do you believe her?"

The doctor looked at Shindler with surprise.

"Oh, yes. Quite possible. Mrs. Pegalosi could be suffering from amnesia. Certain types of people will repress a very threatening experience that they wish not to be identified with or not to have as a part of their life. The conscious mind is not even aware that the material is repressed in some cases. If she witnessed . . . Well, you know what it would have been like for anyone, let alone a girl as insecure as this one, to see that murder."

They walked in silence for a few moments. Shindler puffed erratically on his cigarette.

"Damn it, she knows, Doctor. She knows. And I have got to find a way to make her talk."

"I'm afraid that might be difficult."

"Why? She remembered yesterday."

"Yes, under very unusual circumstances. She was exhausted, medicated and she had just tried to commit suicide. In her weakened state, her ability to repress would be weakened. Her subconscious would be less on guard. It's much like being drunk. Most drunks become garrulous and talk about things they might not under ordinary circumstances."

"Is there any way to bring her back again? Some medical method?"

Dr. Tucker was silent for a moment.

"Memory is an interesting area that is receiving a great deal of attention. We really don't know how it works.

"There are two types of memory: long-term and short-term. Short-term is probably an electrical event within the brain and it may not be long-lasting. It's the sort of thing that happens when you drive to the beach and pass many things along the way. You see trees and farmhouses and so forth, and you can remember them for a short time, but it's unlikely that your brain will record these permanently since they don't have any emotional connotation.

"Long-term memory is probably a basic chemical or anatomical change which may persist as long as the brain cells function, that is for as long as you live. It seems to be more greatly impressed in the mind if it is associated with some emotional stimulus. Long-term memory is stored like books in a library, so, if Esther saw the murder, the memory is probably there. The question is how to get rid of the subconscious guardians that are suppressing the memory.

"I would like to give you the name of a friend of

mine who might be able to help you. He is a psychiatrist and an expert in the use of hypnosis. That is a technique that is often used in the treatment of amnesia. Why don't you get in touch with him and see what he can do for you?"

3

"Franz Anton Mesmer was a Viennese physician who believed that the planets influenced the human body. In 1776, he wrote a paper stating that this action occurred through the instrumentality of a universal fluid in which all bodies were immersed. The fluid, which was invisible, had properties like a magnet and could be withdrawn by the human will from one point and concentrated on another. Mesmer theorized that an inharmonious distribution of these fluids throughout the body produced disease. Health could be attained by establishing harmony of the magnetic fluids. Mesmer believed that a force, which he called 'animal magnetism,' emanated from his hands directly into the patient, thereby enabling him to adjust the internal imbalances in the fluids and to eradicate disease in the patient."

Shindler eased himself quietly into a seat in the last row of the University auditorium and settled back to listen as Dr. Arthur Hollander lectured on "The History of Hypnotism." Dr. Hollander was a portly white-haired gentleman who reminded Shindler of Santa Claus. His lecture never stayed on the podium.

It moved back and forth across the stage punctuated by short jabs of the professor's pudgy fingers or framed in the grandiose sweep of his ever-moving arms.

"Unfortunately for Mesmer, he effected a startling and rapid cure in a young girl suffering from an imposing array of physical symptoms through the use of magnets the very first time he put his theory into practice. Thus buoyed by success, Mesmer embarked on a career aimed at convincing the medical community of the soundness of his theory."

Dr. Hollander took a sip of water from a glass that rested on his podium. Shindler scanned the assembly of attentive students and concluded that the professor had them appropriately mesmerized.

"The Vienna medical fraternity viewed Mesmer as a charlatan and he was forced to flee to Paris, where, in 1781, he founded a clinic. Mesmerism became a popular fad among the wealthy. Eventually, Mesmer was discredited by a commission appointed by the French Government and he retired to Switzerland, an embittered man.

"While Mesmer was being sidetracked by his theories, one of his disciples, Marquis de Puysegur, observed that the 'magnetized' subject could hear only what the 'magnetizer' said and was oblivious to everything else, that he accepted suggestions without question and that he could recall nothing of the events of the trance into which he was put when restored to normal consciousness. De Puysegur called this condition 'artificial somnambulism' and explained that a subject in this condition could accomplish incredible feats like reading sealed messages, suffering needles to be jabbed into his skin and permitting, without flinching, the application of a red hot poker to his body."

The bell rang, ending the period, and several students hurried to the front of the lecture hall to talk with Dr. Hollander. Shindler walked to the front in a leisurely manner and waited until the last of this enthusiastic group had left. Dr. Hollander was gathering up his notes when he noticed Shindler.

"I enjoyed your lecture, Doctor."

"Thank you. I try to be entertaining and I am always gratified when I succeed. I don't believe I have seen you before. Are you a student?"

Shindler fumbled for his badge and managed to flip it open.

"I'm with the Portsmouth Police, Dr. Hollander. My name is Roy Shindler."

Hollander looked intrigued.

"I hope I haven't done anything wrong," he said with a puckish smile.

Shindler laughed.

"No, you're clean as far as I know. Dr. George Tucker gave me your name."

"George. Certainly. Well, I am mystified. How can I help you?"

"Is there someplace we can talk? This is a bit complicated and it may take a while. It concerns a murder case and we may need your specialized knowledge of hypnosis to help us solve it."

Hollander looked surprised, flattered and flustered all at once.

"I'll do what I can, of course. I've never worked with the police before and I don't know what I can do for you, but if you think . . . Say, I know a quiet pub near here. If that is okay. You fellows can drink on duty, can't you?"

Shindler smiled.

"You're a man after my own heart, Doctor."

"Do you teach at the University full-time, Doctor?" Shindler asked.

"No, no. Just one freshman Psychology course to keep me young. My practice keeps me pretty busy, but I enjoy being around youngsters. And you can call me Art. Doctor is way too formal and makes me feel old enough to counter any good I might have gotten out of tonight's class."

Shindler laughed and leaned against the back of the wooden booth. They were seated in the rear of "The Victorian Age," an imitation English pub that catered to a predominantly college clientele.

"Art, what exactly is hypnosis?"

"Nothing magical," Hollander said. He smiled faintly as if he had heard and answered the question a thousand times before. "Simply a form of suggestion. We sit here and I suggest another beer. You weigh the suggestion. The beer is good but you are on duty and you have to think clearly. However, if I suggest that everything I am going to suggest is reasonable, then you will stop evaluating and you will depend on me."

Hollander took a pen out of his pocket and pulled a white napkin in front of him. He placed a dot at the top of the napkin.

"Think of this point as being a state of complete alertness. You are alert now. You can see and hear all

the things that are going on in this pub, as well as listen to our conversation and think your own thoughts.
But there are other states of awareness that are not
total."

Hollander drew a line from the dot straight down
the napkin to the bottom and ended it with another
dot.

"You know the expression 'dead to the world'? A
person is so sound asleep that his mind is practically
completely at rest. This would be a point represented
by the dot at the bottom.

"Okay. Along this line we're going to get various
stages of alertness and somewhere on this line is a
state where a person becomes susceptible to suggestion. This might be a point where the person is at
thirty minutes after he has gone to bed. His eyes
are closed, he's lost contact with the general sounds
around him, but he's still aware of very important
sounds, like a baby crying or, in a doctor's case, that
darn telephone ringing. A person in that state can be
alerted rather easily, because in that state he is paying all of his attention to a single thing."

"If you asked a person in this state a question,
would they respond normally?" Shindler asked. "I
mean, the way you're answering my questions?"

"Oh, yes. It depends on the depth of the hypnosis. The lower the state of awareness, the more their
attention is focused and the more accurate the response."

"Doctor . . . Art. Let's suppose that a person has
seen something so frightening and so upsetting to
them that they have repressed the memory of that
event. They have amnesia. If you ask them about the

event, they deny that they were ever there. If you put that kind of person under hypnosis, could you make them talk about the event, tell what really happened?"

Hollander raised his eyebrows and regarded Shindler with new interest.

"'Repressed,' 'amnesia.' You and George had a nice talk. He must have told you the answer to your questions already or else you wouldn't have come to see me."

Shindler smiled.

"George said he thought you could. What do you say?"

"Possible. Hypnosis is frequently used in amnesia. One of the biggest uses of psychiatry is to recall repressed material of the kind you have just mentioned."

"What would you do in a case like this?"

"Well, you have not given me much information, but I assume you will when you are ready. In the general situation, I would develop a hypnotic state to relax the individual. When the patient is relaxed, the repressive mechanisms in the mind that watches over the forbidden memories are off guard. The relaxation permits the memories to be brought from the subconscious to the conscious.

"Now, this is not an easy process. Especially when we are dealing with amnesia that is due to a very frightening, very threatening experience. The individual might be afraid that they will go crazy, that they will be punished severely or something like that if it is ever discovered that they have been involved in the event that they are repressing. When they come close to the repressed memory, they fight hard. They do their best to avoid contact with it. They

will have bodily reactions we call conversion reactions. They will have headaches, upset stomachs, di-
arrhea. All sorts of physical reactions as well as just
refusing to discuss the matter. It is not easy."

"Do you want another beer?"

"Certainly. It is always a pleasure to live off the
public dole."

Shindler signaled the waitress and ordered two
more beers.

"Can you get through?"

"Not in every case."

"Would you like to take a shot at a very unusual
case?"

Hollander smiled and his eyes twinkled.

"Roy, you know you have me hooked. Tell me
what the facts are."

"Art, this is a case I have been working on for some
time. Have you ever heard of the Murray-Walters
murders?"

          Bobby Coolidge flexed his fingers. He had
developed a cramp in his writing hand and, in the
few seconds in which his attention had wandered
from Professor Schneider's lecture, he had missed
most of what the professor had said about the Budget
and Accounting Act of 1950. Not that he cared about
the Act personally, but he had made a promise to
himself that he would really try this first semester to
see if he could make the grade.

When he first decided to go to college, it had
been a major decision. No one else in his family had
ever done it. College people had always been thought

of as an alien species as different from Coolidges as Martians from Earthmen. Now he was one of the Martians and it wasn't easy.

Bobby was renting a one-bedroom apartment in a crummy area of town. He had saved enough to make it through the first academic year without working. But that meant no frills. His entertainment came from a second-hand portable TV. His meals consisted of several varieties of spaghetti sauce poured over one variety of spaghetti.

And the work was hard. High school had never been this tough. What made it worse was that the other students seemed to understand so much more than he. There had been times when he wanted to quit. Once, he stayed away from school for a week. He was afraid of failure. Afraid that he was out of his depth. Then he had paid another visit to Billy and he had returned to the classroom. On the drive back, he decided that he did have a choice about how his life would end and it was not going to wind up like Billy's had.

The professor announced the end of the period and Bobby still was missing the notes on the purpose of the Budget Act. The girl in the seat next to him was still writing. She was very attractive. Blond, blue-eyed. A cheerleader type, he had decided, during the first few weeks of class. Obviously well off from the cut and variety of her clothes.

Today, she was dressed in a plaid kilt and a red turtleneck sweater. When she leaned over to write, her long blond hair cascaded over her sloping shoulders so that she had to brush it off her writing tablet.

"Excuse me," he said. She looked up and smiled.

"I missed the last few minutes of the lecture. I wonder if I could copy your notes."

"Sure," she said. "Just let me finish them for you."

"I appreciate it. My hand cramped. I just can't write as fast as Schneider talks."

The girl laughed. She had a pleasant laugh that made him think about church bells on clear winter Sundays.

"It isn't just you. I can never keep up with him."

Bobby laughed.

"I'm glad I'm not the only one. Where do you think he learned to talk like that? Maybe his father made phonograph records."

She smiled again and handed him her notes. Not bad, he thought. A laugh and a smile. I'm getting to be a regular comedian.

"What's this word here?" he asked, pointing to a scrawl stuffed between two other illegible words.

" 'Budget.' "

"Right. My name is Bobby Coolidge. I've been sitting across from you all these weeks and I don't think I've ever introduced myself."

"Consider yourself introduced. My name is Sarah Rhodes. Now we're even."

The room was emptying, but Sarah did not seem impatient to leave. Bobby wondered if she would have lunch with him if he asked her. He had not had a real date since he had returned from the army. There had been a few pickups in bars, right after he was discharged, but nothing since his return to Portsmouth. It was partly a lack of money and partly a lack of desire. He was having a difficult time adjusting to civilian life. His values were in a state of flux. His education seemed important, but he had not arrived at a concrete reason why. Emotional attachments seemed frivolous and unsettling. He had decided that women would be a distraction he could not afford, so he had avoided them. Still, lunch would not hurt—if she would go with him.

"Thanks for the loan," he said, handing her the spiral notebook. He walked with her toward the classroom door. The professor was talking to a skinny boy with tortoiseshell glasses. Everyone else had left.

"Are you hungry?" he asked.

He had said it too fast. Blurted it out. Not cool, he thought, uneasily.

"Why?" she asked, hesitantly.

"I thought, if you were, I'd spring you to lunch. I mean, it's a fair trade. Food for thought."

She caught the pun and laughed. He was proud of himself for thinking it up. It was almost intellectual.

"Sure. But we'll go Dutch. My notes aren't worth that much."

The school cafeteria was jammed and they settled for a small table in a corner. Bobby emptied his tray and carried his and hers to an aluminum rack that stood against a wall covered with posters and advertisements about campus affairs. When he returned, Sarah finished taking his sandwich out of its cellophane wrapper and handed it to him.

"Thanks. This place is mobbed. It reminds me of mess hall at boot camp."

Sarah looked interested.

"You were in the army?"

"Just got out," he answered between bites.

"Were you . . . ?"

"In Nam?" he finished for her. "Yes."

"You didn't like it there, did you?" she asked, after looking at the expression on his face.

"It wasn't a pleasant experience. I went. I came back. There's not much in between that I like to talk about."

"Sorry," she said and he realized that he had been too sharp in his reply.

"You shouldn't be. I'm the one who should apologize. You had no way of knowing."

"I only asked because it's in the news so much and you're the first person I ever met who has been there."

"Where have you been? I mean, where are you from?" he asked, changing the subject, artfully, he hoped.

"Toronto."

"You're not American?"

"No," she laughed. "And don't look so shocked. We Canadians don't have horns."

He blushed.

"I didn't mean . . ."

"That's okay. Now we're even."

They smiled at each other and Bobby put down his sandwich and offered his hand. She took it and they shook. He held it a second longer than was necessary, but she did not seem to mind. When he had brought up their trays, there had been a notice that the Student Union was showing *Gone with the Wind* the next evening. One dollar per student. Bobby mentally checked his savings. He could swing two dollars and a couple of bucks for beer.

"Do you like old movies?" he asked.

"Yes. What made you ask?" she said. Her eyes flirted with him, playfully teasing him.

"I noticed . . . They're showing *Gone with the Wind* tomorrow. I've never seen it, but I hear it's good. If you wanted to go . . . ?"

"I have seen it."

"Oh."

"But I'd love to go again."

He brightened up and she smiled again. They had both been smiling a lot, he thought. He glanced at the cafeteria clock and gathered his books.

"I have to run. I have math in five minutes and I can't afford to miss a class. Tell me where you live and I'll pick you up tomorrow at seven."

She gave him an address in the hills. He knew the area. It was expensive. He felt nervous again.

"See you tomorrow," he said as he stood to go.

"Tomorrow."

The detective was here again. Only this time she wasn't as frightened. Yesterday he had sent flowers. She wondered why the doctors would not release her. She did not know that it was Shindler's doing.

"How are you this morning, Esther? I thought I would bring these."

More flowers. A bouquet of roses. Only John and that boy who had taken her to the prom had ever given her flowers. They looked very pretty.

"Thank you. You can put them in the vase on the dresser."

He looked strange carrying the bouquet. He was tall and gangly and his suit didn't fit well. The bouquet was lost in his large hand.

"I sent the flowers as a delayed apology for the way I treated you that time at the station house. I felt awfully bad about that."

She did not know whether to believe him. There was something about Shindler that she did not like. Still, the flowers were pretty and he was acting like a gentleman. Maybe she had been wrong about him.

"That's okay. I . . . I'd almost forgot about it."

"Can I sit down?"

She looked at him for a moment, until it struck her that he was asking her for permission. She wasn't used to that.

"Yeah. Go ahead."

"Are you feeling better?"

"I feel fine now. Except the doctor won't tell me where my boy is."

"Your son is fine, Esther. I checked this morning. Welfare put him with foster parents."

He saw the look of alarm on her face.

"Don't worry. It's only temporary. I'm looking into it for you, Esther. No one is going to take your baby. You believe me, don't you?"

She eyed him warily. There was a trap here somewhere. She was afraid again.

"Do you want a cigarette?"

"The doctor said I shouldn't."

Shindler winked and held one out to her.

"I'll cover for you."

She was going to take it, but she hesitated and drew her hand back.

"No thank you. I'd rather not."

"Do you mind if I . . . ?"

"It's okay."

Shindler lit up.

"You seem to be coming around fine," Shindler said.

"I guess."

"I'm glad we didn't lose you. You're an important person, Esther."

There it was again. Warning signals. There was something about his manner, his questions, that frightened her. She wasn't important to anyone. She never had been.

"Esther, I am here to ask you a favor. Do you think that you would do me a favor?"

"What favor?"

"I know you don't like to discuss it, but I want to talk to you about Richie Walters and Elaine Murray."

She could feel her heart accelerate suddenly. She knew there was something! Why wouldn't he let her be?

"I told you, Mr. Shindler, I really don't know nothin' about that."

"How would you like to clear up everything, once and for all?"

"I would. Honest, Mr. Shindler. You ain't trying to be mean. I know that. But it upsets me a lot when you talk about that."

"Okay. I know you get upset. But think of it this way, Esther. Say you were there." She started to protest and he raised his hand. "I'm not saying that you were. This is something I'm supposing. You know that Richie and Elaine's murders were the biggest murders we've had in Portsmouth, don't you?"

"I suppose," she answered grudgingly.

"Okay. Now anyone who helped us solve those murders would be a pretty important person. She would be famous and everyone would be grateful to her, because of the help she had been to the community. So you can see why I think you are so important."

"But, Mr. . . ."

"Now hear me out, okay?"

Esther gave up and sank back on her pillow.

"Sometimes a person will see something that is so horrible that their own mind won't let them remember it. Have you ever heard of amnesia?"

"Yeah. But I thought you only got that if someone hit you on the head."

Shindler smiled.

"That is one way. But the mind is an unusual machine, Esther. It protects its owner. And it can make a person forget unpleasant things. I think that you saw Richie murdered. I don't think you took any part in the killing. I'm a good judge of character. You get to be that way when you have been a policeman for as long as I have. I think you are too nice a girl to have been knowingly involved in a murder. But let's just say that you and the Coolidge brothers did get drunk after that party. Do you remember telling me that you thought that you went cruising downtown?"

She nodded.

"Well, let's suppose that after you went cruising, the Coolidges got into a drag race with Richie and

Richie forced them off the road. And let's suppose that they got mad at Richie and followed him up to Lookout Park and there was a fight and you saw them kill Richie. Now you are a nice girl. You would never do anything like that. That would have been so horrible to a nice person like you that your mind might blank out that part of the evening."

"But, Mr. Shindler, it wasn't like that at all."

"How do you know, Esther? You told me that you were so drunk that you could not remember what happened that evening."

"Well, I was. But I would remember something like . . . It just didn't happen that way."

She was starting to get upset and Shindler waited for her to calm down.

"Esther, remember I said that we could clear this up once and for all?"

"Yes, I would like that, Mr. Shindler."

"There is a doctor I know. Dr. Hollander. He is a psychiatrist and he is an expert in hypnotizing people."

Esther ran her tongue over her lips. Her anguish was evident. Her slender fingers worked the edge of the sheet anxiously.

"Dr. Hollander could hypnotize you. When you are hypnotized, your mind can't keep your bad memories hidden as easily. Dr. Hollander will be able to tell if I am wrong."

"I . . . I don't know if I want to do that. Why should I see a psychiatrist? I'm not crazy."

"I never said you were crazy, Esther. It just so happens that the best expert I know in hypnosis is also a psychiatrist. No one thinks you're crazy.

"And once you get this business cleared up, you will feel better. If I'm wrong, then that will be the end of it. And if I'm right—why you will become a very famous and important person. Everyone in Portsmouth will be grateful to you for clearing up this horrible crime.

"And it will certainly help when I go to welfare to get your son back, if I can tell them how helpful you are being in clearing up this very serious case."

"You think this would help with the welfare, if I saw the doctor?"

"I'm positive."

"And you think it's important?"

"This is very important, Esther. There are a lot of people who will be very grateful to you."

"Uh, this wouldn't be in the papers, would it?"

Shindler sensed a note of interest.

"If the doctor finds out that you did see the murders, you would be our star witness."

Shindler waited while she mulled it over. She took a while before she spoke. When she did speak, her voice betrayed great nervousness and apprehension. But there was something else hidden below the surface. A sense of excitement.

"I want to think, Mr. Shindler. I can't say now. But maybe I will—if it's so important."

4

"Dr. Hollander, this is Esther Pegalosi."

The doctor was standing in front of an antique roll-top desk when Esther and Roy Shindler entered his office.

"I am pleased to meet you, Mrs. Pegalosi," the doctor said, flashing her his best Kris Kringle smile. "Roy has told me quite a bit about you."

Esther looked up nervously at Shindler. The doctor noticed and added, with a laugh, "Oh, it's all been good. He is quite thrilled that you have consented to help him on this case and I think that you will find all of this quite exciting.

"Now, may I ask you a personal question?" Hollander asked in a serious tone.

"What is it?" Esther asked warily.

Hollander broke into a grin.

"May I call you Esther? I hate calling people by their last names. It's so stuffy."

Esther smiled with relief. She had expected some inquiry into her sex life or early childhood or whatever it was that psychiatrists asked you about. She was surprised at how down-to-earth Dr. Hollander was. He wasn't at all what she had expected.

"Sure. Esther is fine." She lowered her eyes. "No one calls me Mrs. Pegalosi anyway."

"Good. Then Esther it is. Would you like to sit down?" Hollander asked, leading Esther to a comfortable, soft-colored sofa that sat against one oak-paneled wall under the shadow of a multicolored abstract painting.

Esther accepted the doctor's offer as if it had been an order. He watched her move mechanically to the sofa and sit, hands folded, like a wind-up toy. Shindler sat out of sight in a straight-back chair set in a corner of the room.

"That's a nice dress you have on. Is it new?"

Esther brightened at the mention of her outfit. It was a green skirt with a matching green jacket and a white blouse. Shindler had taken her shopping when she agreed to visit Dr. Hollander and she had picked it out herself. It was the first new outfit she had purchased in years.

"Tell me, Esther, I bet you're nervous. Am I right?"

Esther blushed and looked at the floor.

"I'm a little nervous, I guess."

"Good!" Dr. Hollander said with a hearty laugh that startled her. "Everyone who visits me is nervous the first time. So that shows that you're normal. Now why don't you tell me why you're nervous."

Esther worried her lower lip and shrugged.

"I don't know."

Hollander smiled a warm, fatherly smile. She was beginning to like this nice man.

"Are you worried about being hypnotized?"

She did not answer immediately. Hollander waited patiently.

"A little, I guess," she finally answered.

"Okay. That's good. I'm glad you're open and honest with me, because I will always be open and honest with you. Now, I want you to promise me something. Will you do that?"

"What?"

"Will you promise me that any time you have a question, no matter how silly you think it might be, you will ask me that question? I mean it. I want you to know everything that is going on. We will have no secrets from one another. Is that all right with you?"

"I guess."

"Good. Now tell me, have you ever been hypnotized before?"

"No."

"Have you ever seen anyone hypnotized on TV or in the movies or in person?"

"Once on TV and in a movie."

"Okay. Now I want to tell you that what you see in the movies or TV is not the way hypnosis is at all. It is a form of relaxation during which it is possible to follow suggestions more easily. There is nothing mysterious about it. It is a scientific phenomenon and perfectly natural.

"On TV you see evil hypnotists make slaves of people, rob them of their will and make them do all sorts of horrible things. Do you think I am evil, Esther?"

Esther giggled.

"No."

"Good. Well, I can assure you I am not. And all those silly stories you see in the movies are fantastic rubbish. Hypnosis is not possible unless a person willingly participates in it. You can't make a hypnotized person do anything he doesn't want to, because he can refuse to do anything that is distasteful to him. Hypnosis is a way of helping people, not hurting them. It is like medicine."

"What . . . what if I can't be hypnotized?"

"Don't worry about that. Everyone can be hypnotized if they relax and don't resist. Just make your mind passive and unresisting and don't try too hard and I'll do the rest."

Hollander suddenly became serious.

"Esther, you know that we're here primarily to find out what you know about a certain event. Well, that is one thing, but hypnosis has more value than just finding out about something you may have forgotten. Hypnosis is a way of helping you to master yourself and your problems.

"You were recently in the hospital, because of personal problems, weren't you?"

Esther lowered her head and nodded.

"Well, Esther, I will be serious here for a moment. We all want to find out what you know about Richie Walters's murder, but I am also interested in you as a person.

"Roy tells me that you have raised a fine young son, all by yourself. That says something about your character. I can see that you have the potential to be a strong, confident woman. Hypnosis can help you to realize that potential. Through hypnosis, I can help you to be the person I know you can be. So, you see, you will help us and we will help you. Is that fair?"

"Yes," Esther answered in a low voice. She was overwhelmed. No one had ever taken this much interest in her before.

"Well, now. We are getting way too serious. Let's move to that comfortable chair near my desk and we'll begin."

Hollander led Esther to a large armchair. When she was seated, he placed a pillow under her head and drew a seat up in front of her.

"Are you comfortable? Good. Now I want you to relax and keep both feet resting on the floor. I am going to tell you exactly what is going to happen to you as we go along, so that there will be no surprises," he said in a soothing, steady tone. "You will notice, as we proceed, that you will relax. You will probably begin to feel drowsy. It won't be necessary for you to try too hard. All you have to do is make your mind passive and relax. Then you will become aware that certain things are happening to you as you relax. I want you to concentrate on these things. I will bring them to your attention.

"While we are doing this, you must remember that hypnosis is a normal experience. Each night, before dozing off, you go through a state that resembles hypnosis. I don't want you to go to sleep, because I want you to be aware of what I say and aware of what your thoughts are. But, if you do find yourself falling asleep, don't worry. I want you to be comfortable and I will awaken you. I want this to be a relaxing and pleasant experience. I won't ask you any questions that will embarrass you. Make your mind passive and do not analyze your thoughts and sensations. Do you understand?"

"Yes."

"Good. Now lean back. Are you completely comfortable and relaxed?"

"Yes."

Hollander reached over and switched on a tape recorder that sat on a table near Esther's head. Shindler shifted quietly in his seat.

TAPE # 1

DR. ARTHUR HOLLANDER: Okay, Esther. Why don't you place both of your hands palm down on your thighs. No, don't close your eyes. Keep watching your hands. If you concentrate on your hands, you will notice that you can observe them very closely.

When you sit and relax, you begin to notice things that you have never noticed before. They have always happened when you relax, but you have never been aware of them. I am going to point them out to you.

Esther, I want you to concentrate on all the sensations and feelings in your hands, no matter what they may be. Perhaps you may feel the heaviness of your hand as it lies on your thigh, or you may feel pressure. Perhaps you will feel the texture of your new skirt as it presses against the palm of your hand or the warmth of your hand on your thigh. Perhaps you may feel a tingling. No

matter what the sensations are, I want you to observe them.

(PAUSE)

DR. HOLLANDER: Good, Esther. Keep watching your
hand. See how quiet it is. How it remains in one
position. There is motion there, but it is not yet
noticeable. I want you to keep watching your hand.
Your attention may wander from the hand, but it
will always return to the hand, and you will keep
wondering when the motion that is there will show
itself.

It will be interesting to see which of your fingers will move first. It may be the ring finger or the
thumb. One of the fingers is going to jerk or move.
You don't know when or on which hand. Keep
watching and you will begin to notice a slight
movement, possibly in the right hand. There, the
thumb is jerking. It's moving, just like that.

As the movement begins, you will notice an interesting thing. Very slowly, the spaces between
the fingers will widen. The fingers will move apart
and you will notice that the spaces between the fingers will get wider and wider. They will move slowly
apart. The fingers will seem to be spreading wider
and wider and wider. See how they spread. Slowly
moving wider and wider apart.

Good, Esther. You are doing fine. The fingers
are so wide apart. And soon you will notice that
the fingers will want to arch up from the thigh, as
if they want to lift higher and higher. Notice how
your index finger is lifting. As it does, the other

fingers will want to follow upward—slowly rising, up, up.

See how the other fingers are rising now. As they lift, you will become aware of a feeling of lightness, so much so that the fingers will arch up and the whole hand will slowly lift and rise as if it feels like a feather, as if a balloon is lifting it up in the air, lifting, lifting—up, up, up—pulling it higher and higher and higher. The hand is so light, so very light. As you watch your hand rise, you will notice that the arm comes up, up, up in the air, a little higher and higher and higher.

Keep watching the hand and arm as it rises straight up and you will soon become aware of how drowsy and tired your eyes become. As your arm continues to rise, you will get tired and relaxed and sleepy, very sleepy. Your eyes will get heavy and your lids may want to close. And as your arm rises higher and higher, you will want to feel more relaxed and sleepy, and you will want to enjoy the peaceful, relaxed feeling of letting your eyes close and of being asleep.

Your arm is stretched out directly in front of you now. You cannot take your eyes off your hand, yet your lids are getting heavy, very heavy, and your breathing is getting slow and regular. Breathe deeply, in and out.

As you keep watching your hand and arm and keep feeling more and more drowsy and relaxed, you will notice that the direction of the hand will change. The arm will bend and the hand will move closer and closer to your face—up, up, up—and as it rises you will slowly but steadily go into a deep, deep sleep in which you will relax deeply and to your satisfaction. The arm will continue to rise up, up—lifting, lifting up, until it touches your face and you will get sleepier and sleepier, but you must not go to sleep until your hand touches your face. When the hand touches your face, you will be asleep, deeply asleep.

Your hand is now changing direction. It is moving up toward your face very slowly. Your eyelids are getting heavy. You are getting sleepier and sleepier and sleepier. Your eyelids are blinking faster and faster, because you are trying to fight sleep. Do not fight sleep. Welcome sleep. Let your eyes get heavy, very heavy and let the hand move up toward your face. You get very tired and drowsy. Your eyes are closing. When your hand touches your face, you will be asleep, deeply asleep. You are drowsy. Your eyes are like lead. Your hand moves to your face. It is almost touching. It is touching and your eyes close—now.

Good, Esther. Go to sleep, just sleep. And as you sleep you feel tired and relaxed. I want you to concentrate on relaxation, a state of tensionless relaxation. Think of nothing else, but sleep, deep sleep.

(PAUSE)

DR. HOLLANDER: Now, Esther, remember I told you that I was interested in you? That I saw great potential in you?

ESTHER PEGALOSI: Yes.

Q: Well, I said that because I have confidence in you and I feel that you can be the strong, confident person you want to be. That you can be anything you want to be. I am going to begin now to teach you how to be that strong, confident person. Would that be something you want to be?

A: Yes.

Q: Fine. You can put your hand down now. Just relax. You can open your eyes if you want to. Look around and reassure yourself of your surroundings and then let your eyes close again. That's it. That's fine.

   Esther, I am going to touch your wrist now. I want you to pay attention to the feelings in your wrist. Feel completely the touch of my fingers on your wrist and when you feel that you have that feeling firmly in mind so that you can remember it easily, you can indicate that by saying "yes" without disturbing the trance at all.

(PAUSE)

PEGALOSI: Yes.

HOLLANDER: Good. Fine. Now, Esther, if it is all right with you, any time in the future that I take your wrist in this way and the situation is appropriate, you can remember the way you feel now. You can go into a deep hypnotic trance, a trance deep enough to achieve whatever goal is in your mind, whether the goal is remembering a pleasant incident in the past or a goal of ignoring discomfort or the goal of feeling like the strong, confident person that you know you can be. And if your subconscious mind is willing to respond in this way, it will cause the first finger of the right hand to move up into the air, and we can wonder will that finger move, will the unconscious cause it to move. You can think about that finger and it is— it's moving up into the air and it continues to move up into the air, all by itself. Yes. Good. Good! That's it, Esther, just relax. Now at any time in the future that I take your wrist in this way, you can respond fully, you can respond confidently, knowing that when you awaken from such an experience, you will be more capable of being the kind of person you really want to be; the kind of person you have always known you could be. With increasing anticipation, Esther, you will awaken each morning looking forward to behaving, being and looking more like the kind of person you have always known you could be.

Now, I am going to ask you to awaken in a moment bound by each of these three suggestions: the suggestion of responding rapidly to your signal, the sensation of my fingers on your wrist; the suggestion of responding with a deep enough trance to achieve the goal that you have in mind; and the suggestion that you respond confident of being a better person in every way, a little better each day. Not dramatically, but just a little better each day. More like the kind of person you really want to be. Any time in the future that I take your wrist and the situation is appropriate, you can respond easily, profoundly and rapidly.

In a moment, I am going to count from one to three and I will ask you to awaken feeling good,

feeling refreshed and feeling tremendously satisfied. As I count from one to three, your unconscious mind can pay attention to that counting and
those instructions, so that any time in the future,
no matter who introduces the hypnotic experience, whether you bring the experience back by
yourself or whether you permit someone else to
induce the trance, you will be able to terminate
the trance easily and rapidly by simply following
the suggestions that I give you now:

One, you think of awakening. Two, you take a
very deep breath and feel the energy coming back
all through your body. Three, you are awake, wide
awake.

(PAUSE)

HOLLANDER: How about that? How do you feel?
PEGALOSI: Fine. It was . . . I don't know—funny. I got
dizzy watching my finger come up by itself.

(LAUGHTER)

Q: The surprising thing is that it does come up by
itself. And you did it. So you see that when you
go under, you can achieve anything, virtually anything.
A: I guess.
Q: Even things that you don't even realize you have
the power to achieve. Do you see that?
A: Yes . . . I guess.
Q: Okay. Do you remember the instructions that I
gave you on how to put yourself into a trance?

A: To think about my hand, do you mean?

Q: Not exactly. You missed it a bit. You recall the feeling of my fingers on your wrist?

A: Yes. I remember now.

Q: Would you like to try going under just with that?

A: I . . . I'll try.

Q: Good.

A: Can I say . . . talk about it?

Q: Sure.

A: Well, I'm trying to feel the hand on my wrist, but . . .

Q: You just think about it, the way it felt, and I'll help you remember. Just thinking about it is all that is necessary. Imagine that hand and, if you want to, close your eyes so that you can see it more clearly. Does that help you to see it?

A: Yes.

Q: Good. You see the fingers are moving, jerking, and the hand is moving upward. And as it comes toward your face you go deeper and deeper into the trance.

A: And the fingers separate like this?

Q: Yes. You just go right ahead. You're doing beautifully. You're doing just what I want you to do. When the hand begins to move toward your face, say "now."

(PAUSE)

A: Now.

Q: Good. Now I want you to begin recalling a very, very satisfying experience. A very pleasant experience. An experience where you felt strong and good and when all of those who knew you would have been proud and pleased. Can you recall such an episode?

A: Yes.

Q: All right. Would you like to tell me about it?

A: I felt pretty when I got married.

Q: Yes. That is usually a pleasant, satisfying experience.

A: I was so happy.

Q: Good. Tell me how you feel as you recall that experience.

A: Weepy.

Q: Weepy?

A: I cried all through the ceremony. A judge married us. He thought it was sweet that I cried. He said so. How nice it was to see tears of joy. He lent me his handkerchief to dry my eyes.

Q: Is that what you were doing when you wiped your hands over your face just now?

A: Uh-huh.

Q: Good. You can enjoy reliving that joyful experience vividly and accurately and perhaps even enjoy things you have forgotten. Yes. There is a smile on your face. What are you remembering?

A: John, my husband. He brought me flowers for the wedding. I only had flowers once before from a boy before that. They were awful pretty.

Q: You are doing just fine, Esther. You are able to control your trance so well. I am proud of you. Do you think you are ready to go a little further?

A: I think so.

Q: Good. Now let's make use of your own ability again. The more you practice, the better you get.

Start thinking about that sensation in your wrist. How it felt when I touched you. And when you have reached the stage where your hand is moving toward your face, and you feel it moving, say "now."

A: Now.

Q: Good. Now, Esther, there are many pleasant things in one's life. There are weddings and Christmases. What is the nicest birthday gift that you ever received?

A: My . . . One of my fathers took me to dinner and the show.

Q: Who was that, Esther?

A: My real father. Mr. Freemont. I was eleven or twelve and we dressed up. He wore a suit and tie and Momma looked so nice. I had a new dress. It was yellow and Daddy said it was for me, because I was special.

Q: Can you see that dress now?

A: Yes.

Q: Can you imagine that you are wearing that dress?

A: Yes.

Q: You have it on right now, don't you? You can touch it. You feel so good and proud in your new dress. That's right, stroke it. Feel the material in your hand. You're smiling. Are you pleased with the dress?

A: Yes. It feels so nice. Thank you, Daddy.

Q: Okay, Esther. Relax. Good. That was fun, wasn't it? Good. Relax. Now, perhaps, we can remember some other things. Do you remember a party in November, 1960? Can you remember that party?

A: A party?

Q: Yes. In November, 1960.

A: There were a lot of parties I went to.

Q: Do you remember two boys named Coolidge?

(PAUSE)

Q: Esther, do you remember two brothers named Bobby and Billy Coolidge?

A: Yes.

Q: Could you tell me if you were ever at a party with Billy and Bobby.

A: Well, I hung around with their crowd, you know. I probably was at a lot of parties where they were.

Q: Do you remember a girl named Alice Fay?

A: Uh-huh.

Q: What do you remember about Alice?

A: She was pretty. She was the Junior Prom Queen.

Q: You went to a party at Alice's house in November of 1960, didn't you?

A: In November?

Q: Yes.

(PAUSE)

Q: Esther, can you remember the party at Alice Fay's house?

A: I . . . A little.

Q: Good. Now, would you relax and lean back and close your eyes and just review that evening and that party as much as you can remember. When you do this, I want you to feel confident that you may remember, misremember or forget anything and everything that happens here today as your unconscious needs require and when you awaken you will feel refreshed and you will feel relieved in proportion to any anxiety you may feel during the experience. Review that evening now, and when you have completed reviewing as much as you recall, I want you to say "now."

(PAUSE)

A: Now.

Q: Good. Now, Esther, I want you to close your eyes and imagine that you are seeing each event that happened on the evening of Alice's party. Are you doing that?

A: Yes.

Q: Esther, I would enjoy reviewing that evening with you. Would you like to tell me what you are seeing?

A: The house.

Q: Whose house?

A: Alice's house.

Q: Do you like the house?

A: It's grand.

Q: What do you like best about the house?

A: They have thick carpets in one room. I walked over there. It was like walking in clouds.

Q: It felt good?

A: The furniture was so pretty.

Q: What is happening in the house? Can you see it?

A: There is music and dancing. Everyone is having fun.

Q: Good. You're doing fine. Now, when you review the events taking place I want you to feel as clearly as you can the way you felt when the events were happening. How do you feel, Esther?

A: I felt nervous.

Q: Nervous?

A: We shouldn't be here.

Q: Why shouldn't you be here?

(PAUSE)

Q: Why shouldn't you be at Alice's house?

A: There was something bad . . . I . . . Oh, I can't say. I'm just nervous.

Q: Did Billy and Bobby make you nervous?

A: Umm.

Q: I couldn't hear you, Esther. You have to talk up.

A: I guess.

Q: What did they do to make you nervous?

A: Pardon?

Q: What did Billy and Bobby do to make you nervous?

A: I . . . I don't know. Is it hot in here?

Q: I don't think so, Esther.

Esther, did Billy and Bobby make you nervous when they fought? Is that why you are nervous.

A: I don't feel well.

Q: What's wrong?

A: Nothing.

Q: Okay, then. Just relax. Feel how good it is to be so in control. To feel confident that you can be the woman that you really want to be. Do you feel that confidence?

A: Yes.

Q: Are you relaxed and in control?

A: Yes.

Q: All right, Esther, I want you to think about the party. To review that night, as I know you have the power to do. Can you see the thick carpet and the beautiful furniture?

A: Yes.

Q: Take off your shoes and walk around in the thick carpeting. It feels good, doesn't it?

A: I didn't do that.

Q: But you wanted to, didn't you?

A: Yes.

Q: Can you see the people dancing?

A: Yes.

Q: You see Bobby and Billy, don't you?

A: By the punch bowl.

Q: Is that where the fight was?

A: The fight?

Q: Do you remember the fight? Billy and Bobby were fighting. Is that what made you nervous?

A: I don't remember.

Q: You don't remember the fight?

A: Billy was always fighting.

Q: Did Billy fight in the park?

A: Pardon?

Q: Did Billy fight in the park?

A: The . . . I didn't go to the park.

Q: You didn't lose your glasses in the park?

A: No. Uh-uh.

Q: When did you lose your glasses?

A: A little before.

Q: Before when, Esther?

A: The . . . you know, the time when Richie was . . . died.

Q: How did you get along all that time without your glasses?

A: I just needed them to read. I didn't need them real bad.

Q: Tell us about the fight.

A: The fight?

Q: You said there was a fight.

A: I did?

Q: Where was the fight?

A: My head hurts.

Q: Your head hurts?

A: It's throbbing and I can't think.

Q: When, Esther? Back in 1960 or now?

A: My ears hurt, too.

Q: Esther, I want you to relax . . .

A: I can't think.

Q: You just can't think?

A: Uh-uh.

Q: Okay. I want to thank you, Esther, for the help and effort that you have made and I know that you will have a full reward for those efforts. You are learning to be the strong, assured, self-confident person that you want to be and your learning today is in proportion to your cooperation. The more you work with me, the sooner you will become the kind of person you want to be.

   In a few moments, I am going to ask you to awaken feeling confident that whenever you wish to develop the hypnotic trance in the privacy of your own home, in the privacy of your bed, or out in the activity of the world, that you can do so easily, rapidly and confidently as I have taught you. Should you wish to enlarge your concentration

you can do so by counting from one to three, as
I have taught you. By counting to yourself, becoming fully awake, fully alert and more confident,
feeling like the kind of person you really want to
be. Now, when I say "now," begin to count, one,
two, three. Now.

Shindler waited until the door closed. He had
moved as little as possible during the preceding hour,
trying to avoid distracting Hollander's subject, blend-
ing into the cool colors of the decor. Now he stretched,
not saying anything until the doctor had completed
his notes.

"This was fascinating for me," Hollander said,
looking up from a stenographer's pad he kept on his
desk. "Did you notice the headache and earache toward the end?"

"Yes."

"She doesn't want to talk about it, so the body cre-
ates pain that makes it impossible for her to think."

"Then you think she knows something."

"I am not positive. It was too soon to tell. But my
instinct tells me that there is something there. When
can you bring her in again?"

"Tomorrow."

"No. Let's make it next week. I want her to take
some time to think."

"Would it help if I drove her to the Fay home and
the park?"

"It might."

Shindler held out his hand.

"Thanks, Art. I can't tell you how much I appreciate the time you're putting into this."

Hollander laughed.

"I'm the one who should do the thanking. This is the most exciting experience I've had in all my years of practice. You can't believe how pleasant and exhilarating a change this is from listening to the complaints of undersexed housewives."

Shindler shook the doctor's hand and closed the office door behind him. Esther Pegalosi was sitting in the waiting room. She looked up nervously as he approached.

5

The night lights of Portsmouth twinkled like grounded stars, then faded in brilliance as the red halo of the sunrise peeked above the horizon. Bobby Coolidge watched all this with dull, tired eyes from the couch in the darkened living room in Sarah Rhodes's apartment. The red tip of a cigarette glowed at the end of loose fingers. His body slouched in the sofa and his legs rested on a glass-topped coffee table.

The process of turning night into day had taken some time, but Bobby's conscious mind had missed most of it as it tried, with painstaking slowness, to piece together the remnants of a dream.

"Is anything wrong?" Sarah asked from the bedroom door.

"I couldn't sleep. It's nothing."

Sarah watched his silhouette in the half light. They had been living together for the last month and she was still getting used to Bobby and his moods.

Bobby heard her bare feet pad across the hardwood floor and felt the cushions give way beside him.

"Is something bothering you, Bobby?" she asked

softly. "This is the third night in a row that you haven't slept."

He turned to look at her. The weather was mild and she was sleeping in bikini panties and one of his tee shirts. The way she was leaning made the cotton fabric outline her nipples.

"It's just the pressure of exams, that's all," he said, telling a half truth. He hoped she would accept his explanation and stop there, because he knew that he could not explain to her that the dreams had started again, creeping insidiously into his unconscious mind at night, when he had no defenses.

He thought that he had left them in Vietnam, but the pressure of finals had begun to build. Everything, his new life, his relationship with this girl, seemed to center on his staying in school. If he did not pass . . . If he failed . . . It was something he thought about all the time.

"Are you sure there's nothing else?" she asked. He appreciated the sincerity of her concern. He had never had anyone care about him before. He felt her fingers run lightly through his hair and he leaned back and closed his eyes.

"It's the tests. I think about them all the time. It's just getting me down."

"There's nothing to worry about, Bobby. I know you. You'll do fine."

She stroked his hair and he shifted his head to her shoulder. He was tired. It was the same cycle again. Not enough sleep at night and too tired to work during the day. And behind it all were the dreams.

He felt Sarah's lips brush his cheek and he opened

his eyes. She was staring at him. He brushed her hair aside and stroked her cheek. They held each other.

The sun was up now, bathing the sleepy valley in morning light. He watched the mist floating across the rooftops like steam in a bowl. She felt so soft and yielding.

"I know how to help you sleep," she said, her voice a husky whisper.

He smiled. She did, too. She got slowly to her feet and stripped away her clothing. He followed her slim, naked figure into the bedroom.

But the lovemaking did not help. Even while he was inside her, even when he came, he could not experience the full pleasure of the act. One part of him was watching, unbelieving. What was Bobby Coolidge doing in bed with this make-believe girl? What was he doing in college? He didn't belong here. He could not believe that it was real and that it would not end.

Sarah could see that her efforts to relax him had failed. She could feel the tension in his body and she could see the sadness when he was through. Bobby was a strange boy. Not at all like the boys she had dated in high school. That was part of his attraction. His age, the maturity of his friends. Most of them were veterans or at least older than the boys most of the other freshman girls were dating. It made her feel older and more sophisticated to think that a boy who had been to war—a boy who had killed—found her attractive.

She rubbed her hand across his chest and kissed his cheek. How complicated he was. That was another

facet of the attraction. The boys she had dated before were simple. Carbon copies. The idle rich. Sports
cars. The same past, present and future. But Bobby
could not be read. Not entirely. He had dark corners,
secrets. Like the war, which he would not discuss, or
his past, to which he alluded in only the vaguest of
terms. He seemed so vulnerable at times like tonight.
A combination of strength and weakness that she
found fascinating.

"Bobby, there is something wrong and I want you
to tell me."

Bobby said nothing, staring into the silence and
breathing deeply, like a laborer carrying a heavy load.

"Bobby?" she repeated.

"I get scared that I'll fail and all this . . . You mean
so much to me. I think about what I'll do if I don't
make it and about my brother."

"Poor baby," she said, stroking his cheek and shifting her weight across his right side. Her smooth skin
felt good beneath his hand. "Underneath that tough
exterior you're a rabbit. But I know you, rabbit, and
I know that you are strong and smart and good. And
I know that you will make a success of whatever you
do."

He smiled sadly and held her tight.

"You're steel, Sarah. You are the best part of the
good things that have been happening to me. But
you don't really know me. You know *this* Bobby Coolidge, but you don't know who I was before the war."

"People don't change that much, Bobby. Deep down
you are always the same person."

"No, Sarah. I did things before that I could never
do now. Bad things."

"Oh, Bobby, you like to dramatize so. I know you couldn't do 'bad things.' Not really bad."

"But I did. There's blood on my hands, Sarah, and I can't shut it out of my dreams. Whenever the pressure builds up in me, like now, the dreams start again and I see what I've done."

"What, Bobby?" she asked, concerned now at the sudden change in him.

"I'm sorry I said . . . that I talked like this. Please, do me a favor. There are things about me . . . my past . . . that I don't want you to know about. I can't risk losing you and I know I would, if I told you. I shouldn't have brought it up. I did and, now, I am asking you to forget that I did."

"But, Bobby . . ."

"Please. I . . . You are the most important, most decent thing that has ever happened to me. I don't want to lose you. Respect my wishes, this once."

The look she gave him was peculiar and puzzled.

"Okay, Bobby. I won't ask. I just wanted to help."

"You do help. Just by being here. You are my fairy princess and I love you."

He kissed her softly at first, then harder and his love swelled in him, out of control. This time there were no distractions.

TAPE # 2

DR. ARTHUR HOLLANDER: Well, Esther, do you feel comfortable about going ahead at this time?

ESTHER PEGALOSI: I do.

Q: All right. Good. Let's just see how we do then. Do you want to just relax? That's it. When you feel the hand moving toward your face, I want you to say "now."

(PAUSE)

A: Now.

Q: All right. Let's just keep that pleasant, comfortable feeling while we go back in time. We aren't going to go back too far this time. Just to last week, a week ago today. You were in this office, you were lying on this chair very much as you are now. We had a very, very satisfying hour and after we finished you went out and met Roy, Mr. Shindler. And you went and got into his car.

Now, will you, as best you can, repeat that experience now. Don't tell me about it. Review it in your mind's eye. Exactly what happened until you arrived back at your apartment. Let me know when you've finished by saying "now."

(PAUSE)

A: Now.

Q: Did that disturb you at all?

A: No.

Q: Would you be willing to repeat that experience for me?

A: Uh-huh.

Q: Okay. Tell me, if you wish to, as clearly as you can, as though it was happening right now, what happened. You leave through that door. You hear the screen door bounce back and bounce again.

A: We go out to the parking lot and Mr. Shindler tells me how good you said I did. How he is proud of me. I get in the front seat and we drive out of the parking lot.

Q: What street do you take, Esther?

A: Atlanta Boulevard. Then straight to Monroe. We talked about you. I said I thought that you were a nice man.

Q: Why thank you very much!

A: I said you sounded kind and you kind of understood things.

Then we went up Monroe 'til we got to the park and Mr. Shindler turned off there into the park. When we were driving, he asked me if anything looked familiar. First we looked at a place on a hill near one of the switchbacks where the road goes up. I said it looked familiar, because he took me there once before. To where he had found my glasses. But, otherwise, I said it didn't.

We drove further on up and we went . . . we took a ride on a little kind of dirt road. And I had been watching the road to see if I could remember running down any of them and we went up this little dirt road then. But first, before we got to that road, we passed a place on the side of the road with a fireplace, kind of up on the top of the hill there. It was all grassy and I thought that picnic benches and things used to be there. And Roy said they had been and they moved them.

Then we went up past where some park benches used to be. We went up the dirt road to the right and it was kind of muddy and sloppy and we went up there and Roy was telling me that this was the road that the murder happened on. A little ahead. And I said that it seemed familiar, but I couldn't remember for sure. But I did tell him that I know that there was this big, flat, real smooth place at the end of this road where it had been flattened out and all the weeds and everything were gone and he showed me the place and asked me if I could remember a '55 red Mercury with red and yellow flames along the side parked near the trees at the far corner. But I didn't remember.

Then we parked for a while and Roy asked me if I could remember being with Bobby and Billy that night and I could, but just early in the evening. And he asked if Bobby and Billy dragged on Monroe and I said sometimes.

After that we walked around the meadow and Mr. Shindler took me to the edge of the hill and showed me how, if a girl ran straight down it, she would be near where they found my glasses. But I didn't remember any of it, so we got back in the car.

Q: Where are you going now?

A: We went back down and we didn't go back toward town but to the left at the park entrance and we passed this house that was down a ways from the entrance. I noticed it when we passed it and Roy turned around and parked in front.

We got out and walked up the driveway a bit and Roy took me into the backyard and asked me, "Do you remember anything about dogs barking?" And I . . .

Q: Yes.

A: Well, I had never been here. I know it. But I got really scared. Like when you feel weak and faint. I thought then that I felt like something was going to come out.

Q: Can you feel that now? Would you be willing to re-create that feeling now?

A: I'd rather not.

Q: You said you had never been there before?

A: I can't say for certain. But when I was there it was as if I had been. And when he said about the dogs barking I had this funny thought that he meant a kind of dog.

Q: What kind?

A: A German Shepherd.

Q: Why a German Shepherd?

A: I don't know. Except we had one once. My step-father killed it.

Q: He killed it?

A: It was after my mother divorced my real father. I was thirteen and she married this man. He was real strict and he had been in the psycho ward a couple of times after he got out of the Service. And he was an alcoholic.

He would drink, then he would beat us day and night. He stabbed my mother. I saw him. Then my mother took us away.

Q: You were going to tell me about the dog. The German Shepherd.

A: I was?

Q: Yes.

A: He killed it. It was my pet. We lived near these woods and I would walk with him. He was my only friend. Then he killed him to punish me when I disobeyed once. He shot my dog in the eye and made me watch.

(PAUSE)

Q: Do you want my handkerchief?
A: Thank you.
Q: Are you all right? Can you continue?
A: I'm okay.
Q: Why don't you relax? Why don't you lean back on the cool grass and let the breeze blow across your face? That's it. Take a nice deep breath. When you can feel the breeze and see the cool, puff clouds tell me by saying "now."

(Deep breathing then shallow breathing.)

Q: You're okay.
A: Now.
Q: Okay. You're relaxed and you are drifting back to last week and you are with Roy looking at that backyard and you have a strange feeling. Tell me about the feeling. You can re-create that feeling, because you are a strong and confident woman who is slowly becoming a person like you want yourself to be. A woman who controls her destiny. Do you feel relaxed and confident?
A: Yes.
Q: Then tell me what you feel. You see that dog as though it was happening right now, don't you? Feel that feeling that you got when you saw that big, brown German Shepherd dog. Feel it. Then if

there is something that you want to say, say it. But feel that feeling.

A: I know I've been there before.

Q: You know that you've been there before?

A: And I know that I was scared when I was there before.

Q: I want you to give me your best hunch what scared you. What scared you? First thought! First thought!

A: That we were going to get caught.

Q: Going to get caught? What would you be caught about?

A: Just being there.

Q: Be caught for being there? Why would that be bad? Why would anyone want to catch you for being there?

A: I don't know.

Q: You don't know?

A: I could guess, but I really don't know.

Q: All right. Would you be willing to guess for me?

A: Uh huh. I thought about it and after we left the house to drive me home, Roy told me that the murder happened just straight up the hill from the house and that the lady there had German Shepherds and they were acting up that night and she saw a girl running away. So maybe I thought it was me.

Q: But you were scared before Roy told you.

A: Yes.

Q: So how could you be scared if you didn't know about the dogs yet?

A: I don't know.

Q: You said "we were going to get caught." Why we?

A: That's funny.

Q: What?

A: Well, when I was there—in the driveway—I had the feeling like I was there twice. And once it was in a car.

Q: Oh, you mean you were up that driveway by that house in a car. Were you worrying about being caught because it was after the murder?

A: I don't know when it was. All I can remember is just driving into the driveway and I think I was in the back seat of a car and it seemed like there was someone with me in the back.

Q: Did they pick you up on the road after you ran down the hill?

A: I can't remember!

Q: Relax, Esther. That's fine. Let it come! Let it come! Just let it come! I'm right here.

A: I can't. (Screaming, crying.)

Q: Let it come. I'm right here. Let it all come out of your system. Let all of that feeling leave now. Let it all come out naturally and properly.

A: I can't think. (Still crying.)

Q: All right. It's all right. You're doing a nice job. Don't worry about thinking for a few moments.

(Still crying for a few moments.)

Q: Are you all right now?

A: I can't remember. I can't. I can't remember.

Q: If you can't recall . . .

A: I just can't.

Q: I really appreciate your trying. You know that, don't you, Esther?

A: If I could only get it out.

Q: Get what out?

A: Huh?

Q: What do you want to get out?

A: I . . . I just meant. To see if it really happened or if it didn't. Sometimes I get confused, because we would go to the park all the time when I was in high school and I can't remember if I'm remembering something I really did or if it's from the murder.

Q: You've been to the meadow before?

A: I have been there over and over and over.

Q: I wanted to clear that up. You went there to pitch woo or something . . . and . . .

A: We went up there all the time to party and drink. It was a real good place to play spooks on Halloween because it was real spooky up there anyway. I used to go up there almost every Halloween, scare each other, run through the woods. Stuff like that. Only it didn't seem familiar from that when I was in the driveway. It was so funny . . . that feeling . . . I know I'm afraid to remember.

Q: Well, I don't blame you. I think I would be afraid to remember too.

A: It's like I feel when I'm dreaming and I wake up. I can see the dream a little, but I can't remember it.

Q: You are dreaming about this?

A: A little.

Q: Tell me about your dreams.

A: Sometimes I see Richie's face. It's covered in blood like in the picture Mr. Shindler showed me.

Then I'm running. Whatever has happened has happened already and I run down the hill. And there is someone running with me and I think it is a girl. It didn't seem like I was being chased. Just running. And then we are in a car. In the back seat.

Q: Can you see the girl's face?

A: No. I woke up.

Q: Have you dreamed this more than once?

A: Twice since we went to the park last week.

Q: Do these dreams upset you?

A: Yes.

Q: How do you feel when you wake up from one of these dreams?

A: My heart is beating very fast and I can't breathe. The first time I thought it was real for a moment.

Q: And you have never had these dreams before?

A: Well, I did once or twice.

Q: I thought you said it was since the park. When Roy drove you there.

A: Yes, but I have dreamed about the face. My Mom can tell you. When I was living home.

Q: Okay. Well, Esther, we have had a tiring session today. You have tried very hard and I am proud of you. Now, I am going to tell you something that will help you the next time that you wake up and you are afraid because of one of these dreams or whenever you are under pressure or begin to doubt that you are the strong, mature woman that we know you are. A woman capable of raising a child by herself. Of making it on her own. We can see that you are becoming the strong, confident person that you know you can be.

Now, the next time you are afraid, either here

or at home or anywhere, I want you to relax and remember the feeling of my hand on your wrist. You don't have to see the wrist or close your eyes or anything like that. Just remember how it feels and soon your hand will move toward your face and you will feel comfortable and relaxed and all of your tension will be gone.

Now, I want you to promise me that you will practice this at home. You can do it anytime you want. In your bedroom, while you watch TV. Will you promise me that you will practice?

A: Yes.

Q: Good. Now, in a few moments you are going to awaken from your trance, feeling refreshed, feeling strong and confident . . .

"Eddie!" Gary Barrick yelled, when he spotted Eddie Toller at the other end of the bar. The smoke was heavy in the Satin Slipper and the dim light distorted the features of the young, curly-haired man who was rising from his stool.

"Goddamn!" Eddie said, when he saw who had called his name. "How the hell you been?"

The two men smiled and shook hands vigorously.

"You're lookin' prosperous for a guy who's only been out of the joint a couple of months."

"Hey," Eddie said, looking around to see if anyone had heard Gary's remark. "Keep it down. Most people here don't know I've been in prison."

"Sorry, Eddie. What are you doin'?"

"I work here. I'm assistant manager," he said with a trace of pride.

"No shit! That's great. I'm glad things are workin' for you."

"Yeah, well it's okay." He shrugged. "How about you?"

Gary grinned.

"Same old thing. I ain't got a job now, but I'm lookin'."

Eddie motioned Gary to an empty booth and signaled for a waitress. A good-looking blonde with long legs swayed over to the table.

"What can I get you, Eddie?" she asked.

"Nothing for me, but it's on the house for my friend. What are you drinking, Gary?"

Gary ordered and the blonde wiggled away.

"That's all right," Gary said, impressed. "You gettin' any of that?"

"Sheila? No. I got my own girl. She works in the lounge, but she's off tonight. When did you get into town?"

"Last month."

"You got a place to stay?"

"Yeah. I'm with a chick I met. We'll have to double, huh."

Sheila returned with Gary's drink and Gary and Eddie reminisced about the year they had spent as cellmates.

"So you're straight now?" Gary asked.

"Yeah. I don't mess around. Joyce and me are going to get married as soon as I save enough bread."

"Married. This is serious."

Eddie blushed.

"Yeah. I guess. I ain't getting any younger, as they say."

"Too bad," Gary said wistfully.

"Why?"

Gary looked around the room and hunched forward.

"I got a honey of a job worked out and I could use another guy along."

Eddie thought about it for a second, then shook his head.

"No, I don't want to get mixed up in nothin', Gary. This job don't pay great, but it's enough and it's steady. Besides, I couldn't stand to go back to the joint no more. I'm just getting too old for that stuff."

Gary shrugged.

"To each his own. Say, I'll give you my address and phone number."

"No. I just don't think I'm interested."

"Not for that. To get together. I'd like to meet your chick. Old pals should keep in touch."

Esther folded the baby's wash and set the neat piles next to her own. She looked around the living room. All the ironing was done, the dishes were washed and the baby was asleep. She sagged into the secondhand armchair that sat across from the TV and let out a deep sigh. She was exhausted. All the same, the housework didn't get her down as much as it had before she started going to Dr. Hollander.

He had made her see how important her work was. He had made her realize that not everyone could do the things that she was capable of doing, like raising a child by herself. She had thought that anyone could do it, but he had made her see that that was not so. It took a special kind of person to do what she was doing.

She looked at the clock. It was a quarter to nine. She could watch the last fifteen minutes of a TV show or she could practice her trance. She chose the latter. She had come to look forward to practicing her trance. It helped her to relax when she was tense. It helped her to get rid of her day-to-day anxieties and to become the woman she knew she could be: the strong, confident woman that she really wanted to be. The trance gave her a feeling of contentment that alcohol and pills never did. Her days were easier and her nights filled with deep sleep.

Almost as important, the trance helped her to think about the things that Dr. Hollander wanted her to recall. The shadowy, elusive thoughts that hid around the corners of her subconscious. With each session she was becoming more and more convinced that she was hiding something from herself about that night. She was sure of it. When the doctor or Roy talked about things that they thought she had done, they made so much sense. If it had happened, it must have happened the way they said.

Esther let her eyes close and imagined the doctor's fingers on her wrist. There was a tingling in her limbs and she could begin to feel her body relaxing and her hand floating toward her face.

She looked forward to seeing Dr. Hollander each week. He was so kind, so, well, fatherly was the right word. He wasn't like her other fathers had been, but like she wished they would have been. Always supporting her. Always helping her.

She even liked Roy now. She guessed that she

had been wrong about him that first time, because he seemed so nice now. Always buying her things. Nothing expensive, except for her beautiful new clothes, but little things like flowers or gifts for the baby. He was so considerate. Like John had been. Roy was about the same age as John. Older men always seemed more considerate, although she had been with a few who were not. Roy reminded her of John. Of course, Roy was much smarter. She felt so dumb when she was around him and the doctor, although they never let on that they thought she was dumb. But she was. She always knew it. The only reason the boys had ever paid any attention to her in school was because she was pretty and she would do it with them. John had showed her respect. So had Dr. Hollander and Roy.

She had dreamt about Roy last night. When she woke up, she had felt uncomfortable, because the dream had been erotic. They had both been naked in a large bed. They weren't in a room, she didn't think. It had been hazy. Maybe there were clouds instead of walls. And he was on top and doing it to her.

She realized that she was growing tense and she concentrated on her wrist and the trance. She thought about what Roy and the doctor wanted from her. She wanted to help them very much. Some of their questions puzzled her, though. She wondered why Roy had asked her about Monroe and dragging. Did he think they had dragged Richie that night? She was certain they had not. There had been once that she was with someone who had dragged Richie, only she wasn't sure if it had been Roger or if Billy and Bobby had been there. It was all so long ago.

But, what if it was that night . . . ? Only it couldn't have been. But, what if? Then, she might be wrong about other things. She didn't feel relaxed anymore and she opened her eyes. Somehow, the trance was not working tonight. It was nine o'clock. She got up and turned on the television.

6

TAPE # 5

DR. ARTHUR HOLLANDER: All right. And soon the hand will begin to move toward the face. The hand is now touching the face and the eyes will close when it is comfortable to do so. There we are. Fine. Good. Completely relaxed.

Now, Esther, I wonder if you would be willing to forget whatever might be unpleasant in today's episode, and you can indicate so by a "yes."

ESTHER PEGALOSI: Yes.

Q: Good. And then if we need that information at some time in the future, when you are ready, you can remember it either alone or with my help. But any information that might be unpleasant and you might not be ready to consciously remember, you can forget just as you forget a dream a few minutes after awakening. And you can do the same with any unpleasant phase of today's work.

Now, Esther, I want you to imagine that the window in front of you is actually a screen, a movie screen. And can you in your mind's eye clearly see a movie screen there in front of you?

A: Uh-huh.

Q: Good. Now if you look at the bottom of that movie screen, you will notice a little counter, something like the mileage counter on an automobile.

A: Uh-huh.

Q: Can you see it? And can you see that the mileage counter says 1967?

A: Uh-huh.

Q: All right. I want you to just imagine that counter running backwards, '67, '66, '65, at whatever convenient speed you want. And when that counter has moved back to the year 1960, I would like you to let me know by saying the number.

A: 1960.

Q: Good. Now, as you watch that screen, you will see things that have happened in 1960, as though you were in the audience watching a movie screen. It could be that you will see yourself as one of the stars or actors and when you begin to see action on the screen, I want you to say "now."

A: Now.

Q: Good. And would you like to tell me what you see.

A: We are at Bob's.

Q: Bob who?

A: It's a restaurant. Bob's Hamburger Heaven. It's where we used to hang out.

Q: Who do you mean when you say "we," Esther?

A: My friends.

Q: Do you mean the Cobras?

A: Some members.

Q: Billy and Bobby Coolidge?

A: I knew them.

Q: What did you do with the Cobras?

A: I don't know.

Q: Did you ever do anything bad with them?

A: Bad?

Q: Against the law.

A: We robbed the miniature golf once.

Q: Tell me about that. When was that?

A: In '59. In July. There were three boys and me. They robbed the place, then we found we were going to get caught, so they drove the car down the hill. It belonged to one of the boys' brothers. And we were speeding as fast as we could down this curvy road and there were police cars following us and one went in a ditch. We made it all the way down the hill, then we went the wrong way on a one-way street and about five cars finally stopped us.

Q: Police cars?

A: Uh-huh.

Q: Were you scared?

A: Oh, yeah. I couldn't look half the time.

Q: What happened to you?

A: Well, I was young, you know, so they just let me go with Mom. But they kept me at detention for a while.

Q: Why did you do that—rob that place?

A: I was pretty drunk and I could never remember it all. Even in court. I had to testify, but I could never remember if we knew what was gonna happen. We were all plowed. All I know was Bones went to the place where you pay and held a knife at the woman's neck and threatened to rip it. He didn't hurt her though. I think it was all spur of the moment. We were like that then. Live for the moment. The Cobras were always saying something like that.

Q: Did it frighten you to get arrested?

A: I wasn't scared of being arrested. I'd been arrested before. I was scared of detention. I didn't like that.

Q: What's "detention"?

A: Where they keep you if you're a juvenile. I didn't like being locked up.

Q: When were you arrested before?

A: When I stabbed that boy.

Q: You stabbed someone?

A: Andy Trask.

Q: Andy Trask?

A: It was a pocketknife that I carried in my pocket. I didn't really hurt him bad. I just scared him. They let me go when Momma came.

Q: Why did you stab him?

A: It was at a school hop and he wanted to get smart with me and I wouldn't let him.

Q: What do you mean, "get smart"?

A: You know, feel me up and such. I . . . He scared me.

Q: Didn't you like it when he wanted to touch you?

A: I liked that he wanted to . . . That he wanted me, but not how he did it.

Q: How did he do it?

A: He was rough, like my . . . like George. He tried to push me down in the back seat of his car.

Q: Who is George?

A: My . . . my stepfather . . . He would be drunk, you know, and he would beat Momma, then make her, you know, do it and we would have to watch. He would make us.

He was just out of his mind. That was why Momma left him. She could take it, but she was scared for us.

Q: And this boy was like your stepfather?

A: He was drinking, then he pushed me and ordered me. I like boys to be gentle. To say I'm pretty. I'm not . . .

Q: Okay, Esther, you can relax. I can see that this is upsetting to you, so let's go on. Do you think you can do that?

(NOD)

Q: Okay. Let's push ahead now. Let's think about late 1960 and just let things come to mind. Can you still see the movie screen? Good. Now keep watching it and pretty soon the scene will wipe out and a new scene will come on, a little later in the year. In November. You can see a party on the screen. Do you see it?

A: All I can see is a Christmas party.

Q: Well, Esther, we have discussed this party before. This is the one at Alice Fay's house. I want you to see Alice's house on the screen. The thick carpets that you walked on. Do you remember? It felt like walking on clouds.

A: Yes.

Q: You can take your shoes off and walk around in it. How does it feel?

A: Like floating. Like I'm in the sky.

Q: Good. You're smiling. Are there other people there?

A: Oh, sure. It's a party.

Q: What are they doing, Esther?

A: Dancing. Having fun.

Q: Who are you with, Esther?

A: Roger. And Billy and Bobby Coolidge are there too.

Q: Who is Roger?

A: Roger Hessey. He's my boyfriend . . . was my boyfriend, then.

Q: Going steady?

A: Just . . . we dated.

Q: Did Roger stay through the whole party?

A: No. He left when the trouble started.

Q: What trouble?

A: Billy started some trouble.

Q: What did he do?

A: He was fighting. Roger didn't want to fight, so he left.

Q: Why didn't you go with Roger?

A: I don't know.

ROY SHINDLER: Billy used a knife when he fought, didn't he?

A: I don't remember.

Q: Look at the screen, Esther. Can you see the room in Alice's house where the party is?

A: Yes.

Q: Do you see yourself and Billy and Bobby with all the other people?

A: I can see that.

Q: You see Tommy Cooper, too, don't you? See him on the screen?

A: I . . .

Q: Just relax and look hard. You'll see Tommy and Alice by the punch bowl and Bobby and Billy there, too. Tell me when you can see that.

A: I can see them.

Q: Tell me about the fight. On the screen, Tommy and Billy are fighting, aren't they?

A: I can't see the fight. Honest. It was very fast.

Q: But you can see Billy with the knife, can't you? Look on the screen. See the table with the punch bowl. Billy is standing in front of it, isn't he?

A: Yes.

Q: How is he dressed?

A: His colors. His black leather jacket with Cobras on the back. And blue jeans. Tight ones.

Q: You see that clearly?

A: Billy always dressed like that.

Q: Okay. And you see the knife. The switchblade knife in his hand?

A: I don't . . . I can't see that.

Q: Billy had a knife like that, didn't he Esther? Didn't he show it around all the time?

A: I . . . It's been a long time.

DR. HOLLANDER: Relax, Esther. There is no need to get upset. Remember, you are looking at a movie screen. Things that happen on a movie screen cannot hurt you, can they?

A: No.

Q: Good. And I am here to help you, aren't I?

A: Yes.

Q: I have helped you to become the strong, confident woman you have always wanted to be, haven't I? Like I promised you. Isn't that so?

A: Yes.

Q: And you feel confident and strong now, don't you?

A: I . . .

Q: How do you feel now, Esther?

A: Scared.

Q: Okay. Then I want you to alert yourself.

A: Okay.

Q: One, two, three, all right.

A: I was thinking about unhappy things.

Q: I know. You said you were scared. What scared you?

A: I don't know. I'm not sleeping too good. I had a dream last night . . .

Q: The same dream you told me about a few weeks ago?

A: Uh-huh. And I feel bad when I'm awake. You've been so nice to me. Like, I know you want me to remember, and I try, but I wish I didn't have to go back.

Q: You don't have to go back, Esther. We can't force you to come here.

A: I know.

Q: When you are home, do you practice what I told you when you get upset or scared?

A: You mean, remembering your fingers on my wrist?

Q: Yes.

A: I try. Sometimes it's hard to concentrate. The baby is so demanding and I have housework.

Q: That's when you should do it. When you feel the pressure. That is when it will help you the most.

A: I know and I do try sometimes. It's just that I get upset. I know it's all inside me. In there. I want to get it out.

Q: Well, you'll do that. Now relax and get comfortable. Feel those fingers caressing your wrist. Your hand growing light as a feather. I want you to feel, in your whole body, the feeling that every day you are finding yourself a little more like the person you really want to be . . .

* * *

ROY SHINDLER: You remember Billy taking the wine. You remember that, don't you, Esther?

A: Yes.

Q: Then you drank the wine in the car. Can you see that, Esther?

A: Uh-huh.

Q: How long were you drinking the wine?

A: Gee, I don't know. You know how you get when you drink too much. I got tired and time got all stretched out.

Q: Then you go cruising downtown, don't you?

A: I think so.

Q: And you are on Monroe now. Can you see Monroe?

A: I can see Monroe, but I'm not . . . I don't remember if . . .

Q: But you had to go on Monroe to get home, didn't you?

A: No. Usually I would go to Marshall Road from downtown.

Q: But you could go that way?

A: Yes.

(WHISPERING)

Q: Okay, Esther, I want you to picture Monroe Boulevard in your mind and I want you to tell us what you see on Monroe Boulevard. Now this is in November, 1960.
A: Well, I can't remember being there that night.
Q: What night?
A: When the . . . The murder, you know.
DR. HOLLANDER: That's okay, Esther. You can pretend that you are there. See Monroe Boulevard on the movie screen. Can you see it?
A: Yes.
Q: Okay. Now what do you see?
A: Not much. Just some stores, you know.

(WHISPERING)

Q: Yes. What kind of car are you in?
A: What do you want me to say?
Q: Just the truth. What do you see on the screen?
A: Well, I'm really . . . I don't see myself in a car.
ROY SHINDLER: What kind of a car did Bobby and Billy Coolidge have?
A: Gee, I can't . . . A Dodge or a Ford. Something like that.
Q: What color was it?
A: Uh, dark blue or black. Some dark color.
Q: You know what car Richie drove, don't you?
A: I don't remember the make.
Q: But you know it.
A: It was the hottest car in school. I was with Billy and Bobby once when they dragged it.

Q: With them? Was anyone else along?

A: I don't think so.

Q: Did you usually go out alone with the Coolidges?

A: There might have been someone else. Probably Roger. I don't remember, because it was so long ago.

Q: What happened during the drag race?

A: Just a drag race.

Q: There was no accident?

A: Not . . . I don't think so.

Q: What were you going to say?

A: Pardon?

Q: You started by saying "not." Were you going to say "not then"? Was there another time when you were with the Coolidges and they dragged Richie and there was an accident?

A: I don't think so.

Q: Don't think so or there wasn't?

A: I don't know. I'm all confused. I would remember an accident, wouldn't I?

Q: You told me that you couldn't remember what happened that night, because you were drunk.

A: Yes.

Q: So there could have been a drag race with Richie on Monroe.

A: I'm awful tired. I don't think I'll be any good anymore today.

*   *   *

"You're very quiet this evening," Shindler said.

Esther turned away from the window and looked at Shindler. He was smiling. It made her feel worse. She knew that she was letting them down by not remembering and here he was, being so kind to her, as if it didn't matter.

"I'm just tired," she said.

"I can understand that. These sessions must not be very pleasant for you. Both Dr. Hollander and I appreciate how hard you're trying."

Shindler eased the car into the exit lane of the freeway and Esther stared down at her hands. She was tired and she was low. The thought of spending the night in her apartment, alone, left her empty inside. She wished she didn't get so depressed after the sessions. She looked forward to them so much that each time they ended she felt as if she had lost something.

The apartment house loomed ahead and Esther let her eyelids close for a moment. Roy parked in front of the door. She didn't want him to leave her. She remembered that he had mentioned that he was hungry earlier. She wondered . . .

"Do you . . . ? Would you want to come in? I could fix some spaghetti."

Shindler was surprised by the invitation, but pleased that she had given it. During the last few sessions he had noticed that she was less tense in his presence.

She expected him to turn her down. It was foolish anyway. She was a poor cook. What would they talk about? She began to regret that she had asked him. Then he accepted and she was terrified that the evening would be a disaster.

Shindler paid the baby-sitter and Esther went into the kitchen to cook the meal. The baby was asleep for the night. Shindler asked her if there was a store nearby where he could buy some wine. Esther didn't know. She didn't buy wine like that for drinking with

a meal. She felt foolish. Shindler said he would go out
and find a store. When he was gone, she changed
into the outfit he had purchased for her. She did not
realize how inappropriate it looked for the occasion.

"You look very nice," Shindler said when he returned. She blushed, the reaction he had been hoping for. She was so easy to manipulate. Most people
were, if you had the time to study them.

Esther set the table and Shindler poured the wine.
She felt that everything she was doing was wrong.
Besides John, she had never really cooked for a man.
Never had the type of relationship with a man that
would call for that type of occasion. It had been
mostly country and western bar dates, then back to
someone's bedroom in some motel or maybe not even
the preliminary hours at the bar. And she had never
been with anyone like Shindler. He was so intelligent and he talked at times about things that she
didn't understand.

"Are you feeling better?" he asked her after they
had finished eating. The wine had relaxed her and
made her a little giddy.

"I'm feeling good," she replied. He helped her
carry the dishes into the narrow kitchen and their
hips touched. The feel of him that close excited her
and he noticed the reaction.

"You look very pretty tonight," he said.

"Thank you," she said and looked away from him,
frightened by the thoughts that were suddenly flood-
ing her. She remembered her dream and felt guilty
about the desire she felt. She started to wash a dish, to
distract herself, but he took it out of her hands and
turned off the water. She looked up at him. He was so

230   *Phillip Margolin*

tall. He was ugly, yet she did not see that. She saw what
he wanted her to see. What she wanted to see. A father
to take care of her. Someone to tell her what to do.

He stroked her hair. This was so easy.

"You wore this dress specially for me?"

She answered him in a whisper so low he could
barely hear her. He stroked her chin and lifted it
gently so that she had to look at his eyes.

He took her hand and led her, like a child, into the
bedroom. Her heart was pounding so loudly she was
certain that he could hear. She felt like liquid inside.
He removed her clothes and she knew if he touched
her, she would melt away.

Shindler made her lie on the bed and ran his hand
across her body. Her breasts were full and her nipples taut. He was becoming aroused, but even his
desire was under control. Her eyes were closed tight
and he watched her clinically.

Esther moaned and arched under his touch. He
was above her and in her and around her. The pleasure was unbearable. It had never been like this for
her before. With other men, even John, there had
been the smell of sweat and a knowledge of where she
was every moment that they were inside her. With
Roy, she was lost.

Shindler felt her quiver and relax. He came and
stayed inside her. She was crying. He kissed her and
held her. Her tears mingled with the sweat on his
shoulder. He soothed her and petted her, as if she was
a dog. It would be much easier now.

7

"Look, Ted, the Communists have got to be stopped. I would rather do it in Vietnam than Disneyland."

"Jesus, I don't believe this," Ted Wolberg said. "Who writes your scripts, the John Birch Society?"

Ted and Bobby Coolidge were passing the time at George Rasmussen's apartment. As usual, Ted and George were arguing about the war. Bobby was paying little attention to what was being said, because he had heard it all before. It seemed that all anyone ever talked about anymore was Vietnam.

"What do you think, Bobby?" Ted asked.

Bobby looked at Ted. He did not like to get drawn into academic discussions, because he did not feel secure enough yet to venture into the intellectual arena. He never spoke in class. With his friends, he was a listener. The trouble was, with Vietnam the topic, he was considered the resident expert. He was always being put on the spot and he was expected to be knowledgeable in every area connected with the war. In fact, he knew less about Vietnam and its history and politics than George, who had spent his army time in Washington, D. C., or Ted, whose hobby was Far Eastern studies and who was a political science major.

"I think you're both right, in a way," he answered cautiously. "I don't think we should be over there . . ."

"See," Ted interrupted. "That's just what the two P.O.W.s who were just released said."

". . . but I don't agree when you say that the country is like Nazi Germany. I mean, there aren't any secret police coming to take you away for your clearly subversive statements, are there?"

"You are being fooled by the repressive tolerance practiced by the military-industrial complex that runs this country. Marcuse says . . ."

"Who?" George asked.

Ted was about to answer when the doorbell rang. George answered it and returned to the living room with Sarah. She had a letter in her hand. When he saw it, Bobby's heart started to pound and his lips felt suddenly dry. The envelope looked like the type the school used to send out grades. It was intersession and Bobby had been expecting his final first semester marks all week.

He expected the worst and he realized that he did not want his friends finding out, if his grades were poor.

"Uh, George, can I talk to Sarah in your bedroom?"

"Sure, just clean up before you leave."

"You're a pig, George," Sarah said, following Bobby down the corridor to George's bedroom.

"Well?" Bobby asked nervously, when the door was closed. She looked at him without expression for a moment and his heart sank. Then she burst into laughter and flung her arms around his neck.

"You made Dean's List, you dummy. I'm so proud."

He tried to untangle himself from her. What she had said had not sunk in.

"What?" he asked, when he had peeled her off and was holding her at arm's length.

"Dean's List," she shouted. "Three As, a B-plus, and a C-plus in math."

"You're shitting me?"

"If you could see how you look, you idiot."

"Dean's List. Oh, wow! Hey, that's not possible."

He walked back and forth, looking at the grade sheet. It was there in black and white.

"Look, you get real pretty tonight. I am going to take you out on the town."

"You don't have to do that, Bobby," she said, knowing how tight his cash was.

"To hell with that. You don't know what this means to me, Sarah. All my life I always thought that I was stupid. That I would never amount to anything. You don't know how scared I've been in school. I almost quit a dozen times."

She did not say anything, but she knew. She had heard him moaning in the night, seen him sweating over his books, cheered him up when he was too disheartened to go on.

"You know, this is the turning point in my life, Sarah. I won't go back, ever again."

TAPE # 8

DR. ARTHUR HOLLANDER: I'm glad to see you looking so well, Esther.

ESTHER PEGALOSI: I've been feeling so good these last few weeks.

Q: Why do you think that is?

A: I . . . You know, I think it's the . . . these meetings and doing the trance at home. I've been really trying and practicing and everything seems so much better.

Q: In what ways?

A: Well, my baby, you know, I used to, well, not hate him, but I felt he tied me down. Sometimes I thought that he was a punishment.

Q: A punishment for what?

A: I don't know. For losing John, my husband, maybe. I know that doesn't make sense, but I felt that if I hadn't had the baby, John would have stayed with me.

Q: You felt that your husband left because of the baby?

A: Well, I know that's wrong now. I mean he would have split eventually anyway. But, I thought . . . I blamed it on the baby, if you see what I mean.

Q: But you don't now?

A: No, I . . . Well, how could I? I mean, he's just a baby. But before I started seeing you and thinking about myself, and what kind of person I am, I never realized about John and the baby.

Q: So you feel differently about your son now?

A: Yes. I . . . I love him. I mean, I don't think I did before. But now, I sit and watch him. I hug and kiss him more. And he's gotten so much quieter. Less demanding.

Q: Do you think that's because he can sense your change of attitude?

A: Well, I don't know. I'm not a doctor. He might.

Q: And you say there are other changes?

A: Well, you know we always talk about becoming the kind of person I want to be. Well, I feel like that is happening.

Q: How can you tell?

A: I'm more quieter now, less scared. When I feel nervous, I relax and think of my wrist and I quiet down, then I think about what is scaring me and I can usually figure it out—how to do it.

Q: Well, I am pleased to hear this and I am pleased that I . . . that you feel that I have been of some help to you.

A: Well, I am very grateful and I wanted to tell you.

Q: Thank you.

A: And, Doctor, I have been thinking all this week and I have decided that I am going to really try this time to remember, because I know there is something there and I am going to try not to fight it.

Q: Good! I am glad to hear you talk like this. To see you change from a frightened girl into a strong, confident young woman. And I am going to help you along, because today we are going to try something new to help you, if you agree.

A: What's that?

Q: I am going to inject you with sodium amytal. Remember how we talked about the guards your subconscious mind erects whenever we get close to the crucial times?

A: Uh-huh.

Q: Well, sodium amytal will put you into a half-
   sleeping state and reduce your conscious awareness. You will feel sort of drunk and this will make
   it more difficult for those guards to protect you
   from your own memories, just like you do things
   more slowly when you are drunk. Do you understand?

A: I think so.

Q: Do I have your permission to try the drug?

A: Yes, if you think it will help.

Q: Okay. Then we will induce hypnosis as we always
   have and I will fortify that with the amytal and
   then we will picture the movie screen again.

A: You know, at home, I try the screen. I picture it and
   I see so many crazy things. You know that's really
   bothering me. I don't want to make a mountain out
   of a molehill by imagining something that didn't
   happen.

Q: Well, we won't let that happen. The reason we
   use the screen is so you don't have to be involved.
   It takes you out of it. You're watching it, like you
   are watching a movie, and while you are involved
   a little bit, it isn't . . . you feel sorry for the heroine
   that the hero doesn't kiss her or anything, but it
   isn't quite the same. You can report what is happening, but you don't get a personal reaction like
   you would if you were thinking about something
   that happened in the past to you. You don't feel as
   threatened.

A: I can see that. I was just afraid of making things
   up, since it is like a movie.

Q: Well, you aren't, are you?

A: Oh, no!

Q: Okay, then. Now, let's get started. I think I will let you lie down on the couch this time, so make yourself comfortable.

A: Could I have a pillow for my head?

Q: Certainly. Get yourself in the most comfortable position you can. Now after you are in the trance and I give you the amytal, I will ask you to count backward. And when we get to a certain point I will know it has taken effect.

A: Will I be asleep?

Q: You will feel a little drunk and sleepy, but I don't expect that you will feel any more asleep than you were before. You might not remember as much afterward.

Now take a real deep breath and relax. Do that two or three times. Just let yourself relax and when you are ready, why, you can hold your hand up in front of your eyes.

(PAUSE)

Okay. In a second you will feel a little punchy. We will be injecting the medication and you will feel even more drowsy than you feel at the present time. As I inject the medication, I want you to start counting backward from 100. Now. 100.

A: 100.

Q: 99. That's it . . . That's just fine. And as you continue drifting deeper, go ahead counting.

A: 80, 79, 78, 77, 76, 75, 74, 73, 72, 71.

Q: That's good, and you can relax now and you can begin to remember important things. The events of that November evening in 1960 are becoming very clear. And as you begin to recall these events, feeling comfortable and very sure of yourself and relaxed, you find it easy to mention them, knowing that you can forget, you can remember or you can misremember as your personality needs require.

That's it. Let's talk about that evening as best you recall each episode. Pleasant feeling, isn't it? Just review that evening in your mind.

A: Have I finished counting my numbers?

Q: Yes. You can tell me what is in your mind.

A: I don't really have anything in my mind.

Q: Can you recall that evening? Anything about it, like being at Bob's Hamburgers?

A: Uh-huh.

Q: And you decided to go to Alice Fay's party.

A: I didn't, uh-uh.

Q: Huh?

A: I didn't.

Q: You didn't? Well, what did you do?

A: I had a shake. Billy decided to crash.

Q: I see. And then what?

A: I don't know.

Q: Didn't you go to the party?

A: Yes.

Q: This was at Alice Fay's, right?

A: Uh-huh.

Q: There was a fight at the party, wasn't there?

A: Yes.

Q: Who fought?

A: Billy and Bobby and Tommy Cooper and some boys I didn't know.

Q: And Billy pulled a knife?

A: Yes.

Q: You remember that?

A: Yes.

Q: You can see that clearly on the screen?

A: I can see it.

Q: How is Billy when he leaves the party?

A: Angry.

Q: At Tommy Cooper?

A: At rich kids.

Q: Why rich kids?

A: He yelled at me.

Q: Who? Billy?

A: Uh-huh. It scared me.

Q: What did he say?

A: It was how he hated rich kids and they didn't have to work like him.

Q: He said that after you left the party?

A: Uh-huh.

Q: Good. You are really starting to remember. I am very proud of you. Now, where did you go from the party?

A: Uh, to the store.

Q: Where?

A: It's open at night. Billy swiped some wine.

Q: How much?

A: A couple of bottles. And there was some in the car already.

Q: What kind of wine?

A: Cheap stuff. It made me sick later. It was so sweet.

Q: Where did you drink the wine?

A: On some side street, I think. Maybe it was near a park or a schoolyard.

Q: A park or a schoolyard?

A: Well, there weren't houses around, you know. That's why we went there, so no one would see us.

Q: Where do you go after you drink the wine?

A: It's fuzzy. Home?

Q: Do you . . . ? Look at the screen, Esther. Do you see a drag race where someone forced your car to spin around?

A: Gee, there were a lot of drag races.

Q: In this one, you were riding with Billy and Bobby and somebody came along and caused your car to spin around. You are on Monroe Boulevard.

A: Uh-huh.

Q: Do you recall that?

A: Billy got mad.

Q: Why did Billy get mad?

A: Huh?

Q: Why is Billy mad?

A: I don't know.

Q: What does Billy do now that he is mad?

A: He followed the car.

Q: This is Richie's car?

A: I didn't say that.

Q: Do you remember?

A: No.

Q: But you know what Richie's car looks like? You can see it on the screen?

A: Yes.

Q: Could the car that forced you off of the road have been Richie's?

A: I'm not sure.

Q: Is it possible?

A: It's possible.

Q: Okay, so Billy followed the car. Where does he go?

A: I guess I went home.

Q: You think you went home?

A: Uh-huh.

Q: In Billy's car?

A: I don't remember.

Q: All right. You think a little deeper. You will remember. You are there. You were there. You can remember. You are in Billy's car. You are on Monroe. You start driving. Do you go into the park?

A: Maybe.

Q: Okay. And you are driving up a hill. Do you go past a place with a fireplace and picnic benches?

A: Uh-huh.

Q: Did the other car go past there?

A: I don't know.

Q: But you were following them?

A: Uh-huh.

Q: Who else is with you in the car?

A: Bobby.

Q. Anyone else?

A: Maybe Roger.

Q: Roger Hessey?

A: Uh-huh.

Q: Didn't you tell us he left shortly after you arrived at Alice Fay's?

A: I guess so.

Q: So he couldn't have been in the car. Look on the screen. Let your mind review that evening. Picture inside Billy's car. Do you see it?

A: Yes.

Q: Okay. Is Roger there—in the park?

A: No.

Q: Okay. Now, you and Billy and Bobby are in Billy's car and you are following the other car and you go past the place in the park with the fireplace and the picnic benches. Now what happens? Tell me what happens, Esther. You are past the place with the fireplace. Tell me what happens. Billy is mad. You are following that car. It is at night. What happens?

A: I saw it.

Q: You saw it?

A: I saw the car.

Q: Okay. What happens after you see it?

A: Didn't I tell you something?

Q: Yes, you have. You have been telling me.

A: I am waking up.

Q: Yes, I know you are.

A: I thought I was sleeping.

Q: You were sleeping a bit. Now you told me you were following the car and you went past this place in Lookout Park with a fireplace and benches and you saw the car.

A: Did I say that?

Q: Yes, you did, Esther. This car ran you off the road and Billy got mad. He was mad before, after the fight.

A: Did I say that?

Q: Yes, Esther. I can play the tape back if you wish.

A: I think I need some more of that stuff.

Q: You think you need more sodium amytal?

A: Yeah. Didn't I tell you something when I had it?

Q: Yes. You told me a lot of interesting things. But we didn't get far enough.

A: Okay. Well, give me some more.

Q: That's it. It is pleasant. Now you can just go ahead. We can protect you here. Nothing can happen to you, if you tell what happened. The truth.

A: Tell me what I said.

Q: You said that this car forced you off the road and Billy chased it into the park. Then you saw the car after a place with a fireplace and benches in the park.

A: Gee, I said that? Doctor, I know I am drowsy, but could you give me some more?

Q: I just did.

A: Oh. I'm sorry. I don't remember what I was talking about.

Q: You were with Billy and Bobby in the car.

A: I'm supposed to say Billy?

Q: You are supposed to say Billy.

A: Uh-huh.

Q: Well, you are supposed to say what actually happens.

A: Right.

Q: Were Billy and Bobby there?

A: Uh-huh. I'm telling you the truth.

Q: Billy and Bobby were with you?

A: (Coughing)

Q: Why don't you go ahead and clear your throat.

A: Could I have some water?

Q: Here. Does my holding the microphone bother you?

A: No.

Q: You weren't telling us a story, were you, when you told us that Bobby and Billy were with you?

A: Uh-uh. Is that a lie detector?

Q: What?

A: A lie detector?

Q: No, it's not a lie detector.

A: When you asked who was in the car and I said Billy and Bobby, were you checking me with a lie detector?

Q: No. This is a microphone with a tape recorder.

A: Roger wasn't with us. I only said he was because I wasn't sure at first.

Q: Okay. Esther, who was driving? When you were in the park, was it Billy or Bobby?

A: Uh.

Q: Can you see who is driving?

A: I am trying to think of what you've told me.

Q: I am interested in what you can remember, Esther. Remember, now, you want to remember this so you can get it off your mind.

A: Uh-huh. I am really trying. I just don't want to sound like a liar.

Q: Are you saying that you think you told me something before and you aren't sure it is the truth?

A: No, it's just that you said I told you something, but I can't remember it and I don't want you to think I am lying.

Q: Let me worry about that and you worry about what you can remember. Is that all right?

A: I am trying to remember.

Q: Okay, can you remember telling us that you went to a grocery store after the party?

A: Uh-huh.

Q: Okay. Now tell me where you went from the grocery store again.

A: We drank the wine.

Q: Right. Now, where did you go from there?

A: I can't remember.

Q: You were able to tell me before. Can't you re-member what you said before?

A: I remember we went home.

Q: Do you recall telling me about Monroe Boule-vard and Lookout Park?

A: Uh-uh. I probably lied.

Q: You probably lied to me?

A: Could I have lied about what I said?

Q: I doubt it.

A: We went to the grocery and drank the wine, but I can't remember anything except we went home.

Q: Are you pretty much awake now?

A: I think so.

Q: Can you say "Around the rugged rock the ragged rascal ran"?

A: Around the rugged rock the ragged rascal ran.

Q: I guess you are awake. You shouldn't be able to say that. I think we'll stop for the day.

Eddie Toller checked the address, then began climbing a flight of rickety wooden stairs that ran along the outside of a weatherbeaten wood-frame two-family dwelling. When he reached the porch on the second floor, he knocked on the screen door. The conversation inside stopped at the sound of his rapping. He heard footsteps and the door opened a crack, releasing the pungent odor of marijuana into the night air.

"Is Gary in?" Eddie asked the young girl who stared through the crack. The girl looked him over. His age had aroused her suspicions.

"I'm Eddie Toller. He's expecting me."

The girl said, "Oh, yeah," and admitted him. The hallway was lit by candles, but Eddie could see that it was the girl's clothes that were young and he revised his age estimate up ten years. She introduced herself as Laura Kinnick, Gary's girlfriend, and led him through a veil of beads into a living room decorated in Early American Guru. Gary, who was seated on a large pillow covered with an Indian fabric, rose from his lotus position and introduced Eddie to the other couples in the room. Both of the men had long hair and Eddie disliked them immediately. They looked dirty and he bet they would smell, if he could smell them over the scent of the dope.

"How you doin', man?" Gary asked later, when they were off together in the kitchen. Eddie had passed on the joint, raising eyebrows among Gary's friends, and had asked for a beer. He had followed Gary into the kitchen while he broke open a six-pack.

"Not so good, Gary. That's why I wanted to see you tonight."

"What happened?"

"Ah, it's those sons of bitches at Parole. They busted Carl, the guy who owns the Satin Slipper. He was selling dope outta the place. I was arrested too, but I had nothing to do with it, so they dropped the charges, only someone told my P.O. and he said I had to quit. He said he didn't want me working at a place like that. I told him I was legit and that I wouldn't be able to get another job this good with my record, but he wouldn't listen. So now I ain't got a job."

"Those fuckers," Gary said sympathetically, shaking his head.

"Yeah, well, what's done is done. Only I gotta figure a way to make some bread. Joyce is still working, but I ain't gonna live off her."

"I'd lend you some dough, if I could, Eddie, but I'm short myself."

"Hey, I ain't lookin' for no handout, Gary. I want to know more about the job you got planned."

"You want in?"

"If it's good. I want to hear about it first. I'm too old to go back to the joint. With my record, my next fall is gonna be long, hard time. So don't jack me around."

"I won't, Eddie. This is a sure thing and there's plenty of dough in it. I got it all worked out and I'm rushin' into nothin'."

"Okay. Lay it out for me."

"Laura works in the Cameron Street Medical Building. I drive her to work in the morning and I pick her up, so I been inside it a lot. I've been checkin' the offices and stores in the building. Laura has a master key that fits the outside door of her office and the pharmacy on the ground floor. That's what we're gonna hit."

"What's there?"

"Drugs, Eddie."

"I know that, but I don't use drugs no more and I don't have the connections to push."

"I got the connection and we don't have to push, either. This guy will pay top dollar on delivery."

"Who is this guy?"

"Someone I met in the joint. He's big, Eddie. He knows all the right people."

"How do you know this guy ain't feeding you a line?"

"Because I dealt with him before."

Eddie jerked his head toward the living room.

"What about her?"

"Laura? She don't know nothin'. I took her keys one weekend and had duplicates made. She don't even suspect I got them."

"I don't know."

"Hey, what's to know? It's a cinch. We got the keys to the castle. They'll never know what happened."

"I want to think it over and I want to see the lay-out myself."

"Sure, Eddie. I ain't rushin' you. What say we go over the place on Tuesday?"

"Okay. Tuesday. But I have to be sure. You see my position, at my age. I can't afford to foul up again."

"I'm very proud of you," Roy whispered in Esther's ear. She purred and kissed him. She was so content. She only wished that she could help him by remembering everything he wanted her to remember.

It was four-thirty. They would have to get dressed soon and go see Dr. Hollander. She wished she could tell the doctor the secret she shared with Roy, but Roy said that she mustn't tell anyone.

She wished Roy would stay with her more, too. He told her that it was only safe before and after the sessions. He said how it would be misconstrued if anyone found out about them later, when there was a trial. She knew he was right, but the few hours they had together weren't enough when you spent every waking minute thinking about someone.

Roy walked into the bathroom to shower. The sitter would arrive soon and she had to tidy up. She felt very good today. Very positive. She was sure that she would remember today. She had to. For Roy. He had told her that the barriers were almost down. She could sense that too. She had been experiencing strange dreams recently.

But what if she was only imagining? She felt suddenly depressed. She had liked Bobby a lot once. She didn't want to hurt him. If it wasn't true, but she said it was . . . She didn't want to think about it. It was true. Roy had said it was. She shut the bad thoughts out of her mind.

TAPE # 10

ESTHER PEGALOSI: I remember a car race.

ROY SHINDLER: Okay. Was there anything special about the car you had the race with?

A: They made us spin around.

DR. HOLLANDER: Very good! You see, your memory is coming back bit by bit. Can you describe the other car?

A: No. Just that it was bright.

Q: Bright?

A: There was fire on it.

Q: It was on fire?

A: I . . . I know what the car is supposed to look like, but I don't want to be biased.

Q: I don't want you to be biased. I want you to tell me what you remember. Do you remember telling us that today you would tell us the truth?

A: Uh-huh.

Q: Good. Now why do you say there was fire on the car? Was there a decal there? Do you mean the flames were painted on?

A: I know what's supposed to be there and I know how it looks and it's awfully hard not to put it there in my head.

Q: I don't want you to do that.

A: I really can't remember. It seemed like fire. I don't like going that fast. I probably didn't look, 'cause I would be scared.

Q: Okay, after the drag race, then what?

A: They got mad.

Q: Who got mad?

A: Billy. He wanted to catch them. He knew the girl.

Q: Billy knew the girl?

A: Oh . . .

Q: Would you speak up? I can't hear you.

A: It did happen on the same night.

Q: What happened?

A: I don't feel so good.

Q: You were doing fine. Who was the girl, Esther?

(Sobbing)

Q: Relax now. Take my handkerchief. You're doing fine. Are you okay? Have some water. Okay. Take a deep breath. Now, tell me. Tell Roy. Who was the girl?

A: Can I whisper?

Q: No, Esther. Today is truth day. Today you must be the strong, confident woman that Roy and I know you've become. Do you want to tell us?

A: (Sobbing) Could I . . . ?

Q: No, Esther. Just answer my question if you want to help me. Who was the girl?

A: Elaine Murray. Billy saw her and he said it.

Q: Okay. It's all right. Then, Billy got mad?

A: Yes.

Q: What did he do?

A: They were cussing and they couldn't see the car for a while.

Q: Did they chase after it?

A: Uh-huh. But they couldn't find it.

Q: Where did they go?

A: Into Lookout Park.

Q: You went into the park?

A: It seems like it. It couldn't be my imagination.

Q: No. You're doing fine. Your memory is working better than it ever has. What happened next?

A: We . . . I saw the car.

Q: The car you were dragging with?

A: Are you sure that I'm not just remembering this because I want to get it over with and I'm not really remembering it?

Q: I think you are remembering it because you have come to the point where you can. I know you want to get it over with.

A: Is it all right if I smoke?

Q: No. In a few minutes I will let you smoke. Now, you saw the car, and then what?

A: I'll tell you if I can remember. But I'm kind of blank.

Q: You're doing fine. Let's see how good your memory is.

A: It's so hard because I know what they did. I know what I'm supposed to say and I want to make sure that I remember and I'm not just saying it . . . Something that I know.

Q: What you are supposed to say may not be true. I want you to remember what you remember.

A: Okay. We are driving in the park. You see, there are curves out there. Real sharp and woods all around. And Billy was mad, so we were going real fast and dust was just flying. I don't know where we went. We drove for a long time. Then we went back and forth over the same area and we passed a place with a fireplace and some benches and then there was a small road off of that and when we went by the road I saw something.

Q: What did you see?

A: I don't remember . . . I don't like to remember, really.

Q: I know you don't like to remember.

A: I really can't . . .

Q: Did anything happen in the park?

A: Uh-huh.

Q: What was it . . . ? You are shaking your head. What happened?

A: I didn't see it.

Q: What didn't you see?

A: I ran.

Q: What did you run from?

A: I . . .

Q: It's okay. Here's a tissue. We will protect you. You're safe here.

A: I . . .

Q: Take a deep breath. Everything is fine.

A: (Crying)

Q: What made you run?

A: The murder.

Q: I couldn't hear you.

A: The murderer.

Q: You saw the murder?

A: They were yelling.

Q: Who?

A: Everyone. They were going to beat him up.

Q: Beat who?

A: The boy from the other car.

Q: Why didn't he drive away?

A: Because he had been insulted.

Q: He had been insulted?

A: His girlfriend had.

Q: What did they say?

A: Billy said nasty things.

Q: What did Billy say? Did he say prostitute? Do
   you recall?

A: And the boy said to shut up.

Q: The boy told Billy to shut up?

A: I can't tell you whether it's really what's in my
   head.

Q: You keep on because your memory is telling
   you fine. We are very proud of you. You are a fine,
   strong woman.

A: So they started fighting.

Q: How did it start? The fight?

A: Billy said something and he said that is no way to
   talk about a lady. To insult her. And he was going
   to make him take it back and Billy socked him.

Q: Billy socked him?

A: And they were hitting him and they went and got
   the girl.

Q: Where was the girl?

A: In the car.

Q: What did you do?

A: I don't feel well. Can we stop now?

Q: No, Esther. We will stop in a little bit.

A: I don't remember.

Q: You do remember. We are so proud of you, Esther.

A: He had no face.

Q: Who?

A: Richie.

Q: Richie had no . . . ? Take it easy. Do you want a handkerchief?

(Sobbing)

A: I ran. (Crying)

Q: Did you run when you saw Richie's face? You are shaking your head yes. Where was the girl?

A: They were dragging her into the grass. That's all I know. I ran away.

Q: Did you fall while you were running?

A: Uh-huh.

Q: While you were running, did you drop anything or lose anything?

A: My purse. My glasses fell out.

Q: After you fell and got up, where did you run?

A: Down to the road.

Q: Did you . . . were you confronted by dogs?

A: I got in the yard and they chased . . . chased me. I didn't see them at first, then they jumped at me.

Q: How did you get away?

A: They were tied. On a leash.

Q: Okay, so you got away from the dogs. Then where did you go?

A: Onto the road. I started to walk home.

Q: How did you get home?

A: I am too wide awake with this stuff now. I can't remember what I'm supposed to say.

Q: I don't want what you are supposed to say. I want what you remember.

A: 'Cause I know what I'm supposed to say and, well, I am telling you the truth. I am not making it up.

Q: I know, Esther. Shut your eyes for a minute. Just relax. In a minute I will give you some more medicine.

DR. HOLLANDER: How did you get home?

A: Bobby and Billy and . . . They stopped the car.

Q: They got you in a car?

A: I was walking on the street and they stopped. They came up behind me and said to get in.

Q: Who was driving?

A: Bobby, I think.

Q: Where was Billy?

A: In the back, holding a girl.

Q: Elaine?

A: Yes.

Q: Was she all right?

A: She wasn't dead. She was all right.

Q: How did you know?

A: She was sitting up and looking at me, but he was holding her.

Q: How did he hold her?

A: By her arms and around her shoulders. She looked asleep almost.

Q: Dazed?

A: Yes.

Q: Where did they go with her?

A: I don't know. They took me home. They dumped me off in the middle of the street and drove away.

Q: They didn't say anything to you?

A: No. Maybe that's why I didn't remember it the next day when I saw it in the papers.

Q: What do you mean?

A: I saw about Richie being killed, but I never saw the boy close, so I decided it couldn't have been and I forgot about it. I was pretty drunk, too.

Q: Why are you crying?

A: I am tired.

Q: Do you think that what we talked about was all you can remember?

A: I don't know.

Q: But you remember seeing the boy murdered?

A: No, I didn't see that.

Q: Didn't you say that you saw the fight?

A: No, no, I didn't know there was a murder, until later. I didn't know what happened. I thought they beat him up like they usually did.

Q: Didn't you say you saw Richie's face?

A: I saw it later.

Q: Did they ever talk to you, Bobby and Billy, after that? Threaten you?

A: Well, you know, you hung together. You didn't tell. And then, I didn't want to go to a home. You know, there was that robbery thing at the miniature golf and if I got in trouble again the judge said he would have to send me to a home.

Q: After that night did you ever see Elaine Murray again?

A: No. I hardly saw Billy or Bobby, either.

Q: Not even in school?

A: They had a car accident in . . . right after New Years and they was in the hospital. Then I stopped hanging around with the Cobras and stayed home more. They almost didn't graduate, I remember. But I guess the school just wanted to get rid of them.

ROY SHINDLER: When did you run away?

A: From the hill?

Q: Yes.

A: I think when they were kicking the boy and then they ran after the girl. It's confused in my mind, because it was so fast.

DR. HOLLANDER: You are remembering very well today.

A: But I didn't remember before. Honest I didn't.

Q: I am sure you didn't.

A: Why? (Crying)

Q: Why couldn't you remember?

A: Did I do something wrong? I didn't know she was going to get in trouble.

Q: I am sure you didn't.

A: I knew there was a fight, but I didn't think it was possible there would be a murder and . . . and the other thing.

Q: What would you have done if you had known that they were going to rape and murder her?

A: I would have stopped them.

Q: How?

A: Any way. They wouldn't have done nothing . . .
   (Crying).

Q: Go ahead and cry.

A: I don't think . . . I don't think they intended to. I
   don't think they did it.

Q: You can't picture them doing it? Not Bobby?

A: He was a tough little shit, but . . .

Q: Not Billy?

(PAUSE)

A: Maybe. I don't know. Billy loved to fight. Maybe
   he went too far without realizing it. I remember
   him beating people more than once.

Q: What was the last thing you remember seeing on
   the hill?

A: I think they were holding the boy by the car. Like
   they were frisking him.

Q: Like they were frisking him?

A: I think they were going to rob him. Maybe they
   figured this boy would be wealthy if he dated this
   girl.

Q: Did they talk about the girl being wealthy?

A: I don't think so. I'm just guessing now.

Q: Okay. Well, we don't want you to guess. Just say
   what you know. Now, who got out of the car first
   on the hill?

A: Billy and the boy was out, too.

Q: When they were fighting, where was the girl?

A: I don't know. In the car I guess.

Q: Did she scream?

A: I don't remember.

Q: Did Billy or Bobby have anything in their hand when they got out of the car?

A: I don't remember.

Q: Did you see either of them hit the boy over the head?

A: No.

Q: Did they get Richie down on the ground?

A: I didn't see that.

ROY SHINDLER: Esther, when you got back into the car, when they picked you up, the girl was in the back seat with Billy?

A: Yes.

Q: And he was holding her around the arms and shoulders?

A: Uh-huh.

Q: Did he have anything around her neck?

A: No.

Q: No rope or something like that.

A: It was real dark in the car and I didn't see too good. I only looked at her for a minute and I was drunk and not feeling so good from the running and being scared by the dogs.

Q: Where did you drive to then?

A: They drove me home.

Q: Did she try to get out of the car or struggle?

A: No.

Q: She didn't try to get out?

A: Wait a minute. How many times have I lied to you about this? I don't want to . . .

Q: You aren't lying now. Did they have a hand over her mouth?

A: They could have.

DR. HOLLANDER: Do you remember how the girl was reacting to this?

A: She was quiet, dazed.

Q: Did she cry?

A: I didn't look at her that long, you know. She could have been crying, but that may not be true.

Q: Tell us what you remember and don't worry about what's true. What you remember will be true.

8

"Mr. Boggs, are you a homosexual?"

"Objection, Your Honor."

Harry Jamison was on his feet shouting before the last words of the question had carried across the courtroom to the frightened little man in the witness box. Judge Jacob Samuels tried to hide his displeasure with Philip Heider, but the jury could not help but notice the scathing look he flashed at the prosecutor as soon as the question was asked.

Heider, although he did not show it, was delighted with Jamison's reaction. He had planned on it. Now, no matter how the judge ruled on the propriety of his question, the seeds of doubt were sown.

"I will see you gentlemen in chambers," Samuels said as he gathered his black robes around him and disappeared through the door behind his dais.

Harry Jamison waddled after him, his enormous belly shifting with each step. He was a tragicomic figure made more for vaudeville than the courtroom and he heightened this impression by tenting his body in clashing checks and stripes.

Philip Heider, in contrast, was streamlined. He

looked every bit the bright young man. Those who
knew him well, knew that he was cold, ruthless and
pragmatic. Those who saw him in court were usually fooled by the red hair and freckles that gave him
a 'Tom Sawyerish look.

Judge Samuels was seated behind his desk when
Heider and Jamison entered his wood-paneled office.
He had been expecting Heider's question for the
past half hour: ever since Jamison had asked his own
incredibly stupid questions on direct examination of
the defendant, Lowell Boggs. Even so, he found the
whole line of questioning distasteful and he knew
that he had to decide if it was sufficiently prejudicial
to compel his declaring the four-day murder case a
mistrial or sufficiently relevant to permit inquiry.

Samuels looked at the two attorneys with disgust.
Jamison was an incompetent joke. He had not done
one thing right since the case started. It was a sorry
system that even permitted someone like Jamison to
practice.

And Heider . . . That was a different matter. He
was every inch Stewart Heider's son. Vicious, unprin-
cipled. He could go on, but did not. Stewart Heider
had made his money the hard way. He tried to buy
respectability by sending his son to the best schools.
But there was always heredity. The same criminal
streak that was rumored to be behind the money
Heider had made in lumber manifested itself in the
way Philip Heider prosecuted his cases.

The problem was that, like the father, the son
never quite crossed the border of unethical behavior.
And, like the father, Samuels had to admit grudgingly, the son was good—very good. Samuels had

seen a great many lawyers during his seventeen years on the bench and, despite the fact that Heider was relatively inexperienced, having practiced law with the district attorney's office for only two years, he was one of the best the judge had ever seen.

"I want a mistrial. I warned the Court that Mr. Heider would try to go into this. I see no way that Mr. Boggs can get a fair trial, now that Mr. Heider has engaged in this disgusting piece of theatrics."

"Mr. Heider?" the judge asked.

"Your Honor, this goes directly to motive. It is the State's position that Boggs is a homosexual and that he killed Bobby Washington during a lover's quarrel. The ferocity with which Mr. Washington was stabbed indicates great passion on the part of the killer."

"But there is no evidence that Mr. Boggs is a homosexual. It's all speculation," Jamison whined. "He has to produce evidence if he is going to drag in this dirt and he didn't during the State's case."

"Yes, Mr. Heider, I made a ruling on that before we started this trial. I ruled that we were not going into this area without proof."

"I know that, Your Honor, and I did stay away from it, but Mr. Jamison opened the door during his examination of Mr. Boggs when he tried to raise as a defense that Washington was a homosexual who had accosted Mr. Boggs and that Boggs stabbed him in self-defense after wresting the knife from Washington.

"Mr. Jamison went into the sex angle first and I think I have a right to cross-exam on his defense."

As Heider spoke, he watched the expression on

Jamison's face as the older attorney realized what he had done. A quick grin flashed across his face as he savored his moment. Judge Samuels caught the look of triumph and stifled a feeling of anger. Heider was a prick. He had no concept of professional responsibility.

Jamison was babbling now. Grasping at straws, as he tried to explain what he had and had not intended by his question. Samuels let him have his say, because he knew how he would have to rule and he wanted to make sure that Jamison had every chance to make his record.

"I am afraid Mr. Heider is right, Harry. I was astonished when you asked those questions, especially after our discussion in chambers. But you did and I am going to have to allow Mr. Heider to continue along this line for a while."

"I see," Jamison said weakly. He was crushed and he seemed to sag as he lifted himself from his chair and headed back to the courtroom.

Samuels stopped Heider before he could leave the chambers.

"This is a cheap shot, Mr. Heider, and I am watching you at each step. If you don't tie this in, or if you push this too far, I will give Mr. Jamison his mistrial."

"I understand, Your Honor," Heider replied politely. He had won and there was no profit in gloating. He cast a quick glance at Jamison as he returned to his seat. That fat slob was so stupid he couldn't tie his shoelaces without a blueprint, he thought. A good attorney could have made a real fight out of this case. Still, Heider was not one to look a gift horse in the mouth. The win would not hurt his reputation and he would not mind seeing that simpering little fag behind bars anyway. He hated weakness and Boggs was weak. He had sensed it during the trial and on each occasion he had met the defendant. Boggs was a worm, begging the jury for a second chance. And he might have gotten it, Heider mused, if it had not been for the incompetence of his counsel. The jury might have acquitted a sixty-seven-year-old white bookkeeper with no prior record for the murder of a black junkie. But they would never acquit a queer for the murder of his lover. Heider leaned back in his chair and looked across the courtroom at Boggs. Then he glanced at his note pad and asked his next question.

Five hours later Heider strode through the gate next to Fanny Maser's desk and headed for the interior of the district attorney's office with two reporters in tow. Heider was grinning.

"Guilty?" asked a young D.A. who was standing in the corridor as Heider's flying wedge swept by.

"What else?" Heider said and the reporters laughed. They liked Heider. He was colorful and always willing to talk to the press.

"Mr. Heider," Fanny yelled after him, "Mr. Holman wants to see you. He said it was important."

Heider wondered what the D.A. wanted to see him about. Besides being his boss, Herb Holman was an old family friend who owed his present position, in large part, to Stewart Heider's financial and political support.

Heider excused himself and the reporters settled at a small table to jot down notes for their story. Holman's private office was isolated at the far end of the District Attorney's Office. Heider had to pass by several of his colleagues on his way, but few offered congratulations or even bothered to ask about the Boggs verdict. Heider was not well liked by the other deputies. Their attitude stemmed in part from the obvious favoritism shown him by Holman and partly from Heider's superior attitude.

Herb Holman was a little man with a ruddy complexion. He smiled when Phil entered and he extended his hand.

"Very well done. Judge Samuels's clerk called me."

Heider shrugged and grinned.

"With Jamison on the other side, it was like having an assistant."

Holman laughed and they both sat down.

"Phil, are you still serious about trying for state representative next year?"

"Dad and I have talked it over a few times," Heider answered, puzzled by the question. "He thinks Faulk can be had and I agree."

"Okay. Well, something has come up that may help you get the nomination. How well do you remember the Murray-Walters murder case?"

" 'Murray-Walters'? Isn't that the rape-murder in Lookout Park that happened about five or six years ago?"

"Right."

"I remember a little about it. I was in college at the time and I remember it even made the eastern papers."

"I received a call from a Portsmouth detective named Roy Shindler this afternoon. Do you know Shindler?"

"Sure. He's worked on a couple of my cases. Very sharp."

"Yes, I agree. Shindler thinks he has enough to get an indictment in Murray-Walters. I want you to talk to him. If you agree, take it to Grand Jury and all the way after that."

Heider could hear his heart beat. "Murray-Walters" was a household name in Portsmouth. Parents still used it as a bugaboo to keep their teenage children out of Lookout Park at night. Trying the case would mean front-page headlines for months. Assuming that he could get an indictment within a month, and that the trial started within three months, the publicity could carry him right up to the time for filing.

Holman smiled.

"I thought this would interest you. Hell, if I thought I was going to have any opposition next fall, I would have taken the case myself. Shindler will be expecting your call. Treat this one with kid gloves. And, Phil, no leaks."

"I read you."

"Good boy."

Heider was thinking and listening while Shindler talked and drove. The whole thing was fantastic. The problems involved . . . How do you make a jury believe in a witness who did not believe that she was a witness until six years after the crime? The papers would call it trial by voodoo. Still, Shindler was no wild-eyed kid. He was steady, intelligent, not a man to make rash decisions. Everything depended on the girl. That was why he had insisted that Shindler take him to see her. If he did not believe her, the jury would not believe her.

"Dr. Hollander is certain that she's telling the truth?"

"Oh, absolutely. We've been over her story dozens of times."

"And she has an independent recollection now?"

"Yes."

"Independent of the tapes? She doesn't have to listen to the tapes?"

"No. She can tell it from memory now. She remembers it all. Dr. Hollander says that the blocks were removed when she made the breakthrough under the drug."

"Because, if she can't remember it without the tapes, it will look like a put-up job."

"No, this is the real thing. We have other witnesses that corroborate her story. The guy who saw the drag race and the woman who owns the dogs. There are the people at the party who saw Billy Coolidge with the knife."

Heider studied the passing scenery. Shindler reminded himself not to talk too much. It was hard. He was so high. He had worked so long and so hard on this case that had seemed so hopeless and now to see the end in sight . . . he felt an awful calm in his body and a terrible elation of the spirit, as if only part of him was tied to the earth, the other part soaring, unstoppable.

Esther's apartment was just ahead. He had called

her after Heider's call to tell her that they were coming over. He had not spoken to her in two weeks and she sounded like a puppy, overjoyed to hear from him, anxious to know why he had not called. When he told her that he was bringing the district attorney with him, she had become frightened, but he had soothed her by promising to visit her that evening.

"We're here," Shindler said, edging the car into the curb.

"Did you bring the flashlight?" Eddie asked.

"Yeah. Here," Gary said, handing it to Toller. "Don't be so nervous, will ya? It's startin' to get to me."

"I ain't nervous. I just wanted to make sure we had everything."

"Well, I had it."

Eddie zipped up his jacket and turned his collar up to obscure his face. There weren't supposed to be any security guards in the place, but he wasn't taking any chances.

Gary had parked in the rear of the Cameron Street Medical Building. Eddie looked at his watch for the third time in the last two minutes and licked his lips nervously. It was three in the morning and there was no moon. They had cruised the street for a few nights running to check the area for police patrols. The Medical Building was located in a quiet residential area and there was no one about at this hour of the morning.

Gary slipped on his gloves and grabbed the pillow cases they had brought along for the drugs. The rear parking lot was deserted and the car was parked next to the rear door. The back of the building was dark, but Eddie had misgivings, because the pharmacy, which fronted the street, was lit. He had remarked on this to Gary, but Barrick had explained that the room where the drugs were kept was in the rear of the pharmacy and was difficult to see from the street.

Gary took the duplicate keys from his pocket and tested one in the rear door. The door opened easily and Gary smiled as he preceded Eddie into the dark interior of the empty building.

"This is gonna be cake, Eddie," he whispered.

Eddie looked around cautiously. It was bad luck to talk about how easy a job was going to be. Something about this one had made him nervous from the start.

The corridor ended and Gary turned to the right. Eddie could see the street through the glass front door. Gary made a small jog to the left and stopped in front of a heavy, solid wooden door. While Gary tried the keys in the lock, Eddie flashed his light nervously up and down the corridor. He heard Gary curse and he turned to see what was the matter.

"The goddamn key don't fit."

"What?"

"It don't work."

"Let me try." He handed Gary the flashlight and tried both keys in the lock. Neither worked.

"What is this?" Eddie asked, a tinge of panic in his voice.

"I don't know. It was supposed to open the door to the pharmacy."

"What do you mean, supposed to? Didn't you try it out?"

"Jesus, Eddie, someone mightta seen me."

"Oh, shit. You mean you . . . Why did you think it would open the goddamn door?"

"I heard Laura say once that this one opened the street door and this one opened all the offices."

"Oh, no. She probably meant her offices, you dumb . . ."

Gary held up his hand for silence.

"Don't get excited, Eddie. This ain't no big thing. I got this place all cased. I know where they keep a pry bar. It'll just mean some extra work, is all. Just wait here."

Eddie started to say something, but Gary was gone, down the hall and up a flight of stairs by the sound of the echoes. Eddie knew he should get out now. The vibes were bad. He thought he heard a noise in the darkness and turned out the flashlight and tried to squeeze into a corner near the door.

"Turn on the goddamn flash, Eddie, it's me," Gary whispered. He had returned with his arms loaded with tools. He dumped them in front of the door and selected a pry bar. Eddie sat on the floor with his back to the wall and told himself "I told you so" over and over while Gary worked on the door. There was grunting and puffing for a few minutes, then Gary signaled him and the door swung open. Gary crouched down and Eddie followed him in.

He straightened up for a second, then realized the reason for Gary's crouch. The inside of the pharmacy was as bright as day and the front of the pharmacy was all glass. If they straightened up, anyone outside could see them easily.

Gary moved behind some couches to a door in the side of a small room. The lower half of the room was opaque, but the top half was glass. The walls of the room were lined with shelves stocked with drugs. There was a refrigerator in the back.

"Let's start movin'," Gary said as he straightened up and began shoving drugs into one of the pillow cases.

"Wait a minute," Eddie said. "What is this stuff? This stuff ain't worth anything."

"Sure it is," Gary said, moving to the next shelf.

While Gary rummaged through the shelves, Eddie picked up a few boxes and bottles and looked at them. They were pain killers, tranquilizers, cough syrups. No narcotics.

"This guy is gonna pay you for this shit?" Eddie asked unbelievingly.

"Yeah. Sure. Look, Eddie, stop talkin' and get movin'."

"Jesus, Gary. This is worthless."

Gary threw down the pillow case he was holding in a rage.

"Shut up, shut up," he yelled. "You done nothin' but complain since we left tonight. I asked you along because of all that talk in the joint on how you are this big-time burglar. You ain't shit, Eddie. Now get these fuckin' pillow cases full or . . ."

Gary froze and his eyes bugged out. Eddie whirled around and heard Gary make for the rear door. He headed after him. There were two cops staring at them through the front window.

Eddie could only think of the car. He dashed around a corner and realized that he had lost Gary. Well, fuck him. He wouldn't be in this mess if it wasn't for that dumb . . .

He skidded to a halt at a dead end. Damn. He couldn't remember where the back corridor was. He raced around another corner and spotted the rear door. He could hear footsteps behind him. The cops were in the building. He dashed for the door and there was a policeman suddenly framed in it, gun pointed at him in a classic pistol range pose. The footsteps behind were gaining. "Freeze, you fucker," the policeman said through the glass. Eddie sank to the floor and clasped his hands behind his head.

Norman Walters watched his office door remove Shindler from view and wished that the man could be made to vanish that easily.

"Hold my calls," he said into his intercom. He felt very old and very tired. He wanted to close his eyes and go to sleep for a long time, but he knew that, instead, he would have to call on emotional reserves, which had grown smaller and smaller since his son's death and go home to tell Carla.

Carla. To tell her. He felt drained by the thought of it. In the six months following Richie's death he had watched her grow old. The spark that seemed to keep her eternally youthful had been extinguished by Shindler's visit. She had recovered, of course. Time heals, etc. But never fully recovered. She was quieter now. More tired.

He had changed too. A lot of the self-confidence

had gone out of his grip. The things he used to care about so much, his law practice, his cars, his golf game, didn't interest him as much. There was a dimension missing from both their lives.

Still, they had coped and the intervening years had helped to dull the memory of the healthy, loving boy who had been his son. Until now. Until Shindler had made him feel the pain again, just as strongly as he had felt it that first time. And soon—when he could muster the courage—he would have to go home and make Carla feel that same pain.

Detective Avritt slammed the car door on the driver's side and Shindler glanced over at the marked patrol car that had followed them from the courthouse. Heider had called him as soon as the Grand Jury had returned the indictments and he had rushed to the courthouse to get a judge to sign the warrants. On the way he had remembered the shame and frustration he had felt when he was relieved of the case. No one in the department knew about his weekly visits to Dr. Hollander. His investigation had been carried out on his own time. When he had the evidence he needed, he had taken it to the captain. He still savored the apology the captain had made when he returned the case to him.

After securing the warrants, he had driven to Norman Walters's office. He had expected more of a reaction from Richie's father, yet he could understand the emotions the man must have experienced when he received the news that his son was finally to be avenged. Walters had been cool to him in recent years, but Shindler felt that this was a reaction to his failure to solve the case. All that would change now.

Shindler absent-mindedly touched the arrest warrant in his left inside jacket pocket and looked up at the third-floor apartment where Sarah Rhodes lived. His watch showed eleven-thirty. It was a warm, sunny day. The beginning of spring. In a half hour, police detectives carrying a similar warrant would arrive at the State Penitentiary.

The uniformed policemen were out of their car now and Shindler, followed by Avritt, entered the apartment building. The calm was still inside him. It was the feeling of victory, of satisfaction. He had known all along, from the first moment he had seen Billy Coolidge. He thought of the long years when the case had floated in limbo. How often he had despaired of ever proving what he knew in his heart to be the truth.

Shindler paused in front of the apartment door and waited for the others. When they caught up, he rang the bell. A girl answered the door.

"Miss Rhodes?"

"Yes."

He showed her his badge. The girl looked confused. A man's voice called out from the other room and Shindler's pulse began to race.

"Is Bobby Coolidge here?" Shindler asked.

"Yes. Is anything wrong?"

Shindler smiled. He was the fisherman, the hunter. The prey was close, the line was taut.

"We have a matter to discuss with Mr. Coolidge. I wonder if you could ask him to step in here for a moment."

"Of course," she said, hesitantly. She disappeared into another room and the officers filled up the entry way.

Sarah returned. Shindler studied Bobby as he came down the hall. The D.A. haircut was gone and so was the arrogance. He had put on a little weight, but he was the same person Shindler had seen on the night in '61 when they had interrogated the brothers at the station house.

"Robert Coolidge?"

"Yes."

"I have a warrant for your arrest. You will have to accompany us to the station house."

Bobby smiled and looked back and forth between Shindler and the other policemen.

"Is this a joke?"

"I'm afraid not," Shindler said, handing Coolidge a copy of the warrant. Bobby did not look at it.

"Well, what's the charge?"

"Mr. Coolidge, I am here to arrest you for the murders of Elaine Murray and Richie Walters."

Part IV

Shadows

and

Whispers

1

Bobby was in the village again and he was afraid. There were no stars and, like a Hollywood backdrop, the solid black sky seemed to have no dimensions. Mist snaked its way around the circular, grass-thatched huts and shrouded the bodies, creating the eerie illusion that their moans and screams were emitted by the fog.

Bobby looked for the rest of his company, but he saw no one. There was a sound like a spider scuttling in the dark. Another, like Witch's Wind rustling the trees. Bobby clutched his carbine to his khaki-clad chest. He crept forward, bent at the waist, his eyes darting into the ebony mist.

The toe of his boot struck an object and he jumped back, startled. The fog cleared around a patch of ground. There was an old man lying in the dust. He was obviously dead, yet undead. His eyes pleaded with Coolidge and Bobby was seized by an unreasoning terror. He leaped on the old man, stabbing, screaming. His knife struck repeatedly and there was blood everywhere. Fountains of blood, spraying in red streams high into the night sky, as the ancient, sorrow-filled eyes pleaded with him and he listened to the cacophony of his own screams.

"Shut up, goddamn it!"

"What?"

There were several voices yelling for quiet. Bobby's eyes were wide open and he was in his cell and not in the jungle.

"I said, 'Shut up or I'll shut you up,'" someone yelled down the stone corridor.

Bobby mumbled an apology. He was soaking wet. He ran a hand across his face. His heartbeat was rapid. At least he was not in the jungle. He realized that the blanket was clutched around his throat. He released it. He swung his legs over the side of the bunk and let his head fall heavily into the palms of his hands. He could not relax. Deep breathing did not help. Inside was a vacuum. When they had read him the charge, everything that he had been or dreamed had evaporated.

He had been in isolation since his arrest yesterday afternoon. There had been no visitors, except the detectives, and he had refused to talk to them. He wondered why Sarah had not come to see him.

The jail cell was small. There was a bunk bed and a toilet, nothing else. He had enough room to pace, but he had no desire to move. For the last eighteen hours he had been like a rag doll. Every movement was an effort. It was as if his bones had become fluid and his heart a fluttering bird, afraid of the slightest whisper. When they had turned out the lights last evening, he had cried, not out of anger, but in desperation. He was lost.

He wanted someone to hold him and assure him that it was not all going to end. He wanted to bury his head in Sarah's lap and let her stroke his hair and talk about their future together. He wanted to believe.

After he sat on the edge of his bed for some time, his breathing became more regular and he felt very tired. He let himself fall back onto the bed and he covered himself with the blanket and shut his eyes. As soon as he did, a great fear gripped him. It was Vietnam again and even before that. To sleep was to dream. Oh, God, let me rest. Please! But there was a roaring in his head. Wakefulness was the dam that blocked the flood of dreams, sleep the lever that released it. There was no liquor here and no Sarah. Slowly he opened his eyes and stared at the ceiling. He could hear movement in the darkness. The scratching of rat claws on the dry cement floors.

There was an attractive young woman and a man who looked vaguely familiar seated in his waiting room when Mark Shaeffer arrived at his office.

"I don't know if you remember me," the man said. "I'm George Rasmussen. You helped me out of a scrape a few months ago."

The name brought back the event. This was the college student who had been arrested for drunk driving. He wondered if the girl was Rasmussen's wife. He had trouble taking his eyes off her. She was very tense and so was George. He ushered them into his private office.

"What's the problem?" he asked when they were seated. His eyes strayed again to the girl. She was wearing slacks and a tight sweater that showed off her figure. There was a disturbing quality about the girl that struck a sexual chord. She seemed soft and lost and her nearness awakened a desire to protect and to touch. His relations with Cindy had been sporadic lately and he found that he was becoming aroused.

"My boyfriend was arrested yesterday," she said. Her voice quivered when she spoke. Mark took out a yellow note pad and a pen.

"Is he in jail now?"

"Yes. They won't let us see him. I called George and he said that we should see you."

"Have you tried to bail him out?"

"There isn't any bail. We asked."

"There has to be bail. Who did you talk to?"

"I don't remember the name. He was a sergeant."

"Where? At the county jail?"

"Yes."

"He should know better than that."

Mark swiveled his chair and picked up the phone.

"What's your friend's name?"

"Bobby. Bobby Coolidge. It would be under Robert, I guess."

"They said there isn't any bail on a murder charge," George added.

Mark put down the phone. There was a tingling at the base of his scalp.

"Your friend is charged with murder?"

The girl looked nervously at George.

"That's what they told Sarah when they arrested him and that's what they told me when I called."

"I know he couldn't have done anything like that. We've been together almost constantly for the last few months. When could he have done it? It doesn't make sense."

"Who do they say he killed."

"Two people. A man and a woman. I don't remember the names."

The word "murder" has mystical qualities for those who practice criminal law. The sound of it causes a subtle change in the atmosphere. The level of electricity in the air rises. Mark forgot about the girl, for the moment, and dialed the county jail.

"My name is Mark Schaeffer. I understand you have a prisoner named Robert Coolidge in custody."

Sarah watched Mark as he spoke, looking for any sign. He seemed too young to entrust with Bobby's safety, yet George had spoken highly of him and he seemed intelligent and concerned. She heard him repeat a date, 1960, and saw a look of puzzlement cross Mark's face.

"Yes, I'll be out to see him at once. Can you arrange for me to use one of the private interview rooms, instead of the general attorney's room. Thanks, I appreciate that."

Mark hung up and swiveled around to face Sarah.

"Miss Rhodes, do the names Elaine Murray and Richie Walters mean anything to you?"

Sarah could sense a change in Mark. He was tense now too. She began to feel uncomfortable.

"I think those are the names of the people that the police say Bobby killed."

"Yes, but do you know who they are and when they were killed?"

Sarah looked at George. George looked puzzled, as if the names meant something to him, but he could not recall what they meant.

"I . . . No, they don't sound familiar."

"Do you live in Portsmouth? Are you from here?"

"No. I live in Canada—Toronto."

Mark took a deep breath and leaned back in his chair. He was thinking very fast. This could be the case that could make his reputation. In Portsmouth, the Murray-Walters case was like Lizzy Borden and Leopold and Loeb combined. It would mean TV and headlines and enough free advertising to maybe make his business go.

"Miss Rhodes, approximately seven years ago a young man named Richie Walters was murdered in Lookout Park. Several weeks later, his girlfriend, Elaine Murray, was found dead out on the coast highway. Bobby is charged with committing those murders in 1960."

Mark watched the girl's reaction. She turned ashen and appeared unable to speak. George leaned forward.

"That's ridiculous. Why, Bob's almost a pacifist. He won't even talk about his war experiences. I don't believe it."

"I'm not saying that he is guilty, George. I'm telling you what Mr. Coolidge is charged with.

"Miss Rhodes, I hate to bring this up, but I'll have to at some time and, with a case this serious, I think we had better be frank with each other. There is no such thing as a simple murder case. Even the least complicated ones take an incredible amount of an attorney's time.

"From what I know about this case, I think I can safely say that it is going to be very complicated. We are dealing with a crime committed seven years ago. I am going to have to spend an enormous amount of time in investigation and preparation. I may have to obtain the services of expert witnesses. I may have to hire a private investigator to assist me. I will probably have to turn some cases down because I will not have the time to handle them.

"What I'm leading up to is this. Does Bobby have the money to hire an attorney? This will probably cost him several thousand dollars at a minimum."

She spoke haltingly. Mark could see that she was torn. He had seen that look before on the faces of people close to people charged with crime. The look signified the beginning of doubt. The beginning of questioning. She was asking herself who Bobby Coolidge really was. She was having her first look at a dark side that she may not have suspected. When the charge was murder, the questions were harder to answer.

"Bobby doesn't have any money . . . Or not enough to pay that."

"I'm talking about a sum in the area of ten thousand dollars."

Sarah did not answer immediately. She took a good hard look at Mark. What did she really know about Bobby? Ten thousand dollars! To give that sum to this stranger to defend a man who . . . Who what? She was assuming that he was guilty. Why should that be her first reaction? Now it was she who felt guilty and ashamed. Her family had money and she had substantial savings.

"I'm pretty sure I can raise the money. My family is . . . well off. I would need some time to talk to my parents."

"All right. I'm going to go to the jail and talk to Bobby now. I'll call you this evening. Will you know by then?"

"I'll try."

Mark rose and George and Sarah followed him to the door. Sarah turned and held out her hand to him. She looked stunned, but under control. He took her hand and held it.

"Thank you for helping, Mr. Shaeffer. When you see Bobby, would you tell him that I tried to see him. Ask him if there is anything we can do."

"I'll call you tonight and tell you what's going on."

George shook his hand and they left. It was difficult for Mark to control his excitement. He had represented a few people charged with serious crimes before, but a murder case was different from all other types of criminal cases. And this murder case was different from all other murder cases.

And the fee. If she could raise the money, ten thousand dollars would make his first year. It was the type of case that all new practitioners dream of. Maybe even Cindy would be satisfied.

They had had another fight that morning. Rosedale and Collins, a small firm he had interviewed with just before opening his office, had asked him to join as an associate at a salary that was considerably higher

than what he was now making. If he took the job,
Cindy could quit work and they could have their
baby. Cindy had begged him to take the job, but he
had refused. He liked being his own boss and the
business was starting to come in. He wasn't taking
home a lot, but he wasn't worrying about meeting
his overhead anymore either. When he had left for
work this morning, Cindy had been in tears. He was
about to add "as usual," but stopped himself. That
was unfair. He could understand Cindy's point of
view, but, damn it, she had to try and understand his.

Thinking about the fight upset Mark. Then he
thought about Sarah Rhodes. She seemed so different from Cindy. She was thinking of someone other
than herself. She was willing to give up a large sum
of her own money to help Coolidge. Well, maybe
this big fee, if it came through, would help. He didn't
know.

The county jail had been built with massive,
gray stone blocks in an era, before modern architec-
ture, when buildings were constructed to resemble
what they were supposed to be. The jail housed men
awaiting trial and their fear and uncertainty were
visible to all but the most insensitive visitor. The jail
made no distinction between the traffic offender who
could not make bail and the rapist. They were all
housed together, until the courts sent them to the
state penitentiary or set them free.

Because of his special status, Bobby Coolidge
had been housed in one of the rare single cells in

maximum security. Mark waited for him to be escorted to the special interview room in the basement
of the jail. The room was long, narrow and window-
less, and sealed by a large steel door. The only furniture in the room was a long table and several wooden
chairs. Mark had chosen the chair farthest from the
door so that he would have a few seconds for first impressions. He wanted to make sure that he had Coolidge sized up correctly. If Coolidge did not trust
him, he might go elsewhere for a lawyer.

The door to the interview room opened with a
metallic clang. A young man in his mid-twenties
was standing in the doorway in front of a guard.
He was clad in poor-fitting jeans and a blue work
shirt with a partially torn breast pocket. There was
an air of defeat about him that Mark noticed immediately. His eyes were downcast and never looked directly ahead. He made no move to enter the room,
until ordered to by the guard. When he did enter, he
did so slowly. His gaze stopped on Mark, but jumped
away when Mark attempted to make eye contact. He
scanned the room with quick, jerky movements of
his head, as if he expected to find something hidden
in the recesses.

For a brief moment, Mark realized the responsibility he would be undertaking if he represented this
man. The guard slammed the door shut and Coolidge looked behind him. Mark rose and waited for
Coolidge to turn back.

"My name is Mark Shaeffer. I'm an attorney," he
said, extending his hand. Coolidge looked at him for
a moment, then shook hands. There was little life in

his handclasp and both men released quickly, a bit embarrassed.

Mark sat down and indicated a chair. Coolidge sank into it.

"Sarah asked me to tell you that she tried to get in to see you, but they wouldn't let her. George Rasmussen was with her."

"How . . . What does she think about this?"

"She's standing behind you, Mr. Coolidge. She'll come to see you on Sunday."

"Well, that's good," Coolidge said in a tired voice. His hand moved toward his breast pocket and stopped.

"Do you have a cigarette?"

"Sorry, I gave them up a year ago. I can ask a guard." Coolidge shook his head.

"No, that's okay."

He paused before he spoke again.

"Mr. . . . ?"

"Shaeffer. Mark Shaeffer."

"Mr. Shaeffer, before you go any further, I want you to know that I can't pay a lawyer."

"Miss Rhodes is going to take care of that."

Coolidge snapped his head from side to side.

"No. I don't want her involved in this."

"Mr. Coolidge, you are going to have to be practical about this. Innocent or guilty, you are charged with two counts of murder. You need professional help. Miss Rhodes has the money to hire me and you don't. You can reject her help out of pride, but without an attorney the chances are very good that you will spend the rest of your life in a cage. Do you want that?"

Coolidge looked down at his shoes and said nothing. When he looked up, Mark knew that there
would be no more protests.

"Okay," Mark said, "the indictment charges you
with killing a woman named Elaine Murray and a
man named Richie Walters on or about November
25, 1960. Did you do that?"

"Absolutely not. No."

"Did you know them?"

"Of course. Everyone knew about that. I went to
high school with them."

"Why do you think the police arrested you?"

"I don't know. That's what I've been trying to figure out. My brother and I were arrested when this
first happened, but they let us go. Why would they
wait so long to arrest me, if they thought I was guilty?"

"I don't know the answer to that yet. All I have
seen is the indictment charging you and your brother
with the crime."

"Billy! He's arrested too?"

"I assume so."

Bobby ran his hand across his mouth and, for a
few seconds, he was lost in thought.

"Bobby, do any of these names mean anything to
you? These are the people listed on the indictment
as having been witnesses before the Grand Jury.

"Roy Schindler, Arnold Shultz, Thelma Pullen,
Esther Pegalosi, or Dr. Arthur Hollander."

"No. I've never heard of any of them."

Mark thought for a moment.

"Bobby, you mentioned that the police arrested
you when this first happened. Why did they do that?"

Bobby shrugged.

"I don't know. They asked me a lot of questions about that night. I guess what got us in trouble was we had had a fight and Billy pulled a knife at a party we crashed. And I think they mentioned finding some glasses belonging to a girl we knew in the park near where the Walters kid was killed. But that was it."

"Tell me, as best you can remember, what you did on the evening of November 25."

"It's been so long. I don't know. I know I was with Billy—my brother—and . . . uh . . . Roger . . . Roger Hessey. Then there was the girl whose glasses they found, Esther Freemont."

"Wait a second," Mark interrupted. "Could Esther Freemont be Esther Pegalosi. Did she get married?"

Bobby shook his head.

"I don't know. I went into the Army right after high school and I didn't keep track of her. We aren't good friends."

Mark made some notes on his yellow pad.

"Go on."

"Okay. We crashed a party this girl was throwing."

"What was her name? From now on when you mention people, I want names and addresses, if you can remember them."

"I'm not going to be much good on the addresses, but I should be able to give you the names."

Coolidge related the incident at the party and the theft of the wine. Mark took down everything as they went along. He was watching Coolidge closely while the latter spoke, trying to size him up. Bobby was intelligent and articulate. The type of defendant that would be able to assist him in his investigation.

But, was he telling the truth? He had seemed sincere when he denied his guilt. It had been the first time that he had spoken forcefully. Yet, for all his inexperience, Mark had represented enough clients to know that it was very difficult to tell if a person was telling the truth.

"What happened after you drank the wine?" Mark asked. Coolidge shrugged.

"I think we cruised downtown for a bit, then took Esther home, then went home ourselves."

"You think?"

"Well, it's been some time. But that's how it seems to me."

Mark put down his pad and leaned back in his chair.

"Okay. That's enough for today. I'm going to go see the district attorney and try to get a lead on some of these witnesses."

Mark stood up and Coolidge looked at him. He ran his tongue nervously across his lower lip before he spoke.

"Mr. Shaeffer, how does it look?"

"I really can't tell until I find out what the D.A. has."

Bobby looked down at the floor again.

"Do . . . do you think you can get me out of here? I mean, isn't there bail or something?"

"The court doesn't have to set bail in a murder case and even if they did, I'm afraid that they would set it so high that you could never make it."

"Oh," Bobby said in a voice that was almost a sigh. "Well, you try for me, will you, because I had a rough time last night. I'll tell you, I don't think I can take it, being locked up for long."

Eddie Toller entered the attorney's room of the county jail and spotted his court-appointed attorney reading a newspaper at the rear of the room. Eddie wasn't anxious to meet this young jerk again. Their only previous meeting had lasted approximately ten minutes following his arraignment. The gawk had handed him his card, told him not to worry, and rushed out. Eddie had even forgotten his name.

The guy looked reluctant to put the paper down when Eddie reached the interview booth and Eddie said, "Fuck you," under his breath. He doubted this creep would know what he was talking about, even if he did hear him.

"Well, Mr. Toller, I'm afraid I have bad news for you," the attorney said when Eddie was seated.

"Yeah, well what is that?"

"I talked with the district attorney in charge of your case and I am afraid, in light of your extensive prior record, that he is unwilling to plea negotiate. Furthermore, he has told me that he will ask for the maximum, twenty years, if you go to trial and are convicted, which I am afraid is highly likely in view of the overwhelming evidence that the state has against you.

"However, the district attorney did say that he would not recommend a sentence and would leave sentencing entirely up to the judge if you plead to the charge. At this point that seems like our best bet."

"To what? Plead to twenty years?"

"Well, the judge doesn't have to give you twenty years. You were cooperative with the police when they arrested you. That will weigh in your favor."

"Nah. I ain't pleadin' to no twenty years. Look, those cops didn't give me my rights till we got to the station house. Don't that mean something?"

"I'm afraid not, Mr. Toller. You see . . ."

The attorney babbled on about his rights and how they had not been violated, but Eddie wasn't listening. Something on the front page of the newspaper the attorney had been reading caught his eyes. It was a picture of a young girl that he thought he had seen before, many years ago. Eddie craned his neck to get a better look at the headline. The paper was folded over so that he could only see half of the page.

". . . do you want to proceed?"

"Huh?"

"I asked you how you wanted me to proceed," the attorney said, obviously annoyed at Eddie's lack of attention.

"Well, you're my attorney. You tell me. Only, I ain't coppin' to no twenty years."

"Surely you don't want to go to trial. You were caught inside the building and you confessed, not once, but twice."

"Look, who are you working for? Me or the D.A. . . . ? If he ain't gonna deal, I want a trial. This whole thing wasn't my idea anyway. Gary Barrick planned it out and I ain't taking the whole thing on my shoulders."

The attorney started to rise.

"Well, I'll see what I can do. Why don't you think about what I said."

"Sure. Say, can I see your paper for a minute?"

The attorney looked put out, but he handed the paper to Eddie. Eddie unfolded it. The headline read:

TWO ARRESTED IN MURRAY-WALTERS SLAYINGS. SEVEN-YEAR-OLD MYSTERY BELIEVED SOLVED.

Eddie scanned the story quickly. Then he concentrated on the picture of the girl. It had to be her. The attorney was getting impatient, so Eddie handed him the paper. He began to smile.

"Thanks a million," he said, pumping the attorney's hand. The attorney looked confused and smiled back, heading for the door. Eddie sat back down to think. For once the breaks were going to go his way. He could feel it. The attorney stopped at the door and cast a puzzled look at Toller. Toller waved at him.

"So long, asshole," he thought to himself. "I won't be needing you anymore."

Mark found Esther Pegalosi's address listed in the phone book, but decided against calling. Esther's apartment was in an older section of town. The building it was in looked as if it was well maintained. Esther's name was typed on a paper tag that had been affixed to a metal mailbox. Mark rode up in the old cage elevator he found in the lobby. The elevator ascended slowly and Mark could hear the gears and chains clanking and straining. The car shuddered to a stop on the third-floor landing and Mark stepped into the dark corridor. Esther's apartment was at the end of the hall. He knocked, then rang the buzzer.

There was no sound inside and he rang again. This time he could hear the sound of bare feet padding toward the door. There was a snapping sound and Mark guessed that he was being scrutinized through the peephole.

"Mrs. Pegalosi?" he said.

"Who is it?"

"My name is Mark Shaeffer, Mrs. Pegalosi. I'm an attorney and I'd like to talk to you."

"About what?"

"Could I step in for a minute? It's difficult talking through the door. If you want identification, I can slide one of my cards under the door."

Mark heard the snapping of locks and chains and the door opened enough for him to hand in a business card. The woman who took it was attractive in a slutty way. She was dressed in jeans and a tee shirt and her long black hair was unkempt, but the breasts that jiggled under the tee shirt were large enough to attract Mark's attention and her dark complexion and large brown eyes appealed to him. She scrutinized the card through reading glasses, then started to hand it back.

"What is it you want?"

"I was retained to represent Bobby Coolidge, an old friend of yours. He's in jail charged with a very serious crime. You testified at the Grand Jury and I'm interested in what you said."

The woman was obviously alarmed and she looked as if she might shut the door.

"This will only take a few minutes of your time. I am as interested in finding out what happened as the police. Maybe Mr. Coolidge is guilty . . ."

"Yes," the woman almost shouted. "He did it."

"Well, in that case, I certainly want to talk to you so that I will know how to advise my client. Why do you think he's guilty?"

"No, I won't discuss it. They said I wouldn't have to talk to anyone if I didn't want to and I'm not."

"Who said this, Mrs. Pegalosi?"

"Roy . . . Mr. Shindler and Mr. Heider."

"Mr. Heider, the district attorney?"

"Yes. He said I didn't have to talk to anyone if I said no."

"Well, that's right. I certainly wouldn't want to force you to talk to me if you didn't want to, but Bobby has been charged with murder. He could spend the rest of his life in jail. It certainly won't hurt you to talk to me and if there is some mistake, your talking with me might help clear it up."

"I can't talk . . . I won't talk about it."

"Mrs. Pegalosi, you'll have to answer my questions in court if you testify. Why are you worried about talking to me now?"

"Please. Go away. I don't want to talk about it."

There was a tinge of panic in Esther's voice and Mark flinched when she slammed the door. He was angry and, for a moment, he thought about pounding on the door until she opened it. Then he realized that he had no right to talk to her and his anger focused on Philip Heider for having counseled Esther the way he had.

Mark looked at his watch. It was getting late. He had the addresses of Pullen, Shultz, and Hollander. Shindler, he guessed, based on Esther's statement, was probably a cop. He decided to try Thelma Pullen.

Mark arrived back at his office at seven. He took off his jacket, rolled up his sleeves, and called his wife. The phone rang a few times before Cindy answered it.

"Mark?"

"Yes."

"Where are you? I called your office and all they said was that you were out investigating a case."

"Not just a case. You'll never guess who I'm representing."

Cindy sensed the excitement in Mark's voice.

"Who?" she asked, cautiously.

"Did you read the paper today? The front page?"

"Yes."

"I have just been retained to represent Bobby Coolidge, one of the two men charged in the Murray-Walters case."

"The murders?" she asked hesitantly.

"The very same."

There was a pause.

"Mark," she asked, "do you feel that . . . ? A murder is so serious. Do you think you have the experience?"

Mark was disappointed and angry. He had expected Cindy to be as excited as he had been all day.

Now she had killed it for him. It was her insecurity that she was projecting onto him. Her inadequacies.

"Yes, I can handle it," he answered in a more subdued tone.

"Are they paying you a lot?"

"I've asked for ten thousand," he said. This had been his big surprise, but she had deflated his enthusiasm with her fears.

"Ten thousand! Oh, Mark!"

Now she was excited, Mark thought bitterly. Not about the fact that someone thought enough of my ability to hire me to represent someone on a case this big, but because of the money.

"Have they paid you yet?"

"I have to call this evening to make certain that they can come up with the money."

"Then you're not certain you'll get it?" she asked in a disappointed tone.

"No. I have to call now."

There was another embarrassed pause.

"When will you be home?"

The truth was, at this moment, he would rather not have gone home at all.

"In a while. I'll call you before I leave."

"Mark, I'm really happy you got the case."

A little late, he thought. Out loud he said, "I'll see you," and blew her a kiss and hung up.

He took a deep breath and checked the Coolidge file for Sarah's number. He felt a curious excitement when he dialed it. Partly because he would soon know about the fee and partly, he realized, because he wanted to talk to her again.

"Sarah? This is Mark . . . Mark Shaeffer."

"Oh . . . yes?" she asked anxiously.

"I told you I'd call tonight. Remember?"

"Yes. About the money. Did you see Bobby?"

"We talked for about an hour at the jail. I've been out all afternoon talking to witnesses. Tomorrow I'm going to meet with the district attorney."

"How does it look?"

"I can't tell yet. The one witness I wanted to talk to the most wouldn't talk to me. I talked to two other people, but nothing they said seemed to connect Bobby with the crime. I'll learn more about the case tomorrow, hopefully, from the D.A."

"How was . . . is Bobby?"

"Pretty low. I told him you would visit on Sunday. I've arranged for you to see him in a private interview room, instead of with the rest of the prisoners in the visitor's room."

"Thank you."

Mark waited for her to go on, but she didn't.

"Uh, about the fee. Did you talk to your parents?"

"No. I . . . They weren't in. I'll have to keep trying. Can I tell you tomorrow?"

Mark felt a little nervous. He had already gotten involved in the case on her promise.

"Sure. When do you want to come in?"

"Later afternoon? Around five?"

Mark checked his appointment book.

"That's fine. I'll see you then."

They hung up. Mark rested his hand on the phone. He tried to visualize Sarah's features and figure. He could see her breasts pushing against her sweater this morning. For a moment he fantasized her naked, in bed. Then he stopped. He thought about Cindy and what was happening to their marriage. It made him feel sad.

"They sent a man. He said he was an attorney. How did he find me? You said I would only have to talk at the trial."

She was almost hysterical, thought Shindler. He grabbed her shoulders. He couldn't have her cracking up on him. Not when he'd come this far.

"Slow down and calm down," he ordered forcefully. She threw her arms around his neck and started to cry.

"I'm so glad you're here. I was going crazy. He just came. I . . ."

Shindler held her tightly. He was afraid that he would find her like this when he heard the way she sounded over the phone. He had driven from the police station as soon as he had hung up.

"Who came to see you?" he asked when she was calm enough to speak.

"I have his card," she said, breaking away and moving to the kitchen table. She handed him the card and sat down.

"He said he was an attorney," she said in a voice heavy with fear.

"He probably was," Shindler said. He could never understand why people of Esther's type held lawyers in awe. "What did you do?"

"Just like you and Mr. Heider said. I told him I didn't want to talk to him."

He stood behind her and began to massage her shoulders.

"And . . . ?"

"He went away."

"Good," he said softly, feeling her shoulder muscles begin to relax under the thin cotton tee shirt. "That was easy, wasn't it?"

"Yes," she answered sheepishly.

"And you handled that all by yourself, didn't you?" he asked soothingly.

"Yes," she said in an embarrassed whisper. "But I got scared. I didn't know how he found me and I was alone."

"You're not alone, Esther. You have me. And he could have gotten your name in a thousand ways: old newspapers, the indictment, a lot of places."

"I guess," she said. "It's just, I haven't seen you so much, lately. And I've been getting scared, again, like before I saw Dr. Hollander."

"There's nothing to be scared of," Shindler said softly. "Now, stand up and turn around."

She obeyed, but she would not look him in the eye. He cupped her chin in his hand and tilted her head until their eyes met.

"Are you still afraid?" he asked.

"No, Roy," she answered woodenly. She wanted him so bad. She wanted to feel him holding her, inside her. She wanted to cling to him and be safe.

"Is the baby asleep?" he asked. His voice was soft and soothing.

"Yes, Roy."

Her mouth was dry and she was trembling. He reached out and caressed her naked breast through her shirt. Her knees were weak and she felt herself growing moist. He stepped back so he could see her.

She pulled the shirt over her head and stepped out of her jeans so that all she wore were the red silk bikini panties he said he liked. She stood almost at attention, her head bowed, because she was afraid to look at him. He reached out and stroked her hair and she began to weep.

The intercom buzzed and Albert Caproni answered it. Philip Heider was on the other end and he wanted to see Al immediately. Al stacked his work neatly, marking pages with slips of torn paper and placing writing tablets in proper order. Then he headed down the hall to Heider's office.

When a major case like Murray-Walters came along, it was the office practice to assign one deputy, with no other duties, to that case. Often, the deputy would have an assistant, who would be given fewer day-to-day duties. Al considered it an honor to have been chosen from all the district court deputies to assist Heider on this important case. He was sure that a promotion to circuit court would follow when the case was over.

Al had never worked as enthusiastically as he had these past few weeks. He was enjoying the luxury of taking his time on a case. He had already been through the mountains of police reports that had accumulated over the last seven years. Now that they had two suspects, it was amazing how relevant some of the small details he had found buried in those reports had become.

Heider motioned Al into a chair across the desk from him and finished dictating a letter. Heider was not an easy person to work under, but Al appreciated his thoroughness and admired his intelligence. Heider was a perfectionist. There was precision even in his dictation. He would be willing to bet that Heider never misspelled a word. If he was working harder than he ever had before, he was also learning more about the proper way to try a case than he could have in any other way.

"Do you know a lawyer named Mark Shaeffer?"

"I think so. I had a trial with him a few months ago and we negotiated on several cases."

"What are your impressions? He's coming up here in a few minutes."

"I don't know. He seems competent. No Clarence Darrow, but no idiot either. It's hard to say after just one trial. Why?"

"He's representing Bobby Coolidge."

"He is?" Caproni said, surprised. "I figured someone with more experience would have been handling it."

Heider shrugged.

"It will make things easier for us. Do you know if he's ever tried a felony?"

Al shook his head.

"I don't know. I can check."

Heider made some notes on a scratch pad.

"Al, I want you to sit through this meeting and help me size him up. Then I have a small assignment for you. One of the prisoners out at the county jail—a fellow named Toller, Eddie Toller—contacted a guard yesterday. He claims to have some information on the Murray-Walters case and he says he'll only talk to a D.A. This is probably nothing, but Coolidge is housed out there and he may have said something to this guy. When we're through with Shaeffer, take a ride out there and talk with him.

"I've had Toller's record checked. It's long. Nothing violent. Mostly burglaries of businesses, car theft, some drugs. We have an airtight case against him. He probably is going to tell you a fairy story in hopes of making a deal. Find out what he knows. Promise him nothing. If it looks like he has something to offer, tell him that you are my assistant and that I have to give approval on any plea negotiations. You have all that?"

Al smiled and nodded.

"Okay. Now back to Shaeffer. How much do you think we should tell him?"

"I don't know. I think we should at least give him an outline of our case. I don't think we should give him the transcript of Esther's hypnosis interviews, because there is too much there that he could play with."

"I agree, Al. I'm thinking of telling him just enough to get him worried, but no reports or transcripts of interviews. Now, we have to give him copies of the statements his client made when he was interrogated in '61 and I'll have to give him witness statements the day before they testify, but he'll be too busy with the trial to do much with those statements when he gets them."

A buzzer rang and Heider pressed down on his intercom switch.

"Send him back," Heider said. A few moments later, Mark Shaeffer was seated next to Al.

"What can I do for you?" Heider asked with an expansive smile.

Mark was nervous. He knew Heider by reputation and he felt out of his league. He was unsure of himself dealing with someone with the experience Heider had. He also realized that under the state's discovery laws he was entitled to damn little information. He did not want to antagonize Heider or the D.A. might not talk with him at all. Still, he knew that sometime during the meeting he would have to bring up the refusal of Esther Pegalosi and, this morning, Dr. Arthur Hollander, to discuss the case with him.

"I've been retained to represent Bobby Coolidge."

"So I understand. You know that Bobby and Billy are going to get you great press. They sound like a country and western duo. Good-looking boys, too. It's this type of case makes me wish I was in private practice."

Heider winked and Mark laughed. Maybe Heider would be all right after all. He certainly wasn't coming on strong.

"Say, Mark, can I get you some coffee?"

"No thanks."

"Well, what do you want to know?"

"Well, I guess, why you've arrested Mr. Coolidge after all these years."

Heider laughed.

"That's simple. We have the goods on him."

Mark watched the easy way Heider had spoken

that sentence. He saw the D.A. leaning back in his chair, his jacket open, and at ease. There was none of the tension or nervousness about the man that Mark was experiencing. He wished that he could have just a fraction of that self-assurance.

"What are the goods?" he asked, trying to hide his nervousness with an ineffectual smile.

Heider leaned forward in his chair.

"You know, Mark, I'm under no obligation to reveal our case, but this is such an unusual case that I'm going to tell you a little about it.

"Back in 1960, when Richie Walters was murdered, the police found a pair of glasses and some other objects that obviously belonged to a woman down the hill from the boy's body. You can get all this out of the newspaper accounts. The glasses were traced to a girl named Esther Freemont, who claimed that they had been stolen before the murders.

"It turns out, now, that Esther suffered amnesia caused by the trauma of seeing that boy murdered. We had a psychiatrist work with her . . ."

"Dr. Hollander?"

Heider nodded.

"And he was able to break through her resistance. She now has an independent memory of the events. We can put her in the presence of your client and his brother, through their own statements, at approximately the time of the murders. We have independent witnesses who will testify that Billy Coolidge pulled a switchblade knife during a fight earlier in the evening of November 25, a few hours before the murder. The coroner will testify that a knife of the type described would have been capable of causing the wounds that killed Richie Walters."

"You're saying that Esther saw the Coolidges kill Walters and the girl?"

"She saw the events on the hill."

"What does . . . ? How did she say it happened?"

Heider leaned back in his chair, tilting it precariously, so that he was able to rest his heels on his desk. He smiled.

"I'm afraid that you'll have to wait for the trial for the answer to that one. Or, you can ask Esther."

"I tried to do that yesterday, Phil," Mark said, feeling uncomfortable about using Heider's first name, "and she said that you told her she shouldn't talk to me."

"Whoa," Heider said, holding up his hand. "I never told her that. I told her that she had to make up her own mind who she talked with. I guess she just decided that she doesn't want to discuss this case more than she has to. She's a frightened girl, you know. You can't see something as savage as those killings and not be affected. Don't forget, that experience was so horrible for her that she developed amnesia because her conscious mind couldn't deal with it."

"Dr. Hollander wouldn't talk with me either."

Heider shrugged.

"Some people are like that. I'm sorry I can't help you there."

"You can call and tell him it's okay to talk to me."

"Well, Mark, I feel that this is a choice each individual should make on his own. I certainly don't want to influence the man one way or the other."

"In other words, you won't tell him it's all right to discuss this case with me," Mark said, beginning to get angry.

"That's exactly what I did tell him when he asked me. I guess he just decided that he would rather not talk with you."

"I see," Mark said.

"Good," Heider smiled. It was a smile of smug satisfaction, made by the man with the whip hand. Mark felt an overriding desire to get out of Heider's office. They discussed some preliminary matters concerning trial dates and length of trial and Heider gave Mark copies of the police reports concerning Bobby Coolidge's statements when he had been interviewed in 1961. When Shaeffer had gone, Heider turned to Albert Caproni and laughed.

"Candy," he said.

        Sarah Rhodes had not slept much the night before. She had been doing some hard thinking. What did she know about Bobby Coolidge? He seemed to be a nice boy. An older man, really. That, she guessed, had been the attraction. He had traveled, been in the army, the people he associated with were not the same type of people that most of the other freshman girls knew. It made her feel more mature to be seen in the company of someone like Bobby.

But there was another side to Bobby. A dark side. His arrest for murder had brought back vivid memories of his sleepless nights and the conversation they had had in the early dawn hours one morning. She could still hear his sorrow-filled voice quietly telling her about the person he had been before the war. The person who had done "bad things." It had been such a childlike statement. So out-of-place coming from such a strong man. Almost as if the voice had been pitched through him by an unseen ventriloquist.

And was he such a strong man? Yes, on the surface. It took a strong man to go through the war the way Bobby had. In weak moments, he had told her of some of his experiences and she knew that she could never have endured them. It took a strong man to try to get an education, given Bobby's background.

But there was the other, hidden side to him. The feeling she had from time to time that he was like a delicate china vase that could shatter at any moment, if the right type of pressure was applied. There was guilt hiding in the closets and the attics and eating away ever so slowly. Guilt that could be easily explained by the personal knowledge that he had stabbed a young man to death and raped and strangled a young woman. And, if that was true—if he was the type of man who could do such a thing, with premeditation, in cold blood—then how could they go on? How could she possibly hold such a man, let him touch her, knowing what his hands had done?

These were the things that she had thought about last night when she debated with herself about calling her parents. She had read the account of the Murray-Walters case in the paper. She had seen the headlines after she and George had left Mark's office and purchased a paper. The details were graphic and they had shaken her. Could she ask her parents for the money to defend a person who may have done such a thing? Yes, if—and it was a big if—she loved him. But did she? That was the question that was tearing her apart.

Bobby was different from any man she had ever known; he was handsome, their sex was good, but all these things were parts of love, not love itself. She did not know what love was, or whether she was capable of it, and she did not know if what she felt for Bobby was love.

So, she had cried, but she had not called her parents. Instead, she had drawn three thousand dollars out of her personal savings account and she was sitting in Mark Shaeffer's office prepared to lie. She could not abandon Bobby, and the three thousand dollars, she was sure, would keep Mr. Shaeffer on the case. But, at this time, before she had confronted Bobby, she did not have the courage to involve her family.

"My father was away on business when I called. He will be back in a week and I can ask him then, but I'm sure that he'll say it's okay."

Mark looked at the three thousand dollar check and missed most of what Sarah had said. He had never had a fee anywhere near this big and it did not even dawn on him that the rest of the ten thousand might not follow.

"That will be fine. This is more than enough to get me started."

It was after five and Mark's secretary had left for the evening.

"What did the district attorney tell you?" Sarah asked anxiously. Mark noticed that she seemed less self-confident tonight. The quiet in the office and her presence there alone had made him feel mildly uncomfortable. He wanted to reassure her, but his fantasies of where that could lead made him afraid.

"The district attorney didn't tell me much that I didn't know already, except that he says that they have an eye-witness—a girl who was supposedly with Bobby and his brother at the time of the killings."

"She saw them do it?" Sarah asked in disbelief.

"She says she saw them do it, according to the D.A. That doesn't mean that she's telling the truth. There are some funny things going on that I want to know more about.

"For instance, why didn't she come forward seven years ago? The prosecutor says she had amnesia caused by seeing the people killed, but why, all of a sudden, does her memory come back?

"Also, why is Heider keeping his key witnesses so quiet? If there wasn't something wrong with their case, I don't think he would have done that."

"Do you . . . do you think that Bobby did . . . ?"

"That he's guilty?" Mark said, leaning toward her across his desk. "I have no opinions right now. Bobby said that he didn't and that's good enough for me."

Sarah felt ashamed of herself for having voiced her doubts.

"I'd better go now," she said, starting to rise.

"Can I give you a lift? I'm leaving too."

"Oh, I couldn't put you out."

"No trouble. I'm going in that direction anyway."

He smiled and she noticed how handsome he was. She smiled back and accepted his offer.

* * *

During the ride to Sarah's apartment, Mark tried not to mention the case, because he could see how upset Sarah was. When he had maneuvered his car out of the parking lot and into city traffic, he asked her,

"Why did you come to an American school for your education?"

"It seemed adventurous to study in a foreign country," she said with a smile. The windows were rolled down and the wind tangled and lifted her golden hair.

"Do you enjoy studying among the natives?"

"It's okay."

"Are your parents filthy rich?" he asked.

Sarah's mouth opened in surprise. Then she threw her head back and laughed.

"You are bold."

Mark shrugged.

"You said you were well off and you live in a ritzy part of town."

"Yes. We have scads of money," she answered. She was beginning to like Mark. She was glad that she had hired such a nice person to represent Bobby. "Are you jealous?"

Mark thought about it.

"I wouldn't mind being rich. It would solve a lot of problems."

"Oh, you'll soon be rolling in the dough. Lawyers make a lot of money."

"Some do."

"I have faith in you," she said, smiling. "If I didn't, I wouldn't have hired you."

Mark looked at Sarah and their eyes met for a moment. He looked away, feeling very unsure of himself. Was it his imagination or had she meant more than she said?

Mark drove up into the hills. Sarah looked out the window, not wanting to meet Mark's eyes, because the look he had given her confused her. She was glad when they arrived at her apartment. She didn't want to come on with Mark, but it would be to her advantage to have him interested in her, because of her indecision about the money. Besides, it wouldn't be hard to make Mark think she found him attractive, because she did. He had cheered her up on the ride home and, until that moment when she had looked into his eyes, he had made her forget her problems.

She watched Mark's car disappear over the hill and she suddenly felt guilty. Bobby was her boyfriend and he was in jail charged with murder. The situation was getting too complex for her. Too many things were happening at once. It would be better not to think for a while. She put on a record and sat in the dark, listening to the music.

"Mr. Toller, I'm Albert Caproni and I'm with the district attorney's office. I understand that you have some information on the Murray-Walters case."

Toller looked Caproni over and looked past him toward the door of the private interview room.

"Where's Heidman? Ain't he tryin' the case?"

"I'm Mr. Heider's assistant. Mr. Heider would have come himself, but a matter came up that required his personal attention."

"Yeah? Well this matter's gonna require attention

too, if you want to find out what happened to that girl."

"What girl?"

"The one you say those Coolidge boys killed. I know it wasn't them."

"You mean Elaine Murray?"

"I don't remember the name, but she's the right one. I seen her picture in the paper and I knew her right off."

"If the Coolidge brothers didn't kill Elaine Murray, who did?"

Toller leaned back in his chair and took a long look at Albert Caproni. Then he started to laugh.

"Jesus, you must think I'm awful stupid. I'm sittin' here with the evidence on the biggest case that hit this town in years and I'm sittin' here lookin' at possibly twenty years and you want me to give you what I know for nothin'. Well, I ain't givin' this away. I want to deal, understand?"

"Mr. Toller, I am not authorized to make any 'deals.' Mr. Heider has the authority to plea negotiate any case, but he won't even consider negotiating until he knows what you have to offer."

"If I tell you everything, what guarantee do I have that you won't just tell me to screw off?"

"You don't have any guarantee. On the other hand, if I walk out of here I can guarantee you one thing—no other district attorney is going to come back."

Toller's bravado began to dissipate and Caproni could see that he was thinking hard.

"Mr. Toller, why don't you just tell your attorney what you know and let him handle this?"

Toller waved his hand at Caproni, brushing the suggestion aside.

"He's some young kid that's wet behind the ears. I don't think he has the brains to remember it all. Look, if I tell you, and the information checks out, what can you do for me? I was plannin' to get married before I got busted. Then I lost my job. I knew I was actin' stupid, but I was real down and I never act smart when I'm down."

"Mr. Toller, you really shouldn't be discussing the facts of your case with me. It's my office that will be prosecuting you."

Toller laughed again. Only this time the laughter was bitter.

"Son, there's no way I can beat this one. I know that. I just want a break for once. I'm desperate. I found this girl, Joyce, for the first time. A real stand-up girl, ya know? Then I went ahead and blew it. I don't even know if she'll still stick by me, even if I do get out. But, I'm just gettin' too old for prison and I know that's where I'm headed if I don't make this deal."

"I sympathize with you," Al said, and he really did, "but I can't guarantee anything. You'll just have to trust me. If I think you're leveling with me, I will promise you that I'll try to help you out. That is, if the information is important."

Toller examined his fingernails and Caproni said nothing. Toller raised his head and sighed.

"I guess I gotta take the chance."

Caproni took a writing pad out of his attaché case.

* * *

It was the second week in January, 1961, and Eddie Toller felt like shit. He always felt like shit from late November to late January of every year. Come February the feeling would gradually begin to wear off.

The cause of his spiritual malaise was the cornerstone of American democracy, capitalism, and the commercialism that this theory of economics fostered. From the end of November until the beginning of January, Thanksgiving was followed by Christmas and Christmas by New Year's, and for each one there was a flood of commercials and advertisements that glorified the American family and the joys of spending these holiday seasons with one.

And that was Eddie's problem in a nutshell. He missed his momma, 'cause she was dead, and his daddy was long gone, so that meant no American family, no firesides and two months of depression.

As it was the second week of January, Eddie's depression was on the downswing, but it was still strong enough that he had sought solace in the cups at the bar down the corner from the fleabag hotel he was staying in until he could find work in Portsmouth.

Eddie wasn't alone at the bar tonight. He had made the acquaintance of an unshaven young man who wore a black leather motorcycle jacket and who combed his hair in what was popularly called a "duck's ass." It was the motorcycle jacket that had started the conversation. Eddie knew a lot about 'cycles and so did the fellow in the jacket who introduced himself as Willie Heartstone.

They talked motorcycles for a while, then drifted into other areas of discussion, finally arriving, when they were both good and drunk, at the end point of most male bar conversations that aren't about sports: pussy.

Eddie told Willie about this great black pussy he had eaten in Georgia, while in the army, when he was so drunk that his piss had risen level with his eyeballs, and Willie told him that he wouldn't fuck nigger pussy 'cause he heard it would bite you back. They both howled at that and the bartender had to caution them when they laughed so hard that Eddie knocked the pitcher off the bar.

"I'll tell ya," Eddie said, buying the next round, "a little pussy right now would sure cure all my ills."

Heartstone was as drunk as Eddie. The beer from his mug slopped onto his clothes every time he waved his arm to make a point.

"How about a big pussy," he said, making a point. Eddie roared and Willie spilled some of his beer on Eddie's chino slacks.

"Any old size pussy," Eddie conceded. "Just as long as it don't have teeth."

Eddie started laughing again, but Willie was thinking and starting to look a bit crafty.

"Say, Eddie, I know where you can get some of that good pussy, but it might cost you a bit. You got some dough for some good stuff?"

Eddie had to think about that. He leaned against the bar, almost missing the countertop with his elbow. For some reason the bar stool wouldn't stay in place. When he had steadied himself, he reached back slowly and pulled out his wallet. He had thirty-five bucks, plus, of course, some money he had hidden in his room.

"How much this pussy gonna cost, Willie? 'Cause I'm runnin' low and there still don't look like there's much work in this town."

Willie leaned over and peeked in Eddie's wallet.

"Ah, shit, Eddie. You're a good old boy. Five bucks. How's that?"

Eddie thought about how little money he had left, but then he thought about how he hadn't had a woman since San Antonio and he lurched off the bar stool.

"Let's go. You only live once, I say."

Willie slapped him on the back.

"Only once."

Eddie slapped some change on the bar and they staggered outside. Willie's car was parked in the tavern lot. They drove at breakneck speed over icy roads that threatened to throw them off at every turn. Willie's driving was beginning to sober Eddie up, but speed only served to intoxicate Willie and his driving got crazier as they sped on into the night.

Eddie must have dozed off after a while, because they had started in the city, but they were in the country when he opened his eyes. The car headlights were bouncing off trees and the car was tilted on an incline. Willie was nudging him and he realized that they were parked on a hilly, dirt driveway in front of a one-story weatherbeaten wooden house.

"We here, boy. That good pussy's just around the corner," Willie said with a leer and a grin that revealed several rotting teeth.

Willie tripped over an empty paint can on the

porch and swore loudly. Then he banged the front door open, because of his frustration at not being able to get his key in the lock until the third try. Eddie was giggling and Willie started laughing again, once they were inside.

"Who the fuck is makin' that noise?" a voice yelled from a back room. Eddie peered down the hall to see if he could make out where the voice came from. It was too dark.

"It's me, Ralph. I got my good buddy here and we gonna knock off a piece."

Eddie could hear someone getting out of bed in a hurry. He looked into the front room. The place was a pigsty. Beer cans on the floor, the stuffing poking through a couch cushion.

A man was coming down the hall pulling on his pants. He stopped when he saw Eddie. Anger suffused his face and he grabbed Willie by the arm.

"Who is that, you asshole?"

Willie looked a little put out, but didn't try to pull his arm away.

"Lay off, Ralph. This is my good buddy Eddie. Knows more about pussy and motorcycles than any man alive."

"You brought him here? You crazy? You want to go to . . ." Ralph started. Then, casting a hard look at Eddie he thought better of finishing his thought.

"Listen, get your ass outta here."

Eddie looked at Willie. For the first time, he realized that he didn't know where he was and that he didn't know Willie too well. He decided not to make an issue of it and began to back toward the door. Willie caught his arm and pulled away from Ralph.

"Now wait one fuckin' minute, Ralph. Eddie's okay and he said he could pay ten bucks for some good pussy, didn't you, Eddie?"

Willie winked at him and Eddie thought better of contradicting him on the terms of the contract. He just shook his head.

"Yah. Sure. But I don't want no trouble. If your friend . . ."

"Ain't gonna be no trouble. Now you just wait here while me and Ralph talk. Then you gonna get yourself some fine pussy."

Willie and Ralph walked down the hall. He could hear them arguing in low voices, but he could only make out an occasional word. The door of the room they had gone into opened and Willie and Ralph returned. Willie draped his arm around Eddie's shoulder in a fatherly fashion and led him aside into a corner of the hallway.

"Listen," he whispered in Eddie's ear, "my buddy loves this pussy so much he don't want to share it around, but I talked to him and told him what a good old boy you was, so he's relentin'. Only I had to tell him twenty bucks. That's okay, ain't it?" Willie asked, giving Eddie's shoulder a manly squeeze, "'cause when you taste this pussy, you gonna say it's hundred-dollar stuff."

Eddie was getting frightened. He could smell Willie's stale breath over the beer smell and he did not like the looks of Ralph, who stared menacingly from the hallway.

"Sure, twenty's fine," he agreed, managing a weak smile.

"Good," Willie roared, slapping him on the shoulder. "Now you slip me that twenty and we go do some rootin'."

Eddie gave Willie twenty dollars and Willie handed it to Ralph. Then Willie led him into a darkened kitchen. There was a basement door secured by a strong lock next to the refrigerator. Willie worked the lock and switched on the basement light. There was only a single 60-watt bulb and it left most of the basement in shadow. The rickety wooden stairs squeaked with each step and, in his condition, Eddie had to hold onto the banister to keep from tumbling down them.

Eddie was concentrating so much on the stairs that he didn't notice anything else until he had his feet planted firmly on the concrete. It was cold in the basement, but there was some heat emanating from an old-fashioned furnace that was set off near the far wall. Willie headed toward the furnace and Eddie thought he heard something moving near it.

"How you like that?" Willie asked softly. His voice had changed and his speech was coated with a coarse layer of lust.

It was dark in the basement despite the light, and the corner where Willie was pointing was mostly in shadow, but Eddie could make out a figure, covered by a blanket, huddled on a bare mattress. The mattress gave off a rank odor and there were stains on a corner of it that looked like dried blood. The only part of the person that was not covered by the blanket was the head. He moved closer and he could see that it was a girl. She had not moved since they had come into her line of vision, but her eyes were open and she was watching their every movement. The girl's hair was dirty, stringy and matted and Eddie had trouble making out whether it was black or brown at first. When he got closer, he could see that it was brown.

"We got this one well-trained, Eddie. Yes, sir, don't we?" Willie said, half to Eddie and half to the girl. The girl made no response. Her face was a blank and she seemed past caring.

"This one'll do whatever you so desire, won't you, darlin'?"

Eddie could hear Willie breathing heavily as he stripped off his jacket. Willie was wearing a heavy belt and he drew it out of the loops of his pants as he talked, never letting his eyes stray from the girl's face.

Willie jerked the blanket off with a sudden movement. The girl was dressed in slacks and a blouse. The blouse was unbuttoned and the girl was clutching the halves together with her right hand.

The girl moved for the first time when the blanket was removed. It was not much of a movement. Just a quiver, accompanied by a whimper and a rattling metallic sound. Eddie found the source of that sound in a length of chain that was attached to the girl's right ankle and a metal loop that was fastened to the cellar wall.

Eddie began to feel sick. He didn't go for this kind of thing. He wanted to back out, but he was too scared of Willie and Ralph to say anything.

"You happy to see me, darlin'?" Willie crooned. As he talked, he switched the doubled belt against his thigh. The girl's eyes did not leave the belt and they began to fill with tears. Willie squatted down and cupped the girl's chin in his hand, forcing her to look into his eyes.

"I asked if you was glad to see me."

The girl croaked an answer that sounded like yes. Willie chuckled and released the girl's chin.

"I knew you was. I knew you was. 'Cause you know what's behind these shorts, don't you? You know what good stuff's there."

The girl bit her lip to try to hold back her tears, but the effort was useless. The sight of the girl's helplessness seemed to fuel Heartstone's sadism. He snapped the belt lazily across the girl's hips. Eddie was certain that he had not used enough force to hurt her, yet the girl's buttocks jumped as if she had been struck with great force.

"This here's my friend Eddie, darlin'. I want you to show him what you got."

Eddie wanted to stop it, right here, but he knew that one false move on his part and he would be dead. Knew it for certain.

The girl was removing her slacks with fast, jerky movements. Each effort seemed to cause her pain. When the slacks were to her ankles, Heartsone pulled them off. Underneath, she was naked.

"Now the blouse," Willie said in a husky whisper. "Show this man those fine, fine tits."

The girl obeyed weakly, then lay back on the mattress with her legs spread. Heartstone drew the belt down her stomach, letting the leather touch one of her nipples. The tip of the belt stopped where her curled brown pubic hair began. Willie grinned back at Eddie.

"See how well she learned her lessons. It took some

doin' to get her to lie back and spread those legs. Many a interestin' hour." He shook his head and closed his eyes, savoring the memories. "But she's smart and she learns good. We even gonna feed you tomorra if you treat my friend Eddie okay."

Despite his revulsion, Eddie could not keep his eyes off the girl's body. He noticed how emaciated she looked. Her ribs could be seen easily and there were dark shadows under her eyes.

Eddie was certain that Willie would mount her first while he watched, but all of a sudden, Heartstone seemed to lose interest. He zipped up his pants and stepped back.

"I'm gonna pee. You have fun. If she don't do something you want, you tell me."

Eddie heard Heartstone's footsteps climbing the stairs and the sound of the door closing and locking. The girl shuddered visibly with relief. For a moment Eddie was afraid that he too might be a prisoner and he started to walk toward the stairs.

"No," the girl mumbled feebly. "Don't go, please."

She was begging. He turned back to her.

"Look miss, I . . . I don't know what's going on here, but I won't hurt you. I promise."

He was whispering. As afraid as she that Heartstone might hear them. All he wanted to do was to get away.

"Don't talk," she begged in a whisper. "If he hears me talking, he'll . . ."

She began to sob.

"You don't have to worry. I won't force myself on you," he whispered in an attempt to comfort her. She became terrified when he backed away.

"No. You have to. It will be worse for me if they find out you . . . I didn't do what they said." She turned her head away. "Just be quick."

Toller's voice had gotten lower and lower as he wound toward the end of his tale. As he talked, Caproni began to feel the same fear and revulsion that Toller seemed to be reexperiencing. When the prisoner stopped talking, there was a strained silence in the interview room.

"Did you have intercourse with her?" Caproni asked in a choked voice. Toller shook his head.

"I was too scared to get it up. I done some bad things in my life, but I ain't never done anything like that to no person."

"What did you do when Heartstone came back?"

"He didn't come back. I had to bang on the basement door. He asked me how it was and I made up some story. Then he drove me to town after chargin' me five more dollars for gas. I was scared all the way, but Willie didn't do nothin'.

"The next morning, I packed up and moved out of town. A few days later I read how they found this girl's body in a ditch by the highway. I could see it was her from the picture in the paper."

"Why didn't you tell the police?"

"Look, I wasn't goin' to no police. Not with my record and not after not reporting it first. I was scared and, besides, the cops never did anything for me. She was dead anyway."

Yes, I suppose she was, Caproni thought. Dead long before they killed her. He tried to imagine what it must have been like for the girl, lying in the cold, damp basement, afraid to even speak.

"Did you ever see Heartstone or Ralph again?"

"No, sir. And if I had I woulda gone the other way. Like I said, I done some bad shit in my time, but nothin' like that. I knew what they was capable of."

"Do you know Ralph's last name?"

"He just called him Ralph and I didn't ask."

Caproni made some final notes. Then, he put his pad in his attaché case and stood up.

"What you've told me could be of great importance, Mr. Toller. I'm going to talk to Mr. Heider. If he feels as I do, then we may be able to arrange something for you. Now I'm not promising anything, but I want you to know that I appreciate your coming forward with this information."

Toller seemed flattered and embarrassed by Caproni's sincerity and, for a second, he forgot the real reason he had contacted the authorities. They shook hands and Caproni left. The session with Toller had drained him and he was grateful to be, once again, in the light of day.

3

Shindler was in Heider's office, as he had been each afternoon for the past week, helping Heider sort through the evidence that had been amassed during the years of investigation, when Caproni returned. Heider could see that he was excited and he motioned him into a chair.

"What happened at the jail?" Heider asked.

"Something we should look into. The Coolidges may not be guilty."

Heider cast a quick glance at Shindler. The detective had not moved, but there was a subtle change in his bearing.

"Let's have it, Al. Don't keep us in suspense," Heider said lightly. Inside, wheels were spinning. Tapes preparing to recalculate. The district attorney's office had committed itself publicly and in the press to the theory that the Coolidges had killed Murray and Walters. Heider had been spokesman for the office and it was his credibility and his political future that would be jeopardized if the Coolidges were innocent.

"I spoke to that man at the jail, Eddie Toller. He told me that he was in Portsmouth in 1961, in mid-January. He was in a bar and he met a man named Willie Heartstone. Toller mentioned that he wanted to get laid and Heartstone said he could fix him up for a price."

"Heartstone drove him somewhere in the country, not too far from town, to a house where someone named Ralph was living. Toller thinks Heartstone lived there too, but he is not certain.

"Ralph and Heartstone were keeping a girl locked in the basement. She had a padlocked chain around her ankle. Toller said it looked as if they were beating and starving her. He says that a day or so later, he saw Elaine Murray's picture when her body was found and recognized her as the girl. He said he is certain she was the one. He didn't come forward then, because he had been in trouble with the law before and didn't like the police and because he was scared of Ralph and Heartstone and didn't want to get involved with them again."

"I see," Heider said skeptically. "And what evidence did Mr. Toller offer you to substantiate his story?"

"None, except . . . Just his word. But I believe him. It was the way the man talked. He was upset when he described the girl. His fear communicated. I don't think he could have faked the way he was talking."

Shindler laughed.

"Al, I'm surprised at you. You've been a cop. I suppose you've never been conned before."

Al blushed.

"A million times. I just don't think this guy is conning me."

"Maybe not. Maybe he is telling the truth as he sees it. But it could have been another girl," Heider said.

"No. He was positive. He saw her picture only a day or two later and his description matches the description of the clothes Murray was wearing when she was found and her hair color."

"You have to admit that brown hair, slacks and a blouse is not exactly unusual. Besides, he could have gotten that out of the papers. They're rehashing this whole thing all over the front pages every day," Shindler said.

"And you're forgetting one very important point," Heider said smugly.

"What's that?"

"When was it that Toller is supposed to have seen this girl alive?"

"The second week in January, a few days before her body was found."

"Al, according to Dr. Beauchamp's autopsy report, Elaine Murray was killed four to six weeks before she was found. How could she be alive during the second week in January?"

Caproni looked confused for a moment. Then he remembered something.

"The body. The girl's body. It didn't appear to have deteriorated the way you would expect if it had been outside all that time. That was in one of your reports, Roy. Maybe Beauchamp made a mistake. If I remember, his report theorized that the cold weather had kept the corpse preserved."

Heider shook his head.

"No go, Al. This Toller is just another con trying to make a deal."

Al shook his head vigorously.

"I just don't believe that. You had to be there. That man was actually scared when he was retelling that story. I think it should be checked out."

"Okay, Al. You get back to those transcripts and I'll have Roy get on it."

Caproni seemed mollified by Heider's assurances. They discussed a few other matters and he left. When the door closed behind him, Heider spoke.

"What do you think?"

"Bullshit. Another con with a story."

"You better hope so. I've got my ass on the line with this one and I can't afford any screw-ups. Go out to the jail. Talk to Toller. If there are any problems, get back to me. They can be taken care of."

Roger Hessey was doing okay. He had married a real sweet girl, fathered two great kids and gotten in on the ground floor when his father-in-law purchased a franchise in a chain that sold fried chicken. No one expected the restaurant to do as well as it had and Roger earned enough money to set his family up in a comfortable suburban tract home a few minutes' drive from a shopping center, a golf course and a neighborhood school.

"Some change for me from those high school days," he said, wagging his head. "We did some crazy things then. Say, can I get you a beer or something?"

"No thanks, Mr. Hessey," Mark Shaeffer said. They

were seated in lawn chairs on Roger's patio and his two daughters were running and yelling in the backyard. Roger smiled nostalgically and nodded his head again.

"I'll tell you, I was shocked when I read that Billy and Bobby had been arrested, but I wasn't surprised."

"Why do you say that?"

"Well, you're Bob's lawyer, so I can tell you, but they were pretty wild kids. I mean we all were in those days. Always fighting. Billy was one of the worst of the lot. He was even into dealing a little narcotics. Pot mostly, but don't forget this was back in 1960. Everyone thought that stuff was worse than heroin back then."

"I notice you didn't mention Bobby just now."

"Well, Bobby was a wild kid, but he wasn't mean like his brother. I mean I was wild too. We broke into warehouses and had gang fights. Nothing I'm proud of now. But it was, I don't know how to put it, oh, all in the spirit of good fun, most of the time.

"I mean, most of us, we'd fight a guy and you'd try to whip him good, but you wouldn't try to cripple him or really hurt him permanently. It's hard to explain the line most of us drew, but there was one.

"Then there were kids like Billy. He didn't draw any lines. That's why most of us were a bit afraid of him."

"You knew Esther Freemont, too, didn't you?"

Roger threw back his head and brayed. The little girls stopped playing, startled by the loud noise. When they saw it was only their father laughing, they went back to their games.

"What's so funny?" Mark asked.

"Oh, nothin', I guess. It's just that thinking of Esther brings back some mighty fine memories. She had the biggest set of tits . . ."

Roger shook his head in wonder and Mark shifted uneasily on the plastic netting of his aluminum chair. Roger was reclining. He had on an aloha shirt, dark glasses and a pair of checked bermuda shorts. From time to time, he would pat his beer belly with satisfaction or sip from an open can of Coors. The weekend sun was strong and Mark wished that he was swimming instead of working.

"What can you remember about the night that Elaine and Richie were killed?"

"Not very much, I'm afraid. I told this to the cops a few times. We went over to Bob's. That's a hamburger joint we used to go to. I don't think it's even in business anymore. Then Bobby or Billy, one of them got this idea to crash Alice Faye's party. I knew there was gonna be trouble so I said I wouldn't go, but I didn't want to be called chicken so I went along. Then I changed my mind and left the party before the trouble started. I really didn't see anything."

"Tell me a little about Esther."

Roger leaned over and dropped his voice.

"Not a bad lay, but nothin' between the ears, if you know what I mean. She was what you'd call a loose girl in those days. 'Course that was before the 'sex revolution' and any girl that wasn't a virgin when she got married . . . Well, you know what I mean.

"She used to hang around the Cobras. There was two kinds of girls that did that. Steady girlfriends and girls that just hung around the gang, but didn't go with one guy in particular. Esther was sort of in between. She was good lookin' enough to take out more than a few times, but everyone would get tired of her pretty fast."

"Why is that?"

"Ah, she'd want ya to be in love with her. She'd always be askin' you if you were in love with her. Then there would always be a scene." Hessey shrugged. "You can see what I mean."

Mark made some notes. This was leading nowhere. Mark asked a few more questions, then thanked Hessey and prepared to leave.

"How come they waited so long to arrest Bob?" Hessey asked as they walked toward the backyard gate.

"From what the D.A. tells me, Esther had amnesia all this time. Now she claims to remember the killings."

"What made them think she was involved in the first place?"

"They found her glasses at the scene of the Walters murder."

"You mean Lookout Park?"

"Yes."

"What does that have to do with it?"

"I guess they figure she lost her glasses on the night of the murder."

"She didn't lose them then."

"What?"

"I slapped those glasses off her, up in the park, about a week before those murders."

Sarah glanced at her watch and hoped that Bobby had not seen her. In twenty minutes, visiting hour would be over. She felt as if she would never last.

The visit had been a disaster from the moment the guard had shut the metal door behind them. His kiss had lasted too long and she felt that he was clinging to her the way a drowning man would cling to a piece of driftwood.

Their conversation began with a dozen variations of "how are you" and deteriorated into an inhibited discussion of generalities, punctuated by long, self-conscious silences. The longer she stayed with him, the clearer it became that the man who sat before her, shoulders bowed, eyes never meeting hers, was not the man who shared her bed for the past few months. Her lover was a man of substance. This was a man of shadow. She felt pity for the prisoner. Uncomfortable in his presence.

The guard rapped on the door and yelled, "Five minutes." It was time to ask the question she had come to ask.

"Bobby," she said, interrupting him.

He looked at her and knew what she was going to say by the way her voice trembled. He had dreaded this moment, anticipating it a thousand times in the solitude of his cell.

"Did you . . . ? Those two people . . . I've got to know."

It took all of his courage to take hold of her hand and look into her eyes.

"No, Sarah. I never . . ."

"Remember the night that we talked? The night before exams when you couldn't sleep. Why did you tell me that you had blood on your hands? Why wouldn't you let me ask you any more questions?"

The question struck him like a blow. He remembered the night very well and he had hoped that she had forgotten. He felt as if he was breaking up inside.

"I . . . In Vietnam . . . That's where I . . . killed an old man. An accident . . ."

He continued on, telling her about that night, wondering if she believed him. It was getting to be too much for him. If she loved him, why had she asked? Why couldn't she have just trusted him. He began to cry.

She reached over and let him cry on her shoulder. She felt embarrassed. That was all. She wanted to get away from him, the closeness of this antiseptic room, the smell of defeat.

"Sarah, you're all I've got. You have to believe me. I didn't . . . You're all I've got."

The guard knocked on the door and she helped him to stand and compose himself.

On the freeway, driving home, she thought about their meeting. Had he told her the truth when he denied killing the boy and the girl? As soon as she asked the question, she realized that the answer really didn't matter, because she no longer cared about Bobby Coolidge.

Esther sat in the dark next to the window. She had moved a wooden chair from the kitchen and placed it so that no one looking up from the street could see her. The fingers of her right hand gripped the edge of the window curtain and held it far enough from the window so that she could peek out without attracting notice.

Esther was certain that she was being watched. First, the lawyer had come to her apartment. Then, a few days later, he had called her. She told him again that she would not talk to him and she threatened to call the police.

That evening, she thought she heard someone moving about in her apartment, but there was no one there when she turned on the lights. At times there was a peculiar echo on the phone and she was certain that a blue and white Ford had passed by at least four times since the lawyer's phone call.

She had told all this to Roy and he had told her that it was her imagination. She said that it would all be okay if he would just stay with her. When she was with him, she felt so safe. She didn't want to tell him that she had been thinking about Bobby. How he might feel sitting in jail because of her. In a cell for the rest of his life. That was the sentence Roy had said he would get when she asked.

She thought she saw a movement in a doorway, but there was no one on the street. She must be wrong. Still, she couldn't sleep. She was too upset. She tried to imagine Dr. Hollander's fingers on her wrist, but she could not concentrate long enough to make that work. She kept thinking about Bobby and what it would be like to look at him from the witness stand and say the same things to him that she had told Roy and the doctor in the privacy of the doctor's office.

If Roy was with her—if he would hold her while she talked—she could do it. But she knew, because he had told her, that he would not be allowed in the courtroom. She would have to face Bobby alone. She felt frightened again. She wished Roy would come by again. He was always so kind to her. So gentle. He could make her forget the bad thoughts.

A man rose from his seat at the window of the apartment house across the street. He was an old man dressed in a sleeveless undershirt. A floor lamp situated behind his chair bathed his pale skin in light as he walked away from the window. Esther could see patches of gray hair on his arms. They revolted her. She imagined the old man moving about her apartment in the dark. She could feel the clammy touch of his hand on her cheek. She shuddered.

Why did she feel this way? Wasn't she telling the truth? Dr. Hollander had said so. It was amnesia that had kept her from remembering before. That's why she only remembered now. She knew it was the truth. Bobby would know when he heard her. He couldn't hate her for telling the truth.

She could see the telephone sitting on the end table by the sofa. Maybe she should call Roy. She wanted to. Only he seemed so annoyed the last time she had called. She wanted to hear his voice. Even if he was angry. She got up and stood over the phone. Why shouldn't she call? Weren't they lovers? Hadn't he whispered things to her? Told her about how important she was. If she was important, she could call him.

She touched the cold, black plastic of the receiver. She tried to lift it, but she couldn't. She put her hands to her face and rocked back and forth in front of the phone. She wanted to call so bad. Please, Roy, let me call. Don't be mad. She couldn't stand it if he was mad, 'cause if he was mad he might leave her and she loved him, needed him, so much.

She thought she heard a movement in the bedroom. She was going to look, but she was suddenly afraid. She had to call Roy. If there was a prowler, he couldn't be mad. She sat down on the sofa and dialed his number. Her eyes never left the bedroom door.

4

Mark knocked on the door a second time and wondered if Sarah was home. He was beginning to worry about her. She had broken appointments twice this week and she was evasive on the phone. Cindy had been complaining about the hours he had been putting into the Coolidge case and, every day, she asked him about the rest of the money.

The money worried Mark too, but it was more than that. He wanted to see Sarah. He thought about her constantly. He could picture her pale features and her long blond hair and wanted more and more to touch her.

She was as beautiful as he remembered, but he could not miss the look she gave him. It was a mixture of surprise and embarrassment, as if he had caught her in the middle of doing something she was ashamed of.

"What's wrong?" she asked nervously.

The question surprised him.

"Nothing's wrong. I . . . I wanted to see you. About the case," he said.

"Come in."

She sounded distracted and she brushed at her hair as she led him into the living room.

"I expected to see you at the office on Friday," he said when they were seated on the sofa.

"I couldn't make it. I . . . I'm sorry I didn't call. Something . . . An emergency came up."

"That's okay," he said quickly, not wanting her to think he was criticizing and trying to hide his disappointment in her obvious lie.

"How is the . . . Bobby's case coming? You said you had something to tell me."

"It's coming along just fine," he answered, grateful for a chance to avoid confronting her. "I've uncovered a witness who can help us."

He told her about Roger Hessey, talking quickly, afraid of losing her attention. She pretended to listen, but glanced around the room nervously, hearing only part of what he said. She wished he would leave. She knew he would ask about the money and she wasn't sure how she should handle that.

"That sounds hopeful," she said with what she hoped sounded like enthusiasm.

"Well, I don't want to get your hopes up, but I'm beginning to think I've got something."

They sat in silence for a second. Sarah didn't know what to say. She was getting a headache and she wanted him to leave.

"I . . . Uh, before I forget," Mark started, "did you talk to your parents about the, uh . . . the retainer?"

"About the money, Mark. I never called my parents."

He said nothing, stunned, letting what she said sink in. He looked into her eyes. She was seated so close that he could see the smoothness of her skin and his desire for her made it difficult for him to accept what she had just said.

"But you said you would . . ."

She touched his arm and it was like an electric shock.

"I don't want you to hate me, Mark, but I couldn't. I was going to. I didn't lie to you about that. When Bobby was first arrested, I couldn't believe it. Then I saw him at the jail."

She let go of him and stared into her lap. He wanted to hold her. To comfort her. It hurt him to see her distress.

"Mark, I don't know what to think. If he did kill that girl . . . I don't want you to continue on this case if you don't want to. I don't have the money. I . . . I lied to you. Not at first, but I couldn't ask my parents. What could I say?"

She trembled and tears welled up in her eyes.

"Don't you see? Could I say please help this man who raped and strangled a young girl who could have been me."

She broke down. He moved to her and held her, trying to comfort her while inside his own emotions were in chaos.

He could see the city stretching below through the picture window. A silver plane floated in the blue summer sky. Tears like tiny pearls were flowing over the soft curve of her cheek. He kissed them away and suddenly he was kissing her lips and they embraced with an intensity that left him breathless. What was he doing? He broke away, frightened by the depth of his passion for her.

"Mark," she said.

He got up and walked away.

"I'm sorry. I . . ."

"Don't blame yourself. You've done nothing wrong."

He turned toward her hopefully. She saw the look in his eyes.

"Mark, I can't. Not now. Please understand. It's all too confusing for me. Everything happened so fast. Keep the money I gave you. Tell Bobby to get another lawyer."

"I can't do that," he said. "And I . . . It will be okay about the money. If you just . . ."

She turned away from him. It would have been easier if he had gotten angry at her. She could see how crushed he was and she could no longer bear to be near him. He took a step toward her, then thought better of it.

When the door closed, she sank down on the couch. She looked toward the window and caught sight of herself in the mirror. She looked away. The apartment was suddenly very dark and very lonely. She felt unclean.

Shindler walked past the reception desk toward Phil Heider's office. He was exhausted, because he had spent half the night trying to calm down Esther. He was worried about her. If she cracked up, so did the case and she was beginning to come apart.

So far he had not told Heider about her midnight calls and the scenes he had witnessed at her apartment. He had gotten Hollander to prescribe some sedatives and he hoped those would get her through the two weeks left before the trial.

The trial. He shook his head. There would be no one there to help her when she testified. What if she cracked up on the stand? He had considered moving in with her, but had rejected the idea as too risky. The problem was that she had already tried suicide once. On the other hand, if it ever came out that the chief investigator in the case was screwing the star witness, Heider would never get a conviction.

"Roy."

Shindler stopped and looked around. Al Caproni was hailing him from his office door.

"What can I do for you?"

"I wondered if you'd found out anything about Toller."

"Who?" Shindler asked.

"Eddie Toller. The prisoner who said he saw the Murray girl alive in mid-January."

Shindler's face clouded.

"That's closed, Al. Forget it."

"Did you check it out?"

"There was nothing there."

"I don't know. He sounded so sincere. Maybe we should tell the lawyers for the Coolidges about him. We have a duty to tell the defense about any exculpatory evidence we know about and . . ."

"Listen," Shindler said in a low, angry voice, "there is nothing exculpatory in a wild, unsubstantiated story that some con has made up in order to get his ass out of jail. Those two bastards raped and strangled a defenseless girl and butchered a young man worth ten of them. Have you seen those pictures? Did you see that boy's face? Do you still want to tell the defense attorneys. Because, if you do, we're going to lose this case and you'll be responsible for setting that scum free."

Caproni was stunned by Shindler's outburst. The detective had always seemed so controlled.

"I didn't mean to go tell them now, Roy. Only if there was something to Toller's story."

"I'm sorry I blew up like that," Shindler apologized as soon as he realized what he had done. "I had a rough night last night. Look, I talked with Toller. There's nothing to his story. I questioned him pretty hard and he backed down on a lot of things."

"Like what?"

"Details," Shindler said evasively. "I can't remember any specific examples right now. Look, forget it, huh? I've got to see Heider now."

Shindler walked away and Caproni returned to his office. He did not believe Shindler. Something was wrong here. The question was what to do about it. He didn't want to run off half-cocked to Heider without more proof and he certainly didn't want to tell the defense about Toller if the prisoner's story was a fabrication. Then there was the problem of the time of death. If the coroner was right, Toller had to be mistaken or lying.

Caproni sorted through a stack of papers and picked up Dr. Beauchamp's autopsy report on Elaine Murray. Something in the report had bothered him when he had read it the first time, but he had not thought much of it, because he had not heard of Eddie Toller yet. He found the section and reread it. He didn't know enough about biology to know if he was right or not, but he knew someone who could help him. He picked up the phone and dialed the University Medical School.

The next day, at eleven in the morning, Caproni's intercom buzzed.

"There is a call for you from a Dr. Rohmer. Do you want to take it?"

"Yes," Caproni said, trying to contain his excitement. Kyle Rohmer was a young gynecologist who worked at the Medical School. Caproni had met him at a party approximately a year before and had seen him socially on occasion since then.

"Al," Rohmer said, "I've got the information you wanted. Fortunately, Dr. Gottlieb had actually done some research in the area, so I was able to find my sources pretty fast."

"Shoot."

"Okay. Now you say that the doctor who did the autopsy on the girl said she died four to six weeks before she was found and that morphologically identifiable sperm were found in her vagina. That's just not possible.

"Dr. O. J. Pollak's review of spermatozoa morphological survival time, in an article called 'Semen and Seminal Stains' found in the *Archives of Pathology*, 1943, states that thirty minutes to twenty-four hours is the more usual range. Dr. Bornstein in 'Investigation of Rape: Medico-Legal Problems,' *Medical Trial Technique Quarterly*, 1963, suggests forty-eight hours to be the maximum spermatozoa morphological survival time. Drs. Gonzales, Vance, Helpern, Milton,

Charles and Umberger in *Legal Medicine*, 1954, maintain that spermatozoa can be recovered from the vagina as long as three to four days after their introduction. W. F. Enos, G. T. Mann and W. D. Dolan report finding fragments of spermatozoa on a pap smear four days after an alleged rape in 'A Laboratory Procedure for the Detection of Semen—A Preliminary Report,' *American Journal of Clinical Pathology*, 1950. The longest survival time I was able to find in the literature was fourteen days. Now this was in a living vagina and the report has been discredited by numerous other authorities in the field. Dr. Gottlieb said he thought that seventy-two hours was probably the outside for survival. Does that help?"

"Yes. Very much. Can you mail me copies of the articles you just referred to?"

"Sure. Anything else you want me to do?"

"No. You've been a real help."

Caproni hung up the phone and closed his eyes. How to proceed? He now had concrete evidence to support Toller's story. He could go to Heider and tell him what he had discovered, but a feeling about his superior warned him not to. Heider was in this case to get publicity. Caproni had heard enough office scuttlebutt, and he had seen enough while working with Heider, to realize that Heider needed this case to further his political career. The case was unimportant. It served only as a means of getting Heider's name in the papers every week. He was not going to dismiss a prosecution of this magnitude on the basis of the findings in a few scattered medical journals. Especially when the evidence pointing toward guilt was so strong.

And that was the crux of Caproni's problem. He had gone through the evidence and he believed that the Coolidges were guilty. Toller's story raised a possibility that they were not, but only a possibility and a slim one at that. Even so, under the United States Supreme Court decision in *Brady versus Maryland* the prosecution was obligated to turn over to the defense any evidence in its possession that would tend to clear a defendant and Toller's evidence would meet the criteria, if Toller was telling the truth. If the prosecution kept Toller's story secret and the defense found out, the Coolidges would have grounds for overturning their convictions if they were found guilty. And more important as far as Caproni was concerned, if the prosecution did not reveal Toller's information to the defense, it would be violating the Canon of Ethics. If Toller was telling the truth!

Caproni sighed. He was back where he started. He had to have some way of substantiating the facts in Toller's story. And there was a way that he could do that, he suddenly realized. Find Heartstone. He had an idea. A person like Heartstone would have to have a criminal record. He might have been arrested recently. If he had, there would be a file on his case and, in that file, a police report with the defendant's address. He hurried down to the file room.

Caproni was in luck. Eleven months ago, William Lewis Heartstone had been arrested for "Public Intoxication" and "Carrying a Concealed Weapon." Officer Clark McGivern had responded to a call concerning a disturbance at a skid row bar. Heartstone had been drunk, raving and brandishing a taped broom handle which McGivern found concealed under Heartstone's coat at the time of the arrest. Caproni looked for the section of the report that was used to list the defendant's address. It was blank.

Caproni returned to his office and dialed police headquarters. Officer McGivern was on patrol, but the officer he spoke to promised to have him called on his car radio. Twenty minutes later McGivern was on the phone. At five-thirty that evening, he was seated in a booth in a coffee shop several blocks from the courthouse sipping coffee while Caproni explained a confidential project he wished him to undertake.

"I remember this case vaguely," McGivern said, after studying the copy of the police report that Caproni brought with him. McGivern was young, tall and well built. He had blue eyes, a nice smile that revealed a set of perfect teeth and sandy blond hair that was balding prematurely. "Whatever happened to him? It never went to trial, did it?"

"No. Heartstone was recoged and never showed for trial."

"I'm not surprised he missed his court date. Probably forgot he was arrested by the time the booze wore off."

"Do you think you could find him for me?"

"I can try, but it might take some time. The guy looked like a transient. He might not even be in town."

"I realize that, but it's very important.

"There's one more thing. I want this kept confidential. I don't want you telling anyone what you are doing or who you are doing it for and that includes police officers, district attorneys, anyone."

McGivern's brow furrowed and he looked at Caproni suspiciously.

"This isn't something illegal?"

"No, it's not illegal, but the work I am doing is very sensitive. If word of this leaked to the wrong people, there could be plenty of trouble," Caproni said, failing to add that he was the one who would be in trouble.

Caproni took out his business card and wrote his home phone number and address on the back. He handed the card to McGivern.

"As soon as you locate Heartstone, I want to know. Day or night."

McGivern fingered the card and placed it in his wallet. They shook hands and Caproni left.

Bobby Coolidge was standing on the second-floor balcony of a manor house of a great estate. The manor house was constructed of an odd combination of Ionic columns, stark concrete blocks and un-painted wooden planks. The house was incomplete and furnished rooms, carpeted with Persian rugs and lighted by Tiffany lamps, opened into bare rooms whose western walls did not exist and whose ceiling was the sky.

Bobby gazed across a rolling lawn, lush, green and smelling of new-mown grass. A low hedge separated the estate from a dark and forboding wood and an arched lattice work provided the only means of entrance into the forest. Sarah stood beneath the roses that twined around the thin, white-painted wood sticks of the arch. She was dressed in a white hoop skirt and looked as if she had just attended an antebellum ball given at the home of a Georgia plantation owner.

There was an orchid in Sarah's hair and her blond tresses flew behind her like honey-colored wings as she whirled into the forest, disappearing, then reappearing, in a flash of white petticoats.

Bobby watched helplessly as she danced deeper into the dark woods. Panic seized him and he rushed through the corridors of the empty house looking for a way out. Suddenly he was at the top of a spiral stairway that twisted downward toward the main ballroom. A figure climbed to meet him, its face shrouded in shadow. Its hand stretching out. Bobby screamed as he looked deep into the eyes of the old man.

The young guard listened sympathetically to Bobby's request to see a doctor and promised that he would pay immediate attention to the problem. Later, in the guard room, he noted the request, along with those of several other prisoners, in a report.

In his cell, Bobby lay on his bunk, his forearm pressed tightly against his closed eyelids. How will I make it through another night, he asked himself. How will I survive the trial?

He pondered the significance of the dream. The unfinished mansion—his hopes. The dark and gloomy woods—his future. The fleeting vision of Sarah, far off and fading into the silence of the forest. He refused to dwell on this last component of his dream.

Bobby thought about life in hell. He knew the

subject well, for that is where he resided. Death would be preferable to being caged for the rest of his life, especially now that he had glimpsed paradise.

He thought about getting up and doing some calisthenics. He was losing weight, but his body was becoming flabby. Exercise would keep him in shape. He knew all this, but he had no energy and could see no reason to move.

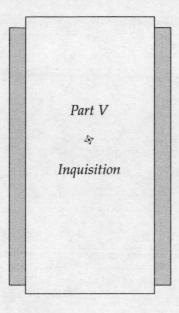

Part V

Inquisition

1

"Yes?" Caproni yawned. The ringing of the phone had roused him from a deep sleep. The phosphorescent hands of his alarm clock indicated that it was one in the morning.

"Mr. Caproni, I'm sorry to wake you, but this is Officer McGivern. I've located Heartstone."

Caproni sat up in bed and switched on a reading lamp.

"What have you got?"

"The Cedar Arms, room 310. It's a transient hotel over on Third and Wallace."

Caproni jotted down the address on a pad on his nightstand.

"I'll be there in half an hour," Caproni said. "Don't wait in front of the hotel or he might see you."

"Don't worry," McGivern said, "I'll be a block away on Prescott, where I can see the front of the hotel."

Caproni hung up and dressed. He wanted to find Heartstone, but he wished that McGivern had found him on some other night. The Coolidge brothers had elected to have separate trials and Bobby's had started last week. It had taken several days to pick a jury and the state was now presenting evidence. While Heider conducted the trial, Caproni was in and out of the courtroom, coordinating witnesses, researching legal points and taking care of emergencies. The pace had been grueling and the work did not stop when court recessed. At five o'clock, he and Heider would go back to the office to prepare for the next day of trial. This evening he had returned home at ten o'clock, completely drained.

Caproni backed his car out of the garage and pointed it downtown. He yawned and switched on the radio for company. So far there had been no deviations from the script that Heider had so carefully orchestrated. Of course, the witnesses to date had all been policemen who were involved in the investigation and a few civilians, like the parents of the victims, who had provided background for the jury. The crucial part of the case that would tie in Coolidge with the murders would begin tomorrow when Heider called Roger Hessey. Hessey would take the jury to the party at Alice Fay's house. He would be followed by the people who had attended the party and witnessed the fight.

After that would come two boys, grown men now, who had talked to Richie Walters and Elaine Murray outside the movie theater on the evening of the crime and who were the last people to see them alive. Mr. Shultz would tell the jury about the drag race on Monroe Boulevard and several people who knew would describe the car that Bobby and Billy were driving on the evening of November 25, 1960.

Thelma Pullen would tell the jury about the girl she had seen running through her backyard on the

evening of the crime, after her dogs had awakened
her. Dr. Webber would explain how Esther's glasses
were traced to her. Dr. Trembler would identify the
glasses as belonging to Esther. Dr. Hollander would
lecture the jurors on hypnosis and amnesia and discuss his treatment of Esther. Esther would testify
and Dr. Beauchamp would wrap up the show with a
graphic description of cause of death, aided by some
of the most gruesome photographs that Caproni had
ever seen.

While Caproni was excited about the way the technical side of the state's case was going, he was disappointed by Mark Shaeffer's poor showing. Shaeffer
seemed confused and preoccupied. He had raised
few of the pretrial motions Caproni and Heider had
anticipated and the points that had been raised were
poorly researched and argued. Judge Samuels, who
had been assigned the case, had lost patience with
Shaeffer on several occasions because of the attorney's lack of preparation.

Caproni felt the urgency of clearing up the mystery
surrounding Toller's story more than ever now. He
had no desire to aid the defense, but he had a strong
sense of justice. Shaeffer was doing such a poor job
that the truth might never come out at the trial. That
made tonight's interview with Heartstone crucial.

Caproni parked behind McGivern's car and
walked over to it. McGivern got out and handed Caproni a mug shot of Heartstone. Caproni was always
astounded at what life could do to human beings. The
face in the picture was long and thin, with sunken
cheeks and rotting teeth that showed through the gap
made by scarred and cracked lips. Heartstone was not

the worst example of the desperate man Caproni had ever seen, but he did evoke strong feelings of revulsion and pity.

"Let's go," Caproni said. "When we get to the hotel I want you to wait outside. I have to talk with him alone."

"He could be dangerous," McGivern said.

"I realize that, but it can't be helped."

The entrance to the Cedar Arms was a narrow glass-paned door with a "Rooms to Rent" sign taped to one of the panes. There was no lobby. A flight of linoleum-covered stairs led up to a landing lit by a low-wattage bulb. The cracked plaster walls exuded an odor of cooked, canned chile. Caproni tried not to breathe.

The metal number three on Heartstone's door was hanging upside down from the bottom nail. Caproni doubted if the door had seen a coat of paint since the building had been completed. He knocked loudly. A radio was playing in a room down the hall. Bedsprings whined and a voice inside Heartstone's room badly slurred the words "Whaddyawant." Caproni said "Mr. Heartstone" in a low voice and knocked again. The voice said, "I'm comin', goddammit" and a shoe worn by a foot out of control thudded on the uncarpeted floor. The lock clicked and the face in the mugshot peered through a crack in the door. Caproni was almost overcome by the man's breath. He did not need to see Heartstone's bleary and bloodshot eyes to know that the man had been drinking heavily. The sight of a man in a suit had a sobering effect on Heartstone. His intelligence was low, but he operated with a certain amount of animal cun-

ning. In his environment suits were worn by people
who wanted to hurt you, usually the law. He said nothing and waited for Caproni to identify himself. Caproni handed him a business card through the slit in
the door.

"Mr. Heartstone, I'm Al Caproni. I'm with the
district attorney's office and I need some help from
you on a case. Could I come in?"

Caproni had used the phrase "need some help" on
purpose. He imagined it had been quite some time
since anyone had asked Willie Heartstone for help
or he had been able to give any.

"About what?" Heartstone asked, his interest
piqued.

"I'd rather not discuss it standing out here where
other people can hear us," Caproni answered in a tone
which he hoped was conspiratorial.

Heartstone tried to weigh his alternatives for a moment, but the task proved too much for him and it
must have appeared simpler to let Caproni in, because
he moved back and opened the door.

The room smelled of stale clothing and unwashed bodies. A bed covered by rumpled sheets was
pushed under the only window. The window was
open and late night street sounds drifted in.

Someone had placed a laced doily on top of the
dresser. Someone else had stained it. There was an
overstuffed secondhand armchair under an ancient
pole lamp and a sink attached to the wall catercorner
from the window. Caproni sat in the armchair while
Heartstone turned on the tap and splashed cold
water on his face. A small mirror was suspended
above the sink from a rusted nail embedded in the

cracked and flaking plaster. The paint on its cheap frame was chipping and the zinc backing showed through in spots, breaking up the face reflected there. Heartstone stared in the mirror and rubbed his eyes as if in disbelief. He turned away from the mirror and dried his face on a towel that hung over the side of the dresser. Then he sat down opposite Caproni on the edge of the bed. There was a half-filled fifth of cheap Scotch and a five-and-dime glass sitting on the nightstand. Heartstone filled the glass and drank from it. He coughed, wiped his mouth and then, suddenly remembering that Caproni was in the room, offered the bottle to him.

"No thank you, Mr. Heartstone," Caproni said.

"Suitcherself," Heartstone replied and poured a refill. The drink seemed to make him more sober.

"I came here to ask you for information about a case I'm working on."

Heartstone eyed him suspiciously.

"I ain't gone talk wit' no cops. Lass time they pulled me in when it was that other damn guy. The son of a bitch."

"This is about a case that occurred some time ago."

Heartstone stood up. He seemed steadier on his feet than he had when he sat down. His face looked meaner.

"Lissen, if this is about that rap where I was falsely accused of a weapon, I ain't talkin' to no cop. That was a frame. That bastard bartender cheated me. Besides," he added sheepishly, the anger in his voice changing rapidly to shame, "I don't remember most of what happened."

"This has nothing to do with that incident, Mr. Heartstone," Caproni assured him. He seemed relieved and sat down again. Caproni checked the door and window for a possible exit if the man got violent. He also checked the room for possible weapons. Heartstone reached for the Scotch bottle and grabbed it by the neck.

"Were you living in Portsmouth in 1960 and '61?"

"Sure," Heartstone said suspiciously, his hand resting on the bottle neck. "I ain't never lived no other place."

"Where were you living at that time?"

Heartstone passed his other hand in front of his face, trying to clear away the cobwebs that draped the corridors of his faded, alcoholic memory.

"Shit, I don't know," he answered finally.

"Were you living with someone named Ralph?"

Heartstone's face clouded and his voice took on an edge of potential violence.

"Why d'you want to know about Ralph? He's long gone. Went to Arizona years ago."

"We want to speak to him."

"About what? What is this?"

Caproni decided that it was time to get to the truth.

"We believe that Ralph murdered a girl in January of 1961."

Caproni did not see the bottle, but he heard the animal roar that escaped from Heartstone's throat at the moment the bottle connected with his temple. For a moment he was blind and falling. Then his head made hard contact with the floor and Heartstone's boot made harder contact with the back of his skull.

When he came to, a half hour had passed and the room was empty. Heartstone had cleared out. The door of a small closet was open and the closet was empty. Two dresser drawers were half open. Caproni could see all this from his position on the floor. There was a terrible pain in his head and it got worse when he tried to sit up. He gritted his teeth and squeezed his eyes shut, but lying down again was the only thing that helped.

He felt like a fool. How had that wino caught him so off guard? He had never expected him to move so fast. He tried to sit up again and made it by rolling to his side and getting his knees under him. He touched his head. It was tender enough to make him grimace, but, miraculously, there was no blood. Scattered pieces of glass lay all over the floor and Caproni tried not to cut himself on them.

When he was on his feet, he washed his face in the sink. He wondered why McGivern had not come up to find him, then he remembered that he had told him to stay downstairs. What an idiot he had been. He assumed that Heartstone was far away by now. There must be a back entrance. If he had gone out the front, McGivern would have apprehended him or come upstairs to see why he had not come down. He was beginning to conclude that he deserved the kick in the head that Heartstone had administered. He had completely botched things.

When he was well enough, Caproni eased himself downstairs. McGivern was leaning against a parked car and he rushed over when Caproni staggered out.

"What happened?"

"He hit me with a bottle of Scotch and a few other things that he had handy," Caproni answered.

"Are you okay?"

"I think so."

"I'll radio his description and we can pick him up."

"No," Caproni said quickly. Everything he was doing was behind Heider's back and potentially damaging to the state's case. He could not risk word of it getting back to Heider.

McGivern gave him a puzzled look, then shrugged his shoulders.

"I think I should take you to the hospital for an x-ray."

"I agree. But first I want to go to the county jail. There's a prisoner there that I have to see."

The front entrance of the county jail looked like the portal of a medieval castle. Caproni rang an electric bell that looked out of place buried in the cold stone blocks and a second later the red iron bars of the front gate swung open.

He walked up a short flight of stairs into a circular reception area. To the right was a counter and, behind the counter, a hallway leading to the office of the jail commander. A guard sat behind the counter. He put down a copy of *True Detective* magazine, took his heels off his desk and stood up.

"I'm with the D.A.'s office. It's urgent that I see one of your prisoners, Edward Toller."

The guard looked at Caproni's identification and handed it back.

"I'll get him in a second," he said and pressed a button on the jail intercom. There was a crackling noise and a voice answered. The guard said, "I need a cell block on an Edward Toller."

There was silence for a second, then the voice on the intercom said, "He's not here. Are you sure you have the name right?"

The guard looked at Caproni and Caproni nodded.

"Check the files on him, will you? I have a D.A. here who wants to talk to him."

There was more silence.

"I got it," the voice said. "He was released a week and a half ago."

"Ask him why," Caproni said. Something was going on here that he did not like.

"Charges were dropped. That's all I know," said the voice.

"Dropped by who?" Caproni asked.

"The court order just says motion of district attorney."

McGivern drove Caproni to the hospital and waited until four o'clock, when he was released. Then he drove him back to his car. Caproni longed for sleep, but he had made a decision that would deny him that pleasure. It wasn't an easy decision for him to make, because he wanted, more than anything, to be a district attorney, and what he was about to do could cost him his job. It wasn't a decision that he was certain was right, not only because he feared that what he was doing might help to set two murderers free, but because his solution was a compromise. In his heart, he knew that he should approach Judge Samuels with what he knew, but that would be the end of his career. Instead, he had chosen a middle road.

There was a night guard on duty at the courthouse. Caproni showed him his identification and took the elevator to the district attorney's office. It was eerie walking the halls of the deserted office at night and Caproni thought he heard footsteps or breathing at every turn. He found what he was looking for and carried the material to the copying machine. At six o'clock, he returned home, showered, shaved, ate a large breakfast and dressed for work.

2

"Your next witness, Mr. Heider," Judge Samuels said.

"The state will call Roger Hessey, Your Honor."

Mark Shaeffer watched the bailiff summon Hessey from the corridor. Hessey walked through the ornate courtroom doors dressed more like a swinging single than a witness in a murder case. He was nervous and his facial expressions moved back and forth between a look of deathlike solemnity and an inappropriate, overdone, smile as Philip Heider led him through his part in the events of November 25, 1960.

Shaeffer rubbed his eyes and wished that he could take a short nap. The trial was exhausting him. He was working late and not sleeping well. He looked at Coolidge, who was seated next to him. He was off in space again and Mark leaned over and whispered to him for no other purpose than to make it appear that the defendant was taking some part in his own trial.

Mark had emphasized the importance that a jury would attach to an attitude of indifference manifested by an accused, but Coolidge had gone through the first week of trial without showing any sign of involvement. At times his eyes appeared glassed over, as if, like a zombie, he was already dead and only his body was on trial. Mark had seriously considered calling a halt to the trial so that Coolidge could be examined by a psychiatrist for the purpose of determining whether or not he could aid and assist in his own defense, but he had concluded that Coolidge was not mentally incompetent, merely defeated.

Yesterday, after court had recessed, Mark watched the guards lead Bobby away down the long corridor to the jail elevator and was suddenly overcome by a dizzying emotion similar to the unnerving disorientation that accompanies *déjà vu*. Perhaps it was the angle of the sun, but the sight of Coolidge in handcuffs, his head and shoulders bowed, his body diminishing in size as it floated down the corridor, a scene he had witnessed on numerous occasions, overwhelmed him. He saw with great clarity his responsibilities in this matter and only a great exercise of will kept him from giving up in despair.

When Shaeffer turned to Coolidge, he caught sight of Sarah sitting in the back of the courtroom. The sight of her angered him. He had arranged for her to visit Bobby any time she chose, but she had refused to see him. Mark had been forced to lie to Bobby to explain why she would not see him.

Sarah had avoided Mark since that day in her apartment and he had slowly come to realize that he had been used by her. He wanted to confront her, but his feelings of guilt over the desire he felt for her made him impotent. He wondered why she insisted on coming to the trial each day and concluded that she wanted to see her belief in Bobby's guilt justified so she could rationalize her desertion of a man who loved her and her lies to him.

"Mr. Hessey, the defendant was a member of a teenage gang called the Cobras, was he not?" Heider asked.

"Yes," Hessey answered.

Judge Samuels looked up from some papers he had been reading and over toward Shaeffer to see what his reaction would be to Heider's last question. Shaeffer seemed oblivious to the danger Judge Samuels saw so clearly on the horizon.

Judge Samuels felt sorry for Shaeffer. He seemed like a nice boy, but he should never have accepted a case of this magnitude. Samuels had tried to give him subtle tips on how to conduct his defense when he realized the boy's inexperience, but Shaeffer seemed distracted and nervous and he never caught on.

"What was the purpose of this gang, Mr. Hessey?"

"What, uh, did we do, do you mean?" Hessey replied uncertainly. He had been a nervous witness, looking at the judge or jury for approval whenever he gave an answer.

"Exactly."

Hessey shifted in his seat and ran his hands along the arms of his chair.

"Well, we got together, you know. Had parties . . ."

His voice trailed off.

"Weren't members of the gang constantly involved in street fights and . . . ?"

"Mr. Shaeffer," Judge Samuels's voice boomed, "aren't you going to object to that question?"

Shaeffer's eyes jerked up from his notes. He had been preoccupied with thoughts of Sarah and he had missed Heider's last few questions. Shaeffer's confusion was apparent to Samuels and the jurist reddened with anger when he realized that Mark did not know what he was talking about. Shaeffer's lack of competence was forcing Samuels to take more of a role in the trial than was proper, yet his conscience and sense of professional ethics made it impossible for him to stand by day after day while Heider ran roughshod over his opponent.

"I'm sorry, I . . ." Shaeffer stuttered. Samuels glared at him for a second, then turned his wrath on Heider.

"It is becoming increasingly apparent to this Court that counsel for both sides have forgotten the rules of evidence concerning examination of witnesses. A person of your experience, Mr. Heider, should know that this entire line of questioning is not permissible."

Heider rose and accepted the judge's challenge. He did not appear to take offense at the judge's remarks and his manner was gracious.

"Your Honor, if this line of questioning is improper, then I will not continue with it. As there was no objection from defense counsel, I assumed the questions were proper."

That little son of a bitch always has the right answers, Samuels thought. He would lose no points with the jury after that response and he had made Shaeffer look bad.

Heider finished his examination of Hessey by leading him through the events at Alice Fay's party. He quizzed him about the attitude of Bobby and Billy toward rich people. Shaeffer, as if to make up for his earlier inattention, made numerous objections, most of which were overruled as improper.

"No further questions," Heider said.

"Your witness, Mr. Shaeffer."

"Thank you, Your Honor."

Mark checked through his notes one last time. He was excited by the prospect of cross-examining Hessey. For the first time in the trial Mark felt that he would be able to score points. The state was basing its case on the credibility of Esther Pegalosi. It had tied her to the murder scene through her glasses. Mark was now prepared to destroy that key link between the star witness and the scene of the crime.

"Mr. Hessey, in 1960, you dated Esther Pegalosi on several occasions, did you not?"

"I guess so."

"You and Mrs. Pegalosi had sexual relations, did you not?"

Hessey hung his head and grinned sheepishly.

"Me and most everyone else I knew."

Heider was on his feet objecting and the spectators were laughing.

"Mr. Hessey, just answer the question," Judge Samuels instructed.

"Mr. Hessey, did Esther wear glasses?"

"Not all the time. She used to wear them when she was in class and at a movie. Times like that. Sometimes she'd keep them on after."

"Is it fair to say that Lookout Park was used as a 'make out' spot in 1960 by large numbers of teenagers?"

Hessey smiled.

"Yes, sir," he said a bit too enthusiastically and several of the spectators laughed.

"Did you ever use Lookout Park to 'make out'?"

"Yes, sir," Hessey answered with even more enthusiasm. Philip Heider and Judge Samuels joined in the laughter this time.

"Did you use Lookout Park to 'make out' approximately one week before the murders of Richie Walters and Elaine Murray?"

Heider's face clouded over and the laughter in the courtroom died down.

"What's he getting at?" Heider whispered to Caproni. Caproni shook his head and concentrated on the questions.

"Yes, sir. About one week before."

"How do you remember that?"

"Well, I remember when they found Richie Walters up there joking about how it could have been me, because I had been right up by the hill just the week before."

"And you are sure of that?"

"Yes."

"Where had you been prior to making out in the park, one week before the murders?"

"To the movies."

"With whom?"

"With Esther."

"When you drove to Lookout Park was Esther wearing her glasses?"

"Yes."

"How do you know?"

Hessey looked suddenly serious and embarrassed.

"Well, uh, I tried to take them off when we parked, but she wouldn't let . . . she, uh, said 'no dice.'"

"To taking off the glasses?"

"She, uh, didn't, uh, want to make out."

"Why was that?"

"Well, I was, uh, dating another girl I'd started seeing." He shrugged. "I guess she was jealous."

"When she said that she wouldn't make out, did you get angry?"

Hessey hung his head.

"I guess so."

"What did you do?"

"Well, she started in on me about this girl. I can't even remember her name now. And I yelled back and she ran out of the car."

"Did you chase her?"

Hessey nodded.

"You'll have to speak up, Mr. Hessey."

"Yes."

"Where were you parked when she ran out of the car?"

"The meadow."

"The meadow? Is that the same meadow where Richie Walters's body was found?"

"Yeah. All the kids used that meadow to make out. In the summer it was usually packed."

"What did you do when you caught Esther?"

Hessey mumbled something.

"You will have to speak up, Mr. Hessey. What did you do?"

"I slapped her."

"And what happened to her glasses?"

"They went flying off."

There was a gasp in the courtroom. Several of the jurors were writing furiously. Heider and Caproni were engaged in a rapid-fire consultation.

"No further questions," Shaeffer said. He could feel a pulse pounding in his ears and his hands were shaking.

"Mr. Heider," Judge Samuels said, secretly amused at Heider's discomfort.

"One moment, if you please, Your Honor."

Shaeffer turned to see how Bobby had reacted to his bombshell. For the first time in the trial, Coolidge was leaning forward, attentive. Mark turned toward Sarah, but she would not meet his eyes. Heider and Caproni ended their conversation.

"Mr. Hessey, were you in the habit of slapping women in your younger days?"

"Like I said, I did a lot of things then that I am not proud of now."

"Had you ever slapped Esther before?"

"Yes."

"Ever knock her glasses off before?"

Hessey paused.

"Once I think."

"What did she do when you did that?"

Hessey looked as if he wanted to crawl into a hole.

"Cried, I guess."

"No, Mr. Hessey, I mean with the glasses. What did she do with the glasses?"

Hessey paused.

"Picked them up, I guess."

"And what did she do when you slapped off her glasses in Lookout Park?"

Hessey stared at Heider open mouthed, then he shook his head from side to side.

"I can't remember."

"Did you drive her home from the park?"

"Yeah. I'm pretty sure I did."

"Is it likely that she would have forgotten her glasses?"

"No," Hessey said thoughtfully.

"Do you remember now whether she picked up her glasses?"

"I don't."

"But you will not swear that she did not?"

"No. I'm not sure."

"Did she drop her purse when you slapped her, Mr. Hessey?"

"No . . . No, I'm pretty sure she didn't."

"Did she drop a cigarette lighter on the evening you slapped her?"

"No, just the glasses."

"Or a blue rat-tail comb?"

"No."

Heider smiled at the witness.

"No further questions."

Judge Samuels looked at Mark to see if he wished to ask any further questions. Mark just shook his head.

"I think that this would be a good time to adjourn," Judge Samuels said. "We will reconvene at nine-thirty tomorrow morning."

"He killed us, didn't he?" Bobby said bitterly as the jury filed out.

"No, I think we scored some real points with

Hessey," Mark said, but he did not believe it. He was crestfallen. He knew that he was not doing a good job, but he had hoped to redeem himself with Hessey. Now he had nothing. Heider had completely neutralized the effect of Hessey's testimony about the glasses. He had also established that Esther had been in possession of her glasses as late as one week before the murders.

"See you tomorrow, counselor," Bobby said sarcastically as the guard led him out. Mark watched Heider leave with a trace of bitterness. He began to gather up his papers.

"Mark, I have to talk to you."

Mark looked up. Albert Caproni was standing behind him. He had spoken so softly that Shaeffer had barely heard him.

"Can I meet you at your office, tonight?"

"Sure," Mark said. Caproni was looking around, as if he was afraid to be seen talking to Mark.

"What's the problem?" Mark asked, puzzled.

"I can't explain here. Promise me you won't mention our meeting to anyone. Not even your wife."

Mark started to ask Caproni what was wrong, then changed his mind. Caproni was scared and Mark respected Caproni enough to accept his request.

"I won't say a word."

"Eight o'clock," Caproni said and walked rapidly from the courtroom.

Albert Caproni was waiting in the shadows of the lobby when Mark arrived at his office building.

He refused to speak until they were safely locked in Mark's office. Once the door was closed, he placed his attaché case on the desk in front of him.

"There are some ground rules I want you to agree to before I tell you anything," Caproni said. Mark noticed the edge in Caproni's voice and the nervous way his fingers drummed on the desk. "First, you must swear to me that under no circumstances will you ever tell anyone about this meeting. If you did, it might cost me my job."

"Al, is this something to do with Bobby's case? Because, if it is, I don't know if I can ethically promise you anything."

"Well, you're going to have to bend your ethics, because what I have to tell you might win this case for you, but I am not going to risk my career and I won't tell you anything until I get your promise."

Mark hesitated, then agreed to Caproni's demand.

"Okay. Now, some of what I am going to tell you could provide grounds for dismissal of the case, but only if I were called as a witness. Do I have your promise that you will never attempt to call me as a witness, no matter what I tell you?"

"You know something that could lead to a dismissal of the charges and you want me to promise you that I won't call you?" Mark asked, aghast.

"Yes. Other information I give you may clear your client, so what I know may not be necessary. But you will get nothing from me."

"What choice have I got?" Mark said. "You have my promise."

Caproni sighed and leaned back in his chair. For the next half hour he recounted the events surrounding Eddie Toller's story and his subsequent disappearance and his meeting with Heartstone in the skid row hotel. He also told Shaeffer about the research that Dr. Rohmer had done for him.

"The problem with all this is that nothing I've uncovered can be substantiated. Toller's gone, so he can't testify and Heartstone has split. There's a good chance, given Toller's background, that his story is a lie he invented to get a deal. And Heartstone might have run away for reasons unconnected with Elaine Murray's murder."

"There must be something we can do," Mark said.

"I've been thinking and I have an idea. The real importance of Toller's story is that it places Elaine Murray in that basement alive almost six weeks after the Coolidges are supposed to have killed her. Does your client have an alibi for the first few weeks in January?"

Mark thought for a second, then his face brightened.

"They were in the hospital. It was a car accident or something. Wait, I have it here in my notes."

He shuffled through some papers until he had the right one.

"January 3, 1961, until early February."

"All right," Caproni said. "If you can prove Elaine Murray was alive in January, you get an acquittal."

"But how do I do that?"

"Have the body exhumed and reexamined."

"What?"

"Make us dig up the body."

Mark looked at Caproni to see if he was serious. Caproni stared back. His face showed no trace of humor. Mark felt that events were getting out of hand. Caproni was asking too much of him.

"How am I going to do that? You say you won't get involved. I don't see how I could get Judge Samuels to sign a court order."

Shaeffer's negative attitude irritated Caproni. He expected Mark to be excited. Instead he seemed afraid of his new responsibilities.

"I've thought of that. Line up several of the top gynecologists in Portsmouth and put them on at a hearing. They'll testify that the acidity in the vagina would have destroyed any trace of sperm shortly after Murray died. Just show Samuels Dr. Beauchamp's autopsy report and you have your grounds."

Mark made hasty notes while Caproni spoke. He wondered where he would get the money to hire the doctors. He could not take it from his remaining fee or he would end up trying the case for nothing.

"I brought something else that might help," Caproni said, laying a thick sheaf of papers on the desk. "This is a copy of a transcript of the hypnosis sessions with Esther Pegalosi. It might help you prepare your cross-examination."

Caproni stood up and closed his attaché case.

"I . . . I'm really grateful for all this," Mark said. "I know what a risk you're taking and I . . ."

Caproni was exhausted. All he wanted to do was get some sleep.

"Don't thank me, Mark. Just pray that I haven't helped set a murderer free."

3

"What do you think?" Mark asked.

"I think that there is an excellent possibility that Esther did not see the Walters boy killed," Dr. Nathan Paris replied.

Mark breathed a deep sigh of relief. He felt well prepared for his cross-examination of Esther Pegalosi, but he needed a medical explanation of her testimony if he was going to convince the jury that she was not worthy of belief. Dr. Paris was a professor of psychiatry at the University Medical School, a Diplomate of the American Board of Psychiatry and Neurology and a respected author and lecturer in the field of memory and hypnosis. In addition to his credentials, he had the boyish good looks and open, forthright manner that impressed a jury.

They had just returned to Mark's office from the courthouse where Dr. Hollander had testified. As part of Dr. Hollander's testimony, the tapes of his hypnosis and amytal sessions with Esther Pegalosi had been played. Dr. Paris had been permitted to listen to them so that he could evaluate the sessions.

Mark had prepared him by giving him the transcript to study over the weekend.

"Why do you think she's lying?" Mark asked.

"She's not necessarily lying. Are you familiar with the term 'confabulation'?"

Mark shook his head.

"'Con' means with and 'fabulation,' coming from fable or fabulary, means talk or discourse. Confabulation may mean just carrying on a conversation or constructing a fable, or it may have the more technical meaning given to it by neurologists when they are discussing the type of story constructed to impress the listener that it is in fact a rendition of reality when the storyteller is suffering from a memory defect. In other words, the storyteller constructs a fable to compensate for a memory defect. You see this with alcoholics who have brain damage and who have been in a hospital for a few months. You ask them where they were the day before and they will tell you they were at such and such a place having a great time."

"Is confabulation limited to people with brain damage?"

"No. Psychiatrists and neurologists use the term to mean making up a tale. There is an interesting study that was conducted in 1954 by two Yale researchers named Rubenstein and Newman. They wanted to check the validity of past memories related by people under hypnosis. They reasoned that one way to check on possible confabulation or suggestibility by people supposedly remembering past events would be to put a person in a hypnotic trance and have them visualize themselves ten years in the future and describe what was happening. If they could describe what was happening in 1979, then it would raise some question as to the validity of their recollections of what had happened in 1939.

"The researchers worked with five subjects and found that they could consistently live out 'future' experiences when an age or date was suggested to them under hypnosis. The futures that they created for themselves were plausible and well within the realm of probability as judged from a personality study that had been made of the subjects prior to the start of the investigation.

"So, you see, you may have memories of things that did occur, things that occurred only in fantasy and things that have never occurred at all."

"And Esther?" Mark asked.

"When a person is given amytal for the purpose of suppressing consciousness in addition to hypnosis, this person is placed in a greater state of suggestibility than if she is fully conscious. If a person is suffering from amnesia, we use hypnosis or drugs to make the guardians of that person's repressed memory lower its guard. When that happens, information comes out more easily. But this is a two-edged sword and the patient becomes more open to the suggestions, intentional or unintentional, of her questioner, because her psychological defenses are depressed and her ability to test reality against unreality is weakened.

"My impression of Esther Pegalosi from hearing the tapes and reading the transcript is that she is a person with an extremely poor self-image. She tried to kill herself once. She longs to be a strong, self-confident woman. She craves love. I think that Dr. Hollander, and to a lesser extent, Detective Shindler, became father figures and love objects during her therapy sessions. As such, anything that they suggested would be eagerly accepted out of a fear of losing their affection as well as a desire to please them.

"Esther originally claimed to have had so much to drink on the evening of the murders that she could not remember what she had done. There is your memory defect, just waiting for a fable to fill up the missing time period.

"I can point to several instances during the hypnosis sessions when questions concerning important information were put to Esther in a manner that suggested the answer. For instance, in Tape #5 Esther is told that she went cruising downtown after they finished drinking the stolen wine. It is then suggested that she took Monroe Boulevard home. She rejects this and states that she usually goes home by way of Marshall Road. The questioner then states, 'But you could go that way,' meaning Monroe. She is then told to fantasize that she is on Monroe Boulevard on the evening of the crime.

"This whole technique, making the subject see what is happening on a movie screen, lends itself to the creation of fantasies.

"And listen to some of the other things Hollander tells her," Dr. Paris said, turning to pages in the transcript he had marked with paper clips.

"Here, in Tape #8, just after he administers the amytal for the first time, he tells her that she can 'forget,' 'remember' or, and this is the important one, 'misremember' as her personality needs require.

"Or on Tape #10. 'Tell us what you remember and don't worry about what's true. What you remember will be true.' Those are open invitations to confabulation.

"And there is one thing more that convinces me that there is a high possibility that Esther's story is the product of her imagination."

"What's that?"

"I find the whole theory that she developed amnesia because of the trauma of seeing Walters murdered unacceptable. This girl has been exposed to violence throughout her life. She discusses seeing her father stab her mother. And there was the incident where the police chased her after the miniature golf robbery. Her father shoots the pet dog she loves and makes her watch. Yet we have no amnesia. No, I . . ."

The phone rang. It was after five and Mark's secretary had left. He answered it.

"Is this Mr. Shaeffer?" a woman asked.

"Yes."

"You're the one that's defending that Coolidge boy?"

"Yes."

"I got some information on the case about how they tortured Esther."

"Excuse me?" Mark said, not sure he had heard the woman correctly.

"Esther wasn't at no murder. She was made to say that by the police."

"I see," Mark said, wondering how he could end the conversation, which was turning out to be one of the numerous crank calls he had received since the start of the trial. "How do you know that the police tortured Esther?"

"I seen what they done. I'm her mother."

The short, thin man who answered the front door walked with a slight stoop. His naked chest was covered with thick hair, in contrast to his head, which was bald except for a fringe of dark hair that started just in front of his ears and worked its way around the back of his skull. A rounded, protruding jaw and disproportionately long arms gave him a slight resemblance to a chimpanzee.

It was bright and sunny outside, but the shades were drawn and Mark could hear a baseball game on a set in the darkened living room.

"I'm Mark Shaeffer. Mrs. Taylor asked me to see her."

"She's inside in the bedroom," the man answered belligerently, as if the request was an insult. He had a can of beer in his right hand and he wiped the sweat from his chest with his left.

"Who is it?" A voice called from the rear of the house.

"She's in the back," the man said. Mark expected to be escorted to the bedroom, but the man went back to his ballgame, leaving Mark to search out the source of the voice.

Mrs. Taylor was a mountain of flesh propped up on a mound of pillows. Her fleshy face was the color of pale candle wax and her gray hair was unkempt. Bottles of pills and potions sat on the nightstand alongside a reading lamp and some confession magazines. A portable television set tuned to a soap opera was perched on a second nightstand.

"Sit down," she said, indicating a chair piled high with dirty clothing. "Just push 'em off. Make that son of a bitch husband of mine do some work."

The last sentence was said in a voice loud enough to be heard in the rest of the house. The only sound from the living room was a broadcaster's voice announcing a three-and-two count.

"I'm sorry I ain't up. I'm under a doctor's care."

Mark nodded sympathetically.

"You said you had some information about Esther Pegalosi," Mark prodded.

Esther's mother shook her head.

"I should never have let her talk with that cop," she said half to herself. "Cops always bring trouble."

"What officer was that?"

"That, uh . . . Shindler. He's the one who tortured her."

"When did this 'torture' happen, Mrs. Taylor?"

"In '61, when it first happened. Now she's a big TV star. But no one came to interview me. I couldda told them a thing or two. That girl's lyin' cause of what he done to her."

"What exactly did Detective Shindler do to her?"

Mrs. Taylor shut her eyes and let her head sink into the pillows. She seemed to have lost interest in the conversation.

"You got a cigarette?" she asked.

Mark shook his head and this seemed to annoy her. For a second, Mark was afraid that she would end the interview.

"Get me one from the drawer," she said, indicating

the end table with the TV. "You can turn that thing off."

Mark walked around the bed and switched off the set. He handed a cigarette to Mrs. Taylor, who ripped a match out of a matchbook and lit up.

"Esther was never on that hill," she said after a moment. "They scared her so bad she'd say anything."

"How did they scare her?"

"With the picture. You know, she had nightmares from that picture until she moved outta the house and that was years after. I was gonna sue. I shouldda done it."

"What picture is this?" Mark asked, feeling himself growing impatient.

"Shindler took her to the station house and showed her a picture of that Walters kid's face after it was bashed in. It was disgustin'. She used to wake up screaming."

"Did you ever ask her if she had seen Richie murdered?"

"Of course. She never seen it. That's what she said every time. Only she said Shindler tried to make her say she was there. And when she wouldn't, he showed her the picture."

"And this happened in 1961, right after the murders?"

"Yeah. That girl's been brainwashed. I can tell that. Ever since she seen that picture she's been different. Only the one thing she always denied was that she seen that boy murdered."

* * *

"I can't do it," Esther cried. Shindler held her tightly, fighting down the impulse to strike her.

"It's all lies," she sobbed.

"It is the truth, Esther. You told me and you told Dr. Hollander. If we thought that you were lying, we wouldn't let you testify."

He tried to sound calm, but he had been in turmoil since her call. She was hysterical and he was afraid she would try to kill herself again. All during the harried ride to her apartment, he thought about the years of planning and investigation. So close. And now to have it ruined by an hysterical child.

"I don't know what's real and what you put in my head."

"I didn't put anything in your head, Esther. You were there . . ."

"No."

"And you saw Bobby and Billy Coolidge beat Richie Walters's head until it was a mass of blood and torn flesh . . ."

"No."

"And then they took that girl and raped her and strangled her. . . ."

Esther's sobbing grew wilder and she began to shake.

"And you'll testify to that, Esther. . . ."

"Oh, God."

"Or I'll leave you and you'll never see me again. Do you understand?"

He lifted her chin and made her look into his eyes. She didn't want to. She was afraid of the fire. She could see hell there. But he forced her to look and held her chin in his hard, callused hand so that she could not avert her eyes. She wanted to die. Her body trembled and her face was tracked by tears.

"Please don't," she begged.

"Never see me, Esther. You'll live alone and die alone."

"No," she sobbed and sank slowly to her knees, catching the thin fabric of his slacks, burying her head against his knees.

He looked down at her kneeling figure and felt only disgust.

4

"Would you state your full name and spell the last, please?" the clerk asked.

"Esther Pegalosi. P-e-g-a-l-o-s-i."

"Thank you. Would you take the stand?"

Esther stepped up into the witness box. She was wearing a new gray knit outfit that Roy had purchased for her. Roy had also sent her to the beauty parlor and her hair felt clean and looked just right. She straightened her skirt when she sat down and absent-mindedly touched the armature of the glasses that Roy had made her wear. She focused her attention on Mr. Heider, as she had been told. She would not have had the courage to look at Bobby anyway.

Her hands began to shake and she grabbed her left hand with her right to stop them. There were so many people in the courtroom. She had been very frightened when Roy and the other policemen led her down the corridor to the courtroom. There had been so many people squeezing around her, pushing and shoving. The reporters all talked at once and she couldn't make out any of their questions. An old woman had tried to touch her. The noise in the corridor sounded like the rumbling of a train approaching in a darkened tunnel.

But her fear in the corridor had been nothing to the fear she felt when the courtroom door closed behind her and she had to walk alone down the row of seats through the bar of the court and to the witness stand. She had fastened her eyes on the judge. He seemed very stern and aloof. She could feel his presence above her and to the right, hovering like God, watching her for lies he would punish with terrible swiftness.

"Mrs. Pegalosi, do you reside in Portsmouth?" Philip Heider asked.

"Yes."

"How long have you lived in Portsmouth?"

"All my life."

"I'm sorry, Your Honor," a voice from in front and to her left said, "but I can't hear the witness."

"Yes, Mrs. Pegalosi," the judge's voice boomed from above, "you are going to have to speak up so that Mr. Shaeffer and the jurors can hear you."

Esther felt ashamed, as if she had done something wrong. She wanted to speak up, but her throat was so dry. Involuntarily, she ran her tongue across her lips.

"Perhaps we could have a glass of water for Mrs. Pegalosi," Mr. Heider said.

The clerk filled a clear glass with water from the judge's pitcher and handed it to her. She was grateful for the excuse to put off talking.

"Were you attending high school in 1960 and 1961?" Heider asked when she was ready.

"Yes."

"Did you hang around with a gang called the Cobras?"

"Objection, Your Honor, to the characterization as a gang," Shaeffer said.

"Oh, Your Honor, . . ." Heider began.

"We've been through this before, Mr. Heider," Judge Samuels said.

"Very well. Did you associate with a group known as the Cobras?"

"Yes."

"Was the defendant a member of this group?" Heider asked, putting emphasis on the last word.

"Yes."

"And his brother, Billy Coolidge?"

"Yes."

"And Roger Hessey?"

Esther nodded.

"Now I am going to call your attention to the evening of the twenty-fifth day of November, 1960, and I ask you whether or not at this time you have an independent recollection of what you did that evening."

Esther could hear a hum in the courtroom. She moved her head, because her neck was beginning to ache from tension and she saw Bobby. He was sitting up in his chair and he was looking right at her. She averted her eyes.

"Mrs. Pegalosi," Heider repeated.

"Yes."

"You do have an independent memory?"

"Yes."

"Will you please relate to this Court and this jury what you did that evening."

"I left my house around six-thirty and went to Bob's, because . . ."

"I'm sorry to interrupt, but what is Bob's?"

"It's for hamburgers, shakes. A restaurant."

"And did members of the Cobras hang out there?"

"Yes."

"Go on."

"Roger was there and Billy and Bobby."

"That is Roger Hessey and the Coolidge brothers?"

"Yes. Anyway, we sat around and then Billy or Bobby said we should crash a party. Roger didn't want to go, but he finally did."

"Whose party was this?"

"Alice Fay."

"When you say 'crash,' what do you mean?"

"Well, we weren't invited, you know, because those kids didn't like us that much. But Billy said let's go anyway."

"What kind of 'kids' were Alice Fay and her friends?"

"They were rich . . . richer than us. They didn't like the Cobras."

"Did Billy and Bobby like rich kids?"

"Billy said . . ."

"Objection. Billy Coolidge is not on trial here."

"Sustained," Judge Samuels said.

"Just confine yourself to the defendant," Heider said.

"No. Bobby didn't like them. He thought they got everything so easy and didn't deserve it."

"What happened at the party?"

"We got there and right off Billy wanted to mess around. Roger got nervous, then he left and we had a fight. When I came back in, Billy went over to the table where they had a punch bowl and some food and there was a fight."

"Who fought?"

"Bobby and Billy fought with Tommy Cooper, Alice's boyfriend, and some of his friends."

"What did the Coolidge brothers fight with?"

"Bobby was just punching, you know, with his hands. But Billy had a knife."

"What kind of knife?"

"A switchblade knife."

"Had you seen that knife before?"

"Sure. We all had. Billy was always bragging with it how . . ."

"Objection. Hearsay," Mark Shaeffer said.

"Your Honor, we are not introducing these statements to prove the truth of the contents. We are trying to show that the defendant's brother used this knife on occasion."

"That's not admissible, Your Honor. Other incidents may have occurred. We are talking about one alleged incident."

"Yes, Mr. Heider. Let's keep this to the events of that evening," the judge ruled.

"Very well. When he was fighting with the knife, did Billy say anything?"

"He . . . he said he would cut one of the boys."

"How did the fight end?"

"Some boys had Bobby down and Billy was waving the knife and Billy said to let Bobby up and we would go and they did."

"When they left the party, how did Bobby and Billy act?"

"Bobby was pretty calm. He acted like he was just glad to get out. But Billy was furious. He was yelling about rich kids and such and when I said he had started it, he stopped the car and said how he would hit me and how the rich kids were worthless. I don't know the exact words."

"He was angry?"

"Very angry."

"Where did you go from there?"

"We drove around and then Billy went into an all-night grocery and stole some wine. Then we went near a school and drank it and I got pretty drunk."

"How much did you have to drink?"

"I don't know. But it was a lot. I was sick when I came home."

"What did you do after you drank the wine?"

Esther hesitated.

"Mrs. Pegalosi, did you hear the question?" the judge asked.

"We drove downtown."

"Did you drive on Monroe Boulevard?"

"Objection, Your Honor. Counsel is leading the witness."

"Yes, Mr. Heider, I will sustain Mr. Shaeffer's objection."

"Tell the jury what happened downtown."

"We drove around downtown for a while. All the movies were letting out and there were crowds on the sidewalks and plenty of cars in the street just showing off or driving around.

"Then I said I wasn't feeling well 'cause of the wine and Bobby said they should take me home. We drove up Monroe Boulevard. We came to a light and there was a car there with a boy and a girl in it and Billy said he knew the girl. He pulled alongside and raced his engine and the light changed and we started racing."

"Did you see who was in the car you were racing?"

"No. Not then."

"Why is that?"

"Well, Bobby had got in the back with me and he was, uh, he tried to, uh, you know, make out, and I was making out too, even though I wasn't feeling so well. Then when the race started, it was real quick and I got scared and wouldn't look."

"What happened then?"

"Billy drove too close and we bumped them. Then the other car bumped us back and we spun around. I screamed, but Billy got the car under control and we stopped."

"How did Billy and Bobby feel about the other car making you spin out?"

"They were very mad. They said they should get them and they drove very fast in the direction the other car had went."

"Did they find the other car?"

"Not at first. At first they went too far up Monroe and there was no sight of them. Then Bobby said he bet they were in the park and we drove back there."

"What park is that?"

"Lookout Park. We drove around, but we couldn't find them. Then I saw the car in the meadow."

"Police officers have driven you to the meadow where the body of Richie Walters was found, have they not?"

"Yes."

"And you were shown the car in which his body was found, were you not?"

"Yes."

"Was the meadow where you saw the car the meadow where Richie Walters's body was found?"

"Yes."

"And was the car you saw Richie Walters's car?"

"Yes."

"What happened then?"

Esther took another sip from her glass of water. She could feel Bobby's eyes on her and she felt her head turning toward the defense table. She had expected to see fear or anger in Bobby's eyes. Instead, she saw nothing in them. It was as if he was looking past her at some scene she could not see.

"Billy drove the car onto the meadow and behind the other car and the car door on the driver's side of the other . . . of Richie's car opened and Richie got out."

"Could you see that it was Richie?"

"I think it was. I couldn't see real well, 'cause it was dark."

"What happened then?"

"They were yelling and all of a sudden Billy hit the boy and Bobby crawled out of the back seat and ran around the car."

"What did you do?"

"I got out to watch."

"Were you frightened?"

"No. Not really. I thought they would just beat him up. I'd seen Billy do that and other fights before."

"What happened then?"

Esther felt suddenly dizzy and nauseous.

"Mrs. Pegalosi, are you all right?" Judge Samuels asked.

"I'm just . . . If I could have some more water."

"Would you like us to take a recess?" the judge asked. She shook her head. She didn't know why, because she suddenly felt that she could not remain in the courtroom any longer. Yet she was equally afraid to move. She wished that Roy was there. If she could only see him . . .

The clerk handed her back her glass. She took a drink and sat back.

"I'm okay, now," she heard herself say. It sounded like someone else's voice.

"What happened after you got out of the car?"

"They hit him a few times and he fell down. Richie fell down. And they kept hitting him."

"Did you see them hit Richie with any object?"

"I don't know . . . remember if . . . I wasn't paying attention, because I was looking at the girl in the car."

"The girl?"

"The light was on in the car because the door hadn't closed and you could see inside. And while they were fighting there wasn't . . . It didn't look like there was anyone else in the car. Then this girl sat up and Billy saw her and Billy and Bobby raced around the car and I walked over to where the boy was lying."

"Did you look at the boy?"

She could feel the tears now and she could feel the pain in her throat when she tried to talk. She could not speak. She could only cry.

"Mrs. Pegalosi, I know this is difficult for you,

but we must know. This jury must know. What did you see when you looked at that boy lying in the grass in that meadow on the evening of November 25, 1960."

"He had no face," she heard herself scream. "He had no face."

They had to recess before she could go on. Mr. Heider and Roy sat with her in a small room next to the courtroom and Roy spoke to her in a soothing voice. She wanted to die. She told them she could never go back in there with all those people staring at her, after making such a fool of herself. They told her everything was all right and she cringed and folded up inside. In the end, she agreed to go on.

"Mrs. Pegalosi, after you saw Richie lying in the grass, what did you do?"

"I guess I ran away. Just kept running down the hill."

"And where did you end up?"

"At first, in a backyard. I ran into it and these dogs started barking and ran out at me. I ran out of the backyard and out onto the highway."

"Which highway is this?"

"Monroe Boulevard."

"What happened then?"

"I started walking and every time a car would come by I would jump in the bushes so they wouldn't see me. Eventually I felt that I couldn't walk all the way home and that I would have to take a ride. So, when I saw lights coming I got out of the bushes and walked out and a car stopped and it was them."

"Who?"

"Billy and Bobby and the girl."

"What girl?"

"Elaine Murray."

"How do you know it was Elaine Murray?"

"Well, I knew her from school. She was very popular."

"Tell us what you observed at that time."

"Bobby was driving and Elaine was in the back with Billy. He had her by her arms and around her shoulders and she looked, I don't know, dazed."

"Did she say anything or try to get away?"

"No."

"What happened to you?"

"They just dropped me by my house. In the street."

"Did they say anything to you?"

"No. Just dropped me."

"And did you see the Coolidges again after that?"

"Not much. They were in an accident shortly after and in the hospital and there was the vacations and my mother said I couldn't hang around with that crowd no more, because I was drunk and sick when I came home."

"Mrs. Pegalosi, did you lose anything on the evening of November 25, 1960?"

"Yes. My glasses, a lighter and a blue rat-tail comb."

Heider handed Esther a plastic bag containing a pair of woman's glasses, a blue rat-tail comb and a cigarette lighter.

"I hand you what have previously been marked as

State's Exhibits 35, 36 and 37 and I ask you if you recognize these items?"

"Yes. I lost these that night."

"Now you were contacted by the police regarding these items shortly after the murder of Richie Walters, were you not?"

"Yes."

"What did you tell the police about the glasses?"

"I told them I lost them three months before they came."

"Why did you tell them that?"

"I believed it."

"All right. Now, you have testified that you dated a Roger Hessey in 1960."

"Yes."

"And can you tell us about an occasion that occurred between you and Mr. Hessey shortly before the Walters murder in 1960."

"Yes. We went to a movie and up to the meadow to make out. It was where everyone would go, you know. And I was mad because he was dating some other girl and I found out, so I wouldn't kiss him and I ran out of the car and he caught me and slapped my glasses off my face."

"What happened then?"

"Well, I got the glasses and he drove me home."

"Did you have several meetings with Dr. Arthur Hollander during which you were hypnotized and, sometimes, put under the influence of sodium amytal?"

"Yes."

"How many meetings were there?"

"Gee, I . . . Several. More than ten, I know."

"Prior to these meetings did you recall what you have told us today?"

"No, I did not."

"And today, when you related what happened on November 25, 1960, was that from your own independent memory?"

"Yes, it was."

"No further questions."

Mark checked over his notes from the tapes and transcript and made sure that the other documents that he would use during cross-examination were in order. They had dressed up Esther, so she looked like a secretary or a schoolteacher. Respectable. But nervous. Very nervous.

He had spent considerable time going over the transcript of the hypnosis sessions. When he heard her, the doctor and Shindler speaking the words he had read, it reinforced the clinical explanation that Dr. Paris had given for Esther's testimony. She was lying or brainwashed and he had to make the jury see that.

"Mrs. Pegalosi, I have tried on two occasions to speak to you about this case, have I not?"

"Yes."

"And you refused to discuss the case with me on both of those occasions, isn't that true?"

Esther looked down at her hands.

"You slammed the door in my face on one of those occasions, didn't you?"

She nodded.

"Well, we'll discuss this case now, won't we? Is it your story that after drinking the stolen wine, you became drunk and did not feel well?"

"Yes."

"And you went cruising downtown and then asked the Coolidges to take you home?"

"Yes."

"And the Coolidge brothers drove from the downtown area of Portsmouth to Monroe Boulevard, so that they could drive you home?"

"Yes."

Mark stood up and carried a map of Portsmouth to an easel that stood next to the witness stand.

"Monroe Boulevard is not the shortest route to your house from downtown Portsmouth, is it?" Mark asked.

Esther stared at the map, then at Mark.

"I . . . I don't know."

"Well, why don't you look at the map and tell the jury what route you usually took home from downtown."

"I don't think I took any route like that."

"You don't, Mrs. Pegalosi? That's interesting," Mark said, returning to counsel table and picking up an index card from the top of a stack.

"Do you remember being asked this series of questions on Tape Number 5 and giving these answers:

Question: Then you go cruising downtown, don't you?

Answer: I think so.

Question: And you are on Monroe now. Can you see Monroe?

Answer: I can see Monroe, but I'm not . . . I don't remember if . . .

Question: But you had to go on Monroe to get home, didn't you?

Answer: No. Usually I would go on Marshall Road from downtown.

"I don't remember that."

"Would you like me to play that tape for you?"

"No, I . . ."

"Is it not a fact, Mrs. Pegalosi, that the normal way, the usual way, for you to go home from downtown Portsmouth in 1960 was Marshall Road?"

"I guess so."

"And is it not true that you repeatedly told Dr. Hollander that you could not remember being on Monroe Boulevard that evening?"

"That was before . . ."

"Before they brainwashed you into believing you were on Monroe?"

Heider was on his feet, objecting.

"I withdraw the question, Your Honor," Mark said and returned to counsel table.

"Is it your testimony that you lost your glasses and your lighter and your comb on the evening of November 25, 1960?"

"Yes."

Mark selected a police report from the top of a stack and turned to one of the pages in it.

"During the second week of January, 1961, do you remember being visited by two police detectives, Roy Shindler and Harvey Marcus?"

"I can't remember the exact date, but they did visit. Mr. Shindler came more than once."

"I am talking about the first occasion. This was at your home and your mother was present."

"I remember that."

"Do you remember telling those officers that the glasses had been stolen from you three months before?"

"I said that, but . . ."

"Just answer the question, please."

"Yes."

"And three months before the second week in January would be right around the time that Roger Hessey slapped those glasses off, not the date of Richie Walters's murder, wouldn't it?"

"I said that because . . ."

"Your Honor," Mark said, "would you please instruct the witness to answer my questions."

"Mrs. Pegalosi, you must answer Mr. Shaeffer," Judge Samuels said.

Esther glanced at the spectators. They were silent, staring at her, accusingly.

"I guess so. I didn't count."

"On direct examination by Mr. Heider, you said that you told the police the glasses had been stolen because you believed that was the truth."

"Yes."

"And when did you stop believing that?"

"After I realized that I had information to give."

"And when was that, Mrs. Pegalosi?"

"After . . . When I met with Dr. Hollander and I began to see that . . . I began to know the truth."

"Was it the truth that you were telling during the sessions you had with Dr. Hollander?"

"Yes."

Mark selected another index card and read it while Esther waited. She was perspiring and she could feel the droplets on her brow. Her stomach was churning and the tension was making her lightheaded. She tried to imagine Dr. Hollander's fingers on her wrist, his soothing voice. She had to relax.

"Mrs. Pegalosi, do you recall these statements on Tape Number 8?

Question: Do you recall telling me about Monroe Boulevard and Lookout Park?
Answer: Uh-huh. I probably lied.
Question: You probably lied to me?
Answer: Could I have lied about what I said?
Question: I doubt it.

Esther licked her lips again and looked over at Mr. Heider. Heider was leaning back in his chair with a bored look. He had told her that he would not give her support during cross-examination, because the jury might interpret it as coaching, but she needed support and wished that he would break the rule, just once.

"Mrs. Pegalosi, I asked you if you remembered that sequence of questions and answers."

"I don't remember that exactly."

"I see. How about this one? This is from Tape Number 10.

Question: Where did they go?
Answer: Into Lookout Park.

Question: You went into the park?

Answer: It seems like it. It couldn't be my imagination.

Question: No. You're doing fine. Your memory is working better than it ever has. What happened next?

Answer: We . . . I saw the car.

Question: The car you were dragging with?

Answer: Are you sure that I'm not just remembering this because I want to get it over with and I'm not really remembering it?

"I don't recall that."

"You don't? Would you like me to play the tape for you?"

"No. It's just that . . . When you are under it . . . The drug makes you dreamy and it's hard to remember what you said."

"Well, do you recall saying this, a bit later?

Question: You're doing fine. Let's see how good your memory is.

Answer: It's so hard because I know what they did. I know what I'm supposed to say and I want to make sure that I remember and I'm not just saying it . . . Something that I know.

"Do you remember saying that?"

Esther kept thinking of Dr. Hollander's fingers.

"No, I don't."

"You don't seem to remember a lot of things."

"I told you," she said, her voice rising a little in panic, "you can't remember with the drug so well."

"Do you remember saying, '. . . I can't remember what I'm supposed to say'?"

Esther shook her head. She concentrated on the fingers. Soothing, relaxing. Don't panic.

"Or 'Wait a minute. How many times have I lied to you about this . . . ?' Do you remember that?"

"No," Esther said. As soon as the word was out of her mouth she realized that she had said it a little too loudly. She had to get a hold on herself.

"How many times did you lie to Dr. Hollander?"

"I didn't."

"How many times have you lied . . . ?"

Mark stopped. He looked at Esther's hands. The right was stroking the left wrist rhythmically.

"Mrs. Pegalosi, what are you doing with your hands?"

She stopped stroking abruptly. The jurors' eyes were on her wrist.

"Nothing," she replied guiltily.

"I saw you stroke your wrist. Are you trying to hypnotize yourself? Your Honor, I ask the Court to instruct the witness that she may not hypnotize herself during cross-examination."

Heider was on his feet.

"This is ridiculous. What is Mr. Shaeffer . . . ?"

Judge Samuels rapped his gavel for order.

"Both of you gentlemen, sit down. We will take a short recess."

The bailiff took the jurors to the jury room and the judge waited until the door was closed. Then he turned his attention to Mark.

"Now, what is your problem, Mr. Shaeffer?"

"The witness was constantly stroking her wrist during my examination, Your Honor. That is how she hypnotizes herself. It was on the tapes."

Samuels leaned back in his chair and seemed thoughtful. He swiveled toward Esther.

"Mrs. Pegalosi, I don't want you to be afraid, but I do want a straight answer. Were you attempting to hypnotize yourself, just now, while Mr. Shaeffer was questioning you?"

Esther looked down into her lap.

"I . . . Yes."

"You cannot do that. Do you understand? If you were under medication or intoxicated, I could not have you testify. You must be fully alert. Do you understand?"

"Yes," she said so quietly that the judge had to ask her to repeat her answer.

"You will not try to hypnotize yourself again, do you understand that?"

"Yes."

"Very well. Bailiff, bring back the jury."

* * *

"Mrs. Pegalosi, why do you think you were unable to remember that you saw the murder of Richie Walters for all these years?"

"I . . . Dr. Hollander told me seeing the body . . . The face . . . like that, you know . . . I couldn't take it. It made me too scared. Plus I was drinking . . ." She shrugged her shoulders. "That's what he said."

"Well, that's understandable," Mark said, smiling. "I would be pretty scared, too, to see all that violence. Tell me, was this the first time you ever saw any violence, Mrs. Pegalosi?"

"No," she said in a low, trembling voice.

"In fact, you have seen quite a bit of violence in your life, haven't you?"

"I . . . I wouldn't say a lot, I've . . ."

"Now don't be modest. Tell the jury about the boy you stabbed with a knife. Andy Trask."

"I wasn't convicted of that."

"I didn't say you were. But you were arrested and put in juvenile detention, weren't you?"

"Yes."

"And that wasn't the first time, was it?"

"No."

"You have been in detention as a runaway and for assault of Andy Trask and for robbery, isn't that correct?"

"Yes."

"And you did stab Andy Trask, didn't you?"

"Yes."

"And you remember that in detail, don't you?"

"Yes."

"Do you remember seeing your father beat your mother?"

She started crying. Mark repeated the question and Heider leaped to his feet.

"Your Honor, counsel is browbeating the witness. This is all irrelevant."

"It is very relevant, Your Honor. Mrs. Pegalosi comes in here and says suddenly after all this time she remembers that this young man is a murderer. Then she says she forgot because she was so scared by the violence. I am entitled to show that she is no stranger to violence. That she remembers incidents of violence very clearly."

"I agree with Mr. Shaeffer and I will overrule the objection. On the other hand, I will not let you harangue this witness."

"Your Honor, I didn't start this crying. If her conscience . . ."

"You have heard what I said, Mr. Shaeffer."

"Yes, Your Honor.

"Mrs. Pegalosi, did you ever see your father stab your mother?"

"Yes."

"Tell the jury what you remember of that incident."

Esther dried her eyes with a handkerchief.

"I was sleeping and I heard yelling from momma . . . my mother's room. He was drunk again and the door slammed open and I could hear her running to the kitchen and he was cursing."

"Go on."

"Momma had a kitchen knife and said she would stab him if he came near her, but he backed her against the refrigerator and got the knife."

"I am having trouble hearing you, Mrs. Pegalosi," Mark said.

Esther sipped some more water.

"That was all. He stabbed her and there was blood on the white refrigerator and momma fell and he dropped the knife and said 'What have I done?' and walked out."

"And you remember that?" Mark asked in a hushed tone.

"Yes," Esther replied and there was no other sound in the courtroom.

"And you remember a man named Bones robbing the miniature golf and racing the police when you were with him?"

"Yes."

"In detail?"

"Yes."

"And you testified on direct that you were not scared initially when Bobby and Billy and Richie Walters were fighting, because you had seen other fights. Have you seen fights where blood was spilled?"

"Yes."

"And could you recount those fights, in detail, to this jury, if I asked you?"

"Some of them."

"Even those where there was blood?"

"Some of them."

Mark paused. He could hear the sound of his own heartbeat in the courtroom. He could see the eyes of the jurors riveted on Esther. He could see her face clearly, drained of color, her cheeks streaked with tears.

"You once owned a pet dog, did you not?" he asked quietly.

"Oh, no," Esther moaned.

"I ask the court to direct the witness to answer the question."

"Mrs. Pegalosi, you must answer."

"Yes," the answer came in a choked whisper.

"Did you love that dog?"

"Yes," she sobbed.

"Tell the jury how that dog died."

Esther paled.

"Mrs. Pegalosi," Mark said.

"I . . . I can't," she said, looking up at the judge. Samuels instructed her to answer.

"My . . . my father shot the dog."

"In the eye?"

Esther was crying and could only nod.

"And you remember that in detail, do you not?"

"Yes."

"And you loved the dog, didn't you?"

"Yes."

"Yet you can remember that."

"Your Honor," Heider shouted.

"Sit down, Mr. Heider. This is appropriate cross." The judge turned to Shaeffer. It was clear that he was restraining himself. "Do you intend to pursue this line of questioning much further, Mr. Shaeffer?"

"No, Your Honor. I believe the point has been made."

Esther was doubled over in the witness box. Someone had given her a handkerchief. The judge ordered a ten-minute recess.

"Mrs. Pegalosi," Mark asked when court resumed, "is it your testimony that you actually saw Richie Walters's battered face shortly after he was murdered?"

"Yes," Esther replied. Her voice was a monotone. She had cried so hard and so long that she had nothing left inside. She knew that court would recess soon and she was just going through the motions until it was over.

"And it was the sight of this face that shocked you into amnesia?"

"That is what Dr. Hollander told me."

"When did you first realize that you had actually seen Richie's face?"

"After . . . When I was given the drug by Dr. Hollander."

"Isn't it a fact, Mrs. Pegalosi, that you did not see Richie's face until some time after the murder?"

"What do you mean?"

"Do you remember this exchange between you and Dr. Hollander on Tape Number 10?

Question: But you remember seeing the boy murdered?

Answer: No, I didn't see that.

Question: Didn't you say that you saw the fight?

Answer: No, no, I didn't know there was a murder, until later. I didn't know what happened. I thought they beat him up like they usually did.

Question: Didn't you say you saw Richie's face?

Answer: I saw it later.

"When was later, Esther?"

"I don't know what you mean."

"Do you remember telling Dr. Hollander that the last thing you remember seeing on the hill before you ran was Bobby and Billy holding Richie against the car like they were frisking him?"

"I told you I can't remember what I said, because I was under the drug."

"Do you want me to play the tape for you?"

"No. If you say that's what it said . . ."

"What you said. Esther, did you ever wake up screaming in the night because of nightmares in which you saw Richie's bloody face?"

Esther looked into her lap again.

"Yes, I did. A lot."

"Those nightmares did not start right after the murder, did they?"

"I can't remember exactly when."

"Have you ever met a detective named Roy Shindler?"

Esther felt as if she had been struck. She looked directly at Shaeffer, her face white. Her hands twisted the handkerchief she was holding into a tight knot.

"Mrs. Pegalosi?"

"Yes," she answered hoarsely.

"Did your nightmares start soon after you met Detective Shindler?"

"I don't know what you mean."

"I think you do, Esther. Detective Shindler is the same detective who made you see Dr. Hollander, isn't he?"

"He didn't force me. I went because I wanted to."

"To what, Esther?"

"To see if what he said was real."

"What did he say?"

"That I saw the murder. He knew it even back then."

"Back when?"

"When they were murdered. He told me."

"Told you and showed the scene."

"Yes."

"Took you up there and suggested how a girl might lose her glasses running down that hill in a certain way."

"It wasn't like that."

"Suggested that you might have dragged Richie that night, even though you couldn't remember."

"It was in my subconscious. Hidden. That's what Dr. . . ."

"Showed you that picture that scared you so much you became hysterical and had nightmares for years after."

Esther stopped.

"What picture?" she asked hesitantly.

"You tell the jury what picture."

"I don't know any picture."

"You don't remember Detective Shindler bringing you to the station house in 1961 and showing you a color picture in one of the interrogation rooms?"

Esther couldn't breathe. She couldn't take her eyes away from Shaeffer's face. He was rising and walking slowly to a table piled high with exhibits that had been introduced into evidence. He was bending slightly from the waist and selecting a manila envelope. There was a roaring in her ears. He was saying, "Perhaps this will help you to remember" and she was back at the police station and it was Roy's hand drawing the color photograph slowly out of the envelope, facedown. And she was peering at it again and it was rotating toward her and she was screaming again.

Sarah had passed him the note as he was leaving the courtroom. It was on yellow note paper and she had obviously written it during the trial. He had slipped it into his pants pocket and retrieved it when he changed back into his prison clothes.

That evening, after dinner, he had stretched out on his bunk, too exhausted from the day's session to do anything but lie there. He had saved the note, even though he wanted so much to read it, because it was the first real communication he had had with Sarah for so long.

She had been in court every day and she had talked to him during recess, but their conversations had been superficial and she always had an excuse for not visiting him at the jail.

When she had handed him the note, she had not looked at him. He tried to speak to her, but she hurried away.

He was afraid of what she had written. When the paper was unfolded, he held it up to the light. It was very short and it said that she was going away and did not want to see him again. It said that she wanted to believe that he was innocent and that the girl was lying, but she had watched Mark Shaeffer torture her today and had come away feeling sick to her stomach that she had ever let him touch her.

He let his hand fall to his side. The yellow paper fluttered to the cement floor.

5

Mark Shaeffer put his attaché case on his counsel table and opened the snaps. Every seat in the courtroom was already filled and more spectators were milling around in the hallway waiting for someone to leave. He smiled in anticipation of today's continued examination of Esther Pegalosi. He was feeling good. The trial seemed to be shifting in his direction and he had already picked up several new clients because of the publicity he was receiving on TV and in the papers.

Bobby wasn't in the courtroom and Mark had some points he wanted to cover with him. He was about to ask the guard to bring Bobby down when Judge Samuels's clerk signaled to him. Mark straightened a file, then walked to the entrance to the judge's chambers.

Caproni and Heider were sitting in front of the judge's desk. Samuels had not donned his robe yet. They all looked grim.

"Sit down, Mr. Shaeffer. I have some unsettling news for you."

Mark looked at Caproni, but Caproni would not look at him.

"Approximately one hour ago I received a call from the jail," Samuels said. "I'm afraid the trial is over. Mr. Coolidge killed himself some time last night."

Esther had been silent during the ride from the courtroom and Shindler was grateful for the chance to think. The trial had ended so suddenly. What did it all mean? For years he had been preparing himself for the moment when a judge would read the jury's verdict. Now that was not to be. He felt vindicated by the suicide, but he also felt as if business had been left unfinished. Without a jury verdict, Coolidge's guilt would remain officially unproven. Already, someone in the press had asked him about the note that had been found in Bobby's cell. The reporter wanted to know about the girl who had written it. They would say he had died for love. Still, there was always Billy. They would do it over again and this time there would be a verdict.

Shindler parked in front of Esther's apartment. She was staring ahead, as she had all during the ride, and she made no effort to leave.

"Are you all right?" he asked. He wanted to be rid of her, but he still needed her for Billy's trial.

"No, I'm not all right."

Her voice was a hard monotone and her intensity surprised him.

"It wasn't your fault, Esther. He killed himself because he knew he had no chance."

"He killed himself because I lied."

"No, Esther. We've been over and over this. You were there. You told the truth on the stand yesterday and you'll tell it again at Billy's trial."

"There won't be another trial, because I won't testify," she said firmly. There was no whine in her voice. No indecision.

"Of course, there'll be another trial. You're just upset."

She shook her head and looked at him. Her eyes did not waver.

"I know what it's like to want to die, remember? To feel like there's nothing left. Now I have to live the rest of my life knowing I made Bobby feel like that because of you, Roy. You used me because you knew I'd do anything to keep you, but I'm through now."

She opened the door and got out of the car. He followed her up the path, catching her at the entrance to the apartment house.

"Esther," he started, taking hold of her arm. She broke free and he grabbed her again. This time she turned toward him. Her eyes were filled with hate.

"Don't ever touch me. Don't ever come near me. If you do, I'll tell everyone what you did to make me kill Bobby. Everyone. How you kissed me and made me kneel. I'll fill the papers with it. I see you, Roy. I see you. Don't you ever come near me or call me or I'll make everyone see what you are."

The door slammed shut. He saw her walk away through the glass. He stood on the path staring, even after she was gone, trying to think of what he would do next.

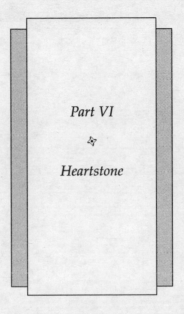

Part VI

Heartstone

Epilogue

Caproni looked through the swirling sheets of snow for a street sign that would tell him how close they were to the Hotel Cordova. He saw none. The car skidded on a patch of ice and Louis Weaver grabbed the door handle for support. Caproni settled back in his seat and listened to the metronomic swish of the windshield wipers.

There had never been a second trial. Esther Pegalosi had retracted her testimony and the charges against Billy Coolidge had been dismissed. Philip Heider did not care. He had won his party's nomination for State Representative and, later, the general election. Now he was a United States Senator.

Mark Shaeffer had not suffered either. The Murray-Walters case had made him one of the best-known criminal attorneys in the state and he had parleyed the publicity into one of the most lucrative practices in the state shortly after he divorced his first wife. Shaeffer rarely touched a criminal case now, concentrating instead on corporate and tax work.

Esther Pegalosi had moved out of state soon after the trial ended and Caproni had heard nothing about her since. Billy Coolidge had served the rest of his prison term and had been shot to death in a half-empty parking lot shortly after his release. Traces of cocaine had been found on the body and there had been some talk about a drug ripoff. The crime had never been solved.

And Roy Shindler. There had been rumors after Esther left town. No one had ever substantiated them. Shindler was still on the force, but he had changed after the Murray-Walters case. He was still good at his work, but he no longer seemed to care. The intensity that had characterized him was gone. Caproni had used him as a witness several times in the past and spoken to him on business on many occasions, but in all those years since the trial Shindler had never once mentioned the Murray-Walters case.

Caproni closed his eyes and reviewed the cast of characters again. There was only one he had not covered: Albert C. Caproni, the youngest elected district attorney in the history of Portsmouth. Would Bobby Coolidge have taken his life if he had gone to Judge Samuels with the information he had? For a while Caproni had deluded himself into believing that he had acted the way he had because he did not want a murderer to go free because of a hasty judgment. But he knew better. What Heider and Shindler had done was wrong whether or not Coolidge was guilty. They had destroyed evidence. That was a criminal and unethical act. He should have gone to the judge, but he hadn't and he knew now that he hadn't because of selfish reasons having to do with his own career. He had been afraid that he would lose his job. It was that simple. So he had taken the middle road when faced with the greatest moral decision of his life. And a man had died.

The Hotel Cordova bore a faint resemblance to the Cedar Arms. As Caproni climbed the stairs to Heartstone's room he felt the same chill he had experienced those long years before when he had walked up the poorly lit staircase to meet William Heartstone that first time.

Louis Weaver opened the door to the room and stood aside to let Caproni and Pat Kelly enter. The odors of disease and death filled the air. The shades were drawn and darkness added to the funereal atmosphere. Heartstone was asleep and Caproni could not make out his features in the dark.

"Willie?" Louis whispered when the door was closed and the shades raised. Caproni found it hard to believe that the man on the bed was still alive. He could almost see the skull beneath the skin. The gnarled hands that so pathetically clutched the soiled blankets looked paper thin.

Heartstone coughed and his eyes opened. It took a moment for them to focus. Then a smile suffused Heartstone's ravaged features.

"You've come," he said in a voice that was barely a whisper.

Caproni pulled a chair over to the side of the bed and leaned close to Heartstone. He started the tape recorder.

"Willie, how did you remember?"

Willie smiled.

"The card," he rasped as a fit of coughing shook him. He motioned toward Weaver and Louis drew a stained and crumpled business card out of his pocket.

It was the card Caproni had given to Heartstone on the evening they had first met. Caproni was astonished.

"You kept it? All these years?"

"As many as received Him to them gave he the power to become the children of God."

Willie's features were serene. He held out his hand. The hand moved with great difficulty. It shook when Caproni took hold of it.

"Tell me, Willie. Who killed Elaine Murray?"

"The wages of sin is death, but the gift of God is eternal life through Jesus Christ our Lord."

"Tell me, Willie."

Tears welled up in the dying man's eyes. Caproni knew that Heartstone was not that much older than he was, yet he could have been one hundred.

"Tell me," he repeated softly.

"Ralph done it. We had her so many days, then Ralph got tired."

It took a great effort for Heartstone to speak and he lapsed into another coughing fit. Caproni wondered if he would last until the doctor arrived.

"Tired, Willie? What do you mean?"

"Feedin' her. Carin' for her, what little we done." He began to cry again.

"It's all right now, Willie. Just tell me."

"He killed her and we left her by the road."

"When?"

"I don't know. It was after New Year's."

"Willie, did you know a man named Eddie Toller?" Willie looked confused.

"A man you sold Elaine to for sex."

"There was so many," Willie sobbed. He grasped

Caproni's hand tightly. "Will I be saved? I sinned so long. I don't want to burn in hell."

"If you tell me everything, God will forgive you, Willie. Now tell me about Toller."

"We sold her to so many. I don't remember. She begged us not to at first, but we beat her and starved her and soon she lost her spirit."

Willie was overcome again. Caproni let him cry and leaned back, exhausted.

"Then Bobby Coolidge was innocent all along," he said.

"No! Guilty! Sinful!"

The words were Heartstone's and the voice was filled with such power that it shocked everyone in the room.

"But you said . . ."

"'He was a murderer from the beginning, and abode not in the truth, because there was no truth in him.' Innocent?" Heartstone laughed, the cruelty of that laugh burning like ice in the stillness of the death room. "Who do you think sold her to us?"

Elaine Murray had been crying ever since they had dropped Esther in front of her house. Billy had grabbed Esther by the throat and had said something to her in a voice too low for Bobby to hear. But Bobby could guess, from the look on her face, what he had said. Esther was very drunk and very scared and Bobby knew that she would keep quiet, if for no other reason than fear of implicating herself in what had happened that night.

Billy was thinking fast as he headed the car into

the country. Bobby had suggested that they take Elaine to a deserted house that the gang sometimes used for parties. The house was isolated and they would not have to worry about prying eyes.

What to do with her once they got to the house was the question. Walters was dead. There was no doubt about that. Billy had stabbed him and Bobby had hit him with the tire iron. They could not let her go, but, even for Billy, killing a girl in cold blood was different from killing a man during a fight.

Elaine's whimpering was starting to get on Billy's nerves. Bobby was holding her in the back seat to make sure that she did not try to get away, but Bobby was almost in a state of shock himself. Billy loved his brother, but Bobby was soft. Oh, he was good enough in most fights, but he did not have the killer instinct. The desire to fight and to inflict pain. Bobby had hit Walters out of panic. Billy had enjoyed it every time he had stabbed that rich bastard. Enjoyed stabbing Walters, who was Cooper and every other rich snob who had looked down on him and treated him like he did not exist. Only Walters knew that Billy Coolidge existed. He knew it every time that the blade struck home. Knew it every time he screamed. Knew that he, Billy Coolidge, was taking—had the power to take—his life.

Billy found the dirt road that led up to the house. A farmer had built it in the late eighteen hundreds and it had been remodeled after that, but the farmer had died and his children had moved away and it was empty now. It was a bulky house. Thick and wide, a two-story silhouette, black space against the early morning night sky.

"Shut her up, Bobby," Billy yelled.

"Easy, Elaine. Everything will be okay. Don't be frightened."

The girl continued to cry. Billy parked in the backyard so that it would be more difficult to see the car. He got out and ran around the side of the house. He peered in the side window that looked in on the kitchen. It did not appear that anyone was living in the house. Last time out they had had to beat up some hobos who were squatting.

Billy was about to double-check through the front window when he heard Bobby curse. He raced toward the back of the house. The car was empty and the door on the back driver's side was open. He could see a vague shape thrashing through the high grass that had once been a wheat field. He ran as fast as he could after the disappearing figure. He heard a grunt and a high-pitched, female scream. Two bodies crashed to the ground. In an instant he was pushing his brother off the fallen girl, straddling her, slapping her face from side to side, screaming "bitch" in a voice filled with animal lust and hate.

"Stop it. You'll kill her."

Bobby was grabbing his arms. His chest was heaving. The girl was moaning. Blood was trickling from her nose. Billy took a deep breath. He glared at the girl. He was sexually aroused by the sight of someone he had desired, but had been denied, now powerless and under his control.

"Let's get her in the house," Billy said.

They forced her to her feet and half dragged, half carried, into the house and up to the second floor bedroom. There were a few mattresses on the floor, carried there during the last party and left for the future.

Billy threw her down roughly on the floor. He turned to Bobby.

"Wait outside."

"But, Billy . . ." Bobby started to say, but one look at his brother's face silenced him.

A half hour later, the bedroom door opened. Billy looked played out, his anger and hatred spent. He nodded toward the naked girl huddled on the floor.

"She's yours, if you want her," he said wearily.

Bobby shook his head. He couldn't. It wasn't just the fear and fatigue. It was the horror of what they had done that night, creeping up on him as he waited for his brother in the darkened hallway. His mind had been racing in a dozen directions, searching for a solution to the problem the girl presented.

"Billy, we have to get rid of her."

"Kill her?" Billy asked. He was too weary to do it tonight.

Bobby shook his head.

"I couldn't."

"We can't let her go. She knows about Walters."

"I have an idea. Remember those two guys you owe the money to on the dope deal."

"Pasante and Heartstone?"

Bobby nodded.

"You still owe them, right?"

"Yeah."

"See if they'll take the girl."

"As payment?"

"Or to . . . to do it for us. Billy, I can't do it. Not like that."

Billy looked at him.

"I can do it."

"Billy, don't," he said desperately. "Besides, if they get caught with Elaine, everyone will think they killed Richie."

"I don't like it. They might let her go or she might get away."

It was then that Bobby broke down. Sobs wracked his body. Billy did not know how to react. It was unmanly to cry, yet he vaguely understood what his brother was going through.

"All right, kid. I'll try it."

Bobby had turned away from him. He let him cry. The girl was out of it. She was curled in the corner, looking at him. He looked at her with contempt.

"He paid us one hundred dollars to kill her. Sold dope for us to cover the debt. We said we'd do it right away, but we didn't. He never knew. Thought we done it the first night."

Heartstone coughed again. This time he spit up blood and the coughing seemed to go on forever. Caproni stood up and walked to the window. Guilty and innocent. It had never occurred to him that two people had done the killings.

"Mr. Caproni," Louis Weaver yelled. He turned from the window and walked rapidly to the bed. It only took him one look to tell that Willie Heartstone was dead.

*   *   *

The snow had stopped falling and the streets were starting to fill with five o'clock traffic. Caproni sat in the back seat of the car with his eyes closed. It was all over. Coolidge had been a murderer after all. Now that he knew, it didn't seem to make any difference. He realized that what he had done in his youth was no more and no less than what all his fellow human beings had done at one time or another. He had been idealistic and naive and he had failed to live up to the goals that he had set for himself because he was a human being. He was not perfect. But he tried to be a good man. If he had failed on that one occasion, he had succeeded on many, many others.

Caproni looked at the tape recorder in his lap and ejected the cartridge. No need to keep this around, he thought. He would erase the tape tomorrow. He was too tired right now.

"Back to the office?" Pat Kelly asked from the front seat.

"No, Pat. I think I'll just go home."

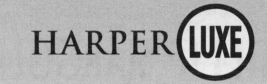